J.C. Wright

Autobiography of Rev. A.B. Wright,

of the Holston conference, M.E. Church

J.C. Wright

Autobiography of Rev. A.B. Wright,
of the Holston conference, M.E. Church

ISBN/EAN: 9783337114053

Printed in Europe, USA, Canada, Australia, Japan

Cover: Foto ©Raphael Reischuk / pixelio.de

More available books at **www.hansebooks.com**

REV. A. B. WRIGHT.

AUTOBIOGRAPHY

OF

REV. A. B. WRIGHT,

OF THE

HOLSTON CONFERENCE, M. E. CHURCH.

PREPARED BY HIS SON,

REV. J. C. WRIGHT, A. M., D. D.,

OF THE HOLSTON CONFERENCE, M. E. CHURCH.

Mark the perfect man, and behold the upright; for the end of that man is peace.—DAVID.

CINCINNATI: CRANSTON & CURTS.

PRINTED FOR THE AUTHOR.

1896.

Williams Printing Company

Printed by
Williams Printing Company
Nashville, Tennessee

DEDICATION.

⚜

To the many toiling Methodist preachers
on hard fields of labor.
That class of men who are meagerly compensated
for their useful work,
and yet are the very salt of the earth,
of whom the world is not worthy,
and whose record is on high,

This Volume

is humbly dedicated

BY THE AUTHOR.

MRS. CYNTHIA S. WRIGHT.

TABLE OF CONTENTS.

PREFACE.

I N young manhood my father began to keep a
journal of his life. His purpose was to leave it
for the benefit of his children. He had no idea that
it would ever be published to the world as a book.
Several years ago it became apparent to him that
its publication would be necessary, so that each of
his children might have a copy. Hundreds of others, outside of our own family, who had a knowledge of his purpose, urged him to publish his life,
in the belief that it would be beneficial to the world.
He finally consented to do so, and requested the
writer to edit and prepare his papers for publication
after his death. I have endeavored to do this hon-
estly and in the fear of God. I have tried, so far
as the rules of good language would at all tolerate,
to retain the mannerisms of my father. He was a
man of fine natural endowment, and had acquired
much by extensive reading, but was without any
literary training.

I anticipate two classes of critics. One class
will object to whatever changes I have made, and
the other will fault me for not making more. I
have in no instance changed the thought of my
father, but only changed the language. I have done
this work amid other heavy labors. To me it has
been a sad but loving task. I prepared the chapter containing his death. If, in it, there shall ap-

pear to any one an unduly high eulogy of my father, let me offer as my apology a strong filial love for a loving, tender father.

I trust that this volume will be useful to his many spiritual children who may read it, and to his many thousands of true friends throughout all of that mountain country where he toiled and spent his life for the Master. Many of the companions and friends of his early life have passed over, and are with him on the other side of the river.

I have now redeemed the promise to my father, and send forth this volume on its mission to humanity.

J. C. WRIGHT.

MARYVILLE, TENN., October 2, 1895.

AUTOBIOGRAPHY

OF

REV. A. B. WRIGHT.

CHAPTER I.

OUR ANCESTRY FOR MY CHILDREN.

MY grandfather's name on my father's side was Moses Wright. I am inclined to think he was born and ever lived in North Carolina. His father came from Ireland. Moses Wright married Margaret Edmondson. I do not know where she was raised, perhaps in North Carolina. Some time after their marriage my grandfather became a local preacher in the Methodist Episcopal Church, and traveled some circuits as supply under Bishop Asbury. He and grandmother reared nine children. Some may have died in infancy; I do not know. I remember hearing my father call over the names of his brothers and sisters. The names of the boys were Jesse, James, John, Robert, Jeremiah, and Aaron. The girls' names were Sarah, Zilphia, and Martha—six boys and three girls.

Uncle Robert and Uncle Jerry Wright died in the War of 1812. They were both soldiers. Uncle Jesse Wright married a Vaughn; Uncle James, a Gravel; Uncle Robert married Nancy Dale; my

1

father married Peninah Dale. I do n't think Uncle
Jerry was ever married. Uncle Aaron married a
Pritchard; Aunt Sarah married a Pierce; Aunt
Martha married a Lynn; and Aunt Zilphia married
a Halbert.

My Grandfather Wright died before my father
was fully grown, leaving some small children on
grandmother's hands to rear. They lived by farming. Grandmother was a very devoted Christian
woman, praying in her family when grandfather
was not at home to pray. My father emigrated to
East Tennessee into what is now Anderson or
Union County, when quite a young man, my father's
name being John Wright.

And now, boys, I will trace up on my mother's
side of the house. On her side my grandfather
was named William Dale. Grandmother was a
Barden before she married William Dale. I do not
recollect her given name. After they were blessed
with five children, grandmother died. The five
children, three girls and two boys, were small. Not
a great while after her death, one of the boys,
named James, died. The girls' names were Peninah,
which was my mother, Nancy and Alsie. Aunt
Nancy married Uncle Robert Wright, and Aunt
Alsie married Timothy Carpenter, a brother of my
wife's mother. Grandfather Dale was born and
lived the early part of his life in North Carolina.
After the death of grandmother he moved and
lived near Augusta in Georgia. Mother's brother's
name was William Dale. He was younger than
either of the girls. After the children were pretty
well grown they emigrated to East Tennessee, near

to where father, and I should have said Uncle
Robert Wright, came—for they came together—and
I think Grandmother Wright and the whole family
were soon in East Tennessee. It was there that
Uncle Robert Wright and Aunt Nancy Dale were
married. A short time afterwards father and
mother were married. Uncle Robert and father
soon, with their wives, emigrated to Wolf River,
into what was then Overton, but now Fentress
County, Tennessee. In a few years Grandfather
Dale married again, and emigrated to Fentress
County. Uncle William Dale remained in East
Tennessee.

And now I will confine myself to father's family.
Father and mother were blessed with fourteen children, seven boys and seven girls. Two girls and
one boy died in infancy. They raised to full-grown
age six boys and five girls. The boys' names were
William D., James M., Edmondson, John F., Absalom B., and Calvin C. The girls' names were
Sarah, Nancy, Freely Ann, Peninah Jane, and
Eliza Emeline. There was but one that died in infancy named. Its name was Margaret. Now I
have brought it down to your own recollection, I
trust, so that, if it is ever needed in a chain of family history, you can come at it easily. Perhaps I
had better say something about marriages and
deaths. William D. married Elizabeth Hopkins,
James M. married Caroline Craft, Edmondson married Naomi Spears, John F. died unmarried, A. B.
married C. S. Frogge, and Calvin C. married Nancy
Atkinson. Sarah married John Price, Nancy married John W. Frogge, your mother's brother, Freely

Ann married Greenberry Brown, Peninah Jane married John Carpenter, Eliza E. married George Y. Carpenter, who was a Federal soldier, and was killed during the civil war; she afterwards married John Davis. The Carpenters, John and George Y., were cousins of your mother.

And now the deaths. Your Grandfather Wright died of heart dropsy, April 21, 1844. Your Uncle William D. Wright died in Arkansas of fever in 1853. Your Uncle John F. Wright died in Arkansas in 1855. Your Aunt Peninah Jane Carpenter died of childbed fever in 1863. Your Grandma Wright died in July 1867 of apoplexy and paralysis. Edmondson Wright died of dropsy, August 16, 1879. James M. Wright died of congestion of the heart and lungs, October 30, 1879. Nancy Frogge died May, 1888. Your Uncle William D. Wright was a licensed local Methodist preacher for five or six years before his death. Your Uncle Edmondson Wright was a local elder in the Southern Methodist Church for years. He traveled in Kentucky on circuits as a supply for seven or eight years. Your Uncle C. C. Wright was a traveling elder for years in the St. Louis and Pacific Conferences of the Southern Methodist Church, and was presiding elder for a time.

As to my own work, I leave it in my life journal. Father and mother died members of the Methodist Episcopal Church. William D., John F., Nina Jane, Edmondson, and Nancy died members of the Methodist Episcopal Church, South. William D. and John F. are buried in the State of Arkansas. Father, mother, three infants, James

M. and Nancy Frogge are buried at the Three Forks of Wolf River, in Fentress County, Tennessee. Peninah Jane is buried in the Poplar Cove in Fentress County, Tennessee. Edmondson Wright was buried in Cumberland County, Kentucky: O how we are scattered!

And now I will tell you something of your mother's ancestry. Her grandfather on her father's side was named John Frogge, born and raised in Virginia; do not know in what county. He married Lucretia Miller. They raised eight children, four boys and four girls. They emigrated from Virginia to Kentucky, into Cumberland County, while their children were young. Your mother's grandfather did not live a great while after coming to Kentucky. He died from a relapse of measles. Their children's names were Cornelius Mitchell, William, Arthur, and John—boys. The girls' names were Elizabeth, Cynthia, Rebecca, and Mary. Her grandmother raised her children until they were grown and married, and she emigrated with her son-in-law, James Spearman, to Washington Territory, and died there. Cornelius M. Frogge, your grandfather, married Deborah Carpenter. William Frogge married Mary Smith. Arthur and John Frogge each married Williams girls, sisters. Soon after they married—that is, Arthur and John—they emigrated to the West. Your grandfather Frogge was reared by his uncle, Arthur Frogge, in Tennessee, on Wolf River. Your great-grandfather, your mother's grandfather, John Frogge, was a first cousin to James Madison, of Virginia, twice President of the United States. Your grandfather Frogge's early life, after marriage, was spent on Wolf River. After they had six children, they moved to Morgan County, Tennessee, on White Oak Creek, where Curtis Stonecipher now lives, and lived there six years; then went back to his farm on Wolf River, where your cousins, the Frogge boys, now live; only the houses were down on the road, where your pa and ma were married. Your Grandmother Frogge had fifteen children. Five died in infancy, and one girl, named Lucretia, died when nearly grown—three boys and twelve girls. One boy and four girls died in infancy, and two boys and seven girls were raised. The boys' names that were raised were Timothy Carpenter and John Wesley. The girls' names that were raised were Hannah Brown, Elizabeth Turley, Lucy Lane, Cynthia Ann Spearman, Deborah Jane, Rebecca Bosley, and Mary Baskett. Two only that died in infancy were named; one was named Nancy, the other Miriam. And now the marriages. Hannah B. married Harrison Williams. After having two children, she died triumphant. Timothy C. married Harriet Wilson; Elizabeth T. married Simon Shelley; Lucy L. married James Crouch; your mother, Cynthia Ann S., married A. B. Wright; Deborah J. married Lewis Shelley; John W. married Nancy Wright; Rebecca B. married T. C. Peters, and Mary B. married James H. McGinnis.

Your uncle T. C. Frogge has been a traveling Methodist preacher from his early youthful days. Your Grandfather Frogge was for years a Methodist class-leader. Every one of his children were members of the Methodist Church; so were all your uncles and aunts on your father's side of the house, except James M. Wright. Your uncle, T. C. Peters, has been an itinerant Methodist preacher from early youth. Your uncle, Lewis Shelley, is a Methodist preacher. So you see, boys, you have some President and a great deal of Methodist preacher blood in you all. But wait till I come now to your Grandmother Frogge's side of the house, and you will find several more preachers.

Your mother's grandfather, on her mother's side, was named Timothy Carpenter, a Yankee, born and raised to manhood in the State of Connecticut. When a young man he wandered into the State of Massachusetts, and was united in marriage to Hannah Brown, who was raised in the city of Boston. He early became an itinerant Methodist preacher. He had a brother named Samuel Carpenter, who was a missionary Baptist preacher. Timothy Carpenter, with his young wife, came as an itinerant to Kentucky. After traveling in that State a few years, he came to Tennessee, and purchased a good farm on the head of Wolf River, and lived near where William Pile now lives. He and wife raised eight children, five boys and three girls. The boys' names were Timothy, Consider, John, Dan, and Cyril. The girls' names were Lucy, Deborah, your grandmother, and Nancy. Your mother's Grandfather Carpenter sold out on Wolf River, and moved and settled on White Oak Creek, in Morgan County, Tennessee, where Schenck now lives. That is the old Carpenter place. Some of Rev. Timothy Carpenter's family married while he lived on Wolf River, and the others in Morgan County.

And now their marriages: Timothy married Alsie Dale, a sister of your grandmother Wright; Consider married Susan Guthrie; John married Sarah Guthrie; Dan married Jane Cisel; and Cyril married Rhoda Cisel, a sister of Dan's wife. Lucy married Middleton Holloway; Deborah, your grandmother, married Cornelius M. Frogge; Nancy married William Potter. Your mother's uncle, Dan Carpenter, has been from early youth a Methodist minister. Your mother's uncle, Timothy Carpenter, went to Texas early in life. We do not know anything of his or John Carpenter's descendants. And now this gives you a pretty good outline of your ancestry. In our lineage may the stream of greatness continually rise!

CHAPTER II.

BIRTH, CHILDHOOD, AND CONVERSION.

I WAS born in Fentress County, Tennessee, November 3, 1826, six miles northwest of Jamestown, the county-seat of said county, on a pike road, at the foot of Cumberland Mountain, on the headwaters of Wolf River. I was the sixth son and ninth child of my parents. I had two brothers quite chums with me, Brothers John F. and Calvin C. Wright; John being not two years older, and Calvin between three and four years younger, than I was. We were all naturally of quite a mischievous disposition of mind. Doubtless I possessed as large, if not the largest, share of that disposition, though of innocent design. I was brought up to labor in the fields from my earliest recollection, my father being a farmer and stockraiser. When quite young, I took pleasure in feeding hogs, calves, sheep, and other stock, thinking it the only way to live in this life.

I was early taught not to tell a lie, nor swear profanely, nor use blackguardish language in any way. I was taught the evils of using ardent spirits or tobacco. However, when quite a boy I ventured to take one chew of tobacco, which made me so sick that I never tried it again. My early home was very unhandy to school and church, having to walk three miles to school and back every day, to get what little education I obtained from the school-room. I have secured more education outside the school-room than in it, for I have been very fond of books. The nearest church-house was four miles off. I learned to spell and read when very young. I can remember when the first free-school law was enacted by the Legislature of Tennessee.

I was of school age—that is, six or more years old—when the first free school was taught in the district where I was raised. The qualifications required of teachers then were very low as compared with what they are now. Teachers were then employed at from ten to fifteen dollars per month. They sat a great portion of their time, and that even while hearing recitations, with a long beech or hickory switch in their hands, for the purpose of keeping the students under good rule. If one violated the school rules, he received the lash on his back in the presence of the school. The severity of the lash, or the number, was according to the magnitude of the offense committed. School terms were generally from one and a half to three months of length in the year. They generally commenced about the first of August, and always had a vacation of two weeks for fodder-pulling.

I had an ambition early in life to obtain a good education, and under the very meager school facilities I had, I would take my school-books in the clearing and fields with me, and while sitting down to rest, or to rest a horse in the plow, I would be studying my books. O how I do sympathize with a poor boy struggling after an education! So soon as I learned to read, and to commit to memory from the New Testament the Lord's Prayer, my father enjoined it on me to repeat the Lord's Prayer before lying down at night to sleep. I bless God for this, and to my latest breath, I trust, I shall never fail to comply with that rule, adopted so early in 'life. I can scarcely remember so far back as when I first learned to sing songs and hymns of praise to God. Frequently in singing, my heart would be so touched and moved that I would shed tears freely under a conscious sense of my unsaved state by nature. Often I would make the fields vocal with my singing, having a strong voice.

My father gave to me, when a boy, the fictitious nickname of General DeKalb. When quite a boy, I would walk barefoot four miles to attend Sunday-school. Facilities, as to Sunday-school literature, were not then what they are now. Then we studied the spelling-book, readers, and the New Testament, and there was no catechising done. We would take our dinner, and the Sunday-school would hold all day, unless there was preaching, prayer, or class meeting. Class-meetings were more frequent then than now. I ever felt great reverence for prayer or class meeting, as well as for preaching. My father and mother strictly enjoined it on me never to stir about or leave the house in time of divine service, but to treat the house of God with great reverence and respect. My mother was a professed Christian long before my existence, my father afterwards.

Having to work so constantly in the fields, through the week, it seemed Sunday was a long time in coming. When not attending Sunday-school or religious services, myself and brothers, and sometimes sisters, would stroll about the garden-walks, the orchards, and fields, and listen to nature's sweet songsters of the feathered tribes, especially in the early spring, when their notes seemed sweetest. Sometimes we would amuse ourselves in innocent plays, until I would be as tired on Sunday night, if not more so, than if I had worked in the field. At our earnest entreaty, my parents would sometimes allow myself and brothers to visit neighboring boys, and we would play base, run foot-races, wrestle, or play Antony over, until I was so tired that I could scarcely walk a mile or two home, and yet I took great delight in these plays. Sometimes neighboring boys would visit us, and that would save me the walk home. I must think that children were governed about as well then as at any time since, and yet I think that it was a sad mistake on the part of their parents to allow them to exert so much physical strength on Sunday.

As I began to move up in age, into my teens, I
became more anxious about my education, and to
possess some property of my own.   I also began to
feel a warm attachment to the feminine sex, and to
love the girls some ; but now began my school days.
At the age of sixteen, in November, the next spring
in April, I was bitten by a large serpent, supposed
to be a copperhead.   Its teeth-holes were fully an
inch from each other.   Myself and brother John,
taking our horses out of the plow one evening,
started for home, being at an old place, on which
father and mother had first lived, before purchasing
a more desirable site, on the road one-half mile
from the old.   We hitched our horses and went into
an old house partly filled with sheaf oats, to carry
some home with us.   I had great fears of snakes, as
they were numerous in those mountains, especially
at that season of the year.   Brother John went in, as
though talking to the snakes, telling them not to bite
him.   It was becoming rather dark in the old house,
and, on putting my hand down to take up a sheaf of
oats, the serpent bit me on the wrist near the pulse
of my right arm.   Being frightened, I did not move
until the serpent had released its hold.   I then spoke
to my brother and told him I was snakebitten.
He said he reckoned not, but I told him I was.   I
left the house at once, without taking any oats, got
on my horse, and started hurriedly for home.
When about halfway, I turned very sick, but
sucked my wrist where bitten, and spit out the
poison until I was somewhat relieved.

On coming opposite the house, I did not go to
the barn as usual with my horse, but lighted off,

went in, and told father I was snake-bitten. My father kept some medical books, and usually did his own doctoring. He bandaged my arm to prevent the swelling from running to my body, while he resorted to everything of which he could think or read, but all seemed to avail nothing. The bandage had to be changed more than once, and finally taken off entirely, my shoulders, neck, and head becoming so swollen as to almost prevent my breathing, until my friends had alarming fears that I would die from suffocation.

No one that has not experienced it, knows the amount of suffering there is from a bad serpent-bite. As a last resort, I was put to drinking strong whisky to counteract the snake poison, drinking a glass tumblerful at a time, which would for a few minutes relieve me from my intense suffering. When the serpent poison would overcome the whisky, and my suffering would return, again I would drink off another glass tumblerful of strong whisky, until I drank three tumblersful, drinking the last about midnight. After this, I was unconscious until next day about ten o'clock, during which time I was in a swooning condition, struggling for breath, the strong fight between serpent poison and whisky poison going on in my system. When I returned to consciousness I was about easy, but could hardly recognize myself. My right arm, lying by my side, was swollen almost as large as my body, and somewhat crooked, from which I could not straighten it for more than two weeks. O how near I came to death! After recovering a little, I felt as though I would rather die than to go through a like suffering again. For three spring seasons that arm changed to the color of a serpent and shed off the outside skin. My friends had serious fears that my arm would have to be taken off; but I was young, and outgrew it.

At that time I was an unsaved boy, and I knew it, and it made me shudder to think how near I was to the gate of death in an unsaved state. I took great delight in singing, and in studying the rudiments of music in the old four-note system. I purchased a cheap little hymn-book called Vedder's Hymns, and would take it in my side-pocket often, when attending church. Sometimes, when at class-meetings, I would take out my book and sing like a good fellow, unless the Christians should get happy and begin to shout, when my own unsaved condition would so impress me that tears would chase each other down my cheeks. If I could retreat and get on a back seat without being observed, I would do so; for I always had a great aversion to being called a coward. My convictions for sin grew heavier all the while, and from early boyhood I had a strong impression of mind that I should do considerable work for the Lord before I died.

My third living brother, Edmondson Wright, became a local preacher in the Methodist Episcopal Church. In his preaching, his very earnest appeals to the sinner often so impressed me that I would weep bitterly. I would think, if some one would only come and take me by the hand, how readily I would go to the anxious-seat and seek salvation; but I was young, and small of my age, and so was overlooked. I very well remember, in the summer of

1843, while attending on Three Forks of Wolf River, at old Pleasant Hill Church—the nearest Church to us—that I was so powerfully convicted for sin that I returned home that evening in great agony of mind.

Next day being Monday, and not having much work to do, I walked the woods all day long, wringing my hands in grief, and it seemed my heart would break because of sin. It has ever been since that time a mystery to me why I did not fall on my knees in that grove and surrender my heart in prayer to God for pardon; but I was afraid to make such a surrender of myself to the good Lord. In a few weeks from that time, in the month of August, a camp-meeting was coming on, to be held by the Cumberland Presbyterians, in the Poplar Cove five miles from my father's. I vowed to the Lord that I would go to that meeting and seek my soul's salvation.

By the time the meeting came on, I had about overcome all my serious impressions, and went to the meeting full of life and mischievous fun. I was a leader in such, if I could have a train of boys to follow me. On this occasion I would especially point out one poor old man, and make many funny and unbecoming remarks about him when he would get happy and shout aloud God's praise. I went to the meeting on Friday, I think, and on Saturday night was sitting in the congregation beside a playmate, Washington Campbell. His father, William Campbell, was a camper on the ground, and an elder in the Cumberland Presbyterian Church. James Campbell, an uncle of my companion, who was a

Cumberland Presbyterian minister, rose up to exhort, after some one had preached. He made earnest appeals to the Christians to pray, which they did; and soon shouts of praise to God began to go up. The hearts of myself and companion were melted in deep penitence. We were sitting not far from the altar, and when penitents were called, James Campbell came to us and urged us to go forward for prayers, which we did. We prostrated ourselves in the altar, on a carpet of straw; and O how I did pray, for I had achieved a great victory over self!

There was a large number of young men and young ladies at the altar, and still they came in crowds. The Christian people sang, talked, and prayed for us until a late hour, but I got no relief. After awhile it was suggested to take the mourners to the camps for sleep; but there was no sleep for me. Next day there was eloquent preaching; but the mourners were not called until night. Again I was at my place at the altar when the mourners were called, and O how humbly and earnestly I prayed to the Lord! At a late hour some lady asked me if I had any friends on the ground whom I would like to have come and pray for me. I answered by saying, "If I have any friends in the world, I would like to have them pray for me;" for I really felt that I was lost, world without end. It seemed so hard for me to appropriate the precious promises of Christ to my own personal good. Again, at a late hour, together with others, I was taken to the camps for rest; but not much sleep for me. The next day (Monday) the people gathered, as usual, under their brush arbor; for that was the kind under which we had been worshiping.

Just after the preacher took his text and began to preach, there came up a heavy rain, which caused the congregation to retreat to the surrounding camps. Religious services now began in every camp, some one serving as public speaker. A very good man by the name of Tyndall began exhorting in Bowden's, Solomon's, and Owen's camp, where I was. Directly he called mourners to come forward. I stood where I was for a short time, when Brother David Guinn, then a Methodist exhorter, afterward a Methodist preacher, came to me, took me by the hand, and said: "Young man, make one more effort." I started, and went about halfway across the camp, when I fell prostrate, crying: "O Lord, here let me die or be saved!" I cried from the very top of my voice: "O Lord, save or I perish!" I was there in that condition for some time; I hardly know just how long. After awhile, the very same old man, old Brother Simms, that I had made fun of for shouting, came and kind of rolled over me, and told me I could get up from there. He laughed, and talked so kindly that my faith laid hold on Christ, and instantly I arose, shouting: "Glory! glory, hallelujah! glory to God in the highest!" My father and oldest brother, hearing of my distress, had come to the meeting that morning without my knowledge. My oldest brother had been praying for me just before I arose, as he prayed in public.

When I arose he was happy; and in my rejoicing over the camp, I came to my father, took him by the hand, and tried to tell him how happy I was. He was sitting in a chair in the camp. He threw himself back in his chair, and shouted, "Glory! glory! glory!" clapping his hands together. He had been converted some four months before this, but this was the first public expression he had made of his conversion, as he had been converted in the woods. I rejoiced all through the camps; ran out into the streets of the camp-ground and shouted at the very top of my voice: "Hallelujah! I'm saved, I'm saved! glory to God and to the Lamb forever!" I was happily converted to God August 28, 1843, on Monday evening, about three o'clock, in Poplar Cove, Fentress County, Tennessee, five miles west of Jamestown, the county-seat. At my conversion, I thought I could tell the way of life so plainly that every one of my old companions—for several of them were on the ground—would certainly be converted; but with all I could say, they were not all saved.

I don't know just where my companion, young Campbell, was at the time of my conversion, but presumed that he was at the altar in some camp. I remember he was a penitent through the meeting, and was not converted until about two months after its close. I remained at the camp-meeting until it closed, which I think was about the middle of the week. During the remainder of the meeting, after my conversion, I labored to influence sinners to come to the altar, and tried to direct mourners to the Lamb of God. I took more delight than ever before in singing. I felt just like singing right up into heaven.

On returning home, I found my father was greatly delighted with my conversion. At that time I had two brothers and one sister professed Christians, also my father and mother. The others—two older brothers and one younger, also several sisters—were as yet unconverted. Brother John had become afflicted with epilepsy. Amid all my trials I prayed the Lord for sustaining grace. My Christian sister, Nancy, was very helpful to me, telling me to endure as a good soldier, and that I would wear a bright crown in heaven by and by. At the time of my conversion I was attending school. My second brother, James M. Wright, was the teacher. My father would take me to his knees and advise me how to deport myself at school, and especially during playtime. I have ever felt thankful for his godly counsel to me.

Having been converted at the Cumberland Presbyterian meetings, I felt quite an attachment to that Church, so I borrowed their "Confession of Faith" and read it closely for the next month. Also, during the same time, I read a Discipline of the Methodist Episcopal Church. Soon after the close of the camp-meeting in Poplar Cove, the Methodists at Pleasant Hill, on Three Forks of Wolf River, determined to build camps and hold a camp-meeting there early in that fall. Although we lived at a distance of four miles, my father and brothers put in, and we built a good frame camp, with different apartments, in which my father and family camped. The meeting began the last week in September, and reached over a few days into October. A number of ministers were in attendance. The new Confer-

ence year was just beginning. Joel Peake was the
new preacher in charge. On Monday of that meeting, October 1, 1843, I gave my hand to the pastor
in uniting with the Methodist Episcopal Church.
My father united with the same Church the next
day. My mother had been a member of this Church
for many years.

CHAPTER III.

EARLY MINISTRY AND MARRIAGE.

AFTER my conversion I began resorting to a
grove for secret prayer, often praying aloud.
The Lord would there bless my soul, and I would
shout aloud his praise. I must think the old limestone rock, where I knelt down to pray, will be
witness of my devotion. Every morning before
breakfast, as regular as the morning came, I repaired about three hundred yards out in the woods,
also every evening about twilight, for my morning
and evening prayers. Nor did I allow anything
to hinder me from my secret devotions. I found
secret prayer a helpful means of grace. It is altogether probable that this habit saved me from falling away. I recommend this duty to all young
converts.

In the spring of 1844, while myself and brother
James were feeding a large herd of cattle belonging
to my father, I was seriously gored by a vicious
bull. I would certainly have been killed by the
maddened animal, but for the timely presence and
intervention of my brother. He tossed me up on
his horns several times. From the injury and loss

of blood I lay helpless at his feet. I was carried into the house, and was sick for a time; also had to go upon crutches for several weeks, but was happy all the time.

On the 21st of April, 1844, after a very brief illness, my father departed this life, in holy Christian triumph, shouting with his latest breath. He died of heart dropsy. I then thought that I had lost my best friend on earth, next to my blessed Savior. His godly admonitions had been a great blessing to me; of them I was now deprived. I lacked one month and three days of being seventeen years of age when I joined the Church. The camp-meeting at which I joined was also the occasion of a quarterly-meeting on that charge. It was called Albany Circuit, in the Louisville Conference of the Methodist Episcopal Church, before there was an organization of the Methodist Church, South. At that meeting George W. Taylor was the presiding elder, and the preacher in charge was Joel Peake, the man to whom I gave my hand in joining the Church, who also baptized me, and issued my license to exhort. Brother Peake was then a man above forty years of age, and a splendid preacher. He lived, traveled, and died in the Louisville Conference. Father G. W. Taylor, the presiding elder at that time, was a strong, theological, soul-stirring preacher. He had but few superiors in preaching in his day.

The Sunday after my father's death I was nominated and appointed assistant class-leader of Mt. Pleasant Church, the class having near one hundred members. I was quite young, and the term of my probation had just expired; but I went to work, singing and praying, and talking to the class. C. M. Frogge, father of the girl who afterwards became my wife, was the principal class-leader. On the 10th day of August, 1844, I was licensed to exhort. The first few efforts that I made at public exhortation were at Mt. Pleasant Church. I then labored on the East and West Forks of Obed's River, in the counties of Fentress and Overton, in Tennessee. I also held meetings in the Poplar Cove.

It is worthy of notice that I was an assistant class-leader nearly four months, and a licensed exhorter one day, before I received the ordinance of Christian baptism. A small strip of Tennessee had been taken into the Louisville Conference, notwithstanding the Discipline on Conference boundaries ever made the State-line of Tennessee and Kentucky the line between the Holston and Louisville Conferences. It may have been by some neglect on the part of the Holston Conference preachers that it was taken in by the Louisville Conference people. I think it was a very fortunate thing at the time; for it gave us a good opportunity to become acquainted with, and to greatly love, a large number of preachers, exhorters, and class-leaders, on the Kentucky side.

Of some of those godly men I can not well forbear making mention in this sketch. In my first Quarterly Conference sittings, which were in Kentucky, I call to mind such preachers as Absalom Davis, Charles Smith, Jordan Hunter, my own brother Edmondson Wright, then living in Kentucky, among the preachers. Old Uncle John Kelley, Elijah Keene, Daniel Shelley, and Peter Shelley, his brother, were the most holy and useful exhorters that I ever knew. I want to say that quarterly-meetings now are not what they were then, especially in this country. It was not uncommon in that day to see twenty, thirty, and sometimes forty Quarterly Conference members together in one Quarterly Conference. Men would ride horseback twenty-five and thirty miles to attend a quarterly-meeting, and O what a loving handshaking time they would have! A love-feast was invariably held on every Sunday morning of the quarterly-meeting.

Father George W. Taylor—for he was an old man—presided for two years after our first camp-meeting where I joined the Church. At that camp-meeting he preached the funeral of Hannah Williams, my wife's sister. At the second camp-meeting there, he preached the funeral of my father, John Wright, he having died in April before the meeting. At the third camp-meeting he preached the funeral of my wife's father, Cornelius M. Frogge, he having died in the summer of 1845, just before the camp-meeting. Father Frogge was the leader of a large class when he died, and although I was a beardless boy, I took charge of the class. Many happy seasons have we enjoyed in class-meeting at old Mt. Pleasant meeting-house.

I have been afraid, so many new institutions are springing up in the Church to meet the progressive age in which we live, that the old landmarks, so essential to the very life and prosperity of

Methodism, will be neglected. The most essential means of grace to the life of Methodism is the class-meeting. Epworth Leagues, Young Men's Christian Associations, and Christian Endeavor Societies may be, and are, all good in their places, but they can never do the work of the class-meeting. Class-meeting is one of the old and very essential landmarks of Methodism. No place can be like it for the growth and permanency of the young convert.

Where class-meetings are regularly kept up, we lose but a small per cent by backsliding, from our revival meetings. Where they are neglected, there is always a fearfully large number of our converts that go back to the world, especially converts among the young. Class-meetings are so essential to the being and prosperity of Methodism that to dispense with them would certainly destroy the life of the Church. I know that Churches may seem to live without them; but their life is only apparent, and they can reasonably adopt the language:

> "And shall we ever live
> At this poor dying rate,
> Our love so faint, so cold to Thee,
> And Thine to us so great ?"

A Methodist Church is certainly in a very sickly state without the blessed means of a class-meeting. The writer of this sketch, being a boy of sixteen years of age at conversion, and of more than an ordinary gay disposition, attributes his success in Christian life to the blessed influence of class-meetings, filling his first office in the Church as class-leader. This office he held without any intermission for more than eight years, though during the time he was licensed to exhort and to preach, and for some years held the office of class-leader, exhorter, local preacher, steward and trustee of Church property. From past experience, I am convinced that parents, the Church, and class-leaders are responsible for fully three-fourths of the backsliding of so many young converts. If all young converts had the proper nursing they should have in the home, the Church, and by the class-leader, we would lose but a very small per cent of the converts from our revival-meetings. O that God would awaken us to our duty!

In the spring 1844, when I had been in the Church only a short time, at the General Conference in New York the James O. Andrew trouble on slavery came up, he being one of the Episcopal Board. He was required by a resolution of the General Conference to desist from his episcopal work until the impediment in his case should be removed. The Southern delegates were greatly excited by this action, and presented a petition to the General Conference, asking for a " provisional plan of separation " of the Church, whereby the Churches in the South might be permitted, if they so desired, to organize themselves into a separate organization. This plan the General Conference granted, and by a Convention, held in Louisville, Ky., in May, 1845, the Methodist Episcopal Church, South, was organized, the opinion of the Churches in the South on this question having been in the meantime obtained.

Doubtless too much clemency was extended by

the Methodist Episcopal Church to the Southern
Churches, by furnishing the "Plan of Separation"
in the General Conference of 1844. This was unfortunate to Methodism, and, no doubt, was an in-
dex to great national troubles. Although but a
boy, and of short experience in the Methodist
Church, I strongly opposed the organization of the
Southern Methodist Church. Could I have had a
vote, I should have voted against it every time. The
vote was not taken so generally nor unanimously
as was reported in the Louisville Convention. Now
let us pray for fraternal union, if we can not have
organic union. The different limbs that have broken
off from the old stalwart Methodist tree have only
been a healthy pruning.

The Protestant Methodist limb breaking off in
1828, the breach was soon healed. The Wesleyan
Methodist limb breaking off in 1843, the breach
was soon healed. The great division occurred in
1844; although incurring a heavy lawsuit, yet the
breach has been fully healed. A small limb, in
that of the Free Methodist, was broken off in 1860.
The old tree sustains no loss, but is yet full of
foliage and fruitage. I will here relate some incidents of my early Christian life. In the neighborhood where I lived, a certain man, the initials
of whose name were W. P., made and circulated a
very scandalous falsehood about me, and exerted
his utmost power to break down my religious character. Having been taught of God to overcome
evil with good, at a night meeting, where God gave
me great liberty to exhort sinners, this man was present, was deeply convicted, wept aloud, and cried for

mercy at the mourners' bench. After this he seemed
to have the warmest friendship for me.

In order to encourage all to overcome evil with
good, I will relate another instance wherein Christian charity subdued the rage of passion. A young
lady, through a jealous disposition, became highly
offended at me, insomuch that she came to where I
was lodging for the night, on purpose to quarrel
with me. I endured her raillery without resent-
ment, remembering that the Bible says, " Charity
beareth all things." Shortly after this, seeing her
deeply affected at a religious service, I went to her,
took her by the hand, and invited her to go with
me into the altar of prayer. She trembled from
head to foot like an aspen-leaf, but went readily to
the altar, and ever afterward was a warm friend of
mine. I mention these two instances, as I could
many others, just to illustrate the power of religious impressions, over a sinful heart, and to convince all young Christians, as well as more aged
ones, that the shortest way to dispose of their difficulties with each other is to pray them out together
at God's mercy-seat.

Not long after I had entered upon Christian
work, I was requested one evening to go to see a
man who was very low with the fever, and was
greatly concerned about his soul. Knowing the man
in health to be noted for wickedness, and the distance to go about five miles, and the natural timidity of my youth, were crosses hard to overcome.
However I went, and lost but little time in offering
to him a loving Savior, ready to receive him. He
cried for mercy while I prayed at his bedside, until

he laid hold of the gospel promises and shouted aloud the praise of a pardoning God; shouting out of his bed until he fainted from weakness.   But happy as he was, the dark side of the story is yet to come.   He got well, and—O the ingratitude of the human heart!—he relapsed into sin again.   Ever afterward, in his wicked revelries, he would refer to that time as the happiest hour of his life, and would affirm that he then enjoyed heartfelt religion, and would wish that he had then died.   Let this be a standing warning to all to watch and pray.

In endeavoring to serve God and the Church, I had great conflicts with the world.   I found youthful association a mighty obstacle to a growth in grace.   With all the care I could take in the selection of pious company, youthful mirth would intrude itself, and often bring me to tears of penitence. Sometimes I exclaimed with the great apostle, "O wretched man that I am, who shall deliver me from this body of death?"   I worked constantly through the week for my widowed mother, and would then hold my meetings somewhere every Sunday.   It was not long until I began to witness the conversion of my other brothers and sisters.   I obtained the best helps that I could, with my limited means, in the way of good books.   I would take a small pocket Testament with me to the field, and while resting the plow-horse, would study it closely, often reading as much as a whole chapter on my knees. I felt that the Lord had done so much for me that I wanted to do a great deal of work for his cause. I labored in this way as a Methodist exhorter for about four years.

When twenty-one years old, my mother gave to me a small horse and some other stock; these I exchanged for a large saddle-horse. My father, in his will, had appointed as his executor my brother, James M. Wright, who took great interest in my welfare, and was very helpful to me in my early ministry. I engaged myself and horse to my brother for one year at wages. I labored on the farm during the week at all kinds of farm labor, and held religious services at different places on Sunday. In the spring of 1845, at Mt. Pleasant meeting-house, I joined the Washingtonian Temperance Society. The public speakers on the occasion were T. C. Frogge, and Edward A. Martin. From that time I have endeavored to promote the cause of temperance the best I could. Since then I have lived a total abstainer from alcoholic drinks.

In the spring of 1847, Jacob E. Williams and myself made a great many temperance speeches throughout the country. We organized lodges of this temperance order, and held three successive temperance exhibitions, on which occasions we had immense temperance processions, and this noble cause was greatly uplifted. From my early boyhood I have endeavored to contribute my influence in favor of every moral institution. My influence and my vote have ever been thrown in favor of the suppression of the great liquor business, the mighty foe of the Church and the country. In the summer of 1848 I was recommended by the third Quarterly Conference to the fourth Quarterly Conference of Albany Circuit, in the Louisville Con-

ference, for license to preach, and on July 31,
1848, at Five Springs, near the town of Albany,
Clinton County, Kentucky, I was licensed to
preach. John S. Noble was the preacher in charge,
and Thomas Lasley was the presiding elder *pro tem.*
With this step came additional responsibility, and
I felt more than ever that I should consecrate myself more fully to the Master's work.

James King, a powerful preacher, had succeeded Father George W. Taylor as presiding elder
on the district. He remained for four years, and
was succeeded by Rev. N. H. Lee, who remained
on the district for only two years. He was succeeded by John F. South. Soon after South came
on the district, the Holston Conference claimed
their territory to the State line, and took it. John
F. South was a very eloquent and able speaker, and
soon after leaving the district he united with the
Baptist Church somewhere in Kentucky. I was
somewhat censured for the Holston Conference
taking its own territory again. I think it was
much for the best interest of the Church at that
time, and has been ever since, doubtless.

In the winter of 1848 I taught a singing-school
on Cumberland Mountain, eight miles southeast of
Jamestown; the only singing-school I ever taught,
however. I took great delight in singing, and in
my young days had quite a good voice for it. In
the spring of 1849 I was arranging for a matri-
monial connection with Cynthia S. Frogge, and had
been for nearly a year. We grew up together, in
four miles of each other, and had been schoolmates,
more or less, from early childhood. I thought I

loved her sufficiently to make her my life companion, and her love to me seemed true. I had a great
attachment to her eldest brother, Rev. T. C.
Frogge, who was then, and had been for a few
years, an itinerant preacher in the Louisville Conference. We were united together in holy matrimony May 27, 1849, by my worthy brother, Rev.
Edmondson Wright, on Sunday morning, about
eight o'clock, at her mother's home. My wife's
mother was the daughter of an itinerant minister
in the early days, Rev. Timothy Carpenter.

CHAPTER IV.

A LOCAL PREACHER.

SOON after our marriage we went to housekeeping. By entering upon a married state, I
thought I took a wise view of life's duties and
dangers. I might have done more for the Lord in
a single life, and yet I feared the slippery path of
youth in a single life, and believed that I could
live more consecrated to God with a good Christian
helpmeet. I had made some secret promise to God
that if I should be so fortunate as to become settled
down in a home of my own that my life should be
given to the Lord in itinerant work. The prospect for this at that time was gloomy; for neither
of us had much to begin with, and no one to aid
us. We went to housekeeping on my brother's
land, known as the Low Gap farm, on the tribu-
tary waters of Wolf River. The very first night
we dedicated our home to the Lord with family

prayers. We held prayers again next morning, a rule of our family which we have faithfully observed ever since. After housekeeping about two months, I took employment to teach school in Morgan County, Tennessee. The school was near where my wife's grandparents and their son, Cyril Carpenter, lived. I boarded with them. It was truly a feast to my soul to listen to grandfather relate the scenes in his early ministry.

Late in the year 1849 I rented land, and moved upon a farm of Miller Atkins, near my wife's mother. This placed us much more convenient to Church. We remained here for two years. We both used great industry, raised good crops, and accumulated considerable property. My wife was a worthy help-meet for me, both in laboring for our own welfare and in my ministerial work. In that day our clothing, both for ladies and gentlemen, was made from the cotton which we grew ourselves, and of wool taken from our own sheep. Our mothers, wives, sisters, and daughters carded, spun, and wove these into cloth of every variety of color and kind, from which our clothing was made. Ready-made clothing, as bought and worn now, was scarcely known then, and I must claim that people appeared about as handsomely dressed then as now. My wife made our clothing in this way. The weaving-loom was her piano in that day. In September, 1850, our first child was born, a girl. My wife came near dying of child-bed fever at this birth. By the mercy of God and the aid of a good physician she recovered.

In December, 1851, our second child, a boy, was

born. In the fall of 1851, I was sorely afflicted, with a chronic affection of the liver, which caused me great suffering. It was several years before I obtained entire relief. All this time, during my very busy work and family afflictions, I endeavored to preach all that I could, and the Lord wonderfully blessed my labors. After living two years on the land of Miller Atkins, I took a lease on land of my mother-in-law, and moved two or three hundred yards across the line onto it. I built another house to the one already there. We made this change in the spring of 1852, and remained there nearly six years. We were taken back into the Holston Conference in about the year 1851. The first presiding elder from this Conference was R. M. Hickey, a strong young preacher, very sympathetic and moving in his sermons. He was succeeded by Rev. David Fleming, a strong preacher and a very good man. His successor on the district was Rev. W. C. Daily, a smooth, good preacher. During his term on the district the War of the Rebellion came up.

In the summer of 1854 I was recommended by the Quarterly Conference of the Jamestown Circuit for local deacon's orders to the Holston Conference of the Methodist Episcopal Church, South, to meet in Cleveland, Tenn., on October 12, 1854. I left home on Sunday morning, October 8th, rode nineteen miles and attended a meeting that Rev. B. L. Stephens was holding at Washington Taylor's.

In company with Brother Stephens and Rev. Ramey Oaks, I rode nine miles from this place, and took supper with Brother Lee Taylor. We rode three miles more after supper, and staid all night with Brother Oaks. At Brother Lee Taylor's there were several lawyers and a circuit judge on their way to hold circuit court in Jamestown. The next day, myself and these two brethren set off for the Annual Conference. We rode out of Fentress through a portion of Morgan and into Bledsoe County, through the Grassy Cove on to Walden's Ridge. On account of the flux raging on Walden's Ridge, we could not procure a lodging-place for the night until a late hour. We were somewhat disturbed with the thought of having to go down Walden's Ridge that night, it being very dark. This would have greatly endangered our lives. At last we came in sight of a light, and went to it. It was from a small cabin. We called to stay all night, but the man of the house said he was not prepared to keep us; yet as it was impossible to go down the mountain after night, he would take us in and treat us the best he could. After feeding our horses and going into the house, I thought the place looked more like the residence of a cut-throat than of any one else. I must confess, I was in some suspense until I heard a little child singing, "I have a home in the promised land." Then I felt safe, for I knew that parents who taught their little children to praise God would harm no one. We soon learned that the family were religious and members of the Methodist Church. They treated us kindly, and did not want to receive any pay from us. However, we paid them.

The next day we rode to Uncle Dan Carpenter's, in McMinn County, remained in that settle-

ment two days, had meeting, and then rode to
Cleveland on Friday evening, having gone about
thirty-five miles that day.   Brother Oaks and I
were assigned our boarding-place by Rev. W. C.
Daily, at Brother Wood's.   Heaven bless that
brother!   On Saturday, myself and Brother Oaks
were elected to deacons' orders, and Brother
Stephens to elder's orders.   On Saturday night
Dr. E. H. Myers, of Charleston, South Carolina,
preached an excellent discourse.   On Sunday morning Bishop George F. Pierce preached a soul-stirring sermon from Matt. xix, 29.   In the evening
Dr. John B. McFerrin, of Nashville, preached a
happy discourse from Psalms lxxxiv, 10–11.   At
the close of Bishop Pierce's sermon, myself and a
number of others were ordained deacons in the
Church of God, and at the close of the evening
service several were ordained elders.   This was October 15, 1854.   On Monday morning we started
for home, rode into McMinn County the first day,
and had meeting at night.   The next day we rode
to the Grassy Cove, and the next day to Brother
Oaks's.   The following day I reached home, and
found my family all well.

In the summer of 1855 I was solicited to preach
in a Campbellite settlement, where there were very
few Methodists.   Opposition upon the part of the
Campbellites was said to be used; but despite all,
the Lord came down in great power, and converted
twelve or fifteen souls.   Fifteen joined the Methodist Church.   Our third child, John Wesley, a
large boy babe, was born October 5, 1857.   In the
fall of 1857 I bought a farm of one hundred and

sixty acres lying near the Kentucky line, in Fentress County, and moved to it on the last day of the
year. This was a body of good land, for which I
paid $800, paying partly money down, and the re-
mainder in installments. The neighborhood was an
excellent community of people, but there were no
Methodists living near. I opened my own private
house for circuit preaching each month, and soon a
class was organized, composed of my family and
some of the neighbors. Circuit preaching was kept
up in our home for years. Our home was also the
resting-place of the itinerant Methodist preacher.
Sometimes they spent a week of rest on each round
in our humble abode. Myself and family became
greatly attached to these godly men, who came each
year to minister to us in holy things. Myself and
wife used great industry and economy to pay for our
home, and to make ourselves comfortable.

During the year 1858, I cultivated a good crop
of wheat, oats, and rye, and tended twenty-three
acres of corn, without hiring any help. My land
was strong, and I raised bountiful crops, and sold a
great deal of grain. I also raised large numbers of
hogs and cattle each year, and raised and sold some
mule colts. Also in this year I cleared up the land
and cultivated a large tobacco-crop, which I was
able to turn into money during the next winter.
We had a large orchard of apple-trees of splendid
fruit. My wife cut and dried in the old-fashioned
way, in the sunshine, large quantities of these, with
which she bought her own better wearing apparel—
calicoes, ginghams, worsteds, shoes, and domestics.
She kept a large flock of geese, and with the feath-

ers from these bought all our groceries, coffee, sugar, and other things. I mention this to show the young people of to-day just how we lived in that day. A happier life has never been lived than we lived in that good old time.

In the summer and fall of this year I taught school four months at the Holly Grove school-house, near John Campbell's, three miles from my home. I worked all day in the school-room—for I had a large number of students—and then till a late hour at night, and in the early, dewy morning in my tobacco-crop. I hired no help, but worked almost day and night. For teaching I received eighteen dollars per month, which was considered liberal wages for a teacher in that day. In August, 1858, the Cumberland Presbyterians held their annual camp-meeting at Lick Creek Camp-ground, in Fentress County. Myself and family attended it. The services began on Saturday. Tuesday following, an event occurred that broke up the meeting. A difficulty arose over business matters between twin brothers, Alexander and Floyd Evans, and their cousin James Reed on one side, and Champ Ferguson on the other, who afterwards became a noted Confederate guerrilla leader during the Civil War. When the difficulty arose, Ferguson left the grounds to prevent disturbing the worship. The other party followed and overtook him one-half mile from the camps, when a deadly battle ensued, in which Ferguson killed James Reed with a knife, and badly injured Floyd Evans. He was on trial for this murder in the circuit court of Fentress County when the war came up.

As I have mentioned Ferguson's name, and because of his notoriety during the Civil War, I will say of him, that before the war he was known as an orderly citizen, honest in his dealings, and a man well-to-do in the world; but a dangerous man when exasperated.

In the fall of this year our babe was greatly troubled in teething, that led to inflammation of the brain. On a fair golden autumn day—September 13, 1858—about one o'clock in the afternoon, he plumed his angel wings, and with a smile bid farewell to a sin-cursed world, and flew home to glory. Thank God, we have a precious babe in the heavenly world. Our family link reaches from earth to heaven.

> "One army of the living God,
>   To his command we bow;
> Part of his hosts have crossed the flood,
>   And part are crossing now."

We take courage when we hear our blessed Lord say: "Of such is the kingdom of heaven."

> "I take these little lambs, said he,
>   And lay them to my breast;
> Protection they shall find in me,
>   In me be ever blessed."

We laid him to rest the next day in Mt. Pleasant churchyard, where I joined the Church. At his burial, singing and prayer were offered by Rev. Willett G. Sherman. During the Civil War the churchyard was neglected, and so overrun by troops and others, that all traces of his grave were lost, and his resting-place is now unknown. In the autumn of this year the celebrated blazing star appeared in the northwestern heavens. Its head was about halfway between the horizon and the zenith, and its brilliant tail reached nearly halfway across the heavens. It lighted up the night, and remained for weeks. Among the superstitious it was regarded as the harbinger of war.

During this year I spent about all my Sundays in preaching, and witnessed many precious meetings in which souls were converted. It was a year of great sadness to our home; but there were many things for which to rejoice. Praise the Lord! The year 1859, I farmed about as I had done in 1858; raised large crops of grain and tobacco; sold numbers of hogs, cattle, and mule-colts, and in the autumn taught a school of three months at Van Buren Academy, two miles from my home, for which I received twenty dollars per month as wages. We were now about out of debt; had improved our home and the farm greatly, and were gathering about us comfort and plenty. Our two living children were healthy, of strong mind, and were attending school. We were looking forward to our coming future, with bright prospects. I spent my Sundays in ministerial work, and held many protracted meetings, with gracious results.

In the spring of 1860 our community was greatly scourged with an epidemic of scarlet fever among the children. A great many among our neighbors died with it. Almost every home was in mourning on the account of a death. I held many funeral services, and endeavored to comfort many sad-hearted. Our then only son was taken with it,

March 1st, and went down to death's door. By the mercy of God, in answer to prayer, and by the assistance of our splendid physician, Dr. Paige, he recovered. This year found me out of debt.

In the summer of 1860 I held a meeting three or four days in the Poplar Cove, Fentress County, Tennessee, which resulted in fifteen conversions, and about as many joined the Church. In July, I witnessed one conversion at Mount Pleasant Church. In the following October, at an evening service which I held at Sulphur Springs school-house, we had eight happy conversions. The result of my ministerial work for the year was twenty-four conversions, and I took about twenty into the Church.

During the fall of this year the exciting Presidential election occurred, that resulted in the Civil War. There were four candidates in the field. Stephen A. Douglas, of Illinois, was the Peace Democratic candidate. John C. Breckinridge was the States' Rights Democratic candidate. Abraham Lincoln, of Illinois, was the candidate of the Republican party. John Bell, of Tennessee, was the candidate of the Union-American party. True to the teachings of my fathers, I had always been a Democrat, and voted, with the other Democrats of my State, for John C. Breckinridge, though the electoral vote of the State was cast for her favorite son, John Bell. Lincoln was elected.

CHAPTER V.

ROUGH TIMES

IN the winter and spring of 1861 the Civil War came upon the land. Eleven Southern States rebelled against the Federal Government. Tennessee seceded in June. I did not vote when the question of "secession" or "no secession" was before the people, but I was opposed to secession. During four years the country was in the throes of an awful strife. Civil courts were suspended in Tennessee. Anarchy prevailed everywhere. Post-offices and post-roads were abandoned. No stores were kept. Calicoes, domestics, coffees, sugars, shoes, hats, ready-made clothing, and all kinds of merchandise were things of the past. Pastors abandoned their Churches. In Fentress County, the people were divided on the great question. Those on the side of the South enlisted in the Confederate army; and those on the side of the North went through the lines into Kentucky, and enlisted in the Federal army. Many homes were abandoned by the entire family, some going to Kentucky, and the opposite side down South, for greater security from the guerrilla bands on either side. Whole plantations were thrown out to the commons, having been deserted. Waste and ruin were upon every hand. I preached for all the Churches, opened the doors of the Methodist Episcopal Church, South, and received members, baptized them, lettered them when they removed, and thus acted as a self-constituted pastor until the return of peace. I held a basket-meeting at Van Buren Academy, commencing on Saturday before the first Sabbath in August, which lasted five days, and resulted in eleven happy conversions and ten accessions to the Methodist Church. We were greatly indebted to the Rev. Timothy C. Peters for very efficient labors performed during the first two days of this meeting, for he preached with the power of the Holy Ghost sent down from heaven. We were also indebted to Daniel R. Reagan for efficient labors, the last three days of the meeting. Brother Peters, in one of his sermons, took occasion to speak of the war as an unholy war, which gave great offense to the leading secessionists, who brought soldiers to the meeting the next day to have him arrested; but he became apprised of their purpose, and escaped into Kentucky. During the latter part of the meeting two home guards, named Williams, greatly disturbed the meeting in an effort to kill Captain Barton, who had recently enlisted in the Confederate army. Captain Barton was a relative of my wife. Such were the times through which we passed. At a subsequent evening meeting at Van Buren Academy, there was one conversion. I realized other happy meetings during the remainder of the year.

In September of this year, Federal troops of the First Kentucky Cavalry came out from Albany in Clinton County, and attacked some Confederate recruits from Wayne County, Kentucky, stationed at Travisville, Tenn., and killed a young man named Henry Sofley, the first blood shed in our community during the war. In the latter part of this year, General Zollicoffer, with a Confederate

army, passed through Fentress County into Wayne
County, Kentucky, and across the Cumberland
River, and took position at Mill Springs. The result of my ministry during the year was twelve
conversions, and ten accessions to the Methodist
Church, just half the amount of success that I had
realized the preceding year. I can not account for
this on any other ground than from the confusion
that the war had spread through the country. It
was now that the muttering tones of the distant
thunders of human woe began to pour their melan-
choly strains upon our ears. O gracious Lord, save
innocent blood from staining a Christian land!
Blessed be God, I am not afraid to die, therefore I
will meet all dangers for the cause of my Master.

In January, 1862, General Zollicoffer was defeated and killed at Mill Springs, Kentucky, and
his entire army routed after a bloody battle. Later
in the spring, Federal troops came into our part of
Tennessee. About this time, Tinker Dave Beatty
organized his guerrilla band, on the Federal side, in
the fastnesses of the Poplar and Buffalo Coves, and
held his ground there during the remainder of the
war. Champ Ferguson, on the Confederate side, occupied Overton, Clay, White, and the valley part of
Fentress Counties, with an independent company.
Between these independent companies a constant
warfare was carried on during the remainder of
the war.

The great battles of Fort Donelson and Shiloh
were fought during the winter and spring of this
year. During the summer, Colonel John H. Morgan
passed through Fentress, and made a very destructive

raid into Kentucky. In the autumn, General
Bragg invaded Kentucky, and the battle of Perry-
ville was fought, resulting disastrously to his army.
I will now relate some of the atrocious scenes that
occurred during this year within my knowledge.
In May, Alexander Huff, an inoffensive Union man
was captured by a Confederate force, and while a
prisoner, was cruelly murdered near the Three
Forks of Wolf River. About the same time, two
men near us, John Duncan and John Rich,
brothers-in-law, were murdered by Confederate
troops. Their offense was that they had joined
a home guard. In the latter part of the year, an
excellent young man, living on Wolf River, John
Riley by name, was murdered by Union bush-
whackers in his father's yard. He was a non-com-
batant and a harmless young man. His only offense
was that he sympathized with the South. Champ
Ferguson murdered Whigge Frogge, shooting him
while sick in bed with measles; his offerse was that
he was a Union man. About the same time, Ferguson murdered Reuben Woods, a most excellent
and inoffensive man, in his own house.

In September, W. L. Allen, a young man of
our community, a Confederate soldier, was killed
from ambush, near Hale's Mills. He left a young
widow, whom he had married about one year before.
His comrades, who were with him, in retaliation
burned a number of the neighboring houses of
Union people, several families, consisting of women
and children, being turned out of doors without a
shelter. Many homes on both sides, during this
dreadful war, were burned in our section. On the

cold evening of October 24th, Tinker Beatty, with about one hundred men, made a raid through our settlement, and killed, at the Poore place near us, a Confederate soldier named Milligan, and fatally wounded another, Henry Richardson. On that night a snow one foot deep fell.

I will now relate my ministerial work for the year. In May, at an appointment I filled at Van Buren Academy, I witnessed one happy conversion. I had witnessed one at the same place a short time before. I held a basket-meeting of three days at the same place, embracing the fourth Sabbath in July. There were no conversions, though a good time with Christians. I also held a basket-meeting at Sulphur Springs school-house for two days, embracing the first Sabbath in August. Here a false report respecting military men greatly injured our meeting. Our most zealous brethren, through fear, left the meeting ground. Here there were no conversions, but a good time with Christians. Glory be to God! Great credit is due the good people at both of these places for bringing a full supply of provisions each day to feed the congregation. I held a basket-meeting at Brother Joshua Story's, near the Kentucky line. This meeting lasted six days, and resulted in twelve happy conversions and fifteen accessions to our Church. It embraced the second Sabbath in August. Never will the heavenly glory of this meeting be erased from many noble Christian hearts, but will blaze upon the archives of memory forever. We pray God that it may be as bread cast upon the waters, that may be gathered for many days to come. What rendered the meeting most interesting was that members of different Churches, and persons holding different views in politics, embraced each other with warmest hearts, and together in the altar shouted, Glory to God in the highest! On Sunday of this meeting I preached the funeral of Sarah Ann M. Harris to an attentive audience. A few weeks after this I baptized twelve persons—three by affusion and nine by immersion—who were converted in this meeting. I held a two days' basket-meeting at Hale's Mills, embracing the fourth Sabbath in September, and here witnessed one happy conversion. The result of the years' work was fifteen conversions, and twenty-three accessions to the Methodist Church. I baptized fifteen persons, and married five couples. Thanks be to the Great Head of the Church for the mercies of the past year!

During the first days of the year 1863, the bloody battle of Stone River was fought in Middle Tennessee. In the summer of this year, General John H. Morgan passed through Fentress County, on his last raid into Kentucky. At Lebanon, Kentucky, he burned up several millions of dollars in Government stores. The smoke of this fire darkened the heavens for days. In August, a part of General Burnside's Federal army passed through our section into East Tennessee. In September the great battle of Chickamauga was fought; and later in the year, the battles of Mission Ridge and of Knoxville were fought. During the summer of this year Peter Beach, one of Tinker Beatty's men, was captured by the Confederates, and killed at

Three Forks of Wolf River, while on his knees praying to God for mercy.

In the autumn of this year Conrad Pile was killed near my home by Confederate troops, having been taken prisoner. He was a noncombatant, but a Union man. Scores of others on both sides, in the same manner, were murdered in our county during this year. On February 22, 1863, our fourth child, a daughter, Deborah Caroline, was born. In the year 1863 my appointments were once or twice every week. I held a basket-meeting on Back Creek, at Mole's school-house, embracing the second Sabbath in August, which lasted three days, and resulted in three happy conversions.

I held a basket-meeting at a school-house in Stockton's Valley, Clinton County, Kentucky, embracing the third Sabbath in August, which lasted two days. We had a happy time with Christians, but no conversions. On Sunday of this meeting I preached the funeral of Martha Savage, to a large congregation. I held a basket-meeting at Brother Joshua Story's, embracing the fourth Sabbath in August, which lasted two days, and resulted in two conversions, and four accessions to our Church. Again I held a basket-meeting at Head of the Cane school-house, embracing the first Sabbath in September, which lasted three days, and resulted in two happy conversions. I closed this meeting, leaving many penitents at the altar, because I broke down and was unable to preach.

During the year 1863 I preached sixty-seven sermons. A copy of the texts I used I have among

my papers. The result of the year was eight conversions, and four accessions to the Methodist
Church. I also baptized during the year three infants and five adults. The great military operations
of 1864 were the battles in Virginia between Gen-
erals Grant and Lee, and the advance of General
Sherman from Dalton to Atlanta in Georgia, and
subsequently the march to the sea; also the battles
of Franklin and Nashville in our own State. Many
were the atrocious scenes in my own immediate section. In January of this year, one-half mile from
my home, in a battle between some of Beatty's and
Ferguson's men, Hiram Richardson, John Smith,
and Thomas Riley, Confederates, were killed. They
were young men from families of my neighbors.
Young Riley was taken prisoner and brutally murdered, while begging of his captors the privilege of
seeing his young wife, who was only one-half mile
away, before they killed him. This was denied
him. The young wife died soon afterwards of a
broken heart.

In the spring of this year, Fountain Frost, a
Confederate soldier, was killed by Beatty's men, at
Gilreath's Mills, near my home, while begging for
his life. In June, Jefferson Pile, a man who had
taken no part in the Civil War, but was a Southern
man, was cruelly murdered by Beatty's men, near
the Three Forks of Wolf River. During the summer of this year my brother-in-law, George Y.
Carpenter, a Federal soldier, who was at home on
a visit to his family in the Poplar Cove, was killed
by Confederate troops. In November, four young
men, Federal soldiers, were killed three miles from

my home, by two of Ferguson's men, whom they had attacked.

During the year, notwithstanding the thundering storms of an awful revolution raged, I endeavored to urge the conquest of Zion. I had constant appointments to preach, and, thank God, he sanctioned my efforts. I labored in Fentress County, Tennessee, and in Wayne and Clinton Counties, Kentucky. At a meeting I held in June, at Brother Thomas Savage's, in Clinton County, Kentucky, there were three happy conversions, and two joined the Methodist Church. I held a basket-meeting near the same place, at Ferguson's school-house, the fourth Saturday and Sunday in August, which continued two days. Several mourners were at the altar, and I took two white persons and one colored girl into the Church. Myself and Rev. Robert Ramsey held a basket-meeting at Van Buren Academy the first Saturday and Sunday in September. Several mourners were at the altar; one was happily converted, and three joined the Methodist Church. The meeting lasted three days, at the close of which I baptized two by pouring and two by immersion. During the year, I held but two basket-meetings. This is explained by saying, that I received so many applications to preach funerals, and some of these at a great distance, I was unable to hold any more. I could not attend to all the applications that I received to preach funerals. We had some precious meetings at funeral appointments. These were held on Otter Creek, Beaver Creek, Carpenter's Fork, and at Bethesda Church, in Wayne County Kentucky; and on Spring Creek and Lick Creek, in

Clinton County; also among the hills and coves of Fentress County, Tennessee.

On December 10th, at night, I preached at James Coil's, in Wayne County, Kentucky, to a large crowd. There were three happy conversions. I had ridden fourteen miles in the morning, and preached at twelve o'clock the funerals of two little children. I went from Coil's to Bethesda Church, and preached the funeral of an excellent young lady, to an attentive audience. During the year, I preached fifty-seven times, took eight persons into the Church, baptized five infants and six adults—four by pouring and two by immersion—and had at my appointments seven happy conversions to God. I also preached the funerals of thirty-three persons.

With the close of this year it was evident that the cause of the Confederacy was rapidly approaching an end. O how grateful I feel to my Heavenly Father for his unspeakable mercies toward me during the past year! The military events of 1865 were the surrender of Lee to Grant in Virginia, and of Johnson to Sherman in North Carolina; also the assassination of President Lincoln, while attending a theater, by J. Wilkes Booth. In February of this year, in one-half mile of my home, Beatty's men killed an old man, Robert Richardson, who was ninety-two years old, and was too feeble to walk across the room without help. He was murdered in the most brutal manner. His only offense was, that his sons were in the Confederate army. In April, Captain Barton, a Confederate soldier, was killed within one mile of my home by Federal troops.

On the fourth Sabbath in March, on the head-

waters of Spring Creek, I preached the funeral of
an infant son of William and Hester Ann Smith.
We had a precious meeting. On the second Sabbath of May, I preached the funeral of Robert
McGhee, at Travisville, Tennessee. Mourners wept
at the altar, and two joined the Methodist Church.

In May of this year, the white-winged angel of
peace once more spread her pinions over our dis-
tracted land. O how welcome was this peace! By
order of Presdent Johnson, the people were asked
to repair to their accustomed places of worship and
return thanks to Almighty God for this blessing
once more upon the land. A few neighbors and
myself met in a building used for a school-house,
near my home, and held a thanksgiving service.

A great change had come to the South. The
Negroes, who had been held as slaves, were now free.
These very generally abandoned their old homes,
and roamed about the country in quest of some
means of support. They were without property, and
without education. They either became tenants upon
plantations, or worked at low wages for the white
race. They were also invested with the right of
suffrage, while the white race were almost entirely
disfranchised. Unscrupulous Northern adventurers
poured into the South, and, supported by Negro
votes and United States troops, took charge of State
Governments, much to the dissatisfaction, oppression,
and distress of the country. This was known as the
period of reconstruction.

On July 31, 1864, our fifth child, William Dudley
Wright, was born.

CHAPTER VI.

GREAT EVENTS.

WHEN peace was fully restored, and the State Government was set up, my sympathy and vote were with the Republican party, because I believed it was not only the champion of human liberty, but had been the savior of the nation in the hour of peril. I have never allowed politics to occupy much of my thought and life. The first Sabbath in June of this year, in Wayne County, Kentucky, I preached the funerals of two infant children of a colored woman, named Maria Miller. The names of the children were Edia and Abel. We had a glorious shout in the camps of Israel.

On the fourth Sabbath in May, I took a good Cumberland Presbyterian into the Methodist Church. I continued preaching funerals at different points. On the fourth Sabbath in July, I preached twice at Sulphur Springs school-house. We had several weeping penitents at the altar, and one happy conversion to God. On the fifth Sabbath in July, at Story's graveyard, we had a great many mourners at the altar, four happy conversions, and one accession to our Church. The following day we had a happy time, and one more conversion. On the second Saturday in August, I commenced a basket-meeting at Ferguson's school-house, which lasted five days. During that time I preached three funerals. We had a glorious move in Israel's ranks. Mourners in crowds wept at the altar. Such deep penitence I never witnessed before, and

the conversions were the brightest I ever saw.
During the meeting, we had eight happy conversions, and seven joined the Methodist Church. In
September of this year, I was taken with a violent
attack of bilious fever, and was in low condition
for a number of days, but by the good providence
of God I recovered.

On the first Sabbath in October, at a meeting I
held at Thomas Savage's, in Clinton County, Kentucky, we had a great time of religious rejoicing. I
felt uncommon liberty in preaching on the resurrection. One joined the Methodist Church. On
the fourth Sabbath in October, after baptizing some
young converts, I repaired to a graveyard, near
Thomas Savage's, and preached the funeral of a
most excellent Christian girl. We had a gracious
time of the overshadowing presence of Jesus in our
midst, and one happy conversion to God. Glory
to Jesus' precious name, this year so far has been a
happy one to my soul! In December I filled four
appointments on the Albany Circuit, for my brother,
E. Wright, who was preacher in charge of that
work.

On my return home I held a night service at
Thomas Savage's, and, praised be Jesus' name, we
had a precious time! While a great many Christians
shouted aloud the praise of God, mourners were
weeping aloud for mercy, and two young ladies
joined the Methodist Church. The result of the
year's labor in Christ's holy vineyard are as follows: I preached sixty-nine times, received twelve
into the Church, and witnessed fifteen happy conversions. I baptized seven sweet infants and two

adults by pouring and six by immersion. I preached
the funerals of thirty-three persons in Wayne and
Clinton Counties, Kentucky, and in Fentress County,
Tennessee. It will be seen that the year 1865 was
a more useful year of my life than 1864. Thanks
be to the Great Head of the Church, for his unspeakable mercies to me! Hail, O hail thou, 1866!

Notwithstanding the inclement wintry blast, I
began my year's labor much earlier than last year.
After passing through January and February, on
the first Sabbath in March, at night, I held a meeting at Brother Thomas Savage's. Thank God, we
had a feast with Christians, three happy conversions
and three accessions to the Methodist Church! At
a meeting I held the 1st of May, at Sister Duncan's
in preaching for her afflicted son, two persons joined
the Church, and at a meeting that I held the first of
May, at Brother P. H. Davidson's, we had several
weeping penitents at the altar and one accession to
the Church. The day following I held meeting on
the Three Forks of Wolf River, where there were
again some penitents, and four joined the Church.

In April I held a meeting at Ferguson's school-
house, in Clinton County, Kentucky, and baptized
two young converts by immersion, after which, in
holding prayers in Mother Ferguson's house before
we parted, the Lord powerfully converted one soul.
The above aged lady was the excellent mother of
the noted Champ Ferguson. At a meeting that
I held at Head of the Cane, the last of May, we had
a number of penitents at the altar, and one conversion.

On Saturday before the second Sunday in June,

after preaching at eleven o'clock, and baptizing one lady by immersion, I preached in the evening at Thomas Hays's. We had a number of penitents at the altar and one conversion. The next day I preached twice at Ferguson's school-house, and witnessed one more happy conversion to God, and took seven persons into our Church. Here I left a goodly number of penitents at the altar. On the fourth Sabbath in June, S. Grear and myself preached a funeral together at Mother Evans's, Fentress County, Tennessee. We had a number of penitents and five happy conversions. In the evening of the same day, I preached at Van Buren Academy. We again had a number of penitents at the altar, and one accession to our Church. In June of this year I changed my Church relations.

Bishop Early held the sessions of the Holston Conference of the Methodist Episcopal Church, South, for the years 1862, 1863, and 1864. A number of the ministers of the Conference were expelled because of their well-known Union sentiments. These, with other Union ministers, traveling and local, together with a large number of Union people among the membership of the Church, felt that, under the circumstances, they could not longer live happily in the Southern Church. Accordingly, under the direction of Bishop Clark, the work of the reorganization of the Methodist Episcopal Church was begun in East Tennessee, in the year 1864. The first Conference session was held in May, 1865, in Athens, Tennessee, Bishop Clark presiding.

I opposed the division in 1844, and all the time regarded the Church South, as built upon the institution of slavery, the sum of all villainies. My mind had been made up to the fact, during the Civil War, that, should the Methodist Episcopal Church return to the South, I would welcome the opportunity of returning to its ranks. I was strongly opposed to secession, as well as the division of the Methodist Church in 1844; and when the first opportunity offered, in June, 1866, I gladly transferred my membership from the Methodist Episcopal Church, South, to the Methodist Episcopal Church. This was the Church which I had joined when a boy, and I felt that I had returned to my old home again. I am not sectarian in making choice of the old Methodist Episcopal Church. It is the Church of my choice. I believe that the doctrines of Methodism are founded upon the Scriptures, and I believe that the Methodist Episcopal Church is the best type of Methodism in the world. It suits me better than any other; hence my choice. I do not fault any one for preferring some other Methodism, or some other Church.

Embracing the first Sabbath in July, beginning the day before, Rev. T. A. Cass, preacher in charge of Jamestown Circuit, and myself held a meeting at Travis school-house, on Caney Creek, Fentress County, Tennessee, which lasted six days, and resulted in fifty happy conversions to God; forty-eight joined our Church. Such an overwhelming power of the presence of Jesus I have scarcely ever seen. Among the converts were some that had stood very remote from the worship of God. Convictions were deep, and conversions were powerful. Christians united in shouting from the top of their voices,

" Victory! victory! victory!" It is due the excellency of this meeting to say, that it occurred in a settlement where the mourners' bench had been ridiculed from the pulpit by the opponents of our methods. Hallelujah! Glory to God in the highest!

Embracing the second Sabbath in July, I labored in a two days' meeting in Poplar Cove, in connection with Rev. Samuel Grear, which resulted in five conversions to God, and about as many joined our Church. To God be all the glory!

Embracing the third Sabbath in July, I labored in a meeting at Van Buren Academy, in connection with Samuel Grear, T. A. Cass, H. C. Huffaker, and Levi Sheppard, where we had a moving time indeed. The Lord came down in chariots of triumph at our first coming together, and before the meeting closed he powerfully converted sixty-five souls; sixty-one joined our Church. The saints of God shouted together the praises of salvation. Glory be to Jesus' name!

On Saturday before the second Sunday in August, I preached at the old Story graveyard, where two joined our Church. The following day I preached some funerals at Travis school-house, and three more joined the Church.

On Saturday before the fourth Sabbath in July, I preached at Ferguson's school-house. We had one happy conversion. The following day I preached some funerals at Thomas Hays's, took one into the Church, and had three conversions.

On the first Sabbath in September I preached at Head of the Cane. We had a melting season, and two happy conversions. At our second quarterly-meeting for Jamestown Circuit, held at Van Buren Academy, I preached twice, and other ministers preached. We had a number of penitents at the altar, and five joined our Church. On the fourth Saturday and Sunday in September, I held a two days' meeting at Concord Church, in Clinton County, Kentucky where four joined the Church. On the 26th of November, in the evening, I held a meeting for George Huckabee, as he was on his death-bed. We had a number of penitents, and one conversion.

On the third Saturday and Sunday in November, I held a two days' meeting at Head of the Cane. On Sunday we had several penitents, and five joined the Church—some by letter, and some new accessions. On Saturday before the first Sabbath in December, at a meeting I held at Andrew Kannatsur's, near Head of the Cane, we had a number of penitents, and two joined the Church. The following day, one joined our Church at my meeting at P. H. Davidson's. On the second Saturday and Sunday in December, I held a two days' meeting in Morgan County, Tennessee, where we had a moving time. On Sunday night there were several mourners at the altar, and two happy conversions to God. On Thursday night following, I held a meeting at Timothy Gauncy's, at the Head of Dry Creek, in Fentress County, where we had a number of penitents, three conversions, and one joined our Church. Timothy Asbury Wright, our sixth child, was born August 21st, of this year, 1866.

The results of the year were as follows: I married three couples, baptized by immersion sixty-two persons, and six by pouring. I received one hundred and fifty-six into the Church, witnessed one hundred and forty-four conversions to God, and preached the funerals of twenty-nine persons, infants and adults. Glory be to God for his great mercies during the past year! My Lord, how grateful I should be that my unprofitable life has been spared to enter upon the duties of another year! Notwithstanding that January and February were very inclement, with falling weather, and the roads were very bad, yet I frequently engaged in fighting the battles of the Lord. On the second Saturday and Sunday in February, at Brother Samuel Ramsey's the third quarterly-meeting for the Jamestown Circuit was held. Rev. T. A. Cass, Rev. S. Grear, and myself preached on the occasion. On Sunday night there was a large number of penitents at the altar, four conversions, and four joined our Church.

On the third Sabbath in April, at Concord Church, in Clinton County, Kentucky, we had several penitents at the altar, and Christians shouted aloud the praises of God. We had one happy conversion, and three accessions to our Church. On the first Saturday and Sunday in May I engaged in a meeting in connection with T. A. Cass, Samuel Grear, and Levi Sheppard. The meeting lasted three days, and resulted in seven conversions and eight accessions to the Church. To God be all the praise! On the third Saturday in May, in the evening, I held a meeting at Isham Richards's. We had a large number of penitents, and one happy conversion to God. On Sunday, the following day,

I held a meeting at the Head of the Cane. Christians had a feast, and there were two happy conversions to God. Hallelujah!

On Thursday before the third Sunday in July, Rev. T. A. Cass and myself held a meeting in the evening at Brother William Cowan's, on Caney Creek. We had a number of penitents at the altar, one conversion, and one accession to the Church. Embracing the third Saturday and Sunday in July, I labored in a meeting at William Hill's, in Fentress County, in connection with Thomas Cass, Samuel Grear, and Levi Sheppard. There were a number of penitents, and the saints of God shouted aloud the praises of the Captain of their salvation. Sixteen souls were happily converted, and about that number joined the Church. Embracing the fourth Saturday and Sunday in July, I held a basket-meeting at Concord Church. Several penitents wept at the altar, there were four happy conversions, and one joined the Church. Embracing the first Sabbath in August, Samuel Grear and myself held a meeting at Otter Creek, in Wayne County, Kentucky. It was an excellent meeting, indeed. Penitents crowded the altar, and up to Tuesday evening, when I left, we had had about twenty happy conversions, and thirteen had joined our Church.

On Friday evening before the third Sabbath in August, I held meeting at Head of the Cane. There were several penitents and one conversion. The following day I began a meeting at A. M. Allan's, in Fentress County, which continued nine days, and resulted in forty-three happy conversions and forty accessions to the Methodist Church. It was a time of deep, serious impressions upon all present; mourners crowded to the altar in large numbers. That which rendered the revival still more congratulating was, several of the first-class ladies and gentlemen of the country were among the converts. The people brought their provisions upon the ground, and remained during the day. There were no services at night.

On Friday before the first Sabbath in September, my brother, Rev. C. C. Wright, and myself, held a meeting at this same place. A number of penitents were at the altar, and one was happily converted. On this occasion my brother preached the funerals of Mrs. Gilreath and her brother, W. L. Allan, who had been killed in the Confederate army. In September, at a prayer-meeting held at Brother J. H. Carter's, we had a refreshing time; several penitents, one conversion, and one accession to the Church. Embracing the second Saturday and Sunday in August, at our last quarterly-meeting for the year, which was held in Jamestown, I was recommended by the Holston Conference, to be held in Knoxville, for admission into the traveling connection. It was through the earnest persuasion of the presiding elder, Rev. J. A. Hyden, and my other brethren, that I did this. I was also recommended at the same time to the Annual Conference for elder's orders.

While I was a local preacher I devoted a great deal of my time to preaching and holding protracted meetings through the summer and fall seasons; for in that place and time there were very few church

houses sufficiently comfortable for services in the
winter.   I preached a great deal in family residences
for the sake of comfort, and have seen hundreds of
conversions in family homes.   I was a poor man,
and had to live by my own labor in the field. Often
I would work while other people were asleep, in
order to obtain time to go and hold my meetings.
Sometimes I would leave home to hold meetings
when I was as tired as I well could be.   I left
home on Monday, September 30, 1867, in company
with my wife and others that were going to attend
preaching at Van Buren Academy.   I attended the
same, and heard Rev. Charles Smith, from Kentucky, preach an excellent discourse on the mode of
Christian baptism.

After the services I rode thirteen miles to
Jamestown, and staid over night with Mr. J. W.
Gauden.   Tuesday, October 1st, I rode to Mont-
gomery, and staid for the night at Brother John H.
Bryant's.   I went next day to William R. Dail's,
my cousin, who lived six miles from Clinton, in
Anderson County.   I was kindly received by my
relatives.

Early in the morning of October 3d my cousin
accompanied me to Clinton, where I took the cars,
and ran to Knoxville.   I went to the Conference-
room just as the Conference was opening, and saw
Bishop Kingsley in the chair.   The bishop opened
the Conference by administering the sacrament of
the Lord's Supper.   In the afternoon of the same
day, I went before the Committee of Examination
for trial into the traveling connection, and was
passed.   By a vote of the Conference I was re-

ceived on trial. Later in the day I heard Rev. J. B. Little preach before the Conference. On the second day I attended the Conference session, and in the afternoon went before the Committee of Examination for Elders' Orders, and was passed.

On Sunday I heard Bishop Kingsley preach an excellent and soul-stirring discourse from John xii, 32, after which he ordained several deacons.

In the afternoon I heard Dr. J. M. Reed, of Cincinnati, preach a noble discourse from Isaiah liii, 5, after which the bishop, assisted by some elders, ordained several persons elders. A very solemn impression rested on my soul; for I was one that stood in the altar, and was ordained an elder in the Methodist Episcopal Church. On Monday afternoon I took the train for Clinton, met my cousin with my horse, rode five miles, and preached to an attentive congregation. I staid that night at Cousin Dail's, and took very sick in the night. Next morning, under some weakness, I started for home, reached Montgomery that day, and staid over night again with Brother J. H. Bryant. The next day I rode to Sister Phillips's. The following day I rode home.

CHAPTER VII.

JAMESTOWN CIRCUIT.

FROM the Conference at Knoxville, I was sent to the Jamestown Circuit. That circuit then embraced Fentress and a part of Morgan County. The appointments were as follows: Lick Creek, Caney Creek, Van Buren Academy, Mount Union (which was at the old Gatewood stand), Head of the Cane, Back Creek, Poplar Cove, Crab Creek, Solomon's Chapel, Indian Creek, Hood's school-house, Jamestown, Ramsey's, and James Paul's on Mill Creek (all of these were in Fentress County), Young's Chapel, White Oak, where the town of Sunbright now is, and Mount Vernon. The last three appointments were in Morgan County.

Some of the leading men and women, who then attended my meetings, I will now mention. Reuben Harmon and J. H. Carter, at Lick Creek; Uncle Mark Jennings, and his wife, Aunt Ann, at Mount Union; G. W. Crouch and P. H. Davidson, on Caney Creek; Uncle James Bookout, on Back Creek; Pleasant Taylor and family, and G. W. Kington, at Jamestown; Uncle Jack Young and family, and Uncle Sid Carpenter and wife, at Young's Chapel; James Peters and his wife, Rachel, at Mount Vernon; Robert and Samuel Ramsey and Robert Alexander, at Ramsey's; Jerry Beatty, at Solomon's Chapel; John Beatty, on Crab Creek. There were hundreds of others that I might mention, who stood by the Church as pillars of strength. The most of these have passed to their eternal reward. I expect to meet them by and by on the shining shores of sweet deliverance.

I began the work on my circuit in October. On my first round on Back Creek, at Brother Bookout's, I received three members by letter. At my first quarterly-meeting I reported forty-two conversions and forty-five accessions. The quarterly-meeting was held in Jamestown, beginning November 17, 1867. Rev. William H. Rogers, the presiding

elder, was present, and preached with great power
and with the Holy Ghost sent down from heaven.
The meeting lasted seven days, and resulted in fourteen happy conversions to God and thirteen accessions to our Church. On my December round at
James Paul's, I received two into the Church, and
baptized one; also at John Galloway's we had a precious meeting. There were two conversions and five
accessions to our Church. At Bookout's, on the same
round, we had a good meeting; one conversion and
one accession to the Church. On the same round, at a
Christmas meeting at Mount Union, we had six
happy conversions and received five on probation in
the Church, and eight others recognized from the
Methodist Episcopal Church, South.

The result of my labor for the year 1867 was as
follows: I witnessed one hundred and twenty-five
happy conversions, and received one hundred and
twenty-four into the Methodist Church. I joined
together in matrimony four couples, baptized thirty-
one adults and one infant. I preached the funerals
of eighteen persons. Glory be to God for his mercies to me the past year! Hallelujah, Amen and
Amen! My God, receive the gratitude of my poor
heart, for the perpetuation of my days and the
preservation of my health! This year finds me an
itinerant on the Jamestown Circuit, Holston Conference. On my January round we had some refreshing scenes at our altars of prayer. On the February round we had some happy seasons, and three
accessions to our Church.

The second quarterly-meeting for this year was held
at Van Buren Academy, embracing the first Sunday

in February, and continued four days. Our beloved
presiding elder, W. H. Rogers, was with us, and
preached with the power of the Holy Ghost. We
had a good meeting, though no conversions. I reported at my second quarterly-meeting twenty-eight
accessions on probation, and nine others recognized
from the Methodist Episcopal Church, South. In
March we had five conversions, received twelve persons into full connection, and organized a Sabbath-
school at Mount Union Church.

On my April round, thank God, we had melting
seasons at the altar. At several places mourners
cried aloud for mercy, and Christians shouted high
the praise of God. We had four happy conversions,
and six joined our Church. I also organized three
Sabbath-schools—one at Young's Chapel, a second
at White Oak, and a third at Mount Vernon Church.
Up to this date, as agent for *The Methodist*, a large
weekly newspaper published in New York, I have
taken nine subscribers, by sending on the money
and receiving the paper in return. I have procured several packages of the *Missionary Advocate*
for free distribution on my charge.

On the May round we had several glorious
meetings. Penitents cried for mercy, while young
converts and old veterans shouted aloud God's
praise. I witnessed fifteen happy conversions to
God, received twelve into the Church on probation,
and three others recognized from the Methodist
Episcopal Church, South; also by letter, the widow
of an honored minister of the West Wisconsin Conference Methodist Episcopal Church. Glory be to
God! While we were pleading in behalf of the poor

heathen, in a missionary meeting in Poplar Cove,
God powerfully converted one soul. The third quarterly-meeting for this year was held at Mount Union,
the third Saturday and Sunday in May. We had a
good time. Rev. W. H. Rogers, the presiding elder,
was with us, and preached with great power and good
effect.

On my June round we had some sweet tides of
glory, and on Back Creek two happy conversions.
I could not get all the way around at this time, because I took sick, and had to disappoint some five or
six preaching places out of about twenty appointments. Thank God, "while the outer man grows
weak, the inner man is renewed day by day!" The
basket-meetings which I held were generally out in
the groves. The people made seats of planks and
logs in some deep shade, near to some good spring,
carpeted the ground with straw, and here, in nature's first temples, we preached, and prayed, and
sang, and shouted, while hundreds of sinners were
converted. The people came in wagons, on horseback, and on foot by thousands to these meetings,
from great distances around. They brought their
dinners to the ground, generally in baskets—hence
the name basket-meeting—and staid all day. We
had no night services, so that the people went home,
and slept and rested at night. These took the place
of the old camp-meetings, and were meetings of great
power. Thousands were converted at these altars.
Many in the great day of eternity will bless God
for the basket-meetings.

I attended a quarterly-meeting on the Clinton
Circuit, Kentucky Conference Methodist Episcopal

Church, held at Concord Church, Clinton County, Kentucky, the fourth Sunday in June, and for the first time since my ordination to the office of an elder, I administered the holy communion, assisted by Rev. Joshua S. Taylor. In July my basket-meetings began. My first basket-meeting began July 4th, at Lick Creek, in Fentress County, and closed July 6th. It resulted in ten happy conversions to God and four accessions to our Church. Brother Byers, from the Livingston Circuit, Tennessee Conference, did noble service in preaching and in the altar. My second basket-meeting began on Saturday before the second Sunday in July, at Crab Creek, and lasted eight days. It resulted in forty-two happy conversions and twenty accessions to our Church. The people took great interest in the meeting, and all denominations labored for its success. My third basket-meeting began on Saturday before the third Sunday in July, at Head of the Cane, and lasted until Tuesday evening, when we were compelled to close on account of other appointments. It resulted in ten happy conversions to God, and nine accessions to our Church. My fourth basket-meeting began on Saturday before the fourth Sunday in July, at White Oak Church, in Morgan County, and closed on Monday. It did not result in any conversions, but in several deep penitents, and in a happy time with Christians. My fifth basket-meeting began on Saturday before the first Sunday in August, on Caney Creek, and closed on Tuesday. It resulted in three conversions to God, and five accessions to our Church. My sixth basket-meeting commenced in Poplar Cove on Wednesday be-

fore the second Sunday in August, and closed on
Friday evening, resulting in five conversions, and a
joyful time with Christians. My seventh basket-
meeting commenced on Saturday, the next day, at
Solomon's Chapel, and resulted in forty-four happy
conversions, forty accessions to the Church, and a
deep work of conviction throughout the community.
It is due to say that all these basket-meetings were
well supplied with provisions on the ground, except
at White Oak Church.

My eighth basket-meeting commenced at Young's
Chapel, in Morgan County, on Saturday before the
third Sunday in August, and closed on Tuesday following. It resulted in ten happy conversions, and
two accessions to our Church. Rev. J. M. Durham,
of the Huntsville Circuit, was present, and preached
and labored with good results.

I attended a basket-meeting on the Livingston
Circuit, Tennessee Conference, held by Brother
Byers, embracing the fourth Sunday in August. It
lasted from Saturday until Tuesday evening, and
resulted in twelve happy conversions.

My tenth basket-meeting began on Indian Creek,
and was held on Tuesday and Wednesday before
the fifth Sunday in August. It resulted in five
conversions, and nine accessions to our Church.

My eleventh basket-meeting commenced at Ramsey's on the following Saturday, and closed on Sunday evening, with no conversions, but with a
number of penitents, and one joined our Church.

At several of my basket-meetings I held love-
feast meetings, with glorious testimony for Jesus.
At Poplar Cove and Solomon's Chapel I adminis-

tered the holy communion service, with the happiest effect.

The fourth quarterly-meeting for the circuit was held at Mt. Vernon, in Morgan County, commencing on Friday, September 11th, and closing on the following Monday. During the meeting there was an unusually heavy rainfall each day. Rev. W. H. Rogers, the presiding elder, was present, and preached with great power. The meeting resulted in one happy conversion and four accessions to our Church. I held a sacramental meeting at Jamestown, September 15th and 16th, which resulted in one conversion and one accession to our Church. Brother Rogers was present and added greatly to the result.

On the first Sunday in September I held a meeting at Lick Creek, and administered the sacrament of the Lord's Supper. The Holston Annual Conference met October 8, 1868, in Chattanooga, Tennessee, Bishop D. W. Clark presiding. I left home October 3d, to attend the Conference, went fifteen miles to Jamestown, and preached at night. We had a good, happy, joyful meeting. The next day being Sunday, I rode three miles, and preached at Pleasant Taylor's. We had a moving time in Israel's camp. I went in the afternoon of the same day nine miles, and remained over night with Samuel Ramsey. On Monday, October 5th, I went into Cumberland County, Tennessee, and remained over night with William Renfro, and was very kindly received. On Tuesday I went from Cumberland County through Bledsoe, Rhea, Meigs, and into McMinn County, having ferried Tennessee

River. I reached Cyril Carpenter's, and spent the
night there. On Wednesday morning I went to
Athens, spent the day, and took supper that evening with brother Moore, one of the preachers of
the Holston Conference, who lived in a lower room
of the Athens College. After supper I went to the
depot, and took the evening train for Chattanooga.
A large number of the Conference members were
on the same train. A number of United States
soldiers were on board the same train. We reached
Chattanooga at about half-past nine o'clock. Rev.
John W. Mann, the stationed minister at that place,
assigned us to our homes. Myself and Brother
G. W. Carder were sent to D. B. Carlin's, where we
found hospitable entertainment with a Christian
family. May God bless brother and sister Carlin
and family! A storm of wind in the night, and
two or three companies of United States troops
leaving the city before day, disturbed my sleep.

The next morning, October the 8th, Conference
met, and was opened with the reading of a Scripture
lesson, singing, and prayer by Rev. T. H. Pearne.
Bishop Clark then administered the sacrament of
the Lord's Supper to a large number of ministers
and people. The Conference proceeded with business until twelve o'clock. At two o'clock P. M., I
went before the committee for examination, and was
advanced to the second year. October 9th the Conference was opened with religious services, conducted by Rev. F. M. Fanning. My name was
called, my collections were reported, my character
was passed, and I was advanced to the second year.
In the afternoon I went out on Cameron Hill,

which overlooks the city, came around by the boat-landing on Tennessee River, and saw the steam-boat *Mary Bird*. At night, at the Presbyterian Church, I heard Dr. Mitchell, of the Virginia Conference, preach. October 10th, the Conference was opened with religious services conducted by Rev. L. F. Drake. I made out, and gave in my statistical report.

In the afternoon I took a walk through the National Cemetery. In a field of about seventy acres, inclosed with a stone wall, there sleep near fifteen thousand noble, Union-loving boys. In the center the Stars and Stripes wave over them forty feet high. The graves are beautifully decorated with a variety of sweet-scented flowers. O Lord, may these brave boys all rise at the first sound of the trumpet!

At night I attended the Conference missionary meeting, which was addressed by Dr. N. E. Cobleigh, Rev. J. A. Hyden, and Dr. J. M. Walden. The missionary collection was taken up, amounting to between forty and fifty dollars. On Sunday morning Bishop Clark preached an excellent sermon; in the afternoon Dr. Pearne preached, and at night Rev. J. L. Mann preached a thrilling discourse. On Monday morning Conference was opened with religious services, conducted by Rev. J. L. Mann. At night Dr. Hitchcock, Book Agent at Cincinnati, preached a thrilling sermon, after which, at about eleven o'clock, Bishop Clark read out the appointments. I was again appointed to Jamestown Circuit.

October 13th I took the early morning train for

Athens, took breakfast at Brother Moore's in the college, and then went out ten miles to Uncle Cyril Carpenter's, and there spent the night. I remained in that neighborhood the next day, and preached at Tranquillity Church at night, to a large congregation, at which time the saints of God shouted aloud for joy. I set off the next morning for home, and after riding for three days, a distance of about one hundred miles, I reached home and found my family well. God be praised!

The Jamestown Circuit was thrown back into the Athens District, over which Rev. J. Albert Hyden was presiding elder. October 31st and November 1st my first quarterly-meeting was held in Poplar Cove. The presiding elder was present, preached most eloquently, and administered the communion service. The meeting continued two days, and resulted in two accessions to our Church. On the November round I received three into the Church, and on my December round I received twelve on probation, and one from the Methodist Episcopal Church, South; also witnessed two conversions. In the same month, on the Clinton and Wayne Circuit of the Kentucky Conference, I witnessed ten conversions, and received sixteen into the Methodist Episcopal Church. The result of my year's labor for the year 1868 was as follows: I witnessed two hundred and twenty-eight conversions, and received into the Methodist Episcopal Church two hundred and twenty on probation and by recognition. I preached two hundred and seventeen times, baptized seventy-one adults and one infant, and solemnized the rites of matrimony be-

tween five couples, three white and two colored
couples; also preached the funeral of sixteen persons. To God be all the praise.

On my January round we had eleven happy conversions, and reported at our second quarterly-
meeting twenty-four accessions to the Church. The
second quarterly-meeting began January 23d, and
closed the 25th, at Van Buren Academy. It resulted in five conversions to God and seven accessions to our Church. Rev. John Forrester presided in place of the presiding elder, and preached
with great acceptability. On the February round,
God was with us of a truth. At my own meetings
and at the meetings of Jackson Franklin, a young
exhorter, we had eighteen conversions, and received twenty-five into the Methodist Episcopal
Church. The saints of God shouted aloud for victory. On the March and April rounds our host
moved on successfully. We had some conversions
and some accessions.

In the autumn of 1868 I sold my farm, and
bought another, three miles nearer the Kentucky
line. It contained one hundred acres of as rich
land as one need to want in this world. I had to
build a house and a barn and do a great deal of
fencing, and made many other improvements. This
was a beautiful home, and was in an excellent
neighborhood. I moved my family to this place
in March, 1869. My third quarterly-meeting was
held at Solomon's Chapel, on Obed's River, May
1st and 2d. My presiding elder was not present,
so I had a great deal of work to do. I held
Quarterly Conference on Saturday evening, and on

Sunday morning at nine o'clock I held love-feast, and at eleven o'clock preached and administered the holy communion, witnessed one happy conversion to God, and took three into the Methodist Episcopal Church. The same day, in the afternoon, I baptized thirteen adults. After the quarterly-meeting, during the month of May, we had·eight happy conversions and four accessions to our Church. During the month of June, God was with us at several places, and much good was realized.

On the 4th of July, it being the first Sunday in the month, I preached the funerals of two brothers, who had died away from home in the Union army, their widows and little children surrounding me. On that occasion the Lord powerfully converted three souls, and three joined our Church. My next meetings of interest were my basket-meetings. My first basket-meeting commenced on Saturday before the third Sunday in July, at Head of the Cane, and closed on the following Thursday. It resulted in twenty-four conversions and eight accessions to the Methodist Episcopal Church. Rev. John S. Keene, preacher in charge of the Albany Circuit, Methodist Episcopal Church, South, was with me and preached with great acceptability. We held a good, old-fashioned love-feast on Sunday morning, when several bore testimony for Jesus. My second basket-meeting was held on Crab Creek, beginning on Saturday before the fourth Sunday in July, and closed the following Friday. In this meeting, thirty-five were happily converted, and twelve joined our Church. My third basket-meeting was held at Mount Union, beginning on Saturday before the first Sunday in August, and closed on Monday evening. On Sunday morning of this meeting, I was taken very sick, and after repeated efforts to stand up and preach, I was compelled to lie down. On Monday morning I had somewhat recovered, and preached the funeral of Elizabeth Jennings. In the evening, Brother Cash, a Cumberland Presbyterian minister, preached. I was compelled to close from lack of strength to continue. The meeting resulted in five happy conversions and one accession to our Church. My fourth basket-meeting was held at Solomon's Chapel, beginning on Saturday before the second Sunday in August, and closed on Wednesday evening, resulting in twenty-five happy conversions and thirty-six accessions to our Church.

On Saturday evening of this meeting, the sun was totally eclipsed, and at the darkest time in the church-house the saints of God shouted aloud for joy, and mourners wept at the altar. On Sunday morning we had a glorious, happy time in the communion service. At this hour mourners were called, and a large number came forward. Among these was a young lady who was deaf and dumb. Glory be to God, she was powerfully converted, and though she could not talk, yet she clapped her hands and laughed. She was as happy as any young convert could be. On Wednesday, when signs were made to her that we had opened the doors of the Church, she came forward and joined our Church, and, notwithstanding her mother and people were Baptists, she made signs to be baptized by pouring, just like the Holy Ghost came down. I complied with her request. Is not this a strong proof of baptism by pouring?

My fourth quarterly-meeting was held at Mount Vernon, in Morgan County, where the Montgomery and Jamestown quarterly-meetings were thrown together. This embraced the third Sunday in August. Rev. J. A. Hyden, the presiding elder, was present, and preached with great earnestness. Four traveling and two local preachers were in attendance. My sixth basket-meeting was held at Lick Creek, embracing the fourth Sunday in August, and resulted in eight conversions and eight accessions to the Methodist Episcopal Church. The following Tuesday and Wednesday I held a meeting in the Poplar Cove. There were a number of penitents. Two were converted, and four joined the Church. My eighth basket-meeting was held at Otter Creek, in Wayne County, Kentucky, embracing the first Sunday in September, beginning on Friday and closing on Tuesday. It resulted in seven conversions and three accessions to the Church. On Sunday of the meeting, I preached one hour and a half on the mode of water baptism, and on Monday morning baptized twenty-one adults, mostly by pouring. My ninth basket-meeting was held at Hood's, in Fentress County, embracing the second Sunday in September. On the Sabbath I preached some funerals, administered the communion, labored with penitents in the altar, received three into the Church, and baptized ten adults. My tenth basket-meeting was held at Paul's, eight miles east of Jamestown, embracing the third Sunday in September, and resulted in five conversions and two accessions to our Church. Rev. Samuel Grear, of the Pikeville Circuit, assisted me. On Sunday, both in the morning and in the afternoon, we preached funerals.

Our Annual Conference for this year met in Jonesboro, Tennessee, October 7th, Bishop Matthew Simpson presiding. My domestic affairs were such that I could not attend it without great inconvenience to myself and family. So I did not attend, and was not received into full connection, as I might have been, could I have attended the Conference.

CHAPTER VIII.

MONTGOMERY CIRCUIT.

BY the Conference at Jonesboro I was appointed to the Montgomery Circuit. This circuit embraced the whole of Morgan County, with three appointments in Scott County, and one in Fentress. The presiding eldership on the Athens District was changed, and Rev. L. F. Drake was my presiding elder. This year I was strongly inclined to cease traveling, as my health had become considerably impaired. I became convinced, however, that it was God's will that I should continue; for whenever I would try to reconcile my convictions to the idea of quitting, I could neither sleep nor rest. So I must go yet a little longer. I asked God to give me a token of my call to the itinerancy on my first round on Montgomery Circuit, which was in November, and—glory be to his precious name!—at my first appointment at Young's Chapel we had one happy conversion to God, and one accession to our Church. At my second appointment at R. Lewallen's we had three happy conversions and four accessions to our Church. At Emory Church we had one conversion, making on the round five conversions and five accessions to the Methodist Episcopal Church. O what would weigh with the worth of five immortal souls!

On this round I visited and prayed with thirty families, and exhorted them to a religious life. I also baptized three infant children. I called in my December round. The result of my labors for God during the fiscal year 1869 are as follows: I preached 169 times, witnessed 167 happy conversions, received 159 into the Methodist Episcopal Church, baptized 122 adults and 10 infants, and solemnized the rites of matrimony between 6 couples. Thus I close another year. Glory be to God! Amen.

On my January round I visited thirty families, and held religious services. I preached thirteen times, and rode one hundred and eighty-six miles. My first quarterly-meeting was held at Emory Church, six miles from Montgomery, embracing the fifth Sunday in January. Rev. L. F. Drake presided, and preached with great power. We had several moving and melting seasons throughout the meeting. The saints of God shouted aloud for joy, a large number of penitents were at the altar, and one lady was powerfully converted to God. We also had one accession to the Church, making during the round, one conversion and two accessions to the Church. Rev. L. F. Drake baptized seven little children, and I baptized four more and one adult. My son, Rev. J. C. Wright, filled my work for me during the months of February, March, and April. He gave general satisfaction, preached with great acceptability, and received some into the Church.

In May I preached twice on Obed's River, on the Jamestown Circuit. A tide of glory moved the congregation, and many shouted glory to God in the highest, and one soul was converted to God. At several appointments on my circuit I left a number of penitents at the altar. On the round I visited about forty families, and held prayers with them. We had two happy conversions. I baptized five children and one adult, and rode one hundred and eighty-three miles. On this round I revived all of our Sunday-schools, and put them in lively operation. Church houses were so few and in such bad condition, and the country was so thinly settled that the Sunday-schools could scarcely be kept alive through the winter. On my June round we had some good meetings at several appointments. Having been invited by the Baptists, I held a meeting of four days at a church of theirs called Union Church, at which we witnessed most gracious seasons of the Divine power. Convictions were pungent, many penitents were at the altar, and one young man was powerfully converted. I trust that attachments were formed during this meeting that the strong arm of death can never sever. The tide of Christian fellowship was greatly strengthened in this community.

Now I come to the labors of my basket-meet-

ings. My first basket-meeting was held at
Young's Chapel, July 30th to August 3d. The
Church was greatly revived, seven souls were
powerfully converted to God, and four joined our
Church. My second basket-meeting was held at
White Oak Church, embracing the first Sabbath in
August. There was deep penitence on the occa-
sion, and a happy time with Christians. My third
basket-meeting was held at Ramsey's, embracing
the second Sabbath in August, and resulted in four
happy conversions, and the membership of the
Church greatly revived. I sent my son, Rev. J. C.
Wright, to attend this meeting for me. I was not
there in person, having to preach the funeral of an
old Methodist father at another place at that time.
My fourth basket-meeting was held at Emory
Church, embracing the third Sunday in August.
The Church was greatly revived, but we had to desist without any further results, because of the
wheat-threshers being in the neighborhood. My
fifth basket-meeting was held at Mt. Zion, on the
Crooked Fork of Emory, embracing the fourth
Sunday in August. There was some opposition
here against us, which greatly lessened the congregation. God be praised, five souls were powerfully
converted to him, and seven joined our Church.
Some of the leading citizens of the community were
left penitents at the altar. This was a good new
Methodist church, built during this Conference
year by a weak membership. My cousin, Rev.
J. I. Dail, of Kingston, did noble service in this
meeting. The meeting held four days.

On Monday of the occasion a heavy thunderstorm came up while I was preaching. The lightning flashed around us, and the muttering thunder shook the earth. A bolt of lightning struck a large tree within fifty yards of the church, and tore it to splinters. Myself and congregation were greatly shocked by it. He who rides upon the storm and says, "Touch not mine anointed, and do my prophets no harm," protected us. Glory be to his name!

My sixth basket-meeting was held at the old camp-ground near Montgomery, embracing the first Sunday in September. We had a very good move for a revival, but were compelled to close. Three joined our Church.

My fourth quarterly-meeting was held at Mount Vernon, embracing the second Sabbath in September, at which Rev. L. F. Drake presided. I should have stated that on my May round, at Moss's Mills, we had two conversions and five accessions to our Church, one of whom was from the United Baptist Church; also, on the same round, at Scutcheon Church, seven joined our Church. Rev. L. F. Drake, my presiding elder, attended all my quarterly-meetings, except the third. At his request, I held the third quarterly-meeting on the Jamestown Circuit, on which occasion I preached, administered the holy communion, and held the Quarterly Conference. Rev. Henry Pyle was the preacher in charge of this work. During the Conference year I received into the Church thirty-two persons, and witnessed twenty-two happy conversions at my meetings. The benevolent collections of the Church were advanced above any previous year.

The Holston Annual Conference for the year 1870 convened in the city of Knoxville, September 28th, Bishop Levi Scott presiding. I left home for the seat of the Conference on Sunday morning, September 25th, and took dinner that day with my sister, Mrs. J. W. Frogge. After dinner I went to see a man very low with the fever; and on the same evening went within one mile of Jamestown, and remained over night with my cousin, Jeremiah Wright. September 26th, I rode sixteen miles, and took dinner with my daughter and son-in-law, Tobias Peters. In the afternoon I rode fifteen miles, and remained over night with Joseph Holloway, two miles from Montgomery. September 27th, I rode fifteen miles, and took dinner with Rev. Richard Hudson, a Cumberland Presbyterian minister. I rode fourteen miles more the same day, and remained over night with my cousin, William R. Dail. September 28th, my cousin Dail and I went five miles to Clinton, where I took the train for Knoxville. I reached Knoxville and the Conference-room just as the Conference had opened. Bishop Scott was in the chair. After adjournment, I was directed by Rev. J. L. Mann, the resident pastor, to my boarding-place on College Hill, with Brother A. K. Foster, a most excellent man, himself a missionary Baptist, and his wife, a Methodist. Rev. James Jorry, of Ducktown, was my boarding partner. In the evening I went before the committee on the second year's course of study, as I had failed to attend the Conference the year before, at Jonesboro; passed an examination, and was promoted to the third year's course of study. At night, in the

Methodist Church, I heard an excellent sermon,
preached by Rev. J. R. Eads, from Matt. xxviii, 20.
I attended the Conference sessions during the day,
and the missionary, Church extension, and educational meetings during the evenings of the week,
and was much profited by them. On Sunday the
pulpits of the city churches were occupied by our
preachers. At the morning service in the Methodist Church, Bishop Scott preached an excellent
sermon from Acts i, 8. In the afternoon, at the
same place, Dr. E. Q. Fuller, editor of the *Methodist
Advocate*, of Atlanta, Georgia, preached a noble discourse. At night, from the same pulpit, Dr. A. J.
Kynett, corresponding secretary of the Church Extension Society, preached a soul-stirring sermon.

The Conference business was all finished up on
Monday afternoon. I left the Conference a short
time before it closed, as I had an appointment to
preach five miles from Clinton on Monday night.
I reached my appointment in due time; met a large
congregation, and preached to them. The power of
God came down upon the people in a wonderful
manner; mourners came to the altar for prayer,
while the saints of God shouted aloud for joy. I
remained that night with my cousin, William R.
Dail. The next morning, October 4th, I set off for
home; rode seventeen miles, and took dinner with
Mrs. Stephens, an excellent Christian lady. I rode
four miles further in the afternoon to a place where
I was to preach; but having been belated, I met the
congregation going away. I got off my horse, and
held religious services with them by the roadside. I
staid that night with John Langley. October 5th,

I rode ten miles to Montgomery, and took dinner
with Brother John L. Scott. In the afternoon I
rode sixteen miles, and staid all night with my
daughter and son-in-law. The next day I came
sixteen miles, and staid over night again with my
cousin, Jeremiah Wright. October 6th, I reached
home, and found my family all well. "Bless the
Lord, O my soul, and all that is within me bless
his holy name!"

I was reappointed for the coming year to the
Montgomery Circuit. My son, Rev. J. C. Wright,
filled the first round for me, embracing the last of
October and the first of November. On my second
round we had a glorious revival of religion at Lee's
school-house, where the people of the country were
mostly irreligious. I held a seven days' and nights'
meeting. Thirty-six souls were happily converted,
and I organized a class of twenty-one members, and
appointed Brother James A. Ervin class-leader.
What rendered the meeting very interesting, the
most prominent citizens of the country embraced
religion. The two justices of the peace for that
civil district were both converted. A heavenly
tide of Christian fellowship united the religious denominations of the community. At Moss's Mills,
on this round, five joined our Church, and at S.
Young's, in Scott County, a number of penitents
were at the altar, and one young man was powerfully converted. On this round I witnessed thirty-
seven happy conversions, and received twenty-six
into the Methodist Church.

During the first days of January, I left home
amidst the greatest perils; for the earth was sheeted

with ice, and I had to ride thirty-three miles over
this ice, and crossed some dangerous rivers to reach
my first appointment, which I met promptly. We
had a good meeting. This was at Young's Chapel.
I met some five or six other appointments, and enjoyed gracious seasons at each of them, and leaving
a number of penitents at some of them. I reached
Scutcheon Creek, and held a meeting of five days,
resulting in nine conversions to God, and five accessions to our Church. Among the young converts
was a young lawyer of fine ability, and two school-
teachers, both of whom prayed in public in the
altar before the meeting closed. The membership
of the Church was greatly revived. On my way
from Palestine Church to Ramsey's, although I had,
as I thought, a sufficient pilot, I became lost in a
dense wilderness. In endeavoring to go about
eight miles, we wandered so far off of our way
as to go about sixteen miles, which kept us on the
road until seven o'clock at night. What added to
our distress, the night was very dark, the wind was
blowing hard, and, being in a dense forest, the
timber was frequently breaking and falling around
us, and there was a cold rain at intervals. We
were so far in the wilderness that we could see
neither house nor light. This was in midwinter,
January 14th. We had serious thoughts of having
to lie out all night in this terrible storm under
some trees. At last we came in sight of a light,
which we found to be from the home of Mr. Ervin
Jones. I almost felt like praising God aloud for
deliverance. Mr. Jones and his family very kindly
received us, and prepared us a good warm supper

and bedding. My only grief then was the disappointment of my congregation, to which I was to preach that night, at Brother Alexander's. Possibly my going there that night was providential, for in the services which I held in their home, Mr. and Mrs. Jones both seemed penitent, for neither of them were Christians; and next morning Mr. Jones volunteered his services to go with me to my appointment that day, six miles from his home, and under the preaching he was very serious. May God bless the occasion to their present and eternal good! I had left a number of penitents at the altar at Lee's school-house, and the brethren of that Church continued the services three or four days after I had gone, and four others were converted, making for this round thirteen conversions and four accessions to the Church.

On my February round I sent my son, Rev. J. C. Wright, who filled the appointments with acceptability. Three persons joined the Church on this round. On the March round we had some interesting meetings. Ten persons joined our Church, and we enjoyed refreshing seasons in nearly all the societies. I held a very interesting leader's-meeting in the town of Wartburg. On the April round I put into operation a number of Sabbath-schools, baptized several infants and adults, and received seven persons into the Church, some of whom came from the Baptist Church, and one lady from the Cumberland Presbyterian Church.

On the May round I held some good, old-fashioned class-meetings with the happiest results. At Mount Zion, while holding a class-meeting service, two young ladies were powerfully convicted of sin, knelt at an altar of prayer, and were both happily converted to God. During this round my third quarterly-meeting was held at Lee's school-house. The presiding elder, Rev. J. W. Mann, from some cause, was not present, so I had to do a great deal of work myself. I had no local preacher with me; but at this Quarterly Conference William Young was duly licensed to preach. On Sunday morning we held a love-feast. This was a very precious service; after which I preached the funeral of a little girl, and administered the holy communion. In the afternoon I baptized nine persons. A number of infants and adults were baptized on this round, and three persons joined the Church. In June, at Solomon Young's, in Scott County, the prospects were such that I held services for five days. Five persons were soundly converted, three joined our Church, and the membership was greatly revived. Persons that had formerly been great enemies, embraced each other in the altar in the warmest forgiveness. At several places we realized Divine blessings in abundance. Penitents came to the altar in great crowds. At Lee's school-house three joined the Church, and I baptized at the same place and time eleven adults.

During the month of June I witnessed five conversions, received six into the Church, baptized one infant and thirteen adults, and returned home on the 17th day of the month. While off from my circuit, and in the country of my home, I preached a number of funerals. At a service of this kind, at Jerry Catron's, in Wayne County, Kentucky, two

persons were converted, five joined our Church,
and a number of penitents were left at the altar.

My first basket-meeting for this year was held on
Scutcheon Creek, beginning July 22d, and continuing four days. Penitents were at the altar at our
first coming together. On Sunday morning, I baptized an infant and preached the funeral of an old
mother in Israel. Six souls were happily converted
to God, and four joined our Church. My second
basket-meeting was held at Mount Zion, embracing
the fifth Sunday in July. There again the arm of
the Lord was revealed in support of his cause.
Penitents came in crowds to the altar, and the
shouts of triumph went up from the people of God.
In the evening of the last day of the meeting the
power of the Holy Ghost came upon us in such a
wonderful manner that many shouted glory hallelujah! In less than one hour seven souls were powerfully converted. Here, I think, I was more sanctified than ever before in my life. I baptized several infants and adults at this meeting. The result
was nine conversions and five accessions to our
Church. My third basket-meeting was held at
Mount Vernon, embracing the first Sabbath in
August. It continued four days, and resulted in
five conversions and five accessions to the Church.
Two small twin-sisters professed religion and
joined the Church at this meeting. They were two
of three sisters born at the same time, the third
one having died when about one year old.

My fourth basket-meeting was held at Boring's
Chapel, embracing the second Sunday in August,
and continued four days. There were three con-

versions, four accessions to the Church, and a
number of penitents left at the altar. Rev. A. L.
Williams, of the Huntsville Circuit, was with me
one day at this place. One soul was happily converted at a service which I held at Mrs. McCart's,
in Scott County, in the latter part of this week. I
met my presiding elder, Rev. J. W. Mann, at
Brother Jack Young's. We both went from there
to my fourth quarterly-meeting at Emory Church,
embracing the third Sunday in August. We had a
very pleaaant meeting, but no conversions.

In the following week I held my sixth basket-
meeting at Lee's school-house. The people came
together with strong faith, and the Holy Ghost
rested upon the congregation. On Thursday morning we had a happy love-feast, wher a number testified for Jesus, after which I preached and administered the holy communion. At this meeting one
soul was happily converted, and I baptized one
young man. My seventh basket-meeting was held
in Montgomery, embracing the fourth Sunday in
August. Great seriousness pervaded the unconverted during the entire meeting; but, with deep
affliction of soul, I must say that the Church did
not take the interest that it should have done.
Official members remained at home during the
meeting, because it was not held in Wartburg. I
really think I never saw the world riper for a revival than during this meeting. One soul was converted, and one joined the Church. My eighth and
ninth basket-meetings came on at the same time,
embracing the first Sunday in September—one at
Young's Chapel, and the other at Ramsey's. My

son, Rev. J. C. Wright, held for me at Young's
Chapel. The meeting was a pleasant one, with a
number of penitents, but no conversions. I held
myself at Ramsey's for two days. There were a
number of penitents, with a flattering prospect for
a good meeting, but we were compelled to close.
On Sabbath morning I preached the funeral of an
infant. Carroll Myatt, a young exhorter in the
Methodist Episcopal Church, South, gave zealous
help in my last three basket-meetings.

I have just now closed another year on the
Montgomery Circuit. During the year the Lord
has graciously converted ninety-seven persons, and
I have received eighty-seven into our Church. I
have sold about $40 worth of books from our own
Concern, and about $200 worth from Goodspeed &
Company. I took more than twenty subscribers for
our periodicals, and visited and prayed in between
four and five hundred families. The Holston Conference met in Greeneville, Tennessee, October 11th,
Bishop Scott presiding. I left home for the Conference, October 3d, and went that night to my
brother's, James M. Wright. The next day, in
company with Rev. Samuel Grear, I preached, and
having been joined by J. C. Grear, we rode to Rock
Creek, in Morgan County, and remained over night
with J. R. Brown. We went next day to Captain
Keith's, three miles from Wartburg, and took dinner. We were here joined by Rev. A. L. Williams.
There were now four of us on our way to Conference. We went that afternoon six miles, and met a
congregation, to which I preached. We remained
that night in that settlement, and rode next day to

W. R. Dail's. I had an appointment to preach, on
the following Saturday and Sunday, at Sulphur
Springs Church near that place. We had a glorious meeting. Brothers Grear and Williams assisted in the pulpit and altar work. The meeting
closed on Monday.

On Monday afternoon, Brother Williams and I
went through Clinton, crossed Clinch River, and,
by request of the Protestant Methodists, attended
a protracted meeting, which they were holding at
Union Church, three miles from Clinton. I
preached, and invited penitents to the altar. A
large number came forward, and one young lady
was happily converted. On Tuesday, October 10th,
we took the cars at Clinton for Knoxville, and in
the afternoon of the same day we left Knoxville,
on the East Tennessee and, Virginia train, for
Greeneville, at which place we arrived about sunset.
I was assigned to stay with A. W. Laymonds.
That night I attended worship in the Methodist
Church, and heard Rev. G. W. Coleman preach
from Daniel xii, 3.

Conference was opened next day, October 11th,
with religious exercises, conducted by Rev. R. W.
Patty and Dr. N. E. Cobleigh. Bishop Scott was
in the chair. That afternoon, I went before the
committee on the third year's course of study,
passed an examination, and was advanced to the
fourth year's class. At night, in the Methodist
church, I heard R. W. Patty preach from John xi, 9.

I attended all the Conference sessions, and the
missionary, Church Extension, and educational an-
niversaries, in the evenings of the week. In the

afternoon of the second day of the Conference, I heard Rev. P. H. Reed preach from Job
xix, 25–27, and in the afternoon of the third day,
heard Rev. T. H. Russell preach from John xv,
1, 2. The speakers at the missionary anniversary were Doctors Mitchell, Taylor, and Cobleigh, and at the Church Extension meeting,
were Doctors Mitchell, Fry, and Cobleigh, and
at the educational meeting, the speakers were Revs.
Mauker, Spence, and Dr. Taylor. On Sunday
morning in the Methodist Church, I heard Dr.
B. St. James Fry, from 1 John v, 5. In the afternoon, at the Presbyterian Church, I heard Rev. F. M.
Fanning preach from 1 Peter ii, 16. At night, in
the Methodist Church, I heard Dr. N. G. Taylor
preach from John xvii, 21. The Conference closed
on Monday morning. At nine o'clock we took
the train and ran to Knoxville, and in the afternoon we ran out to Clinton, and remained over
night with Rufus Dail. Brother Williams and I
remained there the next day, and I preached again
at night at Union Church. We had a good meeting.
Next morning, October 18th, we set off for home,
and rode that day to Mrs. Stephens's in Morgan
County. The next day I rode to James Peters',
and remained over night. On the following day I
reached home, and found my family well.

CHAPTER IX.

JAMESTOWN AND CUMBERLAND CITY.

AT the Conference of 1871 I was appointed to the Jamestown Circuit, in the Athens District. Rev. J. W. Mann was again my presiding elder. On the first round, after I had filled two appointments, I was taken sick, and failed to meet four other appointments, but met all the remaining ones. I witnessed some pleasant meetings, but found the work in a very lifeless state. My health soon returned, and on my second round the congregations began to increase in numbers. I succeeded in organizing weekly prayer-meetings in nearly all the settlements. Sinners began to show interest, and mourners came forward for prayers.

On my third round, at a meeting which I held at Captain Dowdy's, on Christmas day and at night, a large number of penitents were at the altar, and the saints of God, Methodists and Baptists, shouted aloud for joy. One man was powerfully converted to God, while his daughter was left at the altar. During the year 1871 I preached one hundred and ninety sermons, besides the love-feasts, prayer and class meetings which I held. I married one couple, baptized thirty-six adults and eighteen infants, rode more than two thousand miles on horseback, received eighty into the Church, and witnessed eighty-three happy conversions; besides, I held religious services in about five hundred families.

My first quarterly-meeting for the year was held at Paul's Chapel, January 13th and 14th. Rev.

J. W. Mann, the presiding elder, was with us, and preached with great power. May Heaven spare his useful life to the Church for many years to come! Brother Mann left us on Sunday evening. I held four days and nights. Twelve souls were powerfully converted, nine joined our Church, and the membership was greatly revived. Methodists and Baptists were united heart and hand in work, and in the praises of God. A justice of the peace, with his two children, came to the altar, was powerfully converted, and all joined our Church. Another justice of the peace, a member of the Baptist Church, did efficient work in the altar. Rev. J. H. Carter, a local preacher whom I had received into the Church and baptized several years before, preached a number of times, and did other efficient work. During January and February of this year the weather was very cold.

At a meeting which I held at Sulphur Springs, embracing the second Sunday in February, during the period of four days and nights, eight souls were happily converted, and four joined our Church. The convictions were deep, the penitence thorough, and the conversions mighty. My first leader's meeting was held at Mt. Union, at old Pall Mall, February 17th and 18th. A good body of official members was present. We had an interesting leaders' conference. On Sunday night a young man was converted, and, with three others, joined our Church. I left a number of penitents at the altar. My second quarterly-meeting was held at Solomon's Chapel, March 30th and 31st. My presiding elder was not present. Brother S. Grear

came in his place, and preached with Holy Ghost
power. Brother Grear left me on Sunday afternoon. On Monday morning I held an old-fashioned Methodist class-meeting. The power of the
Holy Ghost came upon the people in such a manner that the saints of God shouted for joy, and
two young ladies were mightily converted to God.
There was one accession to the Church.

At my second Quarterly Conference, I reported
twenty-two conversions, and twenty accessions to
the Church. I received five of them from the
Methodist Episcopal Church, South, and the other
fifteen by probation. After filling some appointments in Poplar Cove, I went to Jamestown, where
a criminal was in jail, condemned to be hung the
next day until he was dead. His name was James
Calvin Logston. I had known him when he was
a small boy, and had baptized his mother. He
was sentenced to hang for killing two women and
one child with an ax, the funerals of whom I had
preached at their graves. I had been informed
that Mr. Logston desired me to preach his funeral,
and also wished an early interview with me. On
entering the jail, I told him that he had but little
more than twenty-four hours to live in this world.
I sang a hymn, knelt, and prayed with him. He
wept pitifully, and prayed earnestly, but said that
he was prepared to die. After giving him some
spiritual advice, I left him with the promise to return
in a short time. This I did, after taking dinner
with the jailer, in company with Brother J. C.
Taylor, the sheriff of the county. I advised and
prayed with him again.

Late in the day I returned, and found the poor man deeply absorbed in solemn thought, while the sun was pouring in through the grates of the window, for the last time to him, the closing rays of day. Again I held services with him, and at his request baptized him by pouring, after he had taken upon himself the baptismal covenant. The next morning, taking with me Brother Samuel Grear, I returned to the jail. The poor man told me that he had rested well the night before. After appropriate Scripture reading and song, we all knelt, and Brother Grear led in prayer. In a short time he was shrouded and brought out of jail to a wagon standing at the door. His coffin had been placed in the wagon, which we entered. The driver, Mitchell Wright, and Dr. Graham occupied the seat of the wagon. Dr. J. H. Story and myself occupied the head of the coffin, the criminal the center, and Brothers Grear and Pile the foot. Surrounded by a heavy guard, we moved to the gallows, singing as we went the old hymn, "I would not live alway, I ask not to stay." On arriving at the gallows, the death-warrant from the Supreme Court of the State was read by Mr. S. V. Bowden, a young lawyer of the town. Brother Grear read a Scripture lesson, made a few appropriate remarks, and led in prayer. After this, I preached the funeral of the criminal, from Gen. ix, 6: "Whoso sheddeth man's blood, by man shall his blood be shed." At the close of the sermon the criminal was permitted to shake hands with a large number of his acquaintances. It was a melting scene. He then stated to the crowd that he had come to this end by keeping bad company. At 1.30 P. M. the trigger was sprung; but so soon as he dropped, the rope broke, and he fell suddenly to the ground. Another rope was placed around his neck, and he was drawn up, but had scarcely hung one-half minute when the rope broke a second time, and again he fell to the ground. He then uttered a word or two before they raised him the second time. He hung twenty-five minutes, and was pronounced dead. I remained all this time with him, having promised him that I would do so. His body was cut down, and buried at a short distance west of the town. O, what an awful thing, to see a man in good health so suddenly rushed into eternity!

The night before, Brothers Grear, Pile, and myself held religious services in the court-house, Brother Pile preaching a thrilling discourse. I left Jamestown in the afternoon of the hanging, and preached that evening at the residence of Benjamin Stockton. On my round on the circuit, the last of April and the first of May, we had some glorious meetings. Eight persons joined the Church—two recognized from the State of Illinois, two from the Campbellite Church, and four on probation. On my round in May and June we had some glorious seasons. The fiery pillar of Jesus' presence led us on. At Paul's Chapel, on Saturday before the first Sunday in June, after I had preached, penitents were called to the altar, and nearly all of the congregation, who were not already professors of religion, came forward. Four of these persons were mightily converted in that service. The next morning, at the same place, we held a children's meeting, when I preached to the little folks. We had a glorious service.

My third quarterly-meeting embraced the second Sunday in June. It was held in a large, new church, near my family residence. Rev. J. W. Mann, the presiding elder, was present, and preached with great acceptability. During the meeting the rain fell in such torrents that it held only two days. At the Quarterly Conference I reported six conversions and eight accessions for the quarter. During the remainder of June I preached at a number of places on my circuit, when we had strong evidences of the Divine favor; and I raised collections for the missionary cause. Embracing the first Sunday in July, I had an appointment for a two days' meeting at Cumberland City, in Clinton County, Kentucky. The preacher in charge, Rev. Nimrod R. Davis, lives in this town. He is an old preacher of the Kentucky Conference, Methodist Episcopal Church. He is a precious and most excellent man, but a great invalid in health. I think he will get his great reward in heaven in a short time. I was informed that the state of religion was very low in the town, and that a very bitter feeling was existing between the different denominations. I preached twice on Saturday, as also on Sunday, with happy effect.

On Sunday the power of God came down on the congregation in a wonderful manner. At the evening service a number of penitents were at the altar. I remained over Monday with them. God was with us of a truth. Seven souls were powerfully converted, and a number of penitents were lingering at the altar. I left them protracting the meeting. May Heaven grant them a glorious revival of religion! One of the blessed features of the meeting was the warm love and the affiliations of our Baptist brethren. They came in nobly, and labored in the altar. Among the converts was the principal hotel-keeper of the town, and a Baptist preacher's wife, who had been a mourner for eighteen years. The same week I resumed work on my own circuit.

On Friday I rode twenty-four miles over a very rough road, preached twice, and in the evening, for some time, .labored in the altar with mourners. The next morning I visited and prayed with a number of families, when two joined the Church. On returning home I was very sick for a few days from a bealing on my jaw and throat, caused by some decayed teeth. My first basket-meeting was held at Caney Creek, near Travisville, beginning on Saturday, July 20th, and closing on Wednesday, the 24th. The Church was greatly revived, backsliders were reclaimed, and ten souls were powerfully converted. Among the converts were some of the most influential people of the community. Nine joined the Church. At the close of the meeting I baptized fifteen persons.

On Sunday morning of the meeting we held a good, old-fashioned love-feast, with the happiest result. A number bore testimony for Jesus. My second meeting was on the Livingston Circuit, Overton County, Tennessee, by an exchange of ministerial labor with Rev. T. R. Dodson, preacher in charge of that work. We preached on Saturday, Sunday, and Monday to small congregations.

These services were held near Brother William L. Gillentine's residence. I think there is a great deal of prejudice against our Church in that country. The Kuklux outrages there have been numerous. However, on Monday the good Lord powerfully converted one man, while several others were left at the altar. We spent the greater part of Tuesday at the residence of Mrs. Henson, a very kind-hearted widowed lady, also a member of the Christian Order Church, who lives within one mile of Livingston. By invitation I preached that evening in the town, in the Cumberland Presbyterian Church, to an attentive congregation. I was informed that I was the first and only preacher of the old Methodist Episcopal Church who had preached in that town since 1845. I then went with Brother Dodson, and preached with happy results at Free Communion Church, and at Rocky Ridge Church.

My third basket-meeting was held at Solomon's Chapel, embracing the first Sunday in August, and holding four days. Rev. T. R. Dodson attended with me, and preached with great acceptability. Three were converted, and two joined the Church. I baptized seven persons, and received quite a number into full connection. The Church was gloriously revived, shouting aloud for joy. On Sunday morning we held a most interesting love-feast service, and after Brother Dodson had preached, I administered the holy communion to quite a number, one of the communicants being a deaf-and-dumb girl. My fourth quarterly-meeting was held at Jamestown, August 9th, 10th, and 11th. Rev. J. W. Mann, the presiding elder, was present and

preached. Our brethren of the Methodist Episcopal Church, South, held their quarterly-meeting at
the same time and place. Their presiding elder,
W. W. Neal, did not reach the place until Sunday
morning, and left the same afternoon. Rev. Henry
Pyle, from Wartburg Circuit, was also present. We
had no conversions. One joined the Church. The
meeting closed on Sunday night.

My fifth basket-meeting embraced the third
Sunday in August, at the Head of the Cane. After
holding two days there, with penitents at the altar,
we moved to the riverside for baptisms, and held
there one day. The Lord converted two souls, one
joined our Church, and four young men were baptized by immersion. The next day we moved to
Sulphur Springs, and held there two days. Four
souls were converted at this place. My sixth basket-meeting was held at Paul's Chapel, embracing
the first Sunday in September. It continued four
days. The power of the Most High rested on the
people, mourners came in crowds to the altar, and
the saints of God shouted aloud for joy. Nine souls
were powerfully converted to God, and three joined
the Church. I preached funerals during the remainder of the Conference year.

Just before leaving for Conference, I attended a
Baptist Association one day near Albany, Kentucky,
and was highly pleased with the preaching. On my
route to the Holston Annual Conference, which met
in Cleveland, Tennessee, October 2, 1872, I
preached three funerals in three different counties.
I left home for the seat of Conference September
26th, rode to Jamestown, and took dinner with

James F. Paul. I rode that evening to my son-in-law's, Tobias Peters, and preached that night at Mt. Vernon Church. The next day I rode eight miles, and preached the funeral of R. J. Jones, at White Oak Church. We had a most precious service. In the afternoon I rode twelve miles to Wartburg, where I met with Rev. A. C. Peters, a young man going to Conference, for admission into the traveling connection. We had meeting that night in Wartburg, Brother Peters preaching. The next morning we rode nine miles to Mt. Zion Church, met a congregation, and I preached the funeral of Amanda Jane Eastridge. In the afternoon we rode fifteen miles to Colonel James I. Dail's, my cousin, reaching his house some time after dark in a heavy storm of rain. The next day being Sunday, a bright and beautiful day, I preached the funerals of Nancy E. Peters and her infant babe, from Isaiah sixtieth chapter, ninteenth and twentieth verses, the lady being a daughter of Colonel Dail. The Holy Ghost was present in wonderful power. In the afternoon we rode fourteen miles, and remained over night with David Kelsey, a Methodist exhorter, and a most excellent man.

On Monday morning we rode seventeen miles to Uncle Cyril Carpenter's for dinner, in McMinn County; and in the afternoon rode nine miles to Athens, and stopped with Rev. J. W. Mann, my presiding elder. Brother Mann and wife were very kind to us. I reached Athens almost under prostration from continuous traveling. A good night's rest greatly refreshed me. On Tuesday, at twelve o'clock, I heard Ex-President Andrew Johnson make

a political speech in Athens. I took the evening
train, at about four o'clock, for Cleveland, the seat
of the Conference. I was assigned my boarding
place with P. C. R. Lawson, an excellent man indeed. My boarding partner was Rev. Samuel Grear.

At this Conference I passed an examination on the
fourth year's course of study. On Wednesday morning the Conference was opened, with Bishop Merrill
in the chair. In the afternoon of the same day, Rev.
J. B. Little preached, and at night Rev. A. G.
Watkins preached—both in the Methodist Episcopal
Church. The next morning, at five o'clock, I attended a prayer-meeting for entire sanctification, in
the same Church. In the afternoon of Thursday a
consecration meeting was held, when the preachers
were invited into the altar as seekers for entire sanctification. I bore testimony to the full assurance of
perfect love. I attended the early prayer-service
on Friday morning; but feeling indisposed, did not
attend the Conference session. In the afternoon, I
heard Dr. N. G. Taylor preach a most powerful
sermon from Psalms cxliv, 15. I did not attend the
missionary meeting at night, being sick. On Sunday
morning I attended the Conference love-feast, and
afterwards heard Bishop Merrill preach from John
xvii, 22. In the evening, Rev. J. L. Mann preached
a good discourse from Gal. vi, 14.

On Monday morning, Brother Peters and I left
for home. We went to Athens, met our horses, and
went in the afternoon to Cyril Carpenter's. We
both preached at Tranquillity Church that night.
The Holy Ghost was present. On Tuesday morning we rode eighteen miles, and took dinner with

David Kelsey; and in the afternoon rode nine miles to Kingston, and staid over night with Ellis Devaney. The next day we went four miles, and took dinner with Colonel Dail; and in the afternoon rode thirteen miles to the home of William Eastridge, in Morgan County, where I solemnized the rites of matrimony between J. W. Peters and Elizabeth Eastridge. On Thursday morning we rode twelve miles, and I preached at Scutcheon Church. In the afternoon I rode fourteen miles, and staid over night with my daughter and son-in-law. The next day (Friday) I rode fifteen miles to Jamestown, and took dinner with L. T. Smith, the Circuit Court clerk; and in the afternoon rode eighteen miles to my home. I found all well. I was appointed by this Conference to travel the Madisonville Circuit.

On returning home, I was greatly afflicted with catarrh and pneumonia of the lungs, which reduced me for a time to great weakness. I felt that I greatly needed a winter's rest from labor; and knowing that we had an over-number of preachers, I wrote to my presiding elder, Rev. W. C. Daily, to supply the work and excuse me. One great difficulty in the way of my going to my circuit was, that from a pure zeal for the itinerant ministry, I had sold my farm awhile before going to Conference, which brought me under the necessity of selling off my property and grain. With my best efforts, I could not do this. The move with my family would have been about one hundred and thirty miles, over the Cumberland Mountains and across several large rivers. I thought this would be very hazardous to myself and family. With a sad heart I here say, that this decision has brought more cloud to my moral pathway than anything else that has occurred during my ministry. I pray God to forgive me if I have done wrong in asking to be excused. The good Lord knows my heart, and that I am an intinerant, soul and body. I trust and pray that I may yet do efficient labor for years in the itinerant ranks.

Having been excused from going to my circuit by my presiding elder, I began preaching as my health would allow. Soon after returning from Conference, I preached the funerals of John E. Kanatsure and two infant children, also baptized his widow, and received three persons into the Church. I then preached some funerals in Wayne and Clinton Counties, Kentucky, with occasional appointments in other places. From the third Sunday to the fourth Sunday in December, myself and Brother Harris, a Cumberland Presbyterian minister, held a meeting of seven days and nights on Lick Creek, at Campbell's school-house, which resulted in eighteen conversions, four of whom joined the Methodist Church. Backsliders were reclaimed, and the Churches were greatly revived. A strong current of brotherly love prevailed throughout the neighborhood. A few days before this meeting, I bought a large farm, six and one-half miles towards Jamestown from where I lived, to which I moved my family immediately after the close of the foregoing meeting.

On the 27th of December, 1872, I was elected secretary of Jamestown Lodge, No. 281, of Free and Accepted Masons.

Through the great mercy of God, I have now closed another very eventful year of my life. During the year I preached one hundred and fifty-six sermons, besides prayer and class meetings; witnessed eighty-four conversions, received forty-nine into the Church, and baptized thirty-two adults and four infants. I preached the funerals of fourteen persons, and married one couple. Now, O my God, help me to be faithful in thy cause during the year 1873, if I should be kept on the shores of mortal conflict! My brethren and old friends in Kentucky, knowing that I had been released from labor in my own Conference, strongly insisted that I should serve them as their pastor during the year. Feeling the itinerant fire burning in my soul for the salvation of sinners, I offered myself to the Kentucky Conference, not as a transfer, but as a supply for the Cumberland City Circuit, since it lay contiguous to my residence. The Conference saw proper to give me the work. This is in the bounds of the Lexington District, over which Rev. H. J. Perry was presiding elder.

The Kentucky Conference met February 19, 1873, in Lexington, Kentucky. I began my first round the ninth day of March. We had some manifestations of the Divine presence during this round. God be praised for restoring me to health again, sufficient to be in charge. I had been fearful of one blank year in my life, but now feel like living and dying an itinerant Methodist preacher. My first quarterly-meeting was held at No. 1 Schoolhouse, April 12th and 13th. Brother Perry, the presiding elder, was present. We had a very pleasant meeting. A happy love-feast was held on Sunday morning, a number testifying for Jesus. The sacrament of the Lord's Supper was administered after preaching, a large number communing, and three persons joined the Church.

On my May round, at Concord Church, in the class-meeting the people of God rejoiced, and one joined our Church. During the same round, at Thomas York's, a number of penitents were at the altar, and two souls were powerfully converted to God. The next evening I preached at Hiram Guffey's, after preaching in the forenoon at No. 1 School-house; and notwithstanding it was raining and but few could be in attendance, yet all that were not religious were seekers at the altar; and five souls were powerfully converted, and two joined our Church. Mourners were carried from the ground weeping and almost helpless.

On my June round I held an interesting meeting at No. 1 School-house. In the evening of the first Sunday of June I preached at Thomas York's. Quite a number of penitents were at the altar, one person was converted, and two joined our Church. I preached a sermon to the children at Slick Ford on this round. On June 22d I set off for the District Conference at Somerset, Pulaski County, Kentucky. I left home at six o'clock in the morning, rode twelve miles to Slick Ford, and preached a funeral. I took dinner at Emerson Brown's, rode seven miles in the afternoon, and remained over night with B. W. S. Huffaker. The next day I rode twelve miles to Steubenville, and took dinner with Isaac Hurt. In the afternoon I rode seven-

teen miles, crossing the Cumberland River in a
ferry-boat, and remained over night with Dr.
Parker. Dr. Parker and his wife and children are
most excellent people. The next morning, June
24th, in company with Dr. Parker, I rode four
miles into Somerset. On account of delay in the
arrival of the presiding elder, Rev. H. J. Perry,
the Conference did not convene until the next day.
I found the citizens of Somerset to be a very gen-
erous and friendly people. I was assigned to stay
with Brother Kit Hale. Somerset is celebrated for
churches, there being seven good churches in the
town.

I left Somerset in the evening of June 26th,
rode out and remained over night with Dr. Parker.
June 27th, I rode to Steubenville, taking dinner
on the way with Mrs. Forrester, a most excellent
widowed lady, whose husband was a son of Rev.
John Forrester, of precious memory in the Holston Conference. I remained over night with Isaac
Hurt. The next day in Steubenville, I preached
the funerals of two of his infant children. After
preaching twice that day I rode seven miles, and
remained over night with Mrs. Isabelle, a widowed
lady. May God bless this excellent family! The
next morning being Sunday, I rode ten miles to
Kennedy's school-house, and preached the funeral
of a babe. After preaching and taking dinner with
John Culver, I rode home, eleven miles distant,
and found my family well. God be praised.

My second quarterly-meeting was held at Concord Church, July 9th and 10th. The presiding
elder was present and preached. On the second

morning of the meeting, just after love-feast, I received into the Church two persons by letter, two on probation, and one from the United Baptist Church. My first basket-meeting was held at Slick Ford, in Wayne County, Kentucky. It continued for three days, embracing the third Sunday in July, and resulted in eight happy conversions and nine accessions to the Church. Two persons joined from the Baptist Church. The Church at this place had been for a long time in a low state of religious life, but at this meeting the membership was greatly revived, and a great tide of Christian union prevailed throughout the community.

My second basket-meeting was held near Jamestown, in Fentress County, Tennessee, embracing the fourth Sunday in July. This meeting was held in connection with Brothers Bilderback and McPherson, of the Methodist Episcopal Church, South. On Sunday morning we held a love-feast service, after which I preached a funeral, and administered the sacrament of the Lord's Supper to a large number of communicants. After this, penitents came to the altar for prayer, and three souls were powerfully converted. Fifteen persons were converted during the meeting. My third basket-meeting was held at Concord Church, in Clinton County. It continued three days, embracing the first Sunday in August, and resulted in two conversions and five accessions to our Church.

My fourth basket-meeting was held at the residence of Mrs. Guffey, a widowed lady living in Wayne County, embracing the third Sunday in August. It lasted five days, and resulted in seven happy conversions, and ten accessions to the Church. I baptized fourteen persons during the meeting. On Sunday morning, we held a good love-feast meeting; and on Monday morning, after preaching, I administered the sacrament of the Lord's Supper. A large number communed.

My fifth basket-meeting was held at No. 1 school-house, embracing the fifth Sunday in August. It lasted for six days, and resulted in twenty-two conversions to God and nine accessions to our Church. My sixth basket-meeting was held at Edwards school-house in Wayne County, for four days, embracing the first Sunday in September. It resulted in two conversions and one accession to our Church. My seventh basket-meeting was held at Concord Church in Clinton County, embracing the third Sunday in September and continued about one week. It resulted in ten happy conversions and thirteen accessions to the Church. The convictions were deep and the conversions powerful.

On Friday morning, September 26th, I rode twelve miles and baptized eight persons, rode in the afternoon one mile and preached at Concord Church, then rode seven miles more and preached at night at William Perdieu's; making a ride of twenty miles and holding three services in one day. During this round the power of God was gloriously manifested. Mourners crowded to the altar for prayer, three were happily converted to God, thirteen joined our Church, and I baptized fifteen persons. On my October round through Clinton County, I sent Rev. James H. Carter in my place. One more person joined the Church.

The Holston Annual Conference met this year in Knoxville, Tennessee, October 1st, Bishop Gilbert Haven presiding. I did not attend the Conference this time, as I was very closely engaged in finishing up my work on the Cumberland City Circuit. I was expecting an appointment from the Holston Conference, and was assigned to the Jamestown Circuit, in the Athens District, with W. C. Daily as presiding elder. I now had for awhile two circuits to fill, which I endeavored to do, although the work was very hard.

CHAPTER X.

JAMESTOWN AND WARTBURG.

ABOUT the first of October I held two meetings near Travisville, Tenn., which resulted in four happy conversions and four accessions to our Church. My third quarterly-meeting for the Cumberland City Circuit was held at Edwards schoolhouse, October 11th and 12th. Rev. N. R. Davis was present as presiding elder *pro tem.*

On October 10th I organized a class at Beaver Creek, in Wayne County, Kentucky, consisting of five members. At another meeting, which I held at the same place in November, two others joined the Church. At a service which I held at Captain Dowdy's, in Fentress County, December 26th, two persons joined our Church, and a number of penitents were at the altar. My first quarterly-meeting for the Jamestown Circuit was held at Jamestown, December 20th and 21st. Rev. W. C. Daily was present. Brother Daily is a man of lovely spirit. We had no conversions, though anxious penitents were at the altar.

And now farewell to the year 1873. What an eventful year it has been! In the early part of it, more than one hundred persons perished from cold in Iowa and Wisconsin. In the summer, the Asiatic cholera extended a wide arm of death over the land; and fresh upon its tracks the yellow fever spread desolation in many families of the South. Then followed some serious national difficulties, growing out of finances, which brought many almost to starvation. This was thought to be due to the demonitization of silver by authority of the Government. Thanks be to God, Zion has reaped a large harvest of ingathering! Thousands have been converted during the year. I praise the Lord that I yet live; and O may I live to do good! During the year 1873 I preached one hundred and sixty-seven sermons, witnessed eighty-two conversions, took eighty-six persons into the Church, baptized forty-four adults and ten infants, preached the funerals of nineteen persons, and married one couple. Besides, I held a number of love-feasts and communion services.

My fourth quarterly-meeting for the Cumberland City Circuit was held at the residence of Mrs. Guffey, in Wayne County, January 13th and 14th. Rev. H. J. Perry was in attendance, and presided with great satisfaction to the Conference. Brother Perry has greatly endeared himself to many people on the Cumberland City Circuit. There were earnest penitents at the altar, but no conversions. Two persons joined our Church, one of them coming from the United Baptist Church. We had a good love-feast and a good communion-service, a large number communing. During my labors on the Cumberland City Circuit, sixty-three persons professed saving faith in Christ, and seventy-seven persons united with our Church. The people of the circuit insist that I shall serve them another year as their pastor. O that God may prosper that people more abundantly the coming year!

In connection with Brothers McPherson and Hullett, each of the Methodist Episcopal Church, South, I was in a meeting of five days and nights on the Three Forks of Wolf River, in Fentress County. The membership of both branches of the Methodist Church was greatly revived, and labored together in fellowship and love at the altar. Twelve souls were happily converted, and five joined our Church. The meeting began the 7th day of January, and closed on the 12th. One week after the close of the above meeting I held a service at Sulphur Springs. After I had preached, five persons joined our Church.

My second quarterly-meeting was held at Paul's Chapel, March 11th and 12th. Rev. W. C. Daily, the presiding elder, was present, and preached with great acceptability. We had a glorious love-feast and sacramental-meeting. Embracing the third Sunday in May, I held a two days' meeting at Sulphur Springs, when God's mercy came down in power upon the people, and five persons were converted to God, and one joined our Church. My third quarterly-meeting was held in May, embracing the fifth Sunday, in Poplar Cove, and continued three days. There were a number of penitents, but no conversions. Brother Daily was present, and presided ; also Rev. J. F. Perry, preacher in charge of Wartburg Circuit, was with us, and preached with the power of the Holy Ghost.

On my June round we had precious seasons at several places. At Paul's Chapel two very old persons joined the Church; and the next day at Jamestown, a gentleman united with the Church. On the fourth Sunday in June, after preaching at Sulphur Springs, mourners came to the altar, and two young ladies were powerfully converted. My first basket-meeting was held at Travisville, for three days, embracing the second Sunday in July. I held an interesting leaders' and stewards' meeting on Monday afternoon of the meeting. There were three conversions, and five accessions to the Church. I also baptized five persons, and received them into full connection.

On July 18th I left home for the Athens District Conference, which was to meet in Kingston, four days later. I rode the first day to the home of Tobias Peters, after stopping for dinner in Jamestown with J. C. Taylor, the sheriff. The next day, being Sunday, at Mount Vernon, in Morgan County, I preached the funeral of an infant babe of Rufus and Patience Jones ; and in the afternoon, at the same place, I preached, and baptized four infant children. On Monday morning, at the same place, I preached the funeral of Timothy C. Vann, an excellent, Christian young man. At noon, in company with my son, Rev. J. C. Wright,

who had now come up with me, we set off for
Kingston, the seat of the District Conference. We
rode three miles and took dinner at Edley Galloway's; and in the afternoon rode within two miles
of Montgomery, and staid over night with Preston Holloway. The next day we rode six miles,
and took dinner with Captain G. W. Keith; and in
the afternoon rode into Roane County, within four
miles of Kingston, and stopped with Colonel James
I. Dail. We found that several members of his
family were sick with fever. The next morning we
rode into Kingston, and reached the Conference-
room just as Conference was opening. I found a
good home during my stay with Ellis Devaney.
We had a pleasant Conference session.

Obtaining leave of absence on Friday morning,
we set off on our return trip. We took dinner that
day at Colonel Dail's, and in the afternoon rode to
Brother Fairchild's, four miles north of Montgomery. The next morning my son left me, and set off
direct for home. I turned for Scott County, rode to
Rev. L. H. Mosier's and took dinner. In the afternoon I rode into Scott County, and preached to a
congregation at five o'clock. The next day being
Sunday, I preached the funeral of Rev. Andrew
Lewallen, he having requested me in his lifetime,
should I outlive him, to do so, giving me his
funeral text.

On the same day I married a couple, and bap-
tized three infant children. I staid at night at
Brother Jack Young's. On Monday morning
I rode six miles to Tompkins Chapel, a Baptist
Church, where they were holding revival serv-

ices of great interest. At their request I stopped
and preached for them from Luke xix, 10: "For
the Son of man is come to seek and to save that
which was lost." After which I rode to J. F.
Paul's, and took dinner. In the afternoon I rode
twenty miles, and reached my home.

My second basket-meeting was held at Paul's
Chapel, embracing the first Sunday in August. On
Saturday of this occasion I was detained in Jamestown, to hold the funeral service of Sarah W.
Gould, who had lived near the town. Four weeks
before this I had held a like service for a young lady
in the same place. My meeting at Paul's Chapel
closed on Monday evening. One soul was converted, two persons were baptized, and two received
into full connection.

My third basket-meeting was held on Crab
Creek, embracing the second Sunday in August,
and continued five days. It resulted in ten happy
conversions, and nine accessions to the Church.
At the close I baptized six persons. Convictions
were so deep and the interest was so great that,
learning where I was staying at night, for two
nights the people crowded the house where I was,
so that I had to preach again, and to labor with
penitents until a late hour, after having preached
twice, and held two altar services during the day.

My fourth basket-meeting was held at Halbert's
school-house, in connection with my fourth quarterly-meeting, embracing the fourth Sunday in August. Rev. W. C. Daily, the presiding elder, was
present three days, and preached with the power of
the Holy Ghost sent down from heaven. The meet-

ing continued six days, and was truly a time of refreshing from the presence of the Lord.   Mourners came in crowds to the altar, and Christians shouted aloud for joy.   Twenty-four souls were happily converted to God, and twenty-four joined our Church. I baptized fifteen persons at the close of the meeting, and organized a class of forty members at this place.

On Saturday night before the first Sunday in September I preached at Brother Whittenburg's, and baptized four infant children.   The next day, on Sunday, I preached a funeral to a large congregation at Captain Dowdy's.   The next day I baptized four persons at the same place, and after preaching, mourners came in crowds to the altar, and two young ladies joined our Church.   I occupied the remainder of the Conference year in funeral appointments, which were attended with much good.

On account of afflictions in my family, I did not attend the Annual Conference which met in Chattanooga, Tennessee, September 30, 1874, Bishop E. G. Andrews presiding.   My son, Rev. J. C. Wright, went as an applicant for admission on trial into the traveling connection.   He was received, and appointed to Winter's Gap Circuit.   I was appointed to the Wartburg Circuit, formerly known as the Montgomery Circuit.   On my first round in October, I preached three days at Emory Church. The Lord powerfully converted four souls, and a large number of penitents were left at the altar.   I went from there up onto the Clinton Circuit to Sulphur Springs, to preach the funeral of a good lady. While there the Lord converted two precious souls, and the people of God were greatly rejoiced.

On the second round on my circuit, at a meeting held at J. B. Ketcherside's, several penitents were at the altar, one soul was converted to God, and two joined the Church. My first quarterly-meeting was held at Jack Young's, embracing the first Sunday in December. Brother Daily, the presiding elder, was in attendance, and preached with great acceptability. At this meeting the Lord converted one soul, and two joined our Church. On returning home I was very sick with the mumps and bilious fever for more than two weeks, and had to call in the aid of a physician. In fact, all my family were sick with mumps and fever for some time, which detained me at home for three weeks beyond my regular time.

I left home on January 7th for my third round, on a noted cold Saturday. During that round I witnessed two happy conversions to God, and had two accessions to our Church. On the February round we had some melting seasons, with penitents at the altar; and five persons joined our Church, two of them coming from the United Baptist Church. On the March round I left home the sixth day, and rode twenty miles to Paul's Chapel, on the Jamestown Circuit. This was the time and the place of the second quarterly-meeting for that circuit. I was accompanied by Rev. J. V. Brown, of the Methodist Episcopal Church, South. On reaching the church at a late hour, we found a waiting congregation, without either presiding elder or preacher in charge. I afterward learned that Brother Daily, the presiding elder, was at home sick. Brother Brown and I held services for three days. The membership was greatly revived; two souls were converted to God, and two joined the Methodist Episcopal Church. From this place to my own quarterly-meeting was about ten miles. In going there I had to cross the Clear Fork River, and as the waters were swollen by the heavy rains, I greatly imperiled my own life, and came very near having my horse drowned. He would have drowned, having been entangled in some bushes in the angry waters, had not Thomas Brewster, a young man, gone in to him with a canoe, and brought him out. When he was nearest drowning I fell on my knees to praying. He was saved, and I reached the place of my quarterly-meeting at Mount Vernon in due time. My presiding elder, Brother Daily, did not reach there, and this laid all the burden of the occasion upon myself. Glory be to God! he was with us in great power, converting souls every day of the meeting.

On the second day, after preaching, I administered the sacrament of the Lord's Supper to a large number of communicants, having no minister to assist me. That which rendered the sacramental service remarkable was, that our Baptist friends communed with us. We made up a good collection of money for the presiding elder. The people brought out provisions, and remained all day on the grounds, while the spirit of worship remained upon them all the time. The meeting continued four days. The membership was greatly revived, mourners came in crowds to the altar, twelve souls were powerfully converted to God, and thirteen persons joined our Church. To God be all the glory. On the same round I witnessed, at Lee's school-house, four more conversions, and seven accessions to our Church. On my round before this, near Lee's school-house, I preached at the house of Thomas Taylor, a Baptist brother. A number of penitents were at the altar of prayer. Among these were two very small girls, one of whom was converted that day, the other on this round. The one converted first was a daughter of Rufus and Sarah Bishop. Her name was Sarah Amanda. She was happily converted February 13, 1875, being at that date seven years eight months and nine days old. On the present round she would labor with the penitents in the altar with the judgment of a woman. She, with the other little girl, joined our Church. May Heaven bless the precious little girls!

On the April round, we had some very happy seasons of rejoicing. At Mount Vernon, on the second Sunday in April, three young ladies, sisters, by the name of Vann, were happily converted. They had been mourners for eight years. God be praised. On the May round, at Mount Vernon, Rufus Jones and wife both found peace in believing, which makes seventeen conversions at Mount Vernon this year, up to date. I held meeting three days at Scutcheon Church, near old Montgomery, embracing the third Sunday in May. During the meeting penitents came to the altar in large numbers, and the people of God greatly rejoiced. Five souls were happily converted, and two united with our Church. My third quarterly-meeting was held at Mount Zion Church, in Morgan County, embracing the fourth Sunday of May.

I began the meeting on the evening before, with a class-meeting service. Brother Daily was in attendance, and preached with his usual spiritual ability. We had a pleasant communion service, and raised a good collection for the presiding elder. Upon the whole, it was a pleasant meeting.

On the June round I traveled very hard, being pressed with my farming business at home. I would ride from fifteen to twenty miles a day, and preach twice. The first Saturday and Sunday in June, Rev. Benjamin Summers, a Baptist preacher, and I held a meeting at James McKeathan's, a Baptist brother. On Sunday morning, at the request of Brother McKeathan, I preached the funeral of his son, Jesse L. McKeathan. We had a pleasant service, and four happy conversions to God. The next day, being Monday, I preached twice. In the afternoon, at Langley's school-house, two persons joined our Church, one of them coming from the Cumberland Presbyterian Church. The next day, at Lee's school-house, one more joined the Church.

The second Sunday in June, being Children's-day at Mt. Vernon, I preached to a large congregation of children and adults, and lifted a collection for educational purposes. The power of the Holy Ghost came upon the people in a wonderful manner, and penitents came to the altar of prayer crying for mercy. Six souls were powerfully converted, and eight persons joined the Church. On the second Sunday in July I rode from Jamestown to Mt. Vernon, and after preaching baptized three infants and ten adults, and received twenty persons into full connection.

My first basket-meeting was held at Young's Chapel, embracing the third Sunday in July. It continued four days, resulting in ten happy conversions and three accessions to our Church. The presence of the Holy Ghost was so powerfully present at one of these services that every unconverted person in the house was at the altar crying for mercy.

My second basket-meeting was held at Clear Creek the fourth Saturday and Sunday in July. There were no conversions, but a number of anxious penitents. I baptized five infants, preached the funeral of a lady, and received two persons into the Church. I preached at Scutcheon Church the first Sunday in August. There were a number of penitents at the altar, two conversions, and one accession to the Church. The following Tuesday I held two services at Emory Church. There were indications for a good revival at this place, but I was forced to leave so as to meet other engagements.

My third basket-meeting was held at Ramsey's Chapel, embracing the second Sunday in August, and continued three days. Quite a number of penitents were left at the altar, and one lady was converted. My fourth basket-meeting was held at Mt. Zion Church, beginning on Wednesday after the second Sunday in August, and continuing three days. At this place there were no conversions, but a number of penitents were at the altar. My son, Rev. J. C. Wright, of the Winter's Gap Circuit, was present and preached. My fifth basket-meeting was held at Lee's school-house, embracing the third Sunday in August. It continued three days, and resulted in four happy conversions.

I attended the Jamestown quarterly-meeting on the fourth Sunday in August. On Saturday morning of the meeting I baptized four ladies by immersion. Rev. John Forrester was the preacher in charge of this work. I was baptizing, preaching funerals, and receiving into full connection at nearly all my basket-meetings. My fourth quarterly-meeting was held at Scutcheon Church, embracing the fifth Sunday in August. Brother Daily was with us two days, and presided with dignity. The services held for three days. We had a melting, glorious meeting, earnest penitents were at the altar in large numbers, five souls were converted, and three accessions were made to our Church. From this place I went to Mt. Vernon, and held services from Tuesday evening until Friday evening. There seemed to be a Divine power resting upon the congregation through the entire meeting. Mourners came weeping to the altar of prayer, while the people of God prayed and shouted together. Thirteen souls were powerfully converted, and nine persons joined our Church. From this place I went to Young's Chapel, preached and baptized some persons, and closed the Conference year's work. This makes eight years' work in the itinerancy. Glory!

During the Conference year I preached 152 times, traveled 1,918 miles on horseback, prayed with 424 families, witnessed 80 conversions to God, and received 67 persons into the Church. I secured 63 subscribers for the Methodist *Advocate*, published in Atlanta, Georgia, and obtained the first prize, $10 in cash, offered by Dr. Fuller, the editor, to the pastor that should obtain the largest number of subscribers. I sold about $40 worth of books, baptized 40 adults and 18 infants, and married one couple. I received as a salary $215.85, and raised for benevolence $36.25. To God be all the glory!

I left home September 25th to attend the session of the Conference to meet in Greeneville, Tennessee, Bishop Bowman presiding. I rode to Jamestown the first day, and took dinner with J. W. Gaudin, and in the afternoon rode to Tobias Peters', and remained over night. The next day being Sunday, I rode to Brother James R. Brown's, thinking that I had an appointment to preach the funeral of Father Dawn, father-in-law of Brother Brown. But as they had not received my letter arranging for the appointment, I did not meet a congregation. In the afternoon the family of Brother Brown and myself visited the new-made grave of Father Dawn, and sang that beautiful hymn, "In the resurrection morning you will see the Savior coming," and all knelt in prayer. I then rode six miles, and visited a young man by the name of David Honeycutt, who was nearly off these mortal shores with consumption. After reading an appropriate Scripture lesson, and praying with him, I went a short distance to Mrs. Briant's, and remained over night. The next morning I set off for Clinton, Tennessee, rode fifteen miles, and took dinner with Ezra Russell; and in the afternoon rode fourteen miles, and spent the night with

W. R. Dail. The next morning I rode five miles
to Clinton, and took the train for Knoxville. Here
I met with Bishop Bowman and a number of the
traveling preachers. We took the train at Knoxville, and arrived at Greeneville late in the evening.
I was assigned to stay at W. A. Lamon's. We had
a real pleasant session of the Conference. This
was Bishop Bowman's first visit to us. On Sabbath morning, after preaching an excellent sermon,
he dedicated the new Methodist Church in Greeneville, and in the afternoon of the same day dedicated the new Colored Methodist Church. Rev.
F. M. Fanning and Rev. J. J. Manker were elected
delegates to the General Conference.

The Conference closed on Monday night. Early
the next day, in company with a large number of
the preachers, I took the train for Knoxville. I
was very sick all day. At Knoxville I had to wait
for hours for a train to Clinton. In company with
Brother James Jory, one of our ministers, I visited
and took dinner at the Deaf and Dumb Institute.
Late in the evening I took the train for Clinton,
and staid that night with my cousin, W. R. Hicks,
a lawyer, who lives in Clinton. The next day I
rode five miles through a heavy fall of rain to
William R. Dail's. In the afternoon I rode eighteen
miles, and reached Major Stephens' in Morgan
County, late at night, having had trouble with
swollen streams all the way. At one place I paid a
man fifty cents to assist me over. O what heavy
rains and high waters I had that day! I rode the
next day about fourteen miles to Russell Scott's and
took dinner, and in the afternoon rode fifteen miles

to Tobias Peters', and remained over night. The
next day I rode fifteen miles, and took dinner with
Jeremiah Wright, one mile from Jamestown, and in
the afternoon rode home. I found my family all
well, God be praised!

I was appointed this year to the Crossville Circuit, in the Athens District, W. C. Daily presiding
elder.

CHAPTER XI.

CROSSVILLE CIRCUIT.

I LEFT home October 2d, for my new field of
labor, and after traveling one day and a half
reached my first appointment, on Clear Creek, called
Salem Church. The house, situated between two
very high hills, is built of logs, with clapboard
roof, and a chimney of sandrock built up to about
the joists, without any glass windows, very open,
and unfit for use. I met about a dozen very poor
and attentive people, and preached to them. The
next day being Sunday, my appointment was six
miles away, the whole route being a dense wilderness, with only one house on the way. I reached
this appointment at the proper time. The place
was called Mt. Union. It had once been a camp-
ground; however, the camps and the old shed had
gone down. The people of the neighborhood had
built a shed the previous year. The church is a
small old house, with a stick-and-clay chimney.
Here I met a good congregation, and preached to
them. About the close of the sermon the Holy
Ghost came upon the people, and a number, both

men and women, shouted aloud the praise of God.
I preached at the same place that night and the
next morning. There were a number of penitents
at the altar.

On the following Tuesday I went to Maple
Springs to preach, but found no congregation there,
as my appointment had not been published. I
preached that night, however, to a small congregation at the home of Mr. Woody, a Baptist brother.
The next day I preached at Koontz school-house
to a congregation of seven women and two children. I spent the night at James Tanner's. His
wife is a Christian lady and a Methodist, and he,
I think, is an anxious seeker. Next morning I set
off for Hale's Chapel, at a distance of twelve miles.
The whole route is a dense wilderness, with very
few settlers. After going about four miles, I became
lost in what is called the Wild Meadows. I got off
my horse, knelt down and prayed; mounted, rode
on, and reached Dr. Brown's, five miles from the
church. After holding religious services in the
family, the doctor accompanied me to the church.
I found a large congregation waiting, and preached
to them. That night I preached at the residence
of Brother Hale, the class-leader of this Church.
The next day I preached at Gray Ridge, in a new,
half-finished church, to a small but very attentive
congregation. That afternoon I rode into Sequatchie Valley, in Bledsoe County, and remained over
night with Curtis Hinch. He is a well-to-do man,
but not a Christian.

The next morning I went across the valley and
up Walden's Ridge, a very high mountain, to

Pleasant Hill, a plain old church, and preached to a small congregation. In the afternoon I went down into Sequatchie Valley, to Melville. In this place, at the Masonic Hall, a Baptist minister was holding revival services. At his request I preached, and called for penitents. Four ladies were converted. The next day being Sunday, I preached at the same place. Here I met the family of William Lee, a most excellent people. In the afternoon I went five miles up the valley, to Orme's school-house, and preached to a large congregation. We had an excellent service. The next day I rode over the mountain to Grassy Cove. I had an appointment to preach in this place the following day, but the appointment not having been published, I did not preach. Here I met with an English family named Marston, a good people. On Wednesday night I preached in the Baptist Church to a large congregation.

On Thursday morning I set off for home; and after riding about sixty miles, I reached home on Friday night, to find my family well. I began my second round at Salem Church, by preaching to a congregation of five ladies and a little boy. O what clouds of discouragement! Good Lord, help me "to endure as seeing Him that is invisible." That afternoon I rode nine miles, and remained over night with D. C. Adams. The next morning I rode four miles in a heavy rain, and held religious services with the family of Mr. Lavender; after which, I went to Mr. Winnie's, where I was to preach that day, but found no congregation. I staid that night at Mrs. Vickery's. She is an excellent Christian

lady, and has a nice family. The next day I went
to Swan's, and met a very small congregation. I
prayed with them, and held a class-meeting. That
evening I went down into Grassy Cove, and spent
the night with a family named Stratton. They were
a kind Northern family. That night I was in-
itiated into the Order of Good Templars. I am resolved to go into everything that opposes intem-
perance.

On Sunday I attended my appointment, which
had been consolidated with the quarterly-meeting of
the Southern Methodists. I preached on Sunday
night. I lodged with Brother C. Ford, a local
preacher of the Methodist Episcopal Church, South,
who treated me with great kindness. I also met
Dr. Chamberlain and family, who gave me a royal
entertainment. The doctor is in feeble health. On
Monday I went to Sequatchie Valley, and preached
at Brother Selby's. We had an old-fashioned Holy
Ghost meeting. That night I preached at Mrs.
Davenport's. There were a number of penitents at
the altar. On Tuesday morning I preached at Stony
Point, in a large, old frame church. In the after-
noon I went to Pleasant Hill, on Walden's Ridge,
and met with Rev. G. W. Renfro, of the Methodist
Episcopal Church, South, who preached for me.
On Wednesday, I went up Brown's Gap, of the
Cumberland Mountains, and preached at Rev. C. J.
Croft's. Here I met with the family of Brother
Bennett. I found them a good people. That night
I preached at Brother Whitehead's. The next day
I preached at Hale's Chapel, where I met with Rev.
D. H. Cottrell, a Baptist minister. I spent the aft-

ernoon and night with him and his family. The
next day I rode twelve miles to Koontz school-
house, met a good congregation, and preached to
them. That night I preached at Howard's Springs,
with good results. At this place we have a comfortable little church, and this, with a small, half-
finished parsonage, is all the property that our
Church owns on the entire circuit. The next day
I preached at Maple Springs. Here I found an old,
squatty house, with a door in the side, a stick and
clay chimney in one end, and plenty of light gleam-
ing through the open cracks. Our society at this
place is small. I met a large congregation, who
listened attentively while I preached. Some of the
people of God shouted aloud for joy. The only
excuse for such churches is the poverty and inexperience of the people. I here met with Brother
Elmore, the class-leader, and his family; also with
E. Terrell and family, who are spiritualists. The
next day being Sunday, I rode nine miles, through
a heavy rain, to Mount Union; met a small congregation, and preached to them. I stopped with
Brother William Todd. He and his family showed
me much kindness. The next day I rode thirty
miles, and reached my home.

On Sunday, December 26th, I preached at Salem
Church, on my third round. The congregation was
not large. That evening I preached at Harve Shil-
lings. We had an excellent meeting, and one young
lady was converted. On Monday I rode six miles
to Obed's River, but found it too deep to ford, and
remained over night with Mr. Adams. The next
morning a young man rode my horse over the river,

and I crossed in the canoe. I rode nine miles to Crossville, and took dinner with William Hamby, a hotel-keeper. I rode that afternoon into Grassy Cove, and staid with Brother Brown. I had an appointment to preach that night at the Baptist church, but did not preach because there were no lights. The next day I had to surround Grassy Cove Creek, because it could not be forded on account of high waters. I went to Sequatchie Valley, preached to a large congregation at Brother Selby's, and had a good meeting. That night I preached at J. M. Miller's. The Lord was present in power, and two young men were powerfully converted. The next day I rode eight miles to my appointment, going up Lowe's Gap, of Walden's Ridge, and met a small congregation, but had a good meeting. Three persons joined the Church. In the afternoon I went down in the valley to Melville, and preached that night at the hall. There were only a few in attendance. I remained that night with W. X. Ault, a merchant and a farmer. The next day I visited the family of Mr. Thomas, a Northern family. The next day I preached at Stony Point to a small congregation. From this place I was called to attend the funeral services of Sister Hale, the wife of Thomas Hale. The services were held the following day, New-Year's day.

The following day I preached at Hale's Chapel. We had a glorious meeting. A number of penitents were at the altar, and four persons joined our Church. That night there were two conversions at the same place. The next morning I baptized a lady by immersion. I preached again at Hale's

Chapel, and had a good meeting. I preached again at night, and continued the services until Friday evening. We had twenty-four conversions, and twenty-three accessions to our Church. The meeting continued for two days after I left, and resulted in four more conversions. The next day I rode eighteen miles, passing through Crossville, and reached Brother Elmore's, near Maple Springs, where I spent the night. The Baptists were holding revival services at the church. I went out that night and preached. There were a number of penitents at the altar. The next day I rode fourteen miles to Mt. Union, and preached twice that day at this church. We had a good meeting, penitents were at the altar, and four persons joined our Church. The next day I rode thirty miles, and reached my home. Found my family well. God be praised.

On January 24th I left home for my fourth round, and stayed that night at Harve Peters's. The next day I preached at Winnie's to a fair congregation. That night I preached in Crossville, in a room of a hotel kept by Mrs. Gibson, to a fair-sized congregation. The next day I rode into Grassy Cove, and preached that night in the Baptist church, as also the next morning. In the afternoon, through a heavy rain, I passed through Swaggerty's Cove, and down into Sequatchie Valley, preaching at Brother Selby's at night. We had a good meeting. Two young men joined the Church. The next day I rode eight miles up Walden's Ridge, and preached at Pleasant Hill; and again at night at James Kirley's. My quarterly-meeting occasion embraced the fifth Sunday in January, at Stony Point. Rev. W. C. Daily, the presiding elder, was present; also Rev. C. J. Crofts, of the Jamestown Circuit, and Rev. J. H. Parrott, of the Methodist Episcopal Church, South. On Monday night there were a number of penitents at the altar; but, leaving Brother Parrott in charge, I went on Tuesday, through a heavy rain, up Cumberland Mountain, and preached at Brother Crofts'. That afternoon I rode through a snow-storm to Brother Bennett's, and spent the night. The next morning, when the thermometer stood at ten degrees, I baptized a young man by immersion. I preached the same day at Hale's Chapel, and again at night at Laurel Church; also the next day at the same place, and at night I preached at Thomas Hale's.

Friday was a very cold and snowy day. The snow was deep, and I had to travel nine miles by a strange road, through a dense wilderness. I thought if I should become lost, I should certainly perish from cold. O how I felt the need of Divine help! I reached Howard's Springs in time, and preached in the morning, and in the afternoon at Koontz school-house; also at night at Howard's Springs again, making a ride of fifteen miles in the snow, and preaching three times in one day. I stopped that night with Brother Martin, the class-leader. O how tired I was! "O land of rest, for thee I sigh!" The next day I went to Maple Springs, where I expected to hold revival services. The meeting began on Saturday, and closed on the following Thursday night. It resulted in eight conversions and eight accessions to the Church. The weather was unusually cold all the time. On Friday I rode forty-two miles to reach my home, and found my family well.

On my fifth round, at Salem Church on Clear Creek, I preached to a congregation of two men and one boy. I went that afternoon nine miles, and remained over night with D. C. Adams, in company with Rev. J. V. Brown, of the Methodist Episcopal Church, South. The next day being Friday, I preached at Winnie's to a small congregation, but we had an excellent service. That night I preached in Crossville, in the court-house, to a small congregation. Crossville is the county-seat of Cumberland County, and, though a town of some age, there is not in it nor near it a church-building nor Church organization, but it has two active saloons. I spent a part of the next day in the town, and in the afternoon rode down into Grassy Cove, stopping with L. Stratton. That night I gave a lecture on temperance at the Methodist Episcopal Church, South, and the next morning being Sunday, I preached at the Baptist church, taking a collection to defray the expense of our delegates to the next General Conference. We had a very pleasant meeting. I spent a very pleasant time at the home of Mr. Marston and family, and stopped for the night with Mr. Wilson, lately of Ohio. I find them an excellent family. The next day I spent a time at the home of Dr. Chamberlain; found the doctor still very sick, but I hope improving. That afternoon I crossed over Walden's Ridge into Sequatchie Valley, and preached that night for a lady, very low with consumption, by the name of Ford. We had a very happy meeting, indeed.

The next morning I preached at Orme's school-house to the children, and at night I preached in the hall in Melville to a large congregation. Rev. A. C. Peters, of the Washington Circuit, was present. We had a glorious meeting. I spent the night with Frank Lee. He is an excellent man, and has a nice family. The following day I was to preach at Pleasant Hill, on Walden's Ridge, but on the way was met by a terrific storm of wind and rain, so that I had to stop. I did not reach the appointment. That night I preached at Stony Point to a large congregation, Brother Peters being present and assisting. On Thursday I preached at the residence of Rev. C. J. Crofts in the morning, and in the afternoon at Hale's Chapel. At both places there were large congregations. On Friday, in the morning, I preached at Laurel Church, with happy results; and at night I preached at Zion Hill. The people came to these services in large numbers. On this occasion I organized a class at Laurel Church. This is the first organization of a class at this church.

On Saturday morning, I began a two days' meeting at Koontz school-house. After a ride of fifteen miles, I reached the place in time for morning service; the occasion being the time of the monthly meeting of the Baptist Church at this place. After service on Saturday, they held their Church session, in which they preferred charges against a young preacher for drunkenness and swearing. The charges were not sustained. The young man afterwards joined our Church. They also preferred charges against a young lady for attending parties. She would not acknowledge any wrong, and her case was continued until next meeting; but the next day she joined our Church. My meeting closed at this place on Monday morning. On the same night I preached at John Tabor's. The Lord was present in power. The following day I preached at Maple Springs. I took a good missionary collection. That night I preached at the same place. The Holy Ghost came upon the people in power, and one young lady was converted. On Wednesday morning, after a ride of fourteen miles, I preached at Mount Union, to a small but attentive congregation. The next day I rode thirty miles to reach my home, passing through Jamestown. I found my family well.

On my sixth round I did not reach Salem Church at the appointed hour, but preached that night at John Lowe's. A number were in attendance, and I trust much good was done. Brother Lowe and family are plain, honest, and industrious Christian people. The next day I rode eleven miles, preached a missionary sermon to the Vickery class, and took a good missionary collection. That night, after a ride of five miles, I preached at Crossville, in the court-house. The Masons had their monthly meeting at the same time, and this fact lessened my congregation. I am a Freemason myself, but I never allow my lodge-meetings to interfere with my going to Church. The following day I preached at the home of Mrs. Dorton, who lives eight miles from Crossville. The congrega-

tion was small.   Mrs. Dorton is a member of the
Baptist Church, but had invited me to preach at
her house.

The following day being Sunday, I preached in
Grassy Cove, on the cause of missions, and took a
collection for the same.   After spending some hours
pleasantly in the homes of Messrs. Stratton, Brown,
and Chamberlain, I crossed Walden's Ridge into
Sequatchie Valley, and preached in the afternoon at
Mrs. Davenport's to a large congregation, again
taking a missionary collection.   The following day
being Monday, I drew up a deed for a piece of
ground on which to build a Methodist church, and
had it signed and witnessed.   I ran out the lot, and
marked the corners;   also drew up a subscription
paper and secured some funds for building purposes.
I preached that night at Melville, and after preaching, spent the night at William Lee's.   The next day
I preached in the morning at Pleasant Hill, after
climbing a very rugged mountain to reach the place,
and at night preached at Stony Point.   Here I took
a collection for missions.

On Wednesday I preached at Gray Ridge, and
at night at Hale's Chapel.   On both occasions I
preached on the subject of missions, and took collections.   On Thursday, in the morning, I preached
at Laurel Church, and in the evening at Zion Hill
Church.   At Laurel Church a Second Adventist had
been preaching, day and night, for four weeks.   He
holds that the Jewish Sabbath is the proper day to
observe for Sunday, and that the abstaining from
swine's flesh is essential.   He seems to be an intelligent young man, and has secured some converts

to his views. That night, in going from Church to Brother Burger's, during a heavy thunderstorm, the night being very dark, I was seriously hurt by my horse passing under a limb of a tree, which struck me across the face, making an ugly wound, which bled freely.

The next day, although feeling very poorly, I rode thirteen miles to preach at Pleasant Hill, on the road from Crossville to Sparta. I felt strongly tempted to stop several times on the way; but my zeal rallied, and I went on. However, I did not reach the place in time for the morning service, but preached at three o'clock in the afternoon. Here I met several strange families — Mr. Hubbard and family, who are Congregationalists; Mr. Fry and family, who are Lutherans. Next day being Saturday, my quarterly-meeting began at Howard Springs. Brother Daily was present. The usual services of the quarterly-meeting occasion were held.

The following Tuesday I preached at Maple Springs in the morning, and at Robert Keys' at night. On both occasions I took a collection for the cause of education. The next day I preached at Mount Union. The Lord was present in healing power. On this round three persons joined our Church, coming from the Baptist Church. On Thursday I rode a distance of thirty miles to reach my home, and found my family well. God be praised.

On account of making a trip through Morgan County with my wife, to visit our daughter, Mrs. Peters, I did not reach my appointment at Salem Church May 11th. Traveling a strange road, I be-

came lost, and did not reach the place until too late
for service. I spent that night at Jack Hall's. He,
his wife, daughters, and sons, all work in the corn-
fields. They make about a supply for home use.
They know but little about books or letters, but
are contented and happy. The next day I preached
at Vickery's, to a congregation composed of two
ladies and a gentleman.

On May 13th, after riding fifteen miles, I
reached N. C. Brown's, in Grassy Cove, who lives
near the Baptist Church, where I was to preach that
day. A heavy storm of wind and rain arose, which
prevented a congregation from attending, and so
there was no service. That afternoon I rode nine
miles to reach an appointment at five o'clock in
Sequatchie Valley, having to cross a very high
mountain. I reached the place in time, preached
to a good congregation, and took an educational
collection. The next day, being Sunday, I preached
at Stony Point a sermon especially for children.
The Holy Ghost came upon the people, and shouts
went up from the camps of Israel. That afternoon
I preached in Melville. At both services I took
a collection for education. After preaching I rode
eight miles up Cumberland Mountain, and celebrated the rites of matrimony, that night, between
Reuben Lee and a daughter of Rev. C. J. Crofts,
at the home of her father. The next morning I
had great nervous prostration, caused by excessive
traveling and preaching. However, I rode down
into the valley seven miles to Brother Lee's with
the wedding party. In the afternoon, after a ride
of four miles, I preached at Pleasant Hill to a

small congregation, although I was very hoarse.
That night I staid with Mrs. Roberts, whose husband had been murdered by the Confederates during the late war. The next morning I preached
again at Pleasant Hill, and took an educational
collection. I spent the day visiting a number of
families in the valley, and took W. H. Swofford
into the Church. The next day, riding four miles
up Cumberland Mountain, I preached at Gray
Ridge Church. The congregation was small. The
following day, at Hale's Chapel, I preached a sermon on Christian baptism, in reply to a sermon
preached by Rev. D. H. Cottrell some time before.
Mr. Cottrell is a Baptist minister.

In the afternoon of the following day I preached
to an attentive congregation at Laurel Church. I
remained over night with John Wyatt. Mr. Wyatt
and his wife are members of the Campbellite
Church, while his oldest daughter is a Methodist,
and two others are seekers of religion at the altar.
The next morning I visited an aged couple by the
name of Stone. They were both happy in the love
of God. I held services with them. On arriving
at the church I found the congregation engaged in
an experience-meeting. Although this was Saturday, the Second Adventists were holding their Sabbath services. A large number from the Campbellite Church had been influenced by the Second Adventist preacher into these strange views, and had
created quite a confusion in the neighborhood. I
preached here for two days. Mourners came to the
altar in large numbers, and several joined our
Church. I did what I could to quiet the trouble

in this community. On Sunday afternoon I took an educational collection.

On Monday, May 22d, after a lonely ride of thirteen miles through a wilderness country, I preached in the afternoon, at Pleasant Hill Church, to an attentive congregation. After preaching I visited a young lady who had been afflicted for two years with a lingering disease. I found that she was not a Christian, nor concerned about her soul; but I held religious services with her, and left her. The next day I rode seven miles and preached in the morning at Howard's Springs, and in the afternoon rode five miles, and preached at Maple Springs, on the mode of baptism. After riding fourteen miles the next day, I preached to an attentive congregation at Mount Union. I spent the night with William Todd. His little grandson was in the last stage of dropsy. The next morning I baptized the little boy and his two little sisters, and rode thirty miles during the day, a part of the time through heavy rain, to reach my home.

During this round I traveled, in fifteen days, two hundred and thirty miles, and preached fifteen times. I set off for my work again, June 7th, in the early morning. After riding twenty-four miles, I stopped for the night with William McFarland, who lives by a new, half-finished log church, built by the United Brethren I was to preach there that night. The congregation was attentive, but small, the country being very thinly settled. As they had neither lamp nor candle for making a light, I preached by the light of a pine torch. I spent the night with Mr. McFarland. He and his wife and large family are industrious people, his wife being a neat housekeeper. They had recently moved into the place, which, before their arrival, had been exposed to stock, the hogs having lain about the house and under the floor. I had an all-night hand-to-hand fight with the fleas.

The next day, in the morning, I preached at Mount Union, and in the afternoon at the residence of Mr. Terrell, having ridden eighteen miles and preached twice during the day. The next morning, accompanied by the most of Mr. Terrell's family, I rode five miles through the rain, and preached at Maple Springs to a large congregation. In the afternoon I attended service in a new and unfinished log church, built by the Baptists. Rev. Mr. Wilson, a Baptist minister, preached to a large congregation. The following day I preached at Howard Springs. The following Saturday and Sunday I held a two days' meeting at Pleasant Hill. On the Sabbath I preached three times, and organized a Methodist Church at this place; a number of people, who had been members of the Congregational Church in the North, united with our Church. I also took an educational collection on Sunday.

On Monday I rode eleven miles, and remained over night at James Lowe's. Brother Lowe had a son very sick with typhoid fever. I fear he may not recover. He is a good boy, however, he, with his brother, having been converted. I took them both into our Church in the beginning of the year. The next day I preached at Laurel Church, where the Second Adventists had been producing such a cloud of confusion. I preached on the Christian Sabbath.

It seems to me to be a misfortune with a great many people of this mountain country that they will readily embrace a new theory, though it be in direct conflict with a well-tried and God-approved old theory. These Second Adventists, instead of spreading a gospel of peace, are spreading a gospel of confusion and strife. These Advent preachers have entered a community that was living in peace and harmony, and have brought discord and strife; and, so far as I could learn, they have not awakened nor brought a single soul to Christ. These are stubborn facts in their case.

On Wednesday I preached in the morning at Hale's Chapel, and in the afternoon at Gray Ridge, having ridden twelve miles and preached twice during the day. The next morning I rode down the mountain and into the valley four miles, and preached at Stony Point. I stopped for dinner with Brother Patton. In the afternoon I preached at Pleasant Hill. On Friday I preached at Orme's school-house, and in the afternoon was so prostrated from excessive labor that I was compelled to rest at the home of G. W. Miller. The following Saturday and Sunday was the occasion of my third quarterly-meeting in Grassy Cove. There had been such heavy rains for two days and nights that all the streams were greatly swollen, and the earth seemed submerged with water. I had no trouble, however, in reaching the meeting, as my route lay over a very high mountain, a distance of eight miles. Brother Daily, my presiding elder, after a circuitous route, reached the meeting in due time. The congregations were small, the people

being unable to reach the church because of many
and high waters. The usual services of a quarterly-meeting occasion were held. Brother Daily
did the preaching. The meeting was held by invitation in the Methodist Episcopal Church, South.
On Monday I took dinner with Father and Mother
Renfro, an aged couple. They are the parents of
two distinguished ministers of the Methodist Episcopal Church, South. I then set out for the home
of my daughter, who lives in Morgan County, and
after a ride of two days I reached that place. The
next day, in company with my wife, I traveled
twenty-six miles to reach my home.

During this round of fifteen days I traveled 215
miles, preached 16 times, and prayed in 40 families.
God be praised. It may be helpful to those who
come after to give a true description of mission-
work on the Cumberland plateau. It may not be
without interest, also, to those who may occupy
more favorable fields. I have had the painful opportunity to be appointed to labor on some of the
hardest mountain missions, and on them I have
toiled and endured as seeing Him who is invisible.
However, when God has poured from clouds of
mercy rich salvation upon the people, and when in
religious enjoyment, from the most excellent glory,
I have been lifted to Pisgah's top, and have seen by
faith the goodly land before me, I would not exchange this work for a city station.

On this mission field there live as true-hearted
Christian people as can be found anywhere in the
world. The native people of this mountain will
make greater sacrifices to attend Church than any

other people that I have ever seen. I have known ladies to walk from five to fifteen miles to hear one of the Lord's ministers preach one sermon, and they did not regard this as a hardship; and they were as chaste and respectable people as can be found anywhere. Very often you may see nearly the whole family—husband and wife, brothers and sisters—march into the field early in the morning, and remain all day, in cultivating corn or in harvesting. Their food is plain, palatable, and nutritious. A better-contented people is not to be found anywhere. Their houses are built of logs, chinked and daubed, and are very comfortable in the winter. The fireplaces are large, in which they place heaps of logs for the winter fire. Around these fires they spend their winter evenings in a very pleasant manner. They cook on the fireplaces, for among them a cook-stove is a rare thing. They are generally clear of debt, and have plenty of milch-cows and work-oxen; and many of them have fat horses, and almost all of them own real estate.

On almost all the table-land one can buy thousands of acres of unimproved land at from twenty-five cents to one dollar per acre. A great deal of this land will produce from five to six barrels of corn, or one hundred bushels of Irish potatoes, to the acre. I have known families who had three or four hundred dollars loaned out on interest, and not less than five hundred dollars' worth of fat cattle on the range, who did not own a Bible, or take any religious newspaper, nor any other kind, and did not have any books in their homes, and yet owned

two or three fiddles and three or four rifle guns.
These families are exceptions, however. Thou-
sands of others were great readers and well-posted.
I have sold thousands of books in that country.

The reader discovers that I spend only about one
half of my time in my field of labor. I made it a
point to preach nearly every day, and sometimes as
often as two or three times a day, ride fifteen or
twenty miles, generally over very rough roads, and
along the way visit and pray with a number of families. I have read hundreds of pages and volumes
of books through, riding along a wilderness road on
horseback. About one half of my time I was compelled to labor on my farm to make a support for
my family. Outside of the missionary appropria-
tions, there was little other remuneration on these
missions. Three years ago I traveled a large work
the whole year, and received less than thirty dollars
of salary for the same. This looks like the pioneer
days of Peter Cartwright. The men who have
labored in these fields have their record on high.
Nothing but loyalty to God could lead men to suffer
these things. I have now traveled the Crossville
mission nine months; I have traveled seventeen
hundred miles on horseback over a rough mountain
country; have preached one hundred and forty-one
times; have visited and prayed in four hundred
families, and have received as a compensation thirty-
seven dollars and fifty cents.

On my farm I raised good crops of corn, wheat,
oats, and hay; also had live-stock, horses, mules,
cows, sheep, and hogs. I was educating my children in the best schools of the country. My wife

was wide-awake and knew how to manage the farm in my absence, and my children were industrious, and by it all we made a good living. I never drummed a congregation for my support. I believed this to be the work of the stewards. I have never complained about my support. On my work there are about three hundred members. Many of them are very poor in this world, while quite a number of them hold considerable wealth. Many of them have done all that they could, and possibly some of them have done more than they should have done, while many have not done one-fourth of what they ought to do.

The support of Methodist preachers often comes from the poorer members. Our wealthy members too often are covetous. It seems difficult to have our financial matters properly proportioned. Some of our members have a good-will to do, but lack the ability; while others have the ability, but lack the good-will. Of these two classes I respect the former the more.

On a piece of ground which I had given and deeded to the Methodist Episcopal Church, myself and neighbors had erected a good church-building, one year before this time. It was within two hundred yards of my house, and was called Mt. Union. Rev. J. V. Brown, of the Methodist Episcopal Church, South, and myself began a union meeting at this place, July 8th, he and I preaching alternately. It continued eight days. The power of the Holy Ghost was manifest from the very beginning in deep convictions, in thorough conversions, and in the reclaiming of backsliders. Members of both branches of the Methodist Church worked with commendable zeal in the altar, and shouted aloud the praise of God together. Forty souls were powerfully converted to God, and thirty-two persons united with the two Churches. That which made the meeting of great interest to me was, that it was among my own neighbors, and largely among my own relatives.

After resting one day, Brother Brown and I held another union meeting four miles northwest of my home, in a beautiful grove near the residence of Manson Flowers. We held nine days. The people of that neighborhood, a few years before, built a comfortable union church, but a short time before this meeting it had caught fire, and was reduced to ashes. So we were forced to hold our services in a grove. During the meeting there were frequent showers of rain, which compelled us to repair to some farm-house for shelter. The congregations crowded the houses, porches, and yards, so eager were they for the word of life. Notwithstanding our great inconvenience, mourners came in numbers to the altar, and the people of God of different denominations shouted aloud the praise or their salvation. Thirteen souls were happily converted, and eleven persons joined the two Methodist Churches.

These were great meetings, indeed. I have never seen it fail that where Christian people unite in love and in effort there is always salvation. I have ever been in favor of union, both in Church and State. I hope the day will never come when any other Church will reach out a longer arm for Chris-

tian union than the Methodist Episcopal Church.
I rejoice to believe that the time is near when ostra-
cism and hard terms will give way to kind words
and to a better feeling—when it will no more be
said that the Methodist Episcopal Church is tran-
scending the bounds of her mission to go anywhere
in the world where there are souls to be saved; for
with the best that both Churches are doing in this
country, souls are being lost in our midst. I hope
and pray that Methodism may be one in our land;
for "united we stand, divided we fall." In the
meantime let us cultivate love for each other; for the
Savior has said: "By this shall all men know that
ye are my disciples, if ye have love one to another."

On July 28th I set off from home for my circuit. After riding about seventy miles in two days,
I reached Stony Point, in Sequatchie Valley, where
I was to hold my first basket-meeting. During the
last day of my traveling I passed through a heavy
thunderstorm of wind and rain. The meeting at
this place continued for seven days, and the power
of the Holy Ghost was present all the time. In all
my ministry I never saw so many anxious penitents
with so few conversions. At some of the services
there were most melting seasons. The Christian
people of the different Churches united in the work.
Heavy showers of rain fell every day of the meeting. Four souls were converted, and one person
united with our Church. I baptized three adults
and one infant, and received three persons into the
Church.

My second basket-meeting was held at Hale's
Chapel, in Cumberland County, embracing the first

Sunday in August, and continuing three days. It was held in union with the Baptist Church. Rev. G. W. Pressley, pastor of the Baptist Church, was present all the time. I think he is a very sincere man, but quite illiterate. Rev. D. H. Cottrell, of the Baptist Church, and Rev. M. J. Patton, of the Methodist Episcopal Church, South, rendered valuable aid. Penitents came to the altar in large numbers, one soul was converted, and two persons united with our Church. I baptized ten adults, and received eleven persons into full connection. My third basket-meeting was held at Laurel Church, in the same county, embracing the second Sunday in August. It continued six days. The Holy Ghost came down upon the people in wonderful power. A number of the best young men and young ladies of that country were at the altar. Ten persons were powerfully converted to God, and the same number united with our Church. I baptized five adults, and received six into full connection. This is the place where the Second Adventists had caused so much confusion. The Lord gave to his people a great victory over their false teachings.

My fourth basket-meeting commenced at Maple Springs, August 15th, and continued four days. There was one conversion and one accession to the Church. I baptized three persons, and received five into full connection. At the close of this meeting I set out for my leaders' and stewards' meeting in Sequatchie Valley, and in the afternoon of Saturday traveled seventeen miles over a strange road, through a dense wilderness—not a house, plantation, nor person to be seen on the way. O what solitudes are these! What opportunities for meditation and study in nature's primeval forests! My fifth basket-meeting was held at Orme's school-house, in Sequatchie Valley, embracing the third Sunday in August. It was held in connection with my leaders' and stewards' meeting. We had an old-fashioned, wonderful meeting. This place is in a densely-settled country. The school-house being small, and the congregations being large, we were compelled to worship near by in a grove—nature's first temple. Here for a number of days we sang, prayed, and shouted, while souls were converted. Rev. J. H. Parrott, of the Methodist Episcopal Church, South, was present, and preached with power. The result was eight conversions and ten accessions to our Church. I baptized eleven adults, and received six persons into full connection.

My sixth basket-meeting was held at Mt. Union, in Fentress County, embracing the fourth Sunday in August. This place is in a thinly-settled country; but the people came from great distances, and the congregations were large. The Holy Ghost was present in wonderful power at every service. The meeting continued three days, and resulted in four conversions and ten accessions to our Church. I baptized four adults and one infant, and received one person into full connection. At the close of this meeting I rode thirty miles to reach my home, after an absence of several weeks. After remaining at home about ten days, in company with Rev. W. C. Daily I set out for my fourth quarterly-meeting, to be held at Gray Ridge Church, about seventy-five miles distant. After preaching a number of times along the way, and baptizing several persons, I reached the place of the quarterly-meeting in due time. We had a very pleasant meeting. Brother Daily and I preached in turn. We finished paying the presiding elder his full claim on the work.

This closed my year's work on the Crossville Circuit, and after a ride of two days I reached my home. This has been a most laborious year's work. In the beginning I had started out with the view of elevating the condition of the mission in a spiritual, literary, and financial way. Missionary prayer-meetings were held monthly in each class. I held a number of services in the interest of a sanctified, or higher life. I preached one round on missions and took collections, and I preached one round on education and took collections. I also raised five dollars for the East Tennessee Wesleyan University at Athens. I preached one round on the cause of temperance. I traveled during the year on horseback 2,051 miles, climbing up or going down Cumberland Mountain six times on each round, and Walden's Ridge twice. I preached 181 times, received 105 persons into the Church, witnessed 80 happy conversions, visited and prayed with 500 families, baptized 48 adults and 6 infants. In addition to this, I did a great deal of manual labor in the field as a farmer. I read during the year in books 4,166 pages, besides a number of weekly newspapers, and my Bible, Hymn-book, and Discipline. I was now in my fiftieth year of age. I mention these things in the hope that I may stimulate our

younger ministers to greater industry in the vine-
vard of the Lord. May God save our ministry from
self-indulgence!

This year I raised more money for our benevo-
lences than was raised by any other charge in the
Athens District, though there were several prosperous circuits and stations in the district. I do not
mention this boastingly, but to show that small collections come from a lack of going about the work
in a proper way. There is no need that our missionary treasury should be in debt. The Crossville
Mission consisted of fifteen appointments. Eleven
of them were on the table-lands of the Cumberland, one was on Walden's Ridge, three in Sequatchie Valley, and one in Grassy Cove. The Grassy
Cove is surrounded by mountains, and is a fertile
country, but holds a great deal of stagnant water.
It is largely inhabited by Northern people. Our
Church has a small society there, but no church
building. The surrounding water-shed forms a
large creek, which passes through the cove, plunges
into and under the mountain, passing through a
natural tunnel of eight miles, when it emerges from
the mountain at the head of Sequatchie Valley,
forming the beautiful Sequatchie River.

Sequatchie Valley has a fertile soil, is not more
than five miles wide at any place, and is about seventy miles long. It is densely populated with a
well-to-do and wealthy people. It lies between the
Cumberland Mountains on one side, lifting high
their giant heads, and on the other by Walden's
Ridge. There is not a more lovely or beautiful
valley in the world.

Fully two-thirds of the mountain part of Cumberland County is yet in an uncultivated state. Dense forests of oak, hickory, chestnut, maple, and occasionally some pine, abound. It is well watered with abundant springs of freestone water, and mineral springs of various kinds are numerous. Valuable timber is abundant, coal is plentiful, and I think iron may be found in some places. Natural grass grows luxuriantly everywhere. It is very nutritious for stock; cattle and horses will become fat through the summer and fall. I am told that large cattle will live without any help through the winter, unless during excessively cold weather. I saw some young horses that had lived in the woods on the range through the winter without any help, and they looked well in the spring. The uncultivated land can be purchased at a low rate. A person with a small capital can make a good living in this country, while one with a large capital may do well here. This country lies remote from any railroad.

The native people have been greatly misunderstood by the outside world. It has been thought that one could scarcely pass through that country without the peril of life or property. This is a great mistake. Having spent eight years in mission-work among them, and having lived with them in their homes, and having had the opportunity to study them carefully, I must say that they have done wonderfully well for their advantages. Their population is not sufficiently dense to have the best public schools. It is true that they have not many comfortable school-houses; but they will make as great sacrifices to secure these conveniences, according to their ability, as the people of any other country or city. As large a proportion of the population are worthy Church members as one finds anywhere else; and their religious life is of the highest order. The Methodist, Baptist, Campbellite, and Presbyterian Churches are represented. A more hospitable people lives nowhere else. They esteem it an honor to entertain a minister of the gospel. Their kindness is spontaneous and large. In eight years of labor I have witnessed about one thousand happy conversions among these people; and while some have proven the traitor, like Judas, a great many are living witnesses of Jesus' power to save. A number have crossed the flood, shouting victory in death, and are among the white-robed throng on the other side. Some have been known, when too weak to speak, to raise their hand in token of complete triumph over death. I cherish a happy meeting with many of these people on the other side of the river. In the resurrection morning I expect to see a great number of people rise from their graves on this Cumberland Mountain, in the first resurrection. O what a happy day that will be, when husband and wife, parents and children, brothers and sisters, friends and neighbors, and pastor and flock, shall meet on that happy shore, where " sickness, sorrow, pain, and death are felt and feared no more!" Then shall we all join in one universal song, " Unto him that loved us and hath washed us from our sins in his own blood, and hath made us kings and priests unto God and his father; to him be glory and dominion for ever and ever. Amen."

I left home for the seat of Conference October 2d. The Conference was to convene October 4th, in Kingston, Tennessee, Bishop Scott presiding. I rode the first day twenty-six miles, and remained over night with my daughter, Mrs. Peters. The next day I rode twelve miles, to Brother Brown's, on Rock Creek, for dinner, and in the afternoon rode fourteen miles, and remained over night with F. M. Goddard. The next day I rode eleven miles to Colonel Dail's for dinner, and in the afternoon rode four miles into Kingston. I remained at the Conference two days and nights, stopping with Ellis Devaney. Obtaining leave of absence from the Conference on Friday, I rode out four miles and preached at Swan Pond Church that night, stopping with Colonel Dail. The next day I rode eight miles, and took dinner with Mrs. Cross, who lives at the foot of Whetstone Mountain, and in the afternoon rode fifteen miles, and preached at Scutcheon Church at night. The next day being Sunday, at the residence of J. R. Brown I preached the funeral of Father Dawn, and rode that evening seven miles, and remained over night with Edly Galloway. The next day I rode five miles and remained with my daughter, and the following day rode twenty-six miles to my home.

CHAPTER XII.

WARTBURG AND JAMESTOWN.

BY the Conference of 1876 I was appointed to the Wartburg Circuit. Rev. T. H. Russell was my presiding elder. I set off on my first round, November 3d, it being my semi-centennial birthday. On this round my first quarterly-meeting was held at Wartburg, embracing the third Sunday in November. Brother Russell was present, and presided with great acceptability. On the second round there were some indications for good. At my first appointment a very prominent gentleman united with our Church. At a night service which I held at Mrs. Potter's, penitents were at the altar of prayer, and one young lady joined the Church. This brings me to the close of another year. What an eventful one it has been, being the centennial of American independence, and also the semi-centennial of my mortal life! I am sure I have run much the longer part of the race.

During the year I preached two hundred and one times, baptized forty-eight adults and seven infants, preached the funerals of sixteen persons, and married three couples. Now, with a heart of gratitude to God for past mercies, I start out upon the year of 1877. O, my Lord, help me to do more for thee this year than during any previous year! On the third round of the circuit, on account of the very severe cold and ice over the creeks and roads, I did not reach my first appointments. However, I fell in with and filled the greater part of them; but

from severe cold and uncomfortable houses in which
to worship, I could not accomplish much. However, I had some happy meetings, and saw, as I
thought, some omens of good. On the fourth
round, at Mount Vernon, after preaching in the
day, I preached at night at David McCormick's.
A number of penitents were at the altar, four souls
were powerfully converted, and three persons united
with our Church. The next night I preached at
John Galloway's, near by. The power of convicting and converting grace was present. Four others
were converted, while Christians shouted aloud for
joy. At nearly every appointment on this round
there were anxious penitents at the altar, and at a
night service on Yellow Creek one person was
converted.

On this round, in visiting the family of Hon.
M. T. Atkins, in Wartburg, I baptized an infant,
and received into our Church a young lady,
Miss Walker. At Lee's school-house a lady
united with our Church, coming from the Baptist Church. My second quarterly-meeting was
held at Ramsey's Chapel, embracing the third
Sunday in February. Brother Russell was present,
and preached with power. There were a number
of anxious penitents at the altar. During the
month of March there were still growing indications for good. At a night service which I held
at Dennis Hull's, there were anxious penitents at
the altar, and two persons united with the Church.

On the same round I baptized and received into
full connection a number of persons whom I had
received on probation two years before. The pastor

of the past year had not baptized nor received these probationers, although he was an ordained minister. At Mt. Horr, one brother, a merchant, united with our Church. In April I preached some funerals, organized a number of Sabbath-schools, and at several places held altar services with penitents. At Ramsey's Chapel a lady of the United Brethren Church united with our Church. In May the convicting power of God was manifest at nearly all of the appointments. I preached a number of funerals.

My third quarterly-meeting was held at Scutcheon Church, beginning May 12th, and continuing five days. Brother Russell presided, and remained during the entire meeting, preaching and laboring in the altar, with the power of the Holy Ghost sent down from heaven. During the meeting fifteen souls were powerfully converted, and fourteen persons united with our Church. The conversions and accessions were among the best people of the country. Some of these were Germans who spoke English plainly. From that meeting Brother Russell and I met a congregation in Scott County, and he preached to them. We held an interesting altar service. The next day we met a congregation in Morgan County, and again Brother Russell preached. From that place we went to Paul's Chapel in Fentress County, where the third quarterly-meeting for Jamestown Circuit was held. I remained there until Sunday evening. Penitents were weeping at the altar. Rev. A. B. Hale was the preacher in charge of Jamestown Circuit.

In June I preached a number of funerals, held

several missionary meetings, and raised some very good missionary collections. At a meeting which I held at old Montgomery Camp-ground, I organized a class at that place, held a very precious altar service, baptized a number of adults and infants, and received four persons into the Church. That place was near the present town of Lansing. At Mt. Horr a young lady united with our Church. My son, Rev. J. C. Wright, filled my work during the month of July. On the first day of July I rode under a very hot sun, and over a very rough mountain ten miles, to preach some funerals, but as some of the relatives were sick the funerals were deferred.

On July 6th, in company with Rev. A. B. Hale, I set off from home, to hold the quarterly-meeting for the Crossville Circuit, by request of the presiding elder, to be held at Mt. Union, more than thirty miles from my home. We reached the place early on Saturday morning, and found a large congregation assembled under a newly-built shed. Rev. C. J. Crofts was preacher in charge of this work. The meeting continued two days, Brothers Hale and Johnson and myself doing the preaching. The power of the Lord was present to heal. One soul was converted, and two united with our Church. We had an excellent communion service, and a precious experience-meeting.

On July 13th I left home to meet some funeral appointments in Wayne and Clinton Counties, Kentucky. The next day being Saturday, I preached both in the morning and in the afternoon at Guffey's Chapel. On Sunday morning, the congregation being so large, I preached in a grove the funerals of three ladies, two of them being wives of the same husband, John Allen. In the afternoon I preached the funeral of an aged mother in Israel, at the close of which penitents came to the altar for prayers. Three persons were happily converted, while Christians shouted aloud.

On Monday morning I set off for home, but stopped on the way to baptize two infant children of Marion Pardieu, one of which was a babe not quite twenty-four hours old, the youngest babe that I had ever baptized. It looked as sweet and innocent as a little angel. On July 21st I left home for Wayne County, to preach the funeral of G. W. Upchurch, he having requested just before his death that I should do this. After riding eight miles I stopped and baptized two children of Brother Atkinson. The next morning I baptized three children of Rev. J. H. Carter, then repaired to a large graveyard near by, and preached the funeral of George W. Upchurch to a large congregation. My first basket-meeting was held at Emory Church, embracing the last Sabbath in July. It was also the occasion of my fourth quarterly-meeting. Brother Russell was present, and preached with great acceptability, remaining five days with me. This had seemed to be the most lifeless place on the work; but at this meeting the membership was greatly revived, mourners came in crowds to the altar, twenty souls were converted, and nine united with our Church. At the close I organized a large band of young men and young ladies into a Christian association.

My second basket-meeting was held at Young's Chapel, embracing the first Sabbath in August. I preached four funeral sermons during the meeting. The Lord gloriously revived his work. We held for six days. Ten souls were converted, and ten joined the Church. God be praised. I had great nervous prostration during the meeting, caused by excessive labor and very great heat.

My third basket-meeting was held at Mount Vernon, embracing the second Sunday in August. On the Sabbath of this meeting I moved the services two miles to a private house, so as to accommodate a sick lady, the funerals of whose friends I preached at that service. The meeting continued three days. A large number of penitents were at the altar, six souls were converted, and five united with our Church.

My fourth basket-meeting was held at Montgomery camp-ground, embracing the third Sunday in August, and continuing four days. Four persons were converted, and two joined the Church. During the same week, at Scutcheon Church, I baptized several infants and adults, and received a number into full connection into the Church. At Mount Vernon two excellent persons united with our Church, from the Presbyterian Church.

My fifth basket-meeting was held at Ramsey Chapel, embracing the fourth Sunday in August. During the meeting I was very sick all the time; and though without any preaching help, I continued the services for four days, with penitents at the altar. Five souls were gloriously converted.

From this meeting I returned home very sick.

In a few days I was able to be out again, and assisted in some excellent revival services at the Methodist Episcopal Church, South, at the Three Forks of Wolf River. At the request of the presiding elder of the Lexington District, Kentucky Conference, I held for him the second quarterly-meeting for the Cumberland City Circuit, at Edwards Chapel, during the first days of September, although I was very sick during the time. Notwithstanding I was in very feeble health, I met large congregations, and preached a number of funerals, both in Tennessee and Kentucky, during September.

I have now finished my tenth year's work as an itinerant minister. During the past year, under my ministry seventy persons have been converted to God, and fifty-five have united with our Church. I have baptized twenty-five adults and twenty infants, and have raised sixteen dollars for the benevolent collections.

I set off from home for our Annual Conference, in the afternoon of September 22d, rode twelve miles across Doubletop Mountain, and staid over night with John Albertson, on Obed's River. The next morning, being Sunday, I met a large congregation at a graveyard near by, and preached the funerals of two gentlemen and an infant. In the afternoon I rode to Jamestown, and preached at night. The next day I rode thirteen miles, and took dinner with Walter Vann. In the afternoon I preached at Mount Vernon, baptized three young ladies, and received them into the Church. I staid that night at John Galloway's. His daughter was very low with fever. The next day I rode nineteen miles, and remained over night at Mrs. Nitzschke's, a German lady. Her eldest son, Julius J. Nitzschke, went with me to Conference. We set off next morning, rode sixteen miles, and stopped for dinner with Rev. Richard Hudson. In the afternoon we rode fifteen miles, and remained over night with William R. Dail, my cousin.

The next morning we rode to Clinton, and took the morning train for Knoxville, the seat of the Conference. I reached the Conference-room just as the Conference was opening, Bishop W. L. Harris presiding. I was assigned to stay at Brother E. M. Wheeler's, who lives on Methodist Hill. My boarding companion was Rev. J. B. Seaton. This is a kind Christian family. I visited the deaf and dumb institute twice, on different days, while in Knoxville, and was cordially entertained by the president and faculty. I had a number of acquaintances who were students in the institution.

I left Knoxville in the afternoon of October 2d, reached Clinton late in the evening, and was entertained for the night in the home of Hon. W. R. Hicks, my kinsman. I preached that night in Clinton, in the Methodist Church. My horse had been kept free of charge in the livery stable of a Mr. Brown, a member of the Baptist Church.

The next morning I rode fifteen miles, and stopped for dinner in Winter's Gap, with my old friend and Brother, James Taylor. In the afternoon I rode seventeen miles to Wartburg, and stopped at a hotel kept by Mrs. Jones. This lady treated me with great kindness, giving me a warm room and fire. I had ridden nearly all day in heavy rain, and my clothes were very wet. I had a good night's rest. The next day I rode fifteen miles, and stopped for dinner with my daughter, Mrs. Peters. In the afternoon I rode three miles, and remained over night with Henry Peters. The following day I rode fourteen miles to Jamestown, and took dinner with J. C. Taylor. In the afternoon I rode twelve miles to my home. The second day after reaching home, at Mount Union, near my family residence, I preached the funeral of John T. W. Upchurch, to a large congregation, at the close of which eleven persons joined our Church, and I baptized four infants. I praise the Lord for such prospects at the first appointment of the Conference year! I meet many a warm heart and hand on my old home circuit.

On the second-round, my first quarterly-meeting for the Conference year was held at Jamestown, embracing the fourth Sunday in November. Brother Russell, the presiding elder, was in attendance. We had a glorious meeting. Penitents came in crowds to the altar, believers shouted aloud for joy, ten souls were powerfully converted, and eight united with our Church. God be praised! My health all this time was very poor. I had been sent by the last Conference to the Jamestown Circuit, my home work, because of my feeble health. On my third round there were some indications of coming prosperity. At a night service at Solomon's Chapel, an excellent man united with our Church.

Now I am through another year, the year 1877, which counts off my fifty-one years of mortal life, and ten toiling years in the itinerancy. O, my

God, help me to offer the praise of gratitude for such eminent gifts and love during the past year! I have preached during the year one hundred and sixty-seven times, witnessed eighty conversions, and have received seventy-three into the Methodist Episcopal Church. I have preached the funerals of thirty-five persons, baptized twenty-eight adults and twenty-eight infants, married one couple, and traveled on horseback more than two thousand miles. Now 1878 comes with its duties. Lord, help me to be a faithful steward of thy manifold grace! During the month of January the weather was very cold, and on that account the congregations were somewhat lessened. However, we enjoyed some refreshing seasons of religious power.

Embracing the fourth Sunday in February, my second quarterly-meeting came off at Paul's Chapel. The people of that settlement did not manifest as much zeal for the cause of Christ as they once did. The presiding elder did not attend; and with all heavy clouds of discouragement hung over my pathway; but I called upon the Lord, and he heard me, and we had a very gracious meeting indeed. The usual services of such an occasion were held. Rev. John C. Harmon, a young local preacher on the work, was present, and assisted me.

During the month of March we enjoyed some very happy meetings, the people of the Lord often shouting aloud the praises of God, and some souls were seeking the divine life. At an evening service held at Stephen Halbert's, a justice of the peace for the district united with our Church. My financial help was so meager from the work, that I could not devote sufficient time to the ministry, but was compelled to give a great deal of attention to my farm for a family support. I am fearful that the Church on Jamestown Circuit will meet an awful account in the day of judgment for neglecting the support of their pastors, and thereby greatly hindering the work of the Lord.

On this charge we have many wealthy members who do very little for the support of the gospel. I tremble for the future of this work, unless the people wake up to their duty. I believe our people would do better if the stewards would do their duty. This seems to be our trouble everywhere. The good Lord help us. I now feel that the seeds of death are sown in my system. My health is broken down; and I am candid in the belief, that overwork for the Church and severe labor on my farm, because of a very meager support from my charges, have brought this about. I do not complain at my lot in life; for, with the convictions which I now have at my present age, if I had life to go over, I would seek the salvation of my soul earlier, make the same connections that I did with the Methodist Episcopal Church, and endeavor, by the grace of God, to live a more faithful minister of the gospel, regardless of compensation in this life; for I am happy in the assurance that, though I sow in tears, I shall reap in joy.

Among all the other professions, none can look with such happy anticipations to the recompense of reward as the faithful minister of the Lord Jesus. I love the itinerant work, and the missionary fields, such as those in which I have labored for about eleven years. Next to my blessed Savior, I love the Methodist Episcopal Church. I believe her to be apostolic in her spirit and practice. I sing with the poet:

> "For her my tears shall fall,
>   For her my prayers ascend,
>   To her my cares and toils be given,
>   Till toils and cares shall end."

I can confidently commit all my anxieties and solicitude for my family and Church into the hands of the good Lord, and say with Paul, "For me to live is Christ, but to die is gain." Should I live many years, I want to live more devoted to Christ; and if I should die soon, I want my death to be that of the righteous, and my last end like theirs. I trust that I am living to this end. I feel assured that the Methodist Church will never lack for preachers and means to carry on her work over sin, and that she will never lose her aggressiveness for the conversion of the world.

During April, we enjoyed some refreshing seasons from the presence of the Lord. I preached eight times during the month, besides working a great deal on my farm. At an evening service which I held at Halbert's school-house, two ladies joined our Church. One night, at midnight, I was called to go about two miles to see a young man who was nearing the eternal world. Being too feeble to go at night, I went the next morning to see him, and found him ready and willing to die. I held religious services with him, and again, at night, preached in his room, to the family and a few friends, and received him into the Church. About forty hours afterwards he died. I held his funeral services. His name was John Alvin Johnson.

During the month of May we had some religious prosperity on the work. The third quarterly-meeting services embraced the second Sunday. Rev. T. H. Russell was present in labors abundant. We had an excellent communion-service, and on Monday three young ladies were converted to God and united with our Church. During the month I sold fifty copies of "Moody: His Words, Work, and Workers." I believe that the selling of good books is an effective way of preaching the gospel; and during my ministry I have sold a great many books. I attended a Sunday-school picnic at Yellow Creek Falls, near Jamestown, May 25th, and assisted in the exercises. Yellow Creek is quite a stream of water, and makes a fall at this place of about one hundred feet.

During the month of June, at the request of W. B. Rippetoe, presiding elder of the Nashville District, Central Tennessee Conference, I attended with him a Sunday-school institute at Winneham's Crossroads, in Overton County. Rev. J. B. Ford, Sunday-school agent, was present, and by his spiritual lectures and sermons rendered the occasion very interesting. On Sunday afternoon I preached, when the power of the Holy Ghost fell on the people, and many shouted aloud. I called for penitents, when several came, and two souls were mightily converted.

My first basket-meeting was held, in connection with my fourth quarterly-meeting, at Mount Union, embracing the third Sunday in July, and continued five days. Brother Russell, the presiding elder, was present, and preached and labored with great zeal. The Church was greatly revived; twenty souls were happily converted to God, and twenty-one united with our Church. I baptized four infants and five adults at the close of the meeting.

On the 1st day of August, 1878, I was elected County Court clerk of Fentress County by a large majority over several opponents. My second basket-meeting was held at Solomon's Chapel, embracing the first Sabbath in August, and continued five days. There were eight conversions, and three accessions to our Church. Embracing the second Saturday and Sunday in August, I held a meeting at Guffey's Chapel, in Wayne County, Kentucky. On Sunday morning of the meeting I preached a funeral sermon, when the power of the Holy Ghost came upon the people in a wonderful manner. Three young ladies joined our Church, and I baptized two persons. My third basket-meeting was held on Caney Creek, embracing the fourth Sunday in August. It continued five days, and resulted in three conversions and one accession to the Church. I baptized a lady, and received her into full connection. The membership was greatly revived.

My fourth basket-meeting was held at Paul's Chapel, embracing the first Sunday in September. The result of this meeting was two conversions and the membership greatly revived. I baptized three adults and two infants, and received three persons into full connection in the Church. On the second day of September I gave bond to the County Court of Fentress County to the amount of twenty thousand dollars, and took the oath of office as County Court clerk, and entered immediately upon the duties of the office. I appointed and qualified as deputy clerk Mr. A. M. Garrett, who was to attend to the duties of the office in my absence. In company with Rev. J. C. Harmon, I attended the District Conference at Mount Union, on the Crossville Circuit, beginning September 6th. The Conference was well attended, and the exercises were exceedingly interesting and profitable. There were a number of happy conversions during the meeting. The people had erected cabins for tents, and the meeting took the form of a camp-meeting. The Baptist monthly-meeting came off at the same time and place, and we all worshiped fraternally together.

On the third Sunday in September I preached at Mount Union, on Wolf River, baptized ten adults, and received twelve persons into the Church. On the fourth Sunday in September I preached two funerals at Solomon's Chapel, received a young man into the Church, and married Mark Jennings to Catherine Wright, at the church. On the fifth Sunday in September I preached at Halbert's school-house.

Our Annual Conference met in New Market, Tennessee, October 2, 1878, Bishop Scott presiding. I did not attend. I had been elected County Court clerk, and had promised the people, while a candidate, that I would move my family to Jamestown and do the business of the office myself. I was moving at the time of the Conference session. I trust my zeal for the cause of Christ will not weaken because I have retired from the pastorate for a short time. I trust that, after a few years, I shall do more effective work for the Master than ever before. I am resolved to preach, more or less, every week during my term of office. The Lord help me to be a faithful minister of the gospel!

I have done a great deal of service for the Church in Fentress County, with very little compensation. During the Conference year I have witnessed fifty conversions, received fifty-nine persons into our Church, baptized twenty-nine adults and fifteen infants, and preached the funerals of seventeen persons.

CHAPTER XIII.

A COUNTY COURT CLERK.

ON the second Sunday in November I had an appointment, about fifty miles from Jamestown, to preach the funeral of Michael Hale and babe. I left home on Friday morning, rode thirty-three miles, and preached at night at Maple Springs. The next morning I rode fifteen miles, and preached at Hale's Chapel, in Cumberland County. I preached at the same place at night. On the following day, being Sunday, I preached the funeral of Brother Hale and babe, to a large congregation. I preached again at night, when a number of penitents came to the altar, and there were good indications of a revival; but I was compelled to close. That night I staid with Brother William Lee, and the next morning, at family worship, I baptized Brother and Sister Lee and their two infant children. I then rode home, about fifty miles, occupying a part of two days, to find, on my arrival, Brother Russell protracting his quarterly-meeting in our town, with good results.

I had been at home only a few hours, when I was called to go to the home of Mrs. Bledsoe, and pray for her daughter Josephine, a most excellent young lady, who was greatly concerned about her soul's salvation. While we were upon our knees praying, God spoke peace to her soul, and she rejoiced with joy unspeakable and full of glory. Three other persons were converted during the meeting, and three joined our Church. During the remainder of the year 1878 I preached, more or less, at Jamestown, Paul's Chapel, Barger . Church, and other places. I have now finished another year of work. O how thankful I feel to the Lord for the many evidences of his love during the past year! How many more shall I live to recall his goodness?

During the year I have preached one hundred and eighteen times, baptized twenty-seven adults and thirteen infants, and married six couples. My financial support from the work was very little. However, I raised good benevolent collections. My health has greatly improved. During the months of January and February the weather was intensely severe, yet I preached during the period ten times, with happy results. At some places, penitents were at the altar in large numbers. May God bless his work under my ministry this year, to the salvation of precious souls!

I held the second quarterly-meeting on the Jamestown Circuit for Brother Russell, at his request. It was held at New Liberty, eighteen miles from Jamestown. I preached, held a love-feast, administered the holy communion service, and took a collection for the presiding elder.

On Saturday night before the second Sunday in March I preached at William Jones's, near Paul's Chapel. At the close of the sermon a number of penitents came forward for prayers, and a young lady was happily converted. The next day, at Paul's Chapel, anxious penitents were at the altar. O may God convert those precious souls!

I find great need for watchfulness and prayer while engaged in the business of County Court clerk, that my zeal may not lapse. As God knows my heart when I say it, I would rather be in the work of an itinerant Methodist preacher than in anything else in this world. I trust that a few years of rest will render me efficient again in the work. I greatly feel the need of rest, though I do not know that I shall ever have much until I obtain it in my heavenly home.

At a meeting which I held at Paul's Chapel the third Sabbath in April, a lady united with our Church.

The first Saturday and Sunday in May was the occasion of our third quarterly-meeting, on Caney Creek, near Travisville. Brother Russell was present, as were also a number of preachers. The elements for the Lord's Supper were not prepared, and consequently this service was not held. O how careless our Church officials are sometimes!

On Saturday before the second Sunday in May I left home for Cumberland City, Kentucky. After taking dinner at Travisville, I rode in the afternoon to John R. Davis's, in Clinton County, and found Brother and Sister Davis the same true and faithful Christian people. The next day I preached in Cumberland City, to a large congregation, the funerals of Father and Mother Butram, from 1st Corinthians xv, 53, 54. Here I met Brother Shelton, the pastor of the charge, and several other preachers. I also met a number of warm-hearted friends of other days; for I had been pastor of this charge five years before. That evening I preached at Number 1 school-house. We had a precious service.

In the latter part of May I rode forty-five miles into Cumberland County, Kentucky, to see my brother, Rev. Edmondson Wright, who was very sick. I found him in a low state of health. I think, from the symptoms, he can not live long in this world. However, he is fully ready for the change, having been for a number of years a faithful minister of the gospel in the Methodist Episcopal Church, South. He is considerably older than I am, and was a child of God long before I was. On Sunday morning I preached in the Methodist church in a village near by, called Patonsburg. At the request of my sick brother, I preached that afternoon at his house. The next day, on my way home, I stopped for dinner in Albany, with my old friend, A. J. York.

At a meeting which I held at Barger Church, on the fourth Sunday in June, we had a precious service, and a lady united with our Church. I pray God that my zeal may never become less for the prosperity of Zion and the salvation of precious souls; though I find that, out of the itineracy, it will require a great deal of praying and watching to prevent this.

Our fourth quarterly-meeting was held at Mount Union, embracing the third Sunday in July, and was protracted for several days. I preached on Saturday in the place of the presiding elder, as he had not yet arrived. On Sunday morning I preached the funeral of Rebecca Guin, to a large congregation. In the afternoon, Brother Russell preached, and administered the sacrament of the Lord's Supper. On Monday there were three conversions and several accessions to our Church. God be praised! On Tuesday I preached the funeral of Timothy Absalom West, and rode home in the afternoon. The next day I was called to see a sick grandchild, an infant of my daughter, Mrs. Peters. It died the next morning, and we carried it, the following day, to Mount Vernon Cemetery for burial, Brother Russell, the presiding elder, holding the funeral services. God bless the parents!

I attended with Rev. T. A. Cass at Crab Creek, the fourth Sunday in July, and remained with him four days, preaching and praying for penitents as they came in numbers to the altar. The people of God shouted for joy, and eleven souls were converted to God. I baptized three ladies by immersion.

I left home in August, to meet some appointments in Kentucky, and rode the first day to Travisville, and remained over night with F. M. Johnson. The next morning I crossed the Poplar Mountain, by a very rough way, to the Slick Ford of Otter Creek, where Brother Shelton had been holding services for a week with happy results. I met a congregation of about eight hundred people at a creek, and baptized nineteen persons by pouring and twenty by immersion. I preached that afternoon to the people, when penitents came to the altar in numbers, and Christians rejoiced. The next day, in company with Brother F. M. Atkinson, I set out for Concord Church in Clinton County. After traveling ten miles, and crossing a very rough mountain, and then down into the valley, we reached the church in due time for services. We met a large congregation; and the house not being sufficiently large to hold the people, we repaired to a grove near by, and I preached the funeral of Jane Polston. I preached again in the afternoon, and on the following day twice, with happy results, three souls being happily converted to God. I held a meeting for five days, embracing the third Sunday in August, at Paul's Chapel. Penitents crowded the altar, the people of God shouted for joy, and three persons were converted to God. During this meeting, I first heard of the death of my dear brother, Rev. Edmondson Wright, which gave to me great sorrow, but I sorrow not as those who have no hope; for my brother was a good and true man, and doubtless is among "that great number who have washed their robes and made them white in the blood of the Lamb;" and by the grace of God I feel bound to meet him in that better world.

On the fifth Sunday in August, I preached the funerals of Robert W. Holding and his two little

infant sisters, at Sulphur Springs in Fentress
County, to a large congregation, under a brush
arbor prepared for the occasion. The scene was
one of deep solemnity. A number of people
shouted the praise of God, while penitents came to
an altar and pleaded for pardon. For several weeks
I suffered greatly from sore throat and tongue;
however, I went on preaching and filling my appointments. On Saturday before the first Sunday
in September, I went to Mt. Vernon in Morgan
County, where Rev. A. C. Peters was conducting a
basket-meeting. On Sunday morning, in a grove
near by the church, I preached the funeral of Rev.
Calvin R. Vann, to a large congregation; and in the
afternoon, in the church, I preached the funeral of
a little boy of Dennis Hull's. There was great rejoicing in the camps of Israel, and penitents came
to the altar in numbers. I remained over Monday,
assisting in the services, when six souls were converted.

The second Sunday in September I preached
twice at Paul's Chapel with happy results. Embracing the third Sunday in September, I held a two
days' meeting at Concord Church in Clinton County.
On Sabbath morning I baptized one lady by pouring and twenty-one ladies by immersion. On
Monday after the fourth Sunday in September, I
preached the funeral of Belle Pyle, a daughter of
Brother Pearson Davidson.

On the second Sunday in October, Rev. J. C.
Harmon and myself left Jamestown for the seat of
our Annual Conference, which was to convene on
the following Wednesday in Knoxville, Tenn.

After riding nine miles, we stopped at Barger's Church, and I preached the funeral of a little son of Mr. Hoover. In the afternoon we rode over into Morgan County, and spent the night with my daughter, Mrs. Peters. The following day we rode eleven miles, and stopped for dinner with Brother Fairchild. After holding religious services with them, we passed down the railroad line in the afternoon, the road being then in construction, saw them building the high bridge over Rock Creek—one hundred and twenty feet high—and after passing through Lansing and Wartburg, we stopped for the night with Captain G. W. Keith, who lives three miles from the last-named place. The next morning we rode fourteen miles, and stopped for dinner in Winter's Gap at Brother Taylor's, and in the afternoon rode up the valley to William R. Dail's. Here we were joined by Brother S. Grear and others, on their way to the Conference. I preached that night at Sulphur Springs Church. We had a good service.

The following day we rode to Clinton, and took the train for Knoxville, reaching the Conference room soon after the opening. Bishop I. W. Wiley was presiding. Brother Harmon and I were assigned to stay with Mrs. Walker, who lived on the Clinton Pike, some distance from the First Methodist Church. We were very kindly entertained by this excellent family. I attended the Conference sessions during each day, and Church services each night at the Second Methodist Church, where I heard a number of the Conference brethren preach. Bishop Wiley held the Conference well in hand,

and gave great satisfaction. This was not long before his death in China. On Sunday of the Conference I heard him preach an excellent sermon, in the First Methodist Church, from Psalms xlix, 8. In the afternoon, in the same church, he ordained ten elders, among them my own son, Rev. J. C. Wright. Delegates were elected to the General Conference.

On Monday, in the afternoon, Brother Harmon and Elias Bowden and myself took the train for Clinton, at which place we arrived in due time, and rode out five miles to William R. Dail's. The next day we rode to Major Stephens', and stopped for dinner, and in the afternoon rode twelve miles to Scutcheon, and stopped with J. W. Scott. I preached that night at Scutcheon Church to a large congregation. The next morning, after baptizing the little babe of Russell Scott, we rode to my daughter's, Mrs. Peters, for dinner, and in the afternoon rode seventeen miles to my home in Jamestown.

The fourth Sunday in October I preached at Ramsey's Chapel, on the Wartburg Circuit, the funeral of Tennessee Hicks. Several penitents were forward for prayers; one young lady was converted and joined our Church.

My dear brother, James M. Wright, died suddenly October 30, 1879, at the home of John Davis, our old homestead. He had been somewhat ailing for several weeks, had staid with me at my home in Jamestown two nights just prior to his death, and had left my house not more than two hours before his death. He rode up to the yard fence of Mr. Davis, hitched his horse, walked into the house, remarking to Mrs. Davis, my sister, that he was feeling very badly, lay down across the bed, and was dead in one minute. O how sudden, and how sad! He was buried on the following day at the Three Forks of Wolf River, with Masonic honors, two lodges officiating. It is thought that one thousand people were present at his funeral.

On the fourth Sunday in November I preached the funeral of Mrs. Lane and her two sons, at the residence of her son, Braxton Lane, in Morgan County. A large congregation was present, penitents were called to the altar, while the saints of God shouted for joy. My health during this autumn was very feeble, and I was not able for the best service.

On Saturday before the first Sunday in December, I rode about seventeen miles, and preached at night at William Todd's. Some shouted for joy. The next day I preached at Mt. Union Church, on the Crossville Circuit. Brother Burnett, the pastor, was present. I baptized a lady and received one into the Church. The next day I visited Rev. John C. Tate, an able colored minister of the Methodist Episcopal Church, who had founded a colony of colored people on the table-land in Cumberland County. I think he has made a grave mistake in trying to do this. We had a warm religious service in his home. On the following day I reached home.

I have been greatly afflicted with sore throat for some time, and see that I must be careful where I preach during the winter months. And now farewell to the year 1879. What groans and sighs it

has brought to my life! It has been to me a year
of great bereavement, having had to consign two
dear brothers and a little grandchild to the cold
arms of death. Is the Lord justly reproving me
for taking a supernumerary relation, or shall it all
finally tend to my good? May it incite in me holier
living! Our family is rapidly passing away. None
of us live to a great age. I have five brothers in
the spirit-world. One died in infancy, the other
four in manhood's middle day. I now have only
one living brother, and we are more than three thousand miles apart. How lonely I feel! My dear
brother Calvin is far away from me in California,
and is in poor health, having to take a superannuated relation in his Conference. I am sure that in
a few years none of the old family will be left in
this world. May the Lord help us all so to live
that we may all finally meet in our Father's house
above, and live together forever!

During the year I have preached seventy-four
times, witnessed twenty-seven conversions, received
ten persons into our Church, baptized sixty-eight
adults and nine infants, preached the funerals of
seventeen persons, and married two couples. God
be praised for his goodness and mercy during the
past year! I desire to do better service for the year
1880.

On the fourth Sunday in January I attended a
meeting of Brother Scott, at Solomon's Chapel, and
preached that night at Jerry Beatty's. The Holy
Ghost came down upon the people. Some shouted
for joy, while a number came forward for prayers,
and a young lady was converted.

I attended a prayer-meeting on the last Wednesday night in February, at the home of Pleasant Taylor. After some prayers I preached, called penitents to the altar, when quite a number came, among these the grandfather, with quite a number of his grandchildren, crying for mercy. One young lady was converted, and shouted aloud the praise of God. More than ever I feel like moving out into the active work of the ministry. I would rather be employed in preaching and leading souls to the Lord Jesus than to be doing anything else in this world. If my health shall be restored, I feel that I must enter the effective ranks next autumn. The Lord demonstrate his will to me!

At an afternoon service in April I preached at N. S. Northrup's, three miles from Jamestown. We had a melting season, with penitents at the altar. Three persons united with our Church. On the second Sunday in April I preached at Young's Chapel, in Morgan County, and baptized five children at the altar. I preached at that place again in the afternoon, when the Holy Ghost came upon the people in wonderful power, and praises went up from happy hearts. I staid that night with A. R. Lewallen, and the next morning at family worship baptized two of his children. The following day I passed through Glen Mary, and went two miles from there to the coal-mines, at the home of Bracher Davis, and preached to an attentive congregation. We had a good time, with several penitents at the altar. Here I met with Rev. John Forrester, an aged member of the Holston Conference, and the pastor of this charge. He is doing an excellent work here, although far advanced in life. The following day I preached at White Oak Church, near Sunbright, and the next day preached at Mt. Vernon. Here I stopped with Rev. A. C. Peters, pastor of the Wartburg Circuit. That afternoon I reached my home.

On Friday before the third Sunday in May I left home to attend some funeral appointments in Kentucky. After riding twenty-three miles, I stopped for the night with Jabe Edwards, in Wayne County, where I was very kindly entertained. The next morning I rode eight miles to Bethesda Church, in Sherer's Valley, met a large congregation, and preached the funeral of an excellent young man, named Upchurch, from Isaiah xxvi, 19. In the afternoon I rode a few miles, calling on a number of old friends, and spent the night at Andrew Young's. The following day I rode nine miles, to Pleasant Hill Church, where the Baptist brethren were holding their monthly and sacramental meeting. Here I had an appointment with two Baptist ministers to preach some funerals that day. At ten o'clock I preached the funerals of Charles Dabney and his daughter, Elizabeth Hancock, and her two infant children, from 1 Cor. xv, 53, 54; and Elders Nimrod Stinson and Alvin Butram preached the funeral of Mrs. Tuggle, a sister of Mrs. Hancock. The Holy Ghost came upon the people in power, and Baptists and Methodists rejoiced together. Afterward our Baptist brethren proceeded with their sacramental service. I took leave of absence, as I thought my presence would be embarrassing to our Baptist brethren, since, by

au iron rule of their Church, they could not com-
mune with me. After such a season of rejoicing
together in the altar, it seems inconsistent that
these Methodists and Baptists should be separated
at the communion-table. I shall rejoice when the
Baptist Church can see its way clearly to abandon
this old, erroneous view.

Embracing the fourth Sunday in May, in connection with Rev. S. B. Scott, I held services for several days at Beech Grove Church, twenty miles
from Jamestown. We held the service in the grove
near by, because the church could not hold the congregations. The Lord was present in healing
power. Penitents were at the altar in large numbers. Convictions were deep, and conversions were
mighty. Five souls were happily converted to God,
and the Christian people were greatly revived. Two
persons united with our Church. On Monday morning of the meeting I baptized Mrs. Artemia Huddlesten by immersion in Wolf River, and afterwards,
at her own home, received her into full connection
in the Church. She was the widow of Captain
Huddlesten, who had been killed in the Federal
army.

On the fifth Sunday in May, at Solomon's Chapel,
where Brother Scott and myself were holding a two
days' meeting, two young ladies joined our Church.
Embracing the third Sunday in June, Rev. J. V.
Brown and myself held a two days' meeting at the
Three Forks of Wolf River, where, on Sunday, I
preached two funeral sermons with manifest tokens
of the Divine presence.

On the first Sunday in July, it being the fourth

day, in company with a number of ministers and people, we celebrated the natal day of our Nation in a religious way, by holding religious services in a very large cave or rock-house, seven miles east of Jamestown. The occasion was a very interesting one indeed. On the third Sunday in July I preached the funeral of a child of George Franklin, at the Three Forks of Wolf River, when a lady was happily converted. During the following week I assisted Brother Scott in a protracted service for several days at Sulphur Springs. Nine souls were happily converted, and seven united with our Church.

Embracing the second Sunday in August, I assisted Rev. A. C. Peters in a meeting at Mt. Vernon, in Morgan County. Here there were fourteen conversions and a number of accessions to the Church. On the third Sunday in August, at Fellowship Church, thirteen miles from Jamestown, a union service of the native people, and some Northern people who had come to settle in the country, was held. The meeting was a very fraternal one. In the afternoon of the day I preached at Paul's Chapel and baptized an infant. Embracing the fourth Sunday in August, under a brush-arbor at Beech Grove, I held a basket-meeting of six days. The result was, nine souls were converted and eleven accessions to the Church. At the close I baptized fourteen persons. The Christians were greatly revived. Our Church in this community had been very weak, but was now growing rapidly. I had no ministerial help during the meeting.

I held services the fifth Sunday in August, and

the two succeeding days, at Mt. Union, on Wolf
River. The Church was greatly revived, but there
were no conversions. Embracing the first Sunday
in September, the Methodists and Cumberland Presbyterians, held a union camp-meeting at Mt. Union,
on the Crossville Circuit. I was present, and preached
a number of times during the meeting. The Lord
was present in saving power, and a number of souls
were converted. The different Churches united in
the work, and all were greatly revived. On Sunday I baptized two infant children of Rev. Mr.
Shaver.

On the second Sunday in September, at Young's
Chapel, in Morgan County, I preached the funeral
of a little girl of Brother Stonecipher. The Holy
Ghost was present in wondrous power. The day
before, I visited the town of Rugby, in Morgan
County, an English colony recently established. In
company with Cyrus Clark, one of the proprietors of
the place, I went through the large hotel of thirty-
six rooms. Embracing the fourth Sunday in September, Brother Scott and I held a meeting of several days at Solomon's Chapel. The results were
seven conversions and nine accessions to the Church.
Christians were greatly revived.

On the first Sunday in October, at Mt. Union,
on Wolf River, I preached the funerals of Dicey
Johnson, and her daughter-in-law, Rebecca Johnson, and her son John Alvin Johnson, from John v,
28, 29. A large congregation was present, in-
cluding several ministers. In the afternoon I
rode eight miles and celebrated the rites of matrimony between Rev. J. V. Brown, pastor of

the Methodist Episcopal Church, South, and
Abigail Williams, a daughter of John S. Williams,
of Fentress County. Brother Brown is a noble
Christian gentleman, and is having great success in
his pastoral work. May Heaven grant to him and
his wife a bright and happy life! I rode twenty
miles that night to reach my home, the next day
being County Court, and my presence as the clerk
necessary. On the third Sunday in October, after
preaching the night before at Father Austin Choat's,
I met a large congregation at Obed's River, and
baptized five persons by immersion and five by
pouring. We then repaired to Solomon's Chapel,
and I preached to a large congregation, the Lord
being present in saving power. During the following week I held the funeral service of a little boy
of Dr. Whitney, in Jamestown. On the fourth
Sunday in October, the funerals of my two brothers, Rev. Edmondson Wright and James M. Wright,
were preached at the Three Forks of Wolf River,
by Rev. T. C. Frogge, from 1 Tim. iv, 8–10, to a
large and attentive congregation. The Masons were
present in uniform.

Our Annual Conference met October 20, 1880, at
Greeneville, Tenn., Bishop E. O. Haven presiding.
I did not attend, but the Conference granted me a
supernumerary relation again. Rev. W. C. Daily
was appointed presiding elder of the Kingston District. I believe that I can do a great work for the
Lord in this relation, and not expose myself to the
bad weather. I trust that my zeal for the salvation of souls will not become less. May the Lord
help me!

At this session the colored part of our work was set off into the East Tennessee Conference, a long-felt and much-needed improvement. Also the North Carolina part was set off into the Blue Ridge Conference. By the latter division, a number of leading ministers were lost to our Conference. Both of these divisions had been provided for by the last General Conference.

On the first Sunday in November I rode twelve miles over two rough mountains, and preached to a large congregation the funeral of a Mr. Turner, who had died in the Union army during the Civil War. I rode back home in the afternoon. On Saturday before the second Sunday in November, I left home and rode eighteen miles into Morgan County, and preached in the afternoon at Young's Chapel. The next morning, at the same place, I preached the funerals of a lady and four of her infant sisters, all children of Jerry Jones, to an attentive audience. Revs. John Forrester and A. C. Peters, ministers of the Holston Conference, were present at this service. In the afternoon I preached the funeral of an infant child of Brother Young, baptized two children, and received a most excellent man into our Church.

On the afternoon of Saturday before the third Sunday in November, a very cold day, I rode nine miles, and preached at night at Thomas Crabtree's, and the next day, at the Three Forks of Wolf, I preached the funeral of Dorcas Hatfield, a mother in Israel. The fourth Saturday and Sunday in November I attended the first quarterly-meeting on the Jamestown Circuit, at Halbert's Church. W. C.

Daily, the presiding elder, and S. B. Scott, the preacher in charge, were present. December was a very cold, wintry month, and I preached only once or twice during the time. I have now gone through another year, and, O my soul, I trust I do feel thankful to the good Lord that my life has been spared, and my health graciously preserved! I feel unworthy of such marked favor.

During the year I have preached eighty-four times, witnessed at my own meetings forty happy conversions, have received thirty-six persons into the Methodist Episcopal Church, baptized twenty-five adults and fourteen infants, have preached the funerals of twenty-three persons, and married four couples. I bless God that I have enjoyed a very happy year. Now, in the fifty-fifth year of my mortal life, and in the thirty-eighth year of my spiritual life, I begin the year 1881. I have vowed unto the Lord at the altar, in covenant with God's people, by his grace, to live a better life, and one of more service to him. I am fast running my race, and must soon render an account to God for my stewardship here. The Lord help me, unworthy as I am to glorify his name this year, and to see many precious souls brought into the kingdom. I preached, the second Sunday in January, at Paul's Chapel.

During the months of January, February, and March, I did not get out to preach very often, as our winter was the severest that we had ever witnessed in this country. I attended a quarterly-meeting of the Methodist Episcopal Church, South, the last Saturday and Sunday in January, at Mt.

Vernon, where I formed the acquaintance of Brothers Swaim and Curtis. We preached and labored together in a fraternal manner. During the spring, at my appointments, the Holy Ghost was present in the awakening of sinners, and in the making happy the children of God.

On Saturday before the second Sunday in June, I left home for a funeral appointment in Wayne County, Kentucky. I rode that day to the home of Jabe Edwards, where I was kindly received. The next day, at Coil's Church, to a large congregation, in a beautiful grove, I preached the funeral of Jesse Kennedy. At the close of the sermon several men and women shouted aloud the praises of God, and made the grove ring with loud hallelujahs. I met such a large number of old friends that it took some time to go through the handshaking. It brought to my mind the happy greeting when we shall meet with our glorified friends in heaven. In the afternoon I came back three miles, and held a children's-meeting at Edwards Chapel, and raised a collection for Sunday-school literature. A number of the children expressed an earnest desire for salvation.

On Saturday evening before the fourth Sunday in June, I rode six miles to see Jacky Taylor, an old man eighty-eight years of age, who was praying earnestly for a preparation to meet God in peace. I sang, prayed, and preached for him, when he was mightily converted to God, and praised him with all his strength. He lived about two weeks, and died happy. I preached the next day in Poplar Cove. On June 29th, I left home for the Kingston Dis-

trict Conference, to be held at Rockwood in Roane
County. I rode to my daughter's for dinner in
Morgan County, and in the afternoon, in company
with Rev. A. C. Peters, rode five miles to Sunbright, and took the train for Rockwood, arriving
there late in the evening. The District Conference
was conducted by the Rev. W. C. Daily, the presiding elder. The sessions were harmonious and
pleasant, and the preaching by different brethren
was of a high order. I have never favored District
Conferences, and believe that the General Conference made a mistake in establishing them. I think
that the old-time quarterly-meetings have been de-
stroyed by the District Conference. I regard this
as a grave mistake. Rockwood is a mining town
of considerable interest, situated in a charming valley, at the base of Walden's Ridge. Here the Roane
Iron Company have large iron furnaces, where a
great deal of pig-iron is made. In the vicinity
are coal and iron of the finest grade, in inexhausti-
ble quantities. I was entertained in the homes of
Messrs. Shelow, Roberts, and Sanks, from whom I
received royal kindness. In returning I preached at
Sunbright, in the new Baptist church; also at Mt.
Vernon I preached the funeral of an infant child
of Daniel Jack's, from 1 Cor. xv, 25, 26.

Embracing the second Sunday in July, Brother
Scott and I held a meeting of three days, under a
brush-arbor, at Beech Grove, in Fentress County.
The Church was greatly revived, and penitents
came to the altar in large numbers; but there were
no conversions. One lady united with our Church.
On the fourth Sunday in July Rev. A. C. Peters

preached in our town, and in the afternoon he and I rode seven miles to Solomon's Chapel, to assist Brother Scott in a basket-meeting. We remained for two days, preaching and laboring in the altar, while the people of God shouted for joy. On the fifth Sunday in July I attended a basket-meeting on Crab Creek. I preached the funeral of a sainted babe, at the Three Forks of Wolf River, the first Sunday in August.

On Saturday before the second Sunday in August, in company with Brother Herron, the Presbyterian pastor, I left home for a funeral occasion in Wayne County, Kentucky. We rode eleven miles, and stopped for dinner with Asbury Williams. In the afternoon, near Travisville, I encountered a heavy storm of wind and rain, after which I rode to Brother P. H. Davidson's, in Pickett County, near the Kentucky line, and staid over night. The next morning I crossed over a very rough mountain, and after riding seven miles, met a large congregation at Edwards Chapel, in Wayne County, and preached the funeral of Sarah C. Buck. I preached again in the afternoon at the same place, to a very attentive audience, with good prospects for a revival of religion.

On the third Sunday in August I attended the fourth quarterly-meeting of the Jamestown Circuit, at Paul's Chapel, and heard W. C. Daily preach twice. There was not much spiritual power manifest. Embracing the fourth Sunday in August, I held a basket-meeting of several days at Sulphur Springs, in Pickett County. Three souls were converted, three persons united with our Church, and I baptized three adults and one infant. The Church was greatly revived.

On Friday before the first Sunday in September, myself and wife and Nina Allred left home to attend the camp-meeting at Mount Union, on the Crossville Circuit. Rev. A. C. Peters was the preacher in charge. Mrs. Allred, who was with us, afterwards became the wife of Brother Peters. The camps in this place were built in the most rural style; but a number of campers were on hand. The services were conducted in the old-fashioned camp-meeting style. The Lord was present to save. A number were happily converted to God, and hallelujahs went up from the camps in old-fashioned Methodist style. On Sunday I preached the funeral of an excellent young lady, and at the close of the sermon administered the sacrament of the Lord's Supper.

On Friday before the second Sunday in September, I left home to fill a number of funeral appointments in Wayne and Clinton Counties, Kentucky. I rode the first day twenty-four miles, and preached at night at Edwards Chapel to a large congregation. Here I was greatly disturbed by two drunken men, who talked in the house and on the outside while I was preaching, and tried to raise a disturbance with some peaceable men. Early the next morning the officers had them under arrest for their conduct. One of them was fined twenty-five dollars, while the other came clear.

The next morning being Saturday, in company with A. J. Pearcy, I rode eight miles to Bethesda Church, met a large congregation, and preached the funeral of an excellent lady. The father of this lady, Moses Upchurch, being sick and very low, we repaired to his house near by, and I baptized him, as he sat up in his bed. I felt, while baptizing him, that the head on which my hands then rested, almost cold in death, would soon be crowned with life immortal. I preached at the same church again that night. The next morning I rode five miles to Guffey's Chapel, where the Methodist Episcopal Church has a large organization. I found a large congregation of about one thousand people, and met so many old friends whom I had served as pastor in other years, that it took some time to get through with the handshaking. I then preached the funeral of Absalom C. Guffey and his infant babe, while the saints of God shouted aloud. The people had brought provisions on the ground, and I preached to them again in the afternoon. The next morning I rode four miles, met a large congregation, near Thomas Yorke's, and I preached the funeral of Jefferson Yorke in a grove. We had a glorious meeting. A number of the people of God, both ladies and gentlemen, shouted aloud his praise. At night, at Brother Yorke's, I preached the funeral of a babe of Mr. Clark, to a crowded house. At the close of the sermon, penitents came to an altar of prayer, and two persons were powerfully converted and joined our Church. The next day I rode ten miles, met a congregation at Concord Church, in Clinton County, and preached to them. In the afternoon I rode eight miles, and staid over night with Manson Flowers, an old neighbor, who has an excellent family. The next day I went home. On the trip I rode about seventy miles, and preached eight times.

On Saturday before the fourth Sunday in September I left home to fill a funeral appointment in Morgan County. I rode twenty-one miles the first day, and preached at night at W. B. Paul's. Several penitents were forward for prayers. The next day, at Young's Chapel, I met a good congregation, and baptized eight infants and one adult, Brother Ben. H. Albertson, an excellent man, who has been in feeble health for some time. After the baptisms, I preached the funeral of a little boy of Brother Paul's, at the close of which quite a number of young ladies came to the altar for prayers, while the saints of God shouted for joy. In the afternoon I rode six miles to Fellowship Church, where our Baptist brethren were holding their monthly meeting. I stopped with Rev. John C. Hopkins, the pastor, and preached that night at the church. We had a glorious service. A number of penitents were at the altar, and the people of God shouted for joy. The Baptist Church at Fellowship is doing a good work. They are a noble, earnest Christian people. I enjoy their fellowship very much. May God continually bless them! I rode home the next day.

On the first Sunday in October, I preached the funerals of William Brown and his infant babe, at Jamestown, to an attentive congregation. On Friday before the third Sunday in October, I left home with my wife and younger daughter, to preach a funeral in Morgan County. We rode in a wagon for fourteen miles, and stopped for dinner with Rev. A. C. Peters, and in the afternoon rode three miles

to my elder daughter's, Mrs. Peters. Next day I
rode four miles, and spent a few hours very pleasantly with my old friend and brother, J. C. Douglas, and his family. In the afternoon I rode five
miles, and preached at night at Jones's school-house.
The next day, in a pine-grove near by, the congregation being very large, I preached the funeral of
old Mother Mary Jones. At the close of the sermon, I called for penitents to come to an altar of
prayer, when a number came and knelt on the
ground, and prayed earnestly for salvation. One
young man was happily converted. That night
Brother Robert Ramsey, a local preacher in the
Methodist Episcopal Church, preached in the school-
house. Penitents were again called to the altar,
and such a time of deep convictions and powerful
conversions I seldom ever saw. In a short time
six souls were converted, making seven for the day.
The interest was so great that, notwithstanding I
dismissed the congregation at the proper time, the
people would not go home. The young converts
continued to work after their friends, while penitents kept coming to the altar, and the Christians
sang, prayed, and shouted until a very late hour.
Finally the penitents were carried to a family residence near by. I stopped for the night with Rev.
John Stowers, a Christian Baptist minister, and a
merchant of that place. I did not sleep much; for
parties kept coming in from the meeting and disturbing me. I arose at three o'clock, and rode
eight miles before sunrise to my daughter's. After
breakfast I left for Jamestown with my wife and
daughter, and reached home in the afternoon.

On the fourth Sunday in October, I rode eight miles through a heavy rain to Elias Bowden's on Obed's River, to meet Rev. B. L. Stephens, an old minister with whom I had labored a great deal in former years. He was to preach the funeral of old Father Bowden, and I was to preach the funeral of Emma Bowden. The day being so disagreeable, all the children of Father Bowden could not attend, and his funeral was deferred.' I preached the funeral of Emma Bowden, from John xi, 25, 26. On the fifth Sunday in October, at Loudonville, five miles from Jamestown, I preached the funeral of Elijah Yorke. Rev. John Brewster, a Christian Baptist minister, was present, and assisted.

On the first Sunday in November, at the Three Forks of Wolf River, I preached the funerals of Elizabeth Lavender and her infant babe, to a crowded house of attentive hearers.

The Holston Conference met, October 20, 1881, in Maryville, Tenn., Bishop E. G. Andrews presiding. I did not attend, but was again granted a supernumerary relation. On the first Sunday in December, in an unoccupied family residence about three miles from Jamestown, I preached to a small congregation made up largely of children. At the close of the sermon, a number of penitents came to an altar of prayer, and a young girl was happily converted. At this meeting, Cyrus Clark and his wife, from Pennsylvania, were present. Brother Clark is largely engaged in the real-estate business, and is a warm-hearted Methodist.

This brings me to the close of the year 1881. I trust that I am grateful to God for the great mercies

of the past year, but I tremble under a sense of my
unworthiness and inefficiency. During the year I
have preached sixty-eight times, witnessed at my
own meetings fourteen conversions, received six
persons into the Church, baptized six adults and
eleven infants, preached nineteen funerals, and married four couples. The Lord help me to do better
service during the year 1882!

On the second Sunday in January I preached
at N. L. Northup's, near Jamestown. The congregation was small; but several were penitent, and
asked for prayers.

On the first Sunday in February I preached
again at the same place to the family only. The
snow was so deep that the people did not turn out
to Church. At this service the father and mother
and two little daughters were converted, and his
two little sons were penitent. I preached a number of times during January and February with
happy results.

The third Saturday and Sunday in March I
preached at Ramsey's Chapel. At these services a
number of young men were penitent, and asked an
interest in the prayers of the Christians. The fourth
Saturday and Sunday in March I attended the Baptist monthly meeting at Fellowship Church; I
preached a number of times with happy results.
May God bless and prosper this people!

I attended the Baptist Church meeting at Sinking Springs, on Wolf River, the second Saturday
and Sunday in April. I preached for them on Saturday and Sunday. Being Easter Sunday, I preached
on the resurrection of Christ. The second Saturday

and Sunday in May I preached at Captain M. R. Millsap's, in the Poplar Cove, with good results. Embracing the third Sunday in May, I preached at Ramsey's Chapel. Three persons were converted and one joined our Church. The membership was greatly revived. Since being relieved of pastoral work I attend a great many meetings of the Baptist Church, and am kindly received by them everywhere. God bless the Baptist Church!

The fourth Saturday and Sunday in May I attended the third quarterly-meeting of the Jamestown Circuit, at Solomon's Chapel. W. C. Daily, the presiding elder, and A. C. Peters, the preacher-in-charge, were present. There were no conversions. W. C. Daily did the preaching. On the second Sunday in June, Brother Peters and I preached in the Poplar Cove. We held two altar services with a number of penitents present.

At the East Tennessee Sunday-school Convention, held in the month of May, in Chattanooga, I was appointed Sunday-school vice-president of Fentress County, and did some work in organizing Sunday-schools in the destitute places of the county.

On the third Sunday in June I preached at Hood's Church, at the head of Obed's River. This is a Christian Baptist Church. At the close of the sermon I held an altar service. In the afternoon, at the same place, I organized a Sunday-school, perhaps the first ever organized in that place. The fourth Saturday and Sunday in June I preached on Back Creek; but with my best effort I could not organize a Sunday-school. The people were Hardshell Baptists.

The first Sunday in July I preached the funeral of Sarah Jane Crouch, at Mt. Union, on Wolf River, to a large congregation. On Friday before the second Sunday in July I preached to a small congregation on Crab Creek, and in the afternoon of the same day I preached at a school-house near Hiram Beatty's. I preached at the same place again the next day in the morning, and in the afternoon rode six miles into Overton County, and preached at Bethsaida Church to a good congregation. The following day I preached the funeral of Thomas Hull to a very large congregation, at the same place. Rev. H. Stephens, of that county, assisted me. We had a most excellent service, many of the people of God shouting his praise. The third Saturday and Sunday in July I preached at Pine Springs, a United Brethren Church, in Fentress County. On Sunday morning I took a grand view from what is called High Rock, of Obed's River and its meanderings out of the mountains. The scene beggars description. The fourth Saturday in July I preached in the morning at Julius Johnson's, and in the afternoon at Timothy Gauney's on Dry Creek. His wife was lying very low with consumption, and must die in a few days; but she is ready for the change. On Sunday morning I baptized their youngest daughter in Wolf River, and afterwards preached to a large congregation in a grove near by. The fifth Saturday and Sunday in July I attended, with Brother Peters, at Paul's Chapel. In the afternoon of Sunday I baptized three infant children.

On Friday before the second Sunday in August

I rode eighteen miles, and preached in the afternoon at Mt. Vernon, in Morgan County, and the following day rode ten miles to Scutcheon Church, where I had an appointment to hold a basket-meeting. Here I met with M. C. Bruner, the preacher in charge. The meeting continued five days, and resulted in three happy conversions and five accessions to our Church. The membership was greatly revived. I baptized four infant children. From this meeting I rode up the railroad line on horseback to G. W. Todd's, in Scott County. Brother Daily had employed me to hold the fourth quarterly-meeting on Huntsville Circuit for him. On Saturday morning I took the train at Sedgemoor, and ran up the line twenty miles to Chitwood, near the Kentucky line, the place of the quarterly-meeting. On the train I fell in with Brother Scott, the pastor, and his family, and with Rev. A. L. Williams and his wife, all on their way to the quarterly-meeting. We reached the place in time for the morning service, and I preached from 1 Tim. vi, 12. We had three preaching services and a Quarterly Conference that day. On the Sabbath we had a love-feast and communion service and public preaching. I took a collection for the presiding elder. In the afternoon I attended the Sunday-school, and taught the Bible-class. Afterwards we came down the line to Sedgemoor. The following day, in the morning, I attended services that the Baptist were holding near Glen Mary, and in the afternoon I preached at Black Wolf Church. We had a precious meeting, several penitents coming forward for prayers. I rode home the next day.

The fourth Sunday in August I preached the funerals of an excellent Christian man and his daughter, on the mountain above Dry Creek, in Fentress County. On the first Sunday in September, I preached the funeral of Samuel Cobb, at a Baptist church on Crab Creek. The second Sunday in September, I preached at Paul's Chapel, and the third Sunday at Mt. Vernon.

On Saturday before the fourth Sunday in September, I rode eighteen miles to Young's Chapel in Morgan County, where Brother Bruner was holding services, and preached for him that night. The next day I rode six miles to the coal-mines near Solomon Young's in Scott County, where I met a large congregation with Brother Scott, the pastor, and I preached the funerals of two of Brother Young's daughters. At the close of the sermon three souls were converted. We continued the services four days, with eleven conversions and about that many accessions to the Church. I then returned to Young's Chapel, where Brother Bruner was having a glorious revival, and preached for him that night, when one soul was converted and seventeen persons joined our Church. I rode home the next day.

Embracing the first Sunday in October, I assisted Brother Peters in services at Paul's Chapel. We held for three days, when eleven persons were converted and three joined our Church. I must now record a painful event in my life. I had been County Court clerk for a term of four years, and some of my friends wished me to serve another term. I consented to be a candidate for re-election;

but, at the same time, I asked the Lord to give me a demonstration of his will, that, if it would prove detrimental to my usefulness as a minister to be re-elected clerk, to have me defeated; but if not, to let me succeed. For months before the election, I used the above in my daily prayers. A great many men in the county had become my bitter enemies because I was a temperance man, and had fought the illicit liquor business. Others had become my enemies because I would not let them use myself nor the office for dishonest purposes. Others opposed me on account of my political views. A number should have been my best friends, who had become my bitterest enemies; but I refer it all to the great day of judgment. I was fraudulently defeated. The politics of the country is very unclean. I take it all as the leadings of Providence, and believe it to be for the better. And now I give myself wholly to the work of the ministry.

On Saturday morning, October 14, 1892, I left home for the seat of Conference, Chattanooga, Tenn. My son brought myself and younger daughter in a carriage to the railroad at Glen Mary, where we took the train late in the evening, and ran down to Kismet. We were met at the depot by Mr. McKinney, who took us to his home, and kindly entertained us. The next day I went two miles to Shady Grove Church, and preached, to a large congregation, the funerals of an excellent lady and her two infant children. We continued the services two days with good results, Brother Bruner, the pastor, being present. I spent two days in Kismet, visiting a number of families and praying with them, among

these a young man, a Roman Catholic, who had been
unjustly wounded. I procured a title for a lot from
John White, a land agent, on which to build a Methodist church. Myself and daughter, and Flora
Smith, from our town, took the train and ran down
to Rockwood, and stopped with our old friend and
neighbor, Dr. J. H. Story. I remained over in
Rockwood one day, where I left the two young
ladies, and took the train for Chattanooga, at which
place I arrived in due time. I was assigned to stay
at John F. Bryan's, my companion being Rev. T. A.
Cass. The next morning my daughter and son
Willie and Miss Smith came down on the train from
Rockwood, and stopped at the same place with me.
On Saturday afternoon of the Conference, I heard
Rev. William H. Rogers deliver his semi-centennial
address, having been fifty years in the itinerancy.
On Sunday morning, at James's Hall, I heard Bishop
Simpson preach a great sermon from John xix, 30.
In the afternoon, Dr. Stowe preached in the Meth-
odist Episcopal Church, South, when the bishop or-
dained one deacon and five elders.

On Monday morning the Alabama Southern Railroad gave the preachers of the Conference and their
friends an excursion around Cameron Hill, to see
the large rolling-mills and tannery. A large number availed themselves of the privilege. The Conference closed on Monday. I was appointed to the
Wartburg Circuit. We left Chattanooga late in the
evening and ran up to Rockwood, and stopped with
Dr. Story. We spent the next day in Rockwood,
and I preached at night in the company church.
The next day we ran up to Sunbright, hired a hack,

and went out five miles to my daughter's, Mrs. Peters.

Here I left the two young ladies, and rode home on horseback. I had been at home scarcely one hour when I was summoned by the United States marshal to appear at once as a witness before the grand jury of the Federal Court at Nashville. The next day I went back to Sunbright, took the evening train for Chattanooga, at which place I arrived late at night. I took the early morning train for Nashville, arriving there about noon. I stopped at a boarding-house on Summer Street, kept by Mrs. Mullins. I was very sick for a number of days. I had to remain about one week before my testimony was taken. On Sunday after my arrival I went to the Catholic Church at eight o'clock, and witnessed their mass service. Afterward I attended Sunday-school and preaching at McKendree Methodist Church. I heard the pastor, Dr. West, preach an able discourse to a large audience. At night I attended the Cumberland Presbyterian Church, and heard Rev. Pearson, an evangelist, preach. The lady with whom I boarded, at North 60 Summer Street, was a Christian lady.

On Monday, I took a street-car and crossed the Cumberland River on a bridge into Edgefield, and back. Later in the day, I visited the office of R. L. Hays, a temperance worker, and while there I saw two women drive up in a carriage before a saloon-door and call for drinks, one of them apparently much intoxicated. What a sad sight! May the day come when this shall end! On Tuesday I gave my testimony before the jury, received my witness-check, and cashed it. In the afternoon I witnessed the street-parade of a large circus show. During my stay at the boarding-house, I held prayers a number of times.

Late on Tuesday evening I took the train for Chattanooga, arriving there at night. The next morning I took the train for Kismet. Here I lay over one day, arranging to go into the mercantile business with Mr. McKinney. In the evening I ran up to Sunbright, and from there rode home the following day on horseback.

CHAPTER XIV.

WARTBURG AND SUNBRIGHT CIRCUITS.

I SOLD my property in Jamestown to L. T. Smith, still thinking of going into the mercantile business with Mr. McKinney at Kismet; but on the first round of my circuit, after invoicing the goods of Mr. McKinney, and seeing the great wickedness of the place, and fearing it would endanger the morals of my son, I declined going into the business. I procured the old home place of Mother Peters, as I thought, and moved there November 22, 1882. She was not contented to give up the place, but wanted to live with us; and as we were greatly crowded, I bought eight acres of land, on which was a house, in the border of Sunbright, and moved there, December 20th following. The place was in such condition that it needed much improvement, and feed was so hard to obtain that I was much troubled, and I made two efforts to move to Kismet; but by praying over the matter, I declined both times to do so. I have cut loose for the first time in life, and moved onto my circuit. I have rented out my farm on Wolf River. I have been more perplexed in mind about a proper decision than at any time before in my life. I trust that a brighter sky will open upon my pathway. The good Lord send it!

My first quarterly-meeting was held at Sunbright, November 25th and 26th. W. C. Daily, the presiding elder, was present. A few days before this occasion, I became seriously afflicted with jaundice; but I attended the quarterly-meeting services, and although suffering a great deal, I protracted them four days and nights, with the result of nine happy conversions and five accessions to our Church. Penitents flocked to the altar in great crowds. At nearly all of my appointments there are more or less penitents seeking salvation.

On my second round, at Sunbright I held services for two days, embracing Christmas. Two souls were happily converted, and four persons joined our Church. At this place we worship in the Baptist Church.

The year 1882 is now gone; and when I look back through its months, I view seasons when I have suffered a great many heartaches and heartburdens; but amid them all I have enjoyed many happy seasons of Jesus' presence. During the year I have preached one hundred and three times, have witnessed at my meetings thirty-nine happy conversions, have received twenty-nine persons into the Methodist Church, have baptized one adult and nine infants, and have married one couple.

When I take a retrospect of the years of my life, and the years of my ministry, I see a great many interpositions of God's merciful providence in my behalf. However, my life has been one of great labor and suffering; but amid it all, I have "endured as seeing Him that is invisible." I have lived to see my children all converted to God but one. I am pleased with the success that my two older boys are making in an educational and religious line. I trust my younger one will more than rival them. My two daughters are professed Christians, and members of the Methodist Episcopal Church. My eldest daughter, Mary Jane Peters, is a sweet and kind-hearted child. May Heaven bless her!

I now enter upon another year's labor. May the Lord give grace and glory, and may this be one of the best years of my life!

The month of January was very cold; but I preached, more or less, on my own charge, with some promising prospects. My work has done very little for me in the way of support. I do not know what it may yet do. The Methodist Episcopal Church has never contributed much toward my support during all my pastoral work. However, I have sold a great many books, and worked hard in the fields when at home, and thereby kept myself and family from want. I trust that my children will profit by the experience which I leave to them in this journal of my life.

On January 16th, at night, I was called up from my bed to go up the railroad two miles to see a sick woman, who was thought to be near death's door.

Not feeling very well, I deferred the trip until next morning, and after some difficulty, found the place where the sick woman was. Such a place of poverty and want I had never before visited in my life. After singing and praying and talking with the sick woman, she gave her heart to God, and was sweetly resigned to his will. I thought if the blessed Lord would come down and convert a soul in such a place as that was, that his condescending mercy would reach to the lowest steeps of human degradation. O how good the dear Lord is!

My second quarterly-meeting was held at Young's Chapel, embracing the third Sunday in February. Brother Daily, the presiding elder, was present. Four persons joined our Church, and we had prospects for a good meeting; but on account of my children having the measles at that time, I could not protract it. During February and March I preached constantly, with indications of good results, though February was a very cold month. I have sold more books during these months than usual.

On Saturday before the second Sunday in March, I preached twice on Scutcheon. Penitents wept at the altar, the people of God shouted aloud for joy, one soul was converted, and four persons joined our Church. Kismet was thought to be the most wicked place on the work; but as I have devoted considerable time to this place, in preaching and in visiting from house to house, and praying in the families, and urging them to build a church, they have gone to work to build a house for Church and educational purposes. At a number of my meetings in this place, several have expressed a strong desire for salvation, among these the two saloon-keepers.

On the last day of March my younger daughter was taken very sick, and on the first day of April, after preaching twice and riding fifteen miles, I reached home to find her in a very critical state of health. That night, about one o'clock, her system was congested, and we thought, and she too, that she was dying. She was perfectly ready to go and be with Christ. For several weeks she was right at death's door. Doctor J. H. Story treated her case. She had been in declining health for five or six years. Her afflictions were so complicated, that they baffled the skill of the best physicians. About the first of May her case ran into dropsy of a very alarming nature. I lost a great deal of sleep with her, and was greatly hindered in my work. I could not leave home for any great length of time; however, in April we had some good meetings.

At Young's Chapel four persons joined our Church. God's plans and ways are mysterious to us. I moved to my circuit thinking that I would give to the pastoral work my closest attention; but I have never had so much family affliction. This has been a great trial to my faith and Christian resignation; however, I believe that I can say, The Lord's will be done. Embracing the second Sunday in May, my third quarterly-meeting was held at Emory Church. Brother Daily was present. On Sunday morning we had a most glorious old-fashioned love-feast, many of the people of God shouting aloud for joy.

During the month of May I held a number of missionary meetings, with some happy results. On Children's-day, being the second Sunday in June, I rode fifteen miles over a rough road, and preached three times to the children, taking collections for the cause of education on each occasion, and stopped at night in Wartburg with Mr. Mason. They are most excellent people, who emigrated a few years ago to this county from the city of Philadelphia. I am now in the last days of June, and my dear daughter is still sorely afflicted. Her dropsy symptoms have assumed a very alarming character. I can not tell what the result of her case will be; but I pray God to make me resigned to his will. My faith has never been so tried as in these family afflictions. May God help me now! I shall soon enter upon my basket-meetings. O for great success!

My first basket-meeting was held at Pleasant Ridge, embracing the second Sunday in July, and continued four days. The attendance was good, convictions were deep, and penitents in numbers came weeping to the altar for prayers. Fifteen souls were happily converted, and fourteen united with our Church. The meeting was held in a new church, about three miles from Sunbright, where there had not yet been any Church organization. At the close of the meeting I organized a Methodist Episcopal Church, with a class of twenty members. My second basket-meeting was held at Scutcheon, embracing the third Sunday in July. At this place I preached some funerals. The Church was greatly revived, seven souls were converted to God, and two united with our Church.

Embracing the fourth Sunday in July, I held a two days' basket-meeting at Bethel Church, in Wayne County, Kentucky, where, on Sunday, I preached the funeral of Mother Guffey. The attendance was so great that, although the house was a large one, we were compelled to move out into the grove so as to preach to the vast multitude. Here the people of God shouted for joy, and two souls were happily converted. I left home on Thursday before, to attend this meeting; rode ten miles, and preached at Guffey's school-house, where a lady joined our Church; then rode two miles, and baptized five ladies, and afterwards rode sixteen miles to Jamestown, for the night.

My fourth basket-meeting was held at Young's Chapel, embracing the fifth Sunday in July. It resulted in four conversions, and one accession to our Church, with the membership much revived. My fifth basket-meeting was held at Potter's Chapel, embracing the first Sunday in August. It resulted in four conversions and two accessions to our Church. At several of the above meetings I would have witnessed much greater results had I not been compelled to hurry home to our dear sick daughter. My sixth basket-meeting was held at Mt. Zion, embracing the second Sunday in August, and continued four days. Here convictions were deep and conversions were powerful. From Sunday afternoon until Monday night seventeen souls were powerfully converted to God, and nine joined our Church. The Christians shouted aloud the praises of God almost day and night. On Sunday of this meeting I preached two funeral sermons, and on

Tuesday I baptized a lady, and received another lady into full connection in the Church.

My seventh basket-meeting was held at Mt. Vernon, embracing the third Sunday in August, and resulted in the conversion of eight precious souls, and five accessions to our Church. At this meeting my youngest son, I trust, was happily converted to God. My wife and dear sick daughter went with me to this meeting. My eighth basket-meeting was held in connection with our District Conference, and fourth quarterly-meeting at Sunbright, August 22d to 26th. A large number of the preachers of the district were present, and preached with an unction from on high. On Friday we had an interesting Sunday-school Congress, five schools being in attendance. Rev. W. H. Rogers, our Conference Sunday-school agent, was present, and conducted the exercises. This affair was a great success. At the meeting six souls were converted.

The Baptist Association convened in Sunbright, August 30th, and continued four days. A large number of preachers and delegates were in attendance. I attended all their sessions and services. My ninth basket-meeting was held at Emory Church, embracing the second Sunday in September. I held three days. Mourners came in large numbers to the altar, and one soul was mightily converted. On Monday I was compelled to hasten home to my sick daughter. My tenth basket-meeting was held at Ramsey's Chapel, twenty-five miles from my home, embracing the third Sunday in September. My daughter was so very low I could not attend that meeting; but some local preachers filled the appointment for me.

My eleventh basket-meeting was held at Mill Creek, six miles from Sunbright, embracing the fourth Sunday in September, and continued four days. Three persons were happily converted to God. My twelfth basket-meeting was held at Shady Grove, near Kismet, embracing the fifth Sunday in September. On Sunday morning of the meeting I was taken very sick, and was unable to preach; but Dr. Miller, of Wartburg, preached for me, and Brother Robert McCartt held services in the afternoon, and so the meeting closed. I think we would have had a number of conversions here if I had only been able to protract the meeting. On Monday I rode home on horseback, under the greatest weight of suffering that I ever endured in my life. I suffered under this attack for more than two weeks before I began to improve, and was for quite a time unable for any service.

I was summoned to appear as a witness at the Federal Court in Nashville, October 15th, and was detained at court nearly three weeks. I left home in a low state of health, with a number of friends, for Nashville, October 13th. We took the train late in the evening at Sunbright, and ran down to Chattanooga, arriving there in the night. We took lodging, and I would have slept soundly had I not been greatly disturbed with musquitoes. I lay over in Chattanooga the next day, it being Sunday.

There were two Annual Conferences in session in Chattanooga at that time—the East Tennessee Conference of the Methodist Episcopal Church, with

Bishop Bowman presiding, and the Holston Conference of the Methodist Episcopal Church, South, with Bishop McTyeire, presiding. I attended the love-feast meeting at the Methodist Episcopal Church, South, in the morning, and expected to remain to hear Bishop McTyeire preach; but became so sick that I was compelled to return to my room, where I lay up the remainder of the day. I reached Nashville by due course of time, when I was met at the train by Major John C. Wright, who had heard that I was very sick, and carried to his boarding-place, at Mrs. Mullin's, on Summer Street, where I remained nearly three weeks.

The first Sunday that I was in Nashville, I attended services at the First Baptist Church, and heard Dr. Stricklin, their pastor, preach an excellent sermon. In the afternoon I attended Sunday-school in the State-prison, where three hundred prisoners were in Sabbath-school. At the invitation of the superintendent, I gave the lesson review at the close of the recitations. On the second Sunday in the city I attended Sunday-school at the Cumberland Presbyterian Church, and preaching services at the McKendree Methodist Episcopal Church, South, where I heard the new pastor for the Conference year preach his first sermon to a large audience. In the afternoon I again attended Sunday-school in the State-prison, and, at the request of the superintendent, I taught a class, and afterward gave the lesson review. In the evening I attended the meeting of the Young Men's Christian Association.

I reached home November 1st. I was in very

feeble health while in Nashville, and the day after my arrival I thought I should not live until night. I had only one desire, and that was to die at home with my family. I do n't think that I felt any choice either to live or die. But now that I have reached my home, and my health is improving, I am thankful to God, and if the good Lord restores me to health again, I feel that I shall be his more than ever, both for time and for eternity.

Our Annual Conference met in Knoxville, October 17, 1883, with Bishop Bowman presiding. I did not attend, because I was compelled to be in Nashville at that time. On account of my feeble health and the low state of my daughter, I asked for and received a supernumerary relation for the following year. During the past year the afflictions of my daughter kept me at home so much that I was not permitted to render so much service as I should otherwise have done. However, with what labors I could render, the Lord wonderfully blessed the work. Seventy-six souls were happily converted, and I received eighty persons into our Church. I baptized a number of adults and infants, raised $10 for missions, $5 for Church extension, $3 for Conference claimants, $1.50 for education, and $1 for bishops. My own support, with the missionary appropriation, was $130. God be praised for his wonderful goodness!

I was now a supernumerary preacher. Brother Daily, the presiding elder, was disappointed in making a supply for the Jamestown Circuit, and he removed the pastor from the Sunbright Circuit to Jamestown, leaving Sunbright vacant. At Brother

Daily's request I took charge of this work. At my third appointment at Sunbright I baptized three persons, and four united with our Church, one of them being a minister of the Campbellite Church. This meeting was held the last Sunday in December, 1883.

I am now closing the labors of another year. What clouds of trouble have rolled over my life the past year! My dear daughter Debbie has been right at death's door several times, and I have not thought that she would live through the old year. She now seems to be lingering on the last sands of mortality; but, God be praised, she is ready to go and be with Christ. I myself was brought by affliction near the gates of the Celestial City. O Lord, shall I and my family ever see another such year of affliction! Such deep sorrow I have never seen in one year before. The Lord is too good to do wrong, and too wise to make mistakes; and although I can not read the handwriting of his providence, yet I know he will make all things to work for my good, if I but love and serve him and patiently endure the rod of chastisement. Is it possible that I am a hard child for my Heavenly Father to control? Is he compelled to bring me under this rigid discipline of suffering in order to wean me from the world? While I have been looking on the shady side of life, let me also look on the brighter side.

During the year I have preached one hundred and twenty-six times, and witnessed a large number of happy conversions and accessions to our Church. I baptized sixteen adults and seventeen infants, and married two couples. This closes another eventful year of my life. I am now fifty-seven years old, was licensed to preach more than thirty-five years ago, was ordained a deacon more than twenty-nine years ago, and have been an ordained elder and traveling minister more than sixteen years. I now begin the labors of another year. Great trials appear in store for the near future. O Lord, if I am spared to live through the year, may I have more sheaves for my Master than during any former year! My daughter is so low that I hardly see how I can get off from home to call poor sinners to come home to Christ.

The dark cloud of affliction that has hung so long over my household burst in heaviest sorrow on Sunday morning of January 13, 1884, at fifteen minutes before four o'clock. My dear, dear daughter Debbie, who had been such a great sufferer for nearly a year, plumed her seraph wings, and, leaving a world of suffering behind, went home to glory and to God. How sad was that hour to our hearts! We wept, but bowed submissively to the Lord's will. The following day we carried her lifeless form, all beautiful, to Mt. Vernon Church in Morgan County, where her funeral was preached by Rev. A. C. Peters, to a large congregation, from Hebrews xiii, 14, after which her body was laid to its last resting-place in the beautiful churchyard, to await the trumpet sound of the resurrection angel. Sleep on, sweet Debbie; I shall soon see you again. I now have two children in the good world. The thought comes with strange inquiry to my mind, whether another of my children shall outstrip me to the glory-land, or shall I be the next one of the family to enter in through the gates into the city. God only knows how this shall be; but it is no great matter either way. I am resolved to live more consecrated to God than ever before, since I have greater inducements now to get to heaven. I have precious children over there. May the good Lord help me to be a faithful steward of his!

During the month of January, after my daughter's triumphant death, I met my appointments regularly; but the weather was so cold, and the church houses were so uncomfortable, that our meetings could not accomplish so much as I desired. However, there were anxious penitents seeking salvation at nearly every preaching-place.

My second quarterly-meeting was held in Wartburg, embracing the second Sunday in February. There was such a tide on the waters that we had a very small attendance. Brother Daily was present, and preached twice. During the months of February, March, and April the weather was cold, and the waters were so high from excessive rains, there being a number of deep and rapid streams without any bridges on my charge, I was greatly hindered in the work. I have arranged for two days' meetings throughout the month of May at each place, and I am praying for and expecting showers of blessings from clouds of mercy. These meetings were held with much interest and success. At every place there were penitents at the altar, and the Churches were greatly edified. At a meeting held by Rev. E. H. Walker, a Baptist minister, and myself, at Mr. Moore's, in Sunbright, one person was converted, and soon after, in the same town, two persons united with our Church. At Black Wolf Church, in Scott County, a lady was converted and joined the Church.

At my May meetings I held missionary services at every place, and succeeded in raising very good collections for the cause of missions. Throughout the month of June I preached more or less on the cause of education; and on Children's-day my collectiors were double the same of last year. I am now in the month of July. My next meetings will be my basket-meetings. O may the Great Head of the Church crown them with a number of happy conversions and accessions to his people!

My first basket-meeting was held at Black Wolf Church, embracing the third Sunday in July, and continuing three days. Two souls were happily converted. I baptized one person and received four into full connection. The Church was gloriously revived. The people were greatly interested, and brought out an abundance of provisions on the ground each day. The prospects were good for a number of conversions; but I had to close so as to attend the District Conference, about to convene at Vine Grove Church, near Dayton, in Rhea County. I took the train on Tuesday evening, and ran down the line to the place of the Conference, and on the following night, as had been advertised, I preached the introductory sermon. We had a very interesting District Conference, and were royally entertained by the good people of Vine Grove Church. On Friday morning I took the train at Dayton, and ran up the line to Sunbright, my home. My second basket-meeting was held at Emory Church, embracing the fourth Sunday in July, and continued four days. The people of God drank largely from the well of salvation. I baptized one young lady, received one person on probation and four into full connection. Anxious penitents wept at the altar, but there were no conversions. My third basket-meeting was held at Sunbright, in connection with the fourth quarterly-meeting, embracing the first Sunday in August. We held four days, with two happy conversions to God.

My fourth basket-meeting was held at Mt. Pleasant, on Emory, near Rev. J. M. McCartt's, embracing the second Sunday in August. On Sabbath of the occasion I administered the holy communion to a large number of people. There was great rejoicing in the camps of Israel. My fifth basket-meeting was held at Joe Davis's, near Crooktown, in Scott County, embracing the third Sunday in August. I held four days. Two souls were happily converted, and other penitents were left weeping at the altar.

My sixth basket-meeting was held at Shady Grove, embracing the fourth Sunday in August. There were a number of penitents at the altar, and no doubt there would have been a number of conversions; but I had to close the meeting on Sunday afternoon because school was being taught in the building during the week.

My seventh basket-meeting was held at Mt. Zion, embracing the fifth Sunday in August, and continued three days. Three persons joined the Church on probation, and I baptized three others

and received them into full connection. My eighth
basket-meeting was held at Potter's Chapel, embracing the first Sunday in September. My horse being
disabled from blood poison, I did not attend this
meeting. Rev. H. A. McCartt held the meeting for
me. My ninth basket-meeting was held at Mill
Creek, embracing the second Sunday in September.
I continued the meeting four days, with two souls
happily converted and three accessions to our
Church.

My tenth basket-meeting was held at Scutcheon,
embracing the third Sunday in September. One
soul was converted and joined our Church. The
glory of the Lord was present. My eleventh basket-meeting was held at Pleasant Ridge, embracing
the fourth Sunday in September. I held three days
with happy results. I baptized six young ladies and
received them into full connection, and received
two others on probation. I held an evening service in Sunbright just after this, when one soul was
converted and two person united with our Church
by letter. I preached several funerals before leaving
home for Conference.

The Holston Annual Conference met in Greeneville, Tenn., October 16, 1884, Bishop H. W. Warren presiding. I left home on Tuesday evening
rode eight miles, and staid for the night at Russell Scott's. The next day I rode fifteen miles, and
took dinner with Mrs. Hutson, the widow of Rev.
Richard Hutson; and in the afternoon I rode
fifteen miles, and reached William R. Dail's,
in Anderson County. The next morning I rode
five miles to Clinton, and took the train, arriving

at Greeneville in the afternoon, the first day of the Conference. I was assigned to stay with Rev. John R. Hughes, who was at that time the trustee of Greene County, and was living in the Church parsonage near by. The Conference session was a very pleasant and harmonious one. The preaching and all the religious exercises seemed unusually anointed with the Holy Ghost. Rev. William R. Graves preached his semi-centennial sermon at this Conference.

The Conference closed on Sunday night. I was appointed to Kingston Circuit, with Rockwood attached to it. Rev. L. B. Caldwell was my presiding elder. I left Greeneville on Monday morning, reached Knoxville in due time, and took dinner with Hon. B. O. Bowden. Late in the afternoon I took the train for Clinton, reaching there, and stopping for the night with my kinsman, Hon. W. R. Hicks. The next day I rode fourteen miles to Oliver Springs, took dinner with Brother Taylor, and in the afternoon rode fourteen miles to Wartburg. I reached home the next day, and found my family well. God be praised!

After remaining at home three days, having been summoned to appear as a witness at the Federal Court in Nashville, I left for that place. I took the train late on Saturday evening, and ran down to Chattanooga, where I remained over Sunday. I attended services at the First Methodist Episcopal Church, and heard Dr. Warner, the new pastor, preach his first sermon. I reached Nashville the next day, and stopped at Mrs. Mullin's boarding-house, on Summer Street. I was discharged from court on Wednesday, and came to Chattanooga that night. I was much disturbed on the train by a number of people making a mock of our holy religion. The next morning I ran up the Cincinnati road to Sunbright. On account of having to be at Nashville, and having a funeral appointment about forty miles from home, I did not reach my first three appointments, but had them filled by another party.

Here I wish to drop a few thoughts in regard to our Conference. I am fully convinced that appointments of committees, and of preachers to their work, are not made with regard to their qualifications or merit, but more from favoritism. I find the Conference has some favorites, and, whether they have qualifications or business tact, they are pushed to the front. Ring rule holds high control. The Northern men seem to have great influence with the bishop, and from his arrival until he leaves they have his ear, and in a large measure they dictate the appointments. I do not know whether all Conferences are infested with the same spirit and men or not. I wish I could think our own beloved Conference was free from such; but from years of experience, I am otherwise impressed. May the good Lord in mercy save our Conference! I have never sought appointments from the Conference, but have always held sacred my vows at the Conference altar. My appointments have always been to circuits of about second or third class. I have noticed that some of our preachers had a great aversion for the mountain circuits; but I have found them equal to many of the valley circuits. Under this spirit of appointment, I have seen men of medium ability placed on districts, stations, and first-class circuits, and the work suffer in their hands. It is my deliberate judgment that if this sectional spirit continues in the Conference, our future as a Church in this country is very precarious.

It is not pleasant to me to leave such a record as this behind me, to be read when my body lies cold in the ground; for I am a Methodist, warp and filling, and have given my life to some of the hardest work for the Church. I am profoundly concerned for the future of this work. I know that the good Lord will make it all right in the great day of eternity. This gives me great comfort. May God bless our Church!

CHAPTER XV.

THE KINGSTON CIRCUIT.

I LEFT home for my new field of labor on Friday morning, November 14th, rode nine miles, and took dinner with Rev. H. A. McCartt. In the afternoon I rode eight miles to Liberty Church, where Rev. R. O. Taylor, a Baptist minister, was holding revival services. At his request, I preached and called for penitents, when about twenty-five young men and ladies came to the altar. After the meeting, I went home with Thos. Love, to stay all night, who lived four miles from the church. On the way, Brother Love's dog treed a coon. We shook it out, the dog killed it, and we took it on with us.

The next day I rode eleven miles to Colonel Robert Byrd's, in Roane County, and took dinner.

Colonel Byrd was in a low state of health, and died a short time afterwards. In the afternoon I rode down by Emory Gap and Rockwood into Hines Valley, and stopped for the night at Oscar Thompson's. The next day I rode three miles down the valley to the church, and preached to a large congregation. The Lord was present in great power. After taking dinner with Squire Millican, and holding prayers in the family, I rode five miles up the valley to Rockwood, and preached to a large congregation of people at night. I stopped with E. M. Devaney.

In the afternoon of Monday, I rode up Walden's Ridge and out on the plateau seven miles to Brother King's. I missed my way, and that being a wilderness country, I had serious thoughts of having to lay out that night; but fortunately overtaking a stranger going right by Brother King's, he piloted me. My pilot proved to be the postmaster in the settlement, who, when he had learned that I was the Methodist preacher, turned around and said: " I must shake hands with you." He had lately emigrated from Canada. He and his wife were members of the Congregational Church, but on this round united with our Church at King's school-house. Brother King's folks are true Methodists, and are accustomed to take good care of the Methodist preacher. The next day I preached at Brother King's instead of the school-house, the day being very rainy. We had a good meeting, with some deep penitents in the congregation. In the afternoon I rode two miles, and staid for the night with Joseph Smith. Brother Smith and wife live alone.

They have raised a family, but they are all scattered off, some of them being in the West. They are kind, Christian old people.

The next morning, on my way back to Brother King's, I stopped and held prayers with the family of Mrs. Lingo, a widow. Though they are well-to-do and respectable, I learned that no minister had called on them for years. What a field for ministerial work this is!

I preached that day at Brother King's again. There were a number of anxious penitents at the altar. In the afternoon Brother King geared up his two-horse wagon, and he and his daughter Mary and his granddaughter Alice, with two other little grandchildren, and myself, got in and drove out a few miles, visiting and holding religious services in three families—Hutson, Young, and Sabin.

The next day I rode five miles to Pisgah Church, and preached where a young man, Mr. Farmer, was teaching school. After preaching, I went home with Brother Maupin and staid over night. Brother Maupin is an old man, and a true Methodist. He is now living with his second wife, who is a Baptist. King's school-house and Pisgah are both in Cumberland County. The remainder of the circuit is in Roane County, excepting two appointments, that are in Loudon County. The following day I rode down in the valley to Brother Tedder's, near Rockwood. Late in the evening I walked down into the town, and preached at night to a fair congregation. Rockwood seems to be a hard place religiously. My heart is moved at the wickedness; but I am praying the Lord of the harvest for that place.

The next day I walked up to Brother Tedder's, and rode up the valley three miles to Joel Hembree's for dinner. Brother Hembree is a Southern Methodist, and now, for the second time, a widower, with several small children. He is a well-to-do and kind-hearted man.

In the afternoon I rode up by Emory Gap and out to Dick Isham's. Brother Isham has no children. He and his aged wife are warm-hearted Christians. He is a Methodist, and she is a Baptist. The next day being Sunday, I rode two miles to Swan Pond Church. As the morning had been very rainy, the people were slow in getting out. However, I preached to them at ten o'clock. The Methodist Episcopal Church, South, as well as our own Church, has a class at this place. After preaching, I rode one mile and took dinner with Brother Atkinson, the class-leader. After praying with the family, I went three miles to Emory Gap, and preached in the afternoon, and then went one mile and staid with the family of Rev. G. W. Renfro, who is a traveling minister of the Methodist Episcopal Church, South, and was at this time off on his circuit.

The next morning I rode back to Emory Gap, and stopped and prayed in the family of Mr. Grammar, after which I rode one mile down the valley and stopped with Brother John Martin. In the afternoon I walked up to the Gap, and after visiting several families, I preached again. Two persons came forward for prayers, and one old man joined our Church. I staid that night at Brother Martin's. The next day I rode six miles to Pine Grove

Church, and preached to a small congregation, with happy results.

After taking dinner with, and praying in, the family of Mr. Delozier, I rode one mile and staid over night with J. N. Love, the class-leader. The next day I preached again in Emory Gap, and stopped with Brother Grammar. He and his family are excellent people, members of the Baptist Church. He was at this time in feeble health. The next day being Thanksgiving-day, I rode four miles, crossing Emory River, to Oak Hill Church, where a young lady was teaching school, and preached a thanksgiving sermon. I took dinner with Mr. Roberts. Neither he nor his wife are yet Christians, but they are excellent people. Their two daughters are members of our Church. In the afternoon I rode eight miles into Morgan County, and stopped for the night with Peter Mathis. The next day I rode eight miles to Wartburg, stopped at the Roberts Hotel, and that night addressed an audience at that place on the subject of Temperance.

The next day I rode twelve miles to my home in Sunbright. In a little more than two weeks I had traveled on horseback one hundred and forty-three miles, had preached sixteen times, and had visited and prayed in forty-three families.

I left home for my second round on Kingston Circuit, December 11th, in company with Rev. L. B. Caldwell, the presiding elder. We rode twelve miles the first day to Wartburg, where we remained over night; and at the court-house, to a large congregation, we both gave a talk on the subject of Temperance. The next day we rode eight

miles, and took dinner with Peter Mathis. In the
afternoon we rode twelve miles, and stopped with
the family of Rev. T. H. Russell, he being absent
on his circuit. The next morning Dr. Caldwell and
I separated; he going to his quarterly-meeting on
the Scarboro Circuit, and I going on to my circuit.
I rode nine miles to James Cardwell's, who lives
two miles from Cardwell's Chapel. Here I learned
that my appointment at that place for that day had
not been published, and so I staid with Brother
Cardwell. That night I attended service at a school-
house held by the Baptists, and at their request I
preached. The next morning a cold, heavy rain
was falling; but I rode through it three miles to
Woodlawn Church, and preached to a small congregation; and in the afternoon I rode to Cardwell's
Chapel, and staid over night with Brother Cox.

The next day I rode twelve miles to Kingston,
and took dinner with my dear cousin James I. Dail.
In the afternoon, after holding prayers with the
family, I rode seven miles, and staid over night
with James R. Rankin. The next morning I rode
nine miles down into Hines Valley and preached.
After preaching I held a class-meeting with happy
results. In the afternoon, in company with Rev.
A. E. Barnes, of the Pikeville Circuit, I rode back
to Brother Rankin's for the night, having taken
dinner with, and prayed in the family of, Mr. Dyke.
The next morning Brother Barnes and I rode to
Kingston, where our District Conference was to
meet that day. The Conference met in the Methodist Episcopal Church, Dr. Caldwell presiding. I
was elected secretary. We had a harmonious session

of two days and nights. The weather became bitter cold.

On Saturday Dr. Caldwell and I rode out to Swan Pond Church, where my quarterly-meeting was to be held. There were only two people present. The weather was so cold and the house so open, that it seemed a moral impossiblity to accomplish anything, and so we agreed to hold the quarterly-meeting ten days from that time at Pine Grove Church. After taking dinner at Simeon Hassler's, Dr. Caldwell left for his home at Athens, and I set off for Emory Gap. I rode three miles, and stopped and prayed in the family of George Isham, and afterwards rode one mile below the Gap, and stopped for the night with Elisha Martin. That night I preached at Brother Pope's, for his son, who was in the last stage of consumption. Several turned out to the meeting, and quite a number presented themselves as seekers of religion. There was a heavy fall of rain and sleet all that night, and the next morning being Sunday, the ground was perfectly carpeted with ice, and there was still a heavy rain. I walked up to Emory Gap, took the train, and ran up home to Sunbright, where I remained until Tuesday night. I then took the train and ran back down to Emory Gap, and spent the night at Brother Grammar's.

The next morning I walked down to Brother Martin's, mounted my horse, and rode five miles to Rockwood. I was to preach there that night, but the morning Sunday-school had their Christmas entertainment at the same hour and place, and so I did not preach, but attended and opened the exercises with prayer, and made a short talk on Sunday-school work. The next morning being Christmas-day, although the mercury stood at zero, I rode eight miles to King's school-house, where the people had gathered in a very open house, with about a double handful of fire, for worship. I told them that I could not preach there, but that if they would go to Brother King's house I would preach to them, which they did. I preached again at night at Brother Hutson's, although the weather was stinging cold. Quite a number knelt for prayers. There is good prospect for a revival in this settlement.

The next morning I set off in company with a hack-load of young people, for my appointment at Pisgah. We must have traveled about eight miles to reach there. I preached to a small but attentive audience at that place. After preaching I took dinner with Brother Maupin, and in the afternoon rode four miles, and stopped for the night with a family named White, consisting of four sisters and a brother who is a widower, and his two little children. They are all Christians except the two children, and are members of the Methodist Church. They live at the old homestead, where their parents died in the faith.

The next morning I rode down through Rock-wood, and up the valley to Brother Tedder's for dinner. After praying in the family I rode in the afternoon eight miles, to Brother Gilford Delozier's. I preached that night at Pine Grove Church near by, and again at the same place the next morning. In the afternoon I rode three miles to Emory Gap and preached to an attentive congregation. After Church, while making some pastoral calls, I called at the home of Joseph Davis, and after praying with the family, they invited me to stay over night with them, provided I would stay with sinners. I told them that they were the very people to whom we were sent; that we were "not sent to call the righteous but sinners to repentance." So I staid with them. Although they had been living there for a number of years, and were a well-to-do and respectable people, they said that I was the only minister of any kind who had staid with them.

Next morning I rode back three miles to Pine Grove, and preached to an appreciative audience, with some prospect of good. After taking dinner with Mrs. Elizabeth Isham, an excellent Christian widowed lady, I visited and prayed in the families of two other widowed ladies, one by name Isham, and the other by name Atkinson. I preached again that night at Pine Grove. Here my quarterly-meeting was to be held the following two days.

Dr. Caldwell sent Rev. C. Stuart to assist me in holding the quarterly-meeting. The meeting continued over the following Sunday. We had an excellent Quarterly Conference, an old-fashioned Methodist love-feast, and the sacrament of the Lord's Supper during the meeting. There was one happy conversion, and four persons united with our Church. The membership of the Church put on new life. There had been a great deal of enmity among the people of the Church here for some time. I believe there would have been more conversions but for this fact, but I think we succeeded in breaking up this bad spirit. Nothing stands more in the way of God's work than to have the people at strife with each other. This church is located three miles from Kingston, in the midst of a community of good plain people. During the meeting I visited a numer of families of Ishams, Fritts, Atkinsons, Deloziers, Goddards, and Houghtons. In all of these we had precious family services.

On Sunday evening, after the close of this meeting, I preached to a large congregation, at the residence of a Mr. Millsaps, one mile below Emory Gap. There were a number of anxious penitents at the altar, and two young men joined our Church. On Monday morning I took the train at Emory Gap, and ran up to Sunbright, my home. I have now finished another year. The year 1884 is gone forever. What great clouds of sorrow hung over my head during the first part of the year in the affliction and death of my dear sweet daughter Debbie. She is only gone on before. In a few days or years I shall overtake her. The memory of this year will ever lie heavily upon my heart.

During the year I preached one hundred and ninety-one times, witnessed twelve conversions, received thirty persons into our Church, baptized sixteen adults and thirteen infants, preached ten funerals, and married two couples. I have completed two rounds on the Kingston Circuit before January. At many places there are the marked evidences of coming prosperity. This is a widely-scattered circuit, stretching over a great distance of territory. The church houses are generally poor, and very uncomfortable for winter use. Two large rivers flow through the circuit, the Clinch and the Emory, that have to be ferried, besides a number of smaller deep, rapid streams to be forded. The circuit is bounded on the south by the Tennessee River. On my January round there was a great deal of very severe cold weather, so that I only met six congregations out of eleven appointments. I visited a great many families, and prayed with them, and talked to the children.

I visited several sick persons, among these one young man just ready to die with consumption. A lady at Brownsville professed saving faith in Christ while I was holding prayers in her home, and a young man near Pine Grove joined our Church at a family service. Having been hindered by the severe weather from attending all my appointments, I took this way of being employed in the Master's work. I feel that I must not be idle. I closed this round in the afternoon of the fourth Sunday in January; and although I was suffering from a severe cold, I rode thirty-six miles on horseback to my home through the severest winter weather. I left home on Saturday evening, February 14th, for my work. I took the train at Sunbright, and ran down to Rockwood, and staid over night with a Mr. Cox, an Englishman. They showed me much kindness. God bless them! The next morning I walked down below town a short distance to Mr. Thompson's, who geared up his team, and took a wagon-load of us down to the church in Hines Valley.

The Baptists were holding services at that time in the church, but I preached that night. I preached the next day in Rockwood, and visited and prayed with a number of familes. Having secured a horse from Esquire Millican, I rode up the valley on Monday evening to Joel Hembree's, and the following day went on meeting my appointments at Pine Grove, Swan Pond, and Emory Gap. The weather was so bitter cold, and the roads were so covered with ice, that the congregations were small at each place. I felt that I greatly imperiled my own life in traveling that week.

I reached Rockwood late on Friday evening, suffering greatly from the severe weather. My second quarterly-meeting came off at Rockwood the next day, and continued over Monday night. My presiding elder wished to form a new charge of Rockwood, Hines Valley, and King's school-house, and so I agreed to give up these appointments, and to take up some new ones up the line of railroad. On Tuesday morning I ran up the railroad to Brownsville, and preached to the miners there that night. Quite a number of penitents were at the altar for prayers, and three persons united with our Church. The following night I preached again at the same place. I had to preach in private residences, and these were miners' cabins only; and as the people came out to the preaching in great numbers, we were uncomfortably crowded. I find these humble miners anxious for the Word of Life.

The following day I secured a mule from Colonel Brown, the proprietor of the iron-works, and rode five miles to Oak Hill, to reach my appointment. The weather was so severe that only two persons were present. In the afternoon I rode back to

Brownsville, and preached there again that night. Penitents were at the altar, and a lady joined our Church. Mr. Brown says that he will build us a chapel in which to worship. If he does so, I think we can organize a good class at this place. I organized a prayer-meeting for them. The roads were so bad, and the weather was so unsettled, that I declined to go to my appointments in Loudon County. The winter was the severest that we had witnessed in this country for years. I left home, March 20th, for my work, and met the most of my appointments. In several places there were anxious penitents at the altar.

On Saturday evening before the second Sunday in April, in preaching for a man who had been severely injured in the Rockwood mines by rocks falling in on him, he and his wife both joined our Church. On this round another lady joined our Church at Brownsville. Dr. Caldwell failed to organize his new circuit, and so I had to take back into my work Rockwood, Hines Valley, and King's school-house. From sickness and rain I did not reach King's school-house nor Hines Valley on this round, but preached at Rockwood.

About this time my son Willie came home from college with a relapse of measles, and was in very low health for a time. I left home on the last day of April, reached Emory River at night, and staid with William Crow. His wife is a niece of Rev. W. C. Graves, of our Conference. The next morning I was called to go up into the county some distance, to hold the funeral service of a child of Mr. Overstreet at May's school-house. In going, we

passed through what is known as Clack's Gap,
which is a deep gorge between two high ridges.
Here, in the early settlement of the country, the
Indians waylaid a company of white men, and killed
one of them named Clack; hence the name of the
place.   After holding the services, and taking dinner with Brother Letsinger, I rode to Kingston,
and on to Eblen's school-house, and preached at
night.   I met all my appointments promptly.

As I had a week's rest between two appointments, I spent the time in visiting and holding
services with families and forming new acquaintances.   I visited one family of which I will make
mention—Dr. Eaton's, of Eaton's Crossroads in
Loudon County.   He and his family are excellent
people, and well-to-do.   They showed me great
kindness.   His wife, a son, and a daughter are
members of our Church.   I left his newly-married
daughter very penitent.   In the afternoon of Saturday before the second Sunday in May, in the Masonic Hall at Woodlawn, I conferred the degrees of
the Eastern Star of Adoptive Masonry on ten ladies
and twenty gentlemen.   On the following day, after
preaching at Woodlawn, a young lady joined our
Church.   On Wednesday following, after preaching
and holding a missionary meeting at Emory Gap, a
young lady united with our Church.   I preached
on Thursday night at Brownsville.   Several penitents were at the altar of prayer, and two ladies
joined our Church.

My third quarterly-meeting was held in Hines
Valley, May 16th and 17th.   My presiding elder
was not present.   I held the meeting until Monday

night. On Monday one young lady was converted, and a number of penitents were left at the altar. On Sunday, with the assistance of a local preacher, I administered the sacrament of the Lord's Supper to a large number of people—Methodists, Baptists, and Campbellites communing together. That evening shouts of praise went up to God in hallelujahs. I returned home, May 20th.

On my June round, at Cardwell's Chapel, a young lady united with our Church. I spent a week in visiting in Roane and Loudon Counties; but was quite indisposed in health all the time. The following Sunday was Children's-day, being the second Sunday in June. I held an interesting Children's-day service in the forenoon at Woodlawn, and one in the afternoon at Cardwell's Chapel, and intended holding a third one in the evening at West's school-house; but the congregation dispersed before my arrival. Our meetings in June were all interesting, attended, more or less, with earnest seekers of salvation. At King's school-house, on Friday before the third Sunday, there were quite a number of penitents, and two persons united with our Church. The following Sabbath I held a missionary meeting in the morning, and a Children's-day service in the afternoon, at Hines Valley Church, with happy results. A number of penitents were at the altar, and two persons joined the Church. I returned home, June 23d.

My first basket-meeting was held in connection with my fourth quarterly-meeting at Woodlawn Church, embracing the third Sunday in July, and holding until the next Friday night. Dr. Caldwell

was with us a part of three days. The membership was greatly revived, fourteen souls were happily converted, and ten persons united with our
Church. I left the meeting on a rising tide. My
second basket-meeting was held at Pine Grove
Church, three miles from Kingston, embracing the
fourth Sunday in July. I held the meeting until
Thursday night. Five persons were converted, and
the membership was much revived.

My third basket-meeting was held at Oak Hill,
embracing the first Sunday in August, and continuing three days. I think there were deep convictions planted in the hearts of some sinners, and yet
there was a manifest aversion to coming to the altar
to be prayed for. This was due perhaps to previous
teachings and prejudices. My fourth basket-meeting was held at King's school-house, embracing the
second Sunday in August, and continuing five days.
Eleven souls were converted, and eight persons
joined our Church. The membership of this live
Church was much revived. After closing the
meeting at this place I went two miles, and
preached for a sick young man by the name of
Keelan, who was so low that we could not understand anything that he would say. When I asked
him if he was blessed of the Lord, to squeeze my
hand, he did so, with a radiant smile upon his face,
that gave me to understand that all was well with
his soul.

My fifth basket-meeting was held in Hines Val-
ley, five miles below Rockwood, embracing the third
Sunday in August, and continuing twelve days.
It resulted in thirty-one happy conversions, and in

twenty-two accessions to our Church. This was a great and most glorious revival for that Church. From there I went to Rockwood and to Post Oak, and spent a few days in rest. My sixth basket-meeting was held at Eblen's school-house, six miles above Kingston, on the old stage-road to Knoxville, embracing the fifth Sunday in August, and continuing six days. Eight souls were converted, and one person united with our Church. We have no Church organization at that place, and this doubtless prevented others from joining us. At a service which I held at Woodlawn during the week, three persons united with our Church.

My seventh basket-meeting was held at Cardwell's Chapel, twelve miles from Kingston, embracing the first Sunday in September, and continuing eight days, with the happiest results. Thirty-three persons were converted to God, and fourteen joined our Church. At times convictions were so prevalent that we could scarcely make room for the penitents. These were mostly young men. At all my revivals we held old-fashioned love-feasts, with bread and water passed through the congregation, followed by stirring experiences. We also held class-meetings at each occasion, and it was my happy experience that these were followed by the best results. I am more than ever convinced that these old landmarks of our Church are of vital importance to our people.

My eighth basket-meeting was held at Emory Gap, embracing the second Sunday in September. I was detained at Cardwell's Chapel on account of the uncommon interest there, and did not reach

this place until Sunday night, but had secured
Colonel Dail to hold the services until my arrival.
I continued them until Tuesday night, with a number of deep convictions and earnest penitents, and
four accessions to our Church. Within the bounds
of the Kingston Circuit a number of Methodist
preachers have grown up; among these are Moore,
Derrick, Hughes, and Cardwell. I find two nieces
and several nephews of Rev. R. M. Hickey, formerly a presiding elder in this country, living on
this circuit.

On Friday, after closing my meeting in Hines
Valley, Mrs. Milligan and her granddaughter Addie,
and myself, spent the day with Mrs. Rauhn, a widowed lady, and a member of our Church, living
at Post Oak. She, with her husband in his lifetime, had purchased the large farm of Jack Owens.
About fourteen years ago, Mr. Owens conceived the
idea of having a number of his neighbors form a
community by having all things in common, as in
the apostolic day. He induced a number of them
to sell all that they had, and deposit the money in
one common stock; to live together and work together on the same lands, and to eat at the same
table, the colored people at one end to themselves,
calling his organization a community. Mr. Owens
was at the head of all their affairs. I saw the long
dining-room which they used. In about six months
a dissatisfaction arose, and they disbanded in great
confusion, those having gone into the enterprise going out penniless. It was also claimed that Mr.
Owens was bankrupted by this movement. The
whole affair was a very foolish thing. Mr. Owens

was doubtless sincere, but very unwise in this matter.

I left home on Saturday evening before the first Sunday in October, took the train and ran down to Emory Gap, preached there that night, and during the next three days. There were two happy conversions and five accessions to our Church.

This closes the year's work on the Kingston Circuit. It has been a very happy year, with one hundred and eight conversions, and one hundred and five accessions to our Church. The people, without my consent or knowledge, sent up a large petition to the Conference for my return. I had so many applications to preach funerals, and some of these at a distance, and the Conference meeting at Johnson City, at one edge of our territory, I did not attend.

The Conference met, October 15th, with Bishop Hurst presiding. Dr. Caldwell was reappointed to the Kingston District, and I was reappointed to Kingston Circuit

On the third Sunday in September, to a large congregation in Sunbright, I preached the funeral of Anna J. Summers, wife of Rev. B. T. Summers, of the Baptist Church; and on the following Sunday, at Mill Creek, in Scott County, I preached the funeral of James H. Young. On the second Sunday in October, at a large graveyard near Rugby, I preached the funeral of Mary S. Brown; and on the third Sunday I preached the funeral of John A. Range, at Paul's Chapel, in Fentress County. On the fourth Sunday, at Annadel, I preached the funeral of Braxton Lane and three small children.

The day before, at Sunbright, I preached the funeral of Sallie Jennings.

My wife worries a great deal about my absence from home in the work. I live in anticipation, when all these earthly sacrifices shall pass away, that I shall enter upon my reward in heaven. I want to live so as to meet the King's approval in the Great Day.

October 30th, I left home to meet the first round of appointments for the new year. I rode eight miles, and preached at night at Rev. H. A. McCartt's, and rode the next day to Kingston. The following morning, it being Sunday, I rode twelve miles through a heavy rain, and preached at Cardwell's Chapel, to a fair congregation. I preached again at night at the same place when three ladies joined the Church; and on Thursday night following, at the prayer-meeting, there was another accession to the Church. I met all the appointments on this round, besides preaching twice in Kingston for the station. On the round I suffered a great deal from bronchial affection. I fear that I shall have to desist from preaching much during the winter. I become more conscious of the infirmities of age stealing upon me. Of late years I have had severe attacks of asthma, from which I have suffered a great deal. I hope that I shall not be troubled with this fearful disease until my latest breath; but I pray God to give me the grace of patience. The Lord help me to be faithful to the trust committed to me!

On the fifth Sunday in November I preached for Brother Scott, in Sunbright, when a gentleman joined our Church.

My first quarterly-meeting was held at Cardwell's Chapel, December 19th and 20th. Dr. Caldwell was present. I continued the meeting until Monday night, with happy results. Two persons joined the Church. On this round the congregations were large, the religious interest was strong, and anxious penitents were at nearly every place. At Pine Grove a man joined the Church.

I have now closed the year 1885. I have preached two hundred times, ridden horseback about two thousand miles, preached thirteen funerals, baptized twenty-eight adults and six infants, and married one couple. Farewell to the old year. Each year is bringing me nearer my home. I pray God that 1886 may be crowned with greater victories than the previous year.

On January 7th, at night, at Cardwell's Chapel two men joined our Church. The weather became so intensely cold that the rivers were frozen over, and so remained for a number of days, and this prevented my reaching all the appointments of this round. I reached home during the heavy sleet and frozen weather. I left home, and reached Kingston on Friday night before the second Sunday in February, where I heard an evangelist of the Baptist Church preach to a small audience, with very little effect. The next morning I rode seven miles to Union school-house, where I held revival services for five days. Five persons were converted, and the Christians were much revived—Baptists, Methodists, and Presbyterians uniting in labor, and shouting the praise of God together. Our Church has no organization there at this time, but I expect to have one soon. The prospect for good began greatly to increase all around the work.

My second quarterly-meeting was held at Emory Gap, embracing the second Sunday in March. The presiding elder was not in attendance, but had advertised that Dr. Carter, editor of the *Methodist Advocate*, would be present in his place. He did not show up, and so I had to do the best I could alone. I attended to all the business of such an occasion, and continued the services five days and nights. The Lord wonderfully blessed the work. Seven persons were happily converted and six joined the Church. The conversions and accessions were of the best people of that country. I think there would have been a very large number of conversions, but I was compelled to leave so as to meet other appointments. I left the work in the hands of other ministers, who let the interest run down. A local Southern Methodist preacher did our Church a wrong by misrepresenting us in my absence.

During the April round one person in Hines Valley, three persons at Pine Grove, two at Emory Gap, and one at King's school-house, joined our Church. On the same round I baptized and received nine persons into full connection at Woodlawn, baptized and received thirteen in Hines Valley, at King's school-house baptized two and received seven into full connection, and at Emory Gap baptized two and received four. During the May round I held missionary meetings at every appointment.

On the same round there were four conversions, several accessions, and many times happy

Christians. At some places on the circuit our Church is greatly and unjustly misrepresented. Every prejudice is appealed to, to make enemies to us; but amid it all we are more than triumphant. At all the missionary meetings the people responded liberally. At several places there were anxious seekers of salvation, and the people of God were much revived. In the afternoon of the fourth Sunday in May, at Oak Hill, I called penitents to the altar, and two ladies were powerfully converted. In June I held several Children's-day services, but had to do so in the face of a great deal of opposition; but the collections were liberal notwithstanding. I do n't think I ever saw a country so full of superstition and Church prejudices as some portions of the Kingston Circuit. I never saw so many different kinds of denominations on the same ground. Penitents were at the altar at a number of places, and several persons united with our Church.

My first basket-meeting was held at Oak Hill, embracing the third Sunday in July, and continued nine days. From the very beginning the power of the Lord was present to save. Penitents flocked to the altar, praying for mercy, and soon converts were praising God with joyful hearts. During the meeting twenty-eight souls were happily converted, and ten persons joined our Church. Others will likely join the Baptist Church, and perhaps some will join the Southern Methodist. Our Church is greatly persecuted in that section, and those who joined us did so under severe trial. The Mr. Roberts and family that I took dinner with on my first round here—of whom I said neither he nor his wife were

Christians—was converted at this meeting, with his wife, and both joined our Church and were baptized. This is Esquire Ed. Roberts. They are well-to-do and true people.

My second basket-meeting was at Pisgah, embracing the first Sunday in August. I was so sick that I could not attend. My third basket-meeting was held at Woodlawn, embracing the second Sunday in August, and continuing three days. There were some anxious penitents, and a lady united with our Church. A Rev. Mr. Aldridge, an evangelist, had held a meeting at this place, of several days, just before my meeting, and had left the revival interest rather low, although he had some conversions. He seemed to be a man reformed from a very bad life, and uses language in the pulpit that I believe to be objectionable. During the meeting I was greatly disturbed by some young people who engaged in some very unbecoming conduct. They were young girls, and regard themselves as members of a first-class family. The Lord will bring this haughtiness down. During the week, after the close of my own meeting, I attended a meeting of the Baptist Church, held in the neighborhood.

My fourth basket-meeting was held at Cardwell's Chapel, embracing the third Sunday in August. I found the same difficulty here as at Woodlawn, with Rev. Mr. Aldridge. I baptized two persons and received several into full connection. My fifth basket-meeting was held at Pine Grove, embracing the fourth Sunday in August, and holding nine days. My son Asbury, who had been teaching school near Rockwood, was prostrated by fever, and I had to leave the meeting before it closed, so as to attend him. There were fourteen conversions and seven accessions to our Church. My sixth basket-meeting was held in Hines Valley, embracing the fifth Sunday in August. Here there were five conversions and five accessions to our Church. I was compelled to close and go to my son, who had taken a relapse from the fever, and was very low. My seventh basket-meeting was appointed for King's school-house, but I could not leave my son to attend it.

My fourth quarterly-meeting was held in Hines Valley, embracing the fourth Sunday in September. Dr. Caldwell was in attendance. The meeting held two days, with prospects for good. During the week I held services two days at King's school-house. There were anxious penitents at the altar, but no conversions. I attended a meeting in Sunbright for two nights, where there were three conversions.

Embracing the second Sunday in October, I assisted Brother Peters in a protracted meeting at Oneida, on the Huntsville Circuit. There were several conversions and accessions. I have now finished up my second year's work on the Kingston Circuit. During the year there have been ninety-five conversions and sixty accessions to the Church, and during the two years there have been two hundred and three conversions and one hundred and sixty-five accessions. I left home on Saturday, October 16th, in company with Rev. S. B. Scott, to attend the Annual Conference at Athens, Tenn. We traveled the distance over land with a horse and buggy. The first day we traveled into Roane County; and on the following day, being Sunday, we preached at Swan Pond Church. The following day we drove to Rev. David Kelsey's, and remained over night. The next day we traveled through portions of Roane and Meigs Counties and into McMinn County, and stopped with Uncle Dan Carpenter. The next day we drove two miles to Uncle Cyril Carpenter's, and I preached that night at Tranquillity Church. The next day we drove to Athens. The Conference was in session, with Bishop Mallalieu presiding. We had an interesting Conference session. I staid with Brother Walker, the father-in-law of my son.

The Conference closed on Monday morning. In the afternoon I drove out ten miles, and staid with Fletcher Carpenter. The next day we drove to Kingston, and staid with Colonel Dail. We reached home on Thursday evening. At this Conference I was appointed to New River Circuit, with Dr. Caldwell as presiding elder. On Sunday, after reaching home, I preached in Sunbright, to a large congregation, the funerals of old Father Vardimin Byrd and wife with happy results. I preached again that night, and one person was happily converted.

CHAPTER XVI.

NEW RIVER, SUNBRIGHT, AND OLIVER SPRINGS.

THE New River Circuit lies in Scott County, Tennessee. I began the first round on the first Sunday in November by preaching in the morning at Glen Mary, and in the afternoon at Black Wolf. The first quarterly-meeting was held at Helenwood, embracing the second Sunday in November. Dr. Caldwell was present, and preached three times. We had very interesting services. Helenwood is a growing little town on the Cincinnati Southern Railroad.

On the third Sunday in November I preached in the morning at Winfield, and at night at Oneida, to good congregations at both places. These are little towns on the Cincinnati Southern Railroad, Winfield being near the State line of Tennessee and Kentucky. I spent the day before visiting families in New River. This is also a little town on the Cincinnati Southern Railroad. I left home on November 26th, to meet my appointment at Hatfield's, near the Campbell County line. I rode that afternoon ten miles, and staid for the night with Rev. A. L. Williams, a local preacher of our Church. The next day Brother Williams and I set out for Hatfield's. We rode up and down several large mountains, crossed several streams of water, and came in sight of the Round Mountain, which rises higher than the surrounding mountains. I am told that the view from the summit of this mountain is grand beyond description. We undertook to travel

a road by the side of New River about two miles,
but the tides of the previous spring had so washed
out the banks that our own lives and the lives of
our horses were imperiled. We crossed New River
at a very deep ford, where immense rocks lay all
about in the river, greatly endangering our lives.
We also had trouble with quicksand. We held
services two nights and one day. There were a
number of penitents at the altar, two conversions
and two accessions to our Church.

On the first Sunday in December, because of a
heavy snowstorm, I did not reach my appointments
at Glen Mary and Black Wolf. Glen Mary is quite
a mining town on the Cincinnati Southern Railroad,
large quantities of coal being taken from the mines,
and shipped from this place. On the second Sunday in December I preached at Helenwood in the
morning, and at New River at night. Good congregations were at both places. At New River I
stopped with Mr. Hail, an excellent family, the
parents being Baptists and the children Methodists.
On the third Sunday in December I preached in
the morning at Winfield, and at Oneida at night,
to good congregations. My appointments are on
the railroad line, excepting Hatfield's, and Black
Wolf, which are near the line. At Winfield, Mrs.
Sharp, wife of the hotel proprietor, joined our Church
on this round.

Embracing the fourth Sunday in December, I
assisted Rev. T. H. Russell in a revival-meeting at
Scutcheon, on the Sunbright Circuit. At this
meeting there were several conversions and accessions to our Church. This brings me to the close

of 1886. How fast my years are flying away! I am considerably advanced on the western side of life. The greater part of my work is done. I wish it were better done. There are many happy memories along the past. I have given a great deal of my time to the work of the Lord, and am now sixty years old. When young, I was accustomed to sing that good old hymn:

> "I'll suffer on my threescore years
> Till my deliverer comes,
> And wipes away his servant's tears,
> And takes his exile home."

I did not realize then, as I do now, what three-score years means. I want to give the remainder of my days to the Lord. During the year I preached two hundred and two times, witnessed one hundred conversions, received sixty-five persons into the Church, baptized forty-six adults and sixteen infants, preached five funerals, and married three couples.

On the January round I again failed to reach my appointments at Glen Mary and Black Wolf, on account of severe weather. I left home January 7th, on horseback, preached the following day at Black Wolf in the morning, and at New River at night. The next day I rode through a snowstorm five miles to Helenwood, and preached to a small congregation. I rode back in the afternoon to New River, and preached to a good congregation at night. The following day the earth was carpeted with ice, so that traveling was very difficult; however, I rode home twelve miles.

On the previous rounds I had been traveling by

railroad. I preached on Saturday before the third Sunday in January, at Oneida. Here I found Mr. Kershaw and Mrs. St. Clair, Congregationalist ministers, holding services. They are from the North, and seemed to be chiefly engaged in proselyting people from other Churches. They have taken but few from us, and these are not very valuable members. The following day I preached at Winfield. Here I found that my proselyters had been around. Embracing the fourth Sunday in January, I held a meeting of four days at Hatfield's. There were seven conversions and two accessions to our Church. Rev. A. L. Williams assisted me in the meeting.

On the fifth Sunday in January I preached at Black Wolf Church in the morning, and in the afternoon at Glen Mary. Embracing the first Sunday in February I held revival services at Winfield for several days, with the result of seven conversions and eight accessions to the Church. On the second Sunday in February, and the day before, I preached at New River, where I received several into full connection. At night I preached at Helenwood to a very large congregation. On the third Sunday in February I preached at Oneida. The work here is not very promising. Embracing the fourth Sunday in February I held the quarterly-meeting on Sunbright Circuit for Dr. Caldwell, at Emory Church. The following Tuesday I held the funeral services of Dr. Hungerford at Sunbright. The first Saturday and Sunday in March was my second quarterly-meeting occasion at Winfield. The presiding elder was not present. All the labors of such an occasion fell on me. A minister of the Baptist Church communed with us on Sunday, for which his Church turned him out soon afterwards.

On the second Sunday in March I preached at New River and Helenwood, to good congregations, and on the third Sunday preached at Black Wolf in the morning, and at Glen Mary at night. On the fourth Sunday in March I preached at Oak Hill, in Roane County. The following week I attended the Circuit Court at Wartburg as a witness, and lectured one night at the court-house on "Temperance." On the first Sunday in April I preached at Pleasant Grove Church, three miles from Winfield, and in Winfield at night, to good congregations. The second Sunday in April, by exchange with Rev. A. C. Peters, I preached at Mt. Vernon in the morning, and at Cherry's school-house in the afternoon. The Cherry family had recently immigrated to this place from Ohio, where they were Congregationalists, but are now Methodists. On the third Sunday in April I endeavored to reach my appointment at Black Wolf on horseback, but was prevented by heavy rain. I preached at Glen Mary, however, in the afternoon, to a small audience. Religion is in low state at this place.

On the fourth Sunday in April I preached at Hatfield's. I had much difficulty in reaching this place. The recent rains had greatly swollen the streams, and when I reached Brimstone Creek I found that I could not ford it, and so, after traveling some distance a very rough way, I came to where the narrow-gauge road crosses this stream, and, driving my horse into the creek, he swam over, and I walked across on the railroad bridge. When I came to New River I left my horse with a friend, and crossed in a canoe, this being in the neighborhood of the meeting. One young man was happily converted, and a number of penitents were left at the altar. The fifth Sunday in April I preached at Winfield in the morning, and at Oneida at night. I took good missionary collections at both places.

On Saturday night before the first Sunday in May I preached at Robins Station, where the Congregationalists have a small church. The following day I preached at New River in the morning, and at Helenwood at night, taking missionary collections. On the second Sunday in May I preached at Black Wolf and Glen Mary, and raised good missionary collections at both places. The third Sunday in May I preached at Hatfield's. Here there was one conversion. I baptized two persons and received three into the Church. My third quarterly-meeting was held at Oneida. The presiding elder was not present. We had good services. Two persons joined the Church. The first Sunday in June I preached at Winfield. I had intended to hold a children's service; but the prejudice against our Church at that place is so great that I could not. At night I preached at Oneida to a good congregation. On Monday night Rev. T. H. Russell and myself made addresses in Sunbright, on the Constitutional Amendment, and during the week we held revival services at Huffman's Switch. There were five happy conversions.

The second Sunday in June I preached and held
Children's-day service at New River, and at night
at Helenwood. At both places our Church program was used. The decorations and singing were
excellent. On the third Sunday in June I preached
at Young's school-house, three miles from Glen
Mary, and organized a Methodist class at that place.
On the fourth Sunday in June I preached for
Brother Russell at Scutcheon, and had an excellent
meeting. I delivered a temperance address the day
before at Emory Church.

The first Sunday in July I preached at Glen
Mary to one man, three women, and two children.
Gloomy clouds hang over our work at that place.
July 8th, Rev. T. H. Russell and myself left Sunbright on horseback, to meet appointments in Scott
County. The first day we traveled to New River,
where Brother Russell preached at night. The next
day we rode to Oneida, and began a meeting of
five days and nights. There were five conversions
and seven accessions to our Church. From that
place we rode to Hatfield's, and began services on
Saturday before the third Sunday in July. We
continued until Wednesday night. Four persons
were happily converted, and five joined the Church.

Embracing the fourth Sunday in July, my fourth
quarterly-meeting was held at Black Wolf. Dr.
Caldwell was not present. . During the entire year
he held only my first quarterly-meeting. I held
the usual services of such an occasion, and continued
the meeting until Friday night. Twenty souls were
converted, and fifteen joined our Church. The
fifth Sunday in July I preached the funeral of Mrs.

Morgan, in a grove near Oak Hill Church, in Roane
County, to an immense audience. The following
week I returned to Black Wolf and continued the
revival services there, with eight more conversions
and six more accessions to the Church.

Embracing the first Sunday in August, I held
protracted services in Winfield, without any apparent good result. I baptized and received two ladies into full connection. The second Sunday in
August I preached at Helenwood. This is a saloon
town. Embracing the third Sunday in August,
Brother Russell and I held a revival-meeting at
Pleasant Ridge, in Morgan County. There were
eight conversions and a number of accessions to the
Church. On the night of August 25th I held a
prohibition meeting in Sunbright, and had arranged
for speeches to be made on the Constitutional
Amendment in the Baptist church; but Rev. Ben.
Summers and his father locked us out. However,
we held the meeting in another building near by.

Embracing the fourth Sunday in August, I held
a meeting of seven days and nights at Black Wolf.
There were fourteen conversions and ten accessions
to the Church. One man, a well-to-do farmer, who
had been a seeker for twenty years, was converted;
and a lady who had been adjudged insane was converted, and has been ever since in her right mind.
The day before I began this meeting I preached the
funeral of Belle Peake at Young's school-house.

On the first Saturday in September I rode to
Hatfield's; but on the way I stopped and preached
to a Baptist congregation at Bull Creek. The
house in which I preached was made of logs, notched

together, with from four to six inches space between,
unchinked and undaubed. The building was not
higher than an old-fashioned stillhouse, and looked
very much like one. The following day I preached
twice at Hatfield's, baptized two ladies by immersion,
and received five persons into full connection.

The second Sunday in September I preached at
New River, with a view to protracting the meeting;
but the interest was so low that I did not do so.
September 8th, we held a temperance rally at Wartburg, with the view of bringing out the temperance
vote of Morgan County at the coming election. I
spent about two weeks speaking in school-houses
and churches, in Morgan County, in the interest of
the prohibition cause. I had been appointed
county chairman by the Prohibition Committee of
the State. I found the majority of the voters of
the county were in favor of liquor. September 29th
was the day of election. The State gave a fair majority for liquor; but East Tennessee gave a good
majority against it. Morgan County voted for
liquor. This was a dark day for Tennessee.

Embracing the first Sunday in October, I held
a meeting of three days at Oneida. There were
three happy conversions and one accession to our
Church.

This closes my year's work on the New River
Circuit. I had often had a desire to become acquainted with Scott County. It is a country of fine
natural scenery. Its majestic mountains are the
Round, Jellico, Buffalo, and Brimstone ranges. It
has many creeks and rivers. Among these are
New River, White Oak, Black Wolf, Paint Rock,

Buffalo, Straight Fork, Brimstone, Smoky, Jellico, Indian, No Business, and Bull Creek. Being so well watered, it is a great country for Baptists, there being four different denominations of this kind in the county—the Missionary, the Anti-Missionary, the old Hardshell, and the Freewill Baptist. Taken altogether, they are very numerous. Ours is the only Methodist Church in the county. There are a few Presbyterians and a few Congregationalists. These are the Churches of the county. We have two hundred and twenty members. Our Church does not own any property in the county, and I am told that no other Church does. The houses used for preaching are also used for school-houses, and deeded to no one in particular. The Presbyterian Church has a graded school at Huntsville, that has done a great deal of good for the county.

The illiteracy and inexperience of the most of the people are appalling. Superstition has a strong grasp on many. It is a popular opinion among some, that witches are prevalent and doing a great deal of harm; and some even profess to know how to kill them. Mail facilities are very poor. Some people live miles away from the post-office. The majority never read a newspaper. I found a number of preachers who could neither read nor write. There was one in particular of this kind, who was regarded by his brethren as the leading minister of the county. I was told, by truthful people, that there were ministers who not only drank liquor, but actually became intoxicated. It was no uncommon thing to meet large droves of men, with their guns, boys, and dogs, out hunting on Sunday. Often, while preaching, I have heard the report of guns fired by men out hunting on Sunday. The soil is fertile, and the people raise large quantities of corn and other grain, and much live-stock. A kinder-hearted, more hospitable people are not to be found anywhere else. I never received kinder treatment from any people than I received from the native people of Scott County. I shall ever hold this people in grateful memory. Education and morals are beginning to spread through the county, and the day will soon come when Scott County will not be behind any other county in the State in point of morals and intelligence.

Northern families are moving into the county along the line of railroad, and good towns are growing up. The Cincinnati Southern Railroad runs through the county, and other short lines are built out to different places from this main line. The county abounds in coal and iron. At some day these will be developed, and everything will be different there. During the Civil War this was the most loyal county in the State. Almost all the men able to bear arms were in the Federal army. I am anxious for that people and our Church in that county. It is due this country to say, that many of them are intelligent and well-informed people.

October 10th, Rev. A. C. Peters and myself left Sunbright to travel on horseback to Clinton, and there to take the train to our Annual Conference, to meet in Knoxville, October 12th. We rode the first day to Montgomery for dinner, and in the afternoon we rode into the eastern part of Morgan

County, and stopped over night with Thomas Hutson. The following day we rode in the morning to my dear cousin's, William R. Dail, for dinner, and in the afternoon we rode five miles to Clinton, and remained over night with Judge W. R. Hicks. The next morning we took the early train for Knoxville. We had a rather unpleasant Conference. Some of our preachers, impelled by an unholy ambition for leadership, bring about considerable strife in the Conference. Bishop E. G. Andrews presided. I was assigned a boarding place on Clinch Street, not far from the church, at Brother Miller's. I had a real pleasant stay with these people. Bishop Andrews preached a strong sermon on Sunday.

The Conference closed on Monday morning. On Monday night I ran down to Clinton and remained over night. The next day I rode five miles to Cousin Dail's for dinner, and in the afternoon rode into Morgan County. The following day I reached my home. At this Conference I was appointed to Sunbright Circuit, and Rev. A. C. Peters was made presiding elder of the Kingston District.

On my first round at Pleasant Ridge, a young lady joined our Church, and at Pilot Mountain a young man and a young lady joined the Church. I filled two rounds of the work in the old year. On the second Sunday in December, at a newly-erected church, called Rome, near Deer Lodge, I organized a class of twenty members, receiving eight persons by letter. This Church is made up largely of Northern people, who have recently settled the town. Within the last few months they have built and furnished a good church house.

This will become a strong point on the Sunbright Circuit. I am laboring earnestly to build a church in Sunbright, but meet with some discouragements. My first quarterly-meeting was held at Pleasant Hill the last day of the old and the first day of the new year. The streams were so swollen by heavy rains that the congregations were small. Brother Peters, the presiding elder, was present. All the services of the occasion were very interesting, and were seasons of power. After I had preached on Sunday night, all the unconverted people in the house came forward and knelt for prayers. I have now finished another eventful year of my life.

During the time I have preached one hundred and eighty-seven times, witnessed eighty-four conversions, received sixty-four into the Church, baptized twenty-three adults and three infants, and preached the funerals of ten persons. And now, 1887, farewell. I have lived sixty-one years, and have outlived my father's age by more than a year, and all my brothers except one. I can not tell why God lengthens out my life. In boyhood I was regarded as the sickliest of the family. I have observed healthful and temperate rules for living all my life. I never used any tobacco, except one chew when quite a small boy, and that made me so sick that I never tried it any more. I have never used any ardent spirits, and for the last nine years I have refrained from the use of coffee, or any other stimulants. I want to live and work for the Lord so long as he says work. I believe the Church has never appreciated my labors very much; but I have one consolation, the Lord knows all about it. God be praised! The infirmities of age are pressing me heavily. The good Lord help me to serve him to the extent of my strength during the year 1888!

On Saturday night before the second Sunday in January, while I was preaching at Potter's Chapel, a young man was happily converted. There were additions to the Church during January and February, at different places. At night, on the third Sunday in February, I preached at Shady Grove, when a young lady was converted and a number of others were seeking salvation at the altar. My second quarterly-meeting was held at Lansing, embracing the first Sunday in March. The congregations were small, and there was no apparent religious move among the people. Brother Peters was present, and did the preaching. We are having considerable difficulty in locating the church building in Sunbright. The people appear to be unsettled as to the place. The location has been moved twice. I had a portion of lumber for the building on the ground of the second location, when it was moved to the third. The last place is very unhandy to myself and wife. Each one seems anxious to have the building convenient to his own home. I am afraid that some are real selfish in the matter.

During my ministerial life I have built a number of churches. I have built Bethlehem and Edwards Chapel, on the Cumberland City Circuit; Mt. Zion, Scutcheon, and Emory Chapel, on the Wartburg Circuit; also Pleasant Hill, on the Jamestown Circuit. During my life I have met a number of the bishops of the Church. In 1854 I met

Bishop Pierce in Cleveland, Tenn. Since then I have met of our own Church, Bishops Kingsley, Clark, Scott, Simpson, Bowman, Harris, Wiley, Andrews, Gilbert Haven, Warren, Walden, and Mallalieu. Under the feeling of my present infirmities, I do not know that I shall attend many more Conference sessions.

We have great strife among some of the ministers of our Conference, which makes our sessions unpleasant. There is an unholy ambition for leadership. On the fourth Sunday in March, after having preached the night before at Mill Creek, I set off for my appointment, at Pleasant Ridge, distant six miles. I soon encountered a heavy storm of wind and rain, and took up for the day at Brother Dyden's. Brother Dyden is an Episcopalian, but his wife is a Methodist. As I could not get on to my appointment, I held a religious service in the family, when their two oldest children, being daughters, were converted, and I baptized and received them into the Church. I also baptized their four younger children. So much for a stormy March Sunday.

On the first Sunday of April, being Easter Sunday, I preached two sermons on the Resurrection of Christ, in the morning at Emory Chapel, and in the afternoon at Pleasant Hill. At the latter place a young lady joined our Church, and I baptized and received two persons into full connection. At both places the saints of God shouted aloud for joy. I have been greatly afflicted for some time with nervous affection in my left hip and leg, so that I can scarcely walk or get on or off my horse. My system is rapidly running down, and I feel that my work will soon be done. I shall endeavor to keep my life journal well written up, so that it will be complete at the time of my death. Since I began to preach I have preached the funerals of five hundred and four persons, and since my ordination I have baptized four hundred and eighty-three persons by immersion and three hundred and eighty by pouring. I have also baptized three hundred and thirteen infants, making a total of one thousand one hundred and seventy-six baptisms. I have married eighty couples, among them seven ministers, one lawyer, one doctor, and one railroad agent. I can not tell how much longer I shall be effective in preaching Jesus and the resurrection; but while I can go, I will preach. I am pleased with the success that my three boys are making in life. My eldest, Rev. J. C. Wright, I feel sure will be a power for good in the Church. My other two are lawyers; but I trust and pray that they may live humble Christian men.

At a night meeting which I held at Huffman Switch in April, a young man and a young lady school-teacher joined the Church. Although I was greatly afflicted, however during March and April I witnessed a number of conversions and accessions to the Church. I often preached standing on one foot, while suffering untold agonies.

On the first Sunday in May I rode horseback fifteen miles, and preached twice, holding missionary meetings and taking collections. God only knows how much physical suffering I endured that day. I have a strong desire to finish my year's work, if the good Lord lets me live through it. I held missionary meetings in May at nine appointments, and raised by cash paid in and subscription $41. I trust that my missionary collectors in each place will make good collections. My third quarterly-meeting was held at Rome, embracing the first Sunday in June. Brother Peters was present, and preached three times. The meeting closed on Sunday afternoon.

On the second Sunday in June I preached at Emory Chapel and Pleasant Hill. On the following Tuesday, Rev. F. W. Henck, of Kingston Station, began a series of holiness meetings in Sunbright. These continued for ten days with good results. Three persons were converted, and two joined the Church. Brother Henck is a preacher of great power. On the third Sunday in June I held a children's meeting in the morning, and a parents' meeting in the afternoon, at Rome. On the fourth Sunday in June I preached in the morning at Shady Grove, and in the afternoon at Lansing.

On the first Sunday in July I preached at Emory Chapel in the morning, and at Pleasant Hill in the afternoon. At the latter place a young lady was converted. My first basket-meeting was held at Potter's Chapel, embracing the second Sunday in July. It continued six days, and resulted in nine happy conversions, seven accessions to the Church, and believers greatly revived. Brother J. T. Cummius, a Bible agent, was present at this meeting, and sold and donated eighty Bibles and Testaments.

My second basket-meeting was held at Shady Grove, embracing the third Sunday in July, and holding four days. Three souls were converted,

and one united with the Church. At each of these
meetings the people brought their dinners on the
ground, and spread them together. This is a very
happy way of doing. My third basket-meeting was
held at Pleasant Ridge, embracing the fourth Sunday in July.

My fourth basket-meeting was held at Emory
Gap, in Roane County, on the Kingston Circuit.
There were no conversions, but several seekers of
religion. My fifth basket-meeting was held at
Pleasant Hill, embracing the first Sunday in August, and continuing five days. Ten conversions
and five accessions were the result. My sixth
basket-meeting was held at Rome, five days. There
were four conversions, one accession, and one received into full connection.

My seventh basket-meeting was held at Scutcheon, embracing the fourth Sunday in August.
The congregations were not large, and the discouragement was so great that I held only the two days.
I baptized two young ladies, and received them into
full connection. My eighth basket-meeting was
held at Emory Chapel, embracing the first Sunday
in September. There was such a heavy rainfall on
Saturday that neither myself nor congregation could
attend.

On Sunday morning I set off early, and after a
ride of twelve miles across a rough mountain I
reached the church, and found a large congregation
present. They had a full supply of provisions on
the ground, and so I preached to them twice that
day. A young man, a school-teacher, wept bitterly
at the altar, while the people of God shouted aloud

for joy. During the following week I rode through heavy rain down to Travisville, in Pickett County, and on Saturday, in our new church at that place, I preached the funeral of Nancy Dishman Davidson, from Rev. xx, 12. Here I met a great many of my old friends and neighbors, to whom I had preached in early days. I felt that it was heavenly to shake so many of their hands.

On the following day, being Sunday, I rode up to the Three Forks of Wolf River, and heard Rev. Brother Moody, of the Tennessee Conference, Methodist Episcopal Church, South, preach the funeral of my dear sister, Nancy Frogge. My fourth quarterly-meeting embraced the third Sunday in September. Brother Peters was present, and preached several times with good effect, I trust. There were no conversions. The fourth Sunday in September, at Mt. Vernon Church, I preached the funeral of my dear cousin, Jeremiah Wright, from Isa. lx, 19, 20. The fifth Saturday and Sunday in September I held a two days' meeting at Mill Creek. On the first Sunday in October, to a large congregation at Mt. Zion Church, I preached the funeral of Margaret Langley, from John xiv, 1–3.

On the second Sunday in October, at Potter's Chapel, I preached the funerals of Sarah Bishop and her daughter, Martha Potter, from Psa. l, 5. I continued the services at this place for three days. There were two conversions, and a number of penitents left at the altar.

Our Annual Conference convened in Cleveland, Tenn., October 10th, Bishop FitzGerald presiding. I did not attend, but sent my reports by Brother

Peters. At this Conference I was appointed to Oliver Springs Circuit, Rev. A. C. Peters being my presiding elder again. Embracing the third Sunday in October, I held a two days' meeting at Shady Grove. On Sunday a gentleman engaged in teaching school was powerfully converted. Others were seeking salvation. On the fourth Sunday in October, at Black Wolf Church in Scott County, I preached the funeral of Charlotte Jane Russell, from Acts xxvi, 8. Several shouted God's praise.

The Oliver Springs Circuit lies in Anderson, Roane, and Morgan Counties. Oliver Springs is a famous watering and pleasure resort, lying in the gap of Walden's Ridge, called Winter's Gap. Near the town is located the Big Mountain Coal Mines. It is also on the line of the Walden's Ridge Railroad. I set out for my new field of work, November 2d, drove twelve miles, and took dinner at Wartburg. In the afternoon I drove nine miles, and remained over night with William Langley. The following day I drove nine miles, and took dinner with Brother Richards, at Oliver Springs. This is a Welsh family, wealthy and kind-hearted. In the afternoon I drove nine miles, running up Poplar Creek, and crossing it several times, through Frost Bottom, to William R. Duncan's. Brother Duncan is a strong member of our Church, kind-hearted, and well-to-do in the world.

The next day being Sunday I went back down the valley one mile, and met and preached to an attentive congregation, in the old log church, with happy results. After taking dinner with Moses Duncan, who lives near by, at the old Duncan homestead, which has long been a home for Methodist itinerant ministers, I drove eight miles down Poplar Creek, crossing it several times, to Mrs. Galbraith's, a widow lady. The last time that I crossed the creek the water ran into my buggy, so as to wet all my books and papers; however, I dried them by the fire, and there was no loss. Soon after I arrived a crowd of people gathered, and I preached to them. The following day I visited a number of families in the neighborhood, and late in the evening I drove back three miles to Samuel Duncan's, who lives at Donavan's Station, on the Walden's Ridge Railroad.

The next day was election day for President, governor, congressmen, and legislators. I attended the election-ground near by to form acquaintances. In the afternoon I drove down through Oliver Springs to William Fritt's, class-leader for Middle Creek. I took up the remainder of the week visiting, praying with the people, and getting acquainted. The heavy rains were so incessant that they greatly obstructed my work. The following Sunday I preached three times, and in three different counties; but none of them three miles apart. The counties of Anderson, Morgan, and Roane corner in Winter's Gap. At the afternoon service I baptized a young lady at the altar. The following day I drove home thirty miles.

In the evening of Saturday before the third Sunday in November I took the train at Sunbright, and ran down the line to Knoxville Junction. I remained over night at H. Carter's. The next morning I boarded the Walden's Ridge train, and

ran up that line eight miles, to old Oakdale Iron
Works, where I preached to an attentive audience.
In the afternoon I obtained a horse of Robert
Morgan, rode three miles over a rough mountain,
and preached at May's school-house, a very old and
unfit house for worship. After preaching I returned to Oakdale. There was an appointment at
that place for a Baptist minister that night. He
did not come. I attended and preached, when
quite a number came forward as seekers of salvation. I continued the services through the week.
Nine souls were happily converted, and three persons joined our Church. Among the conversions
was the lady school-teacher of the town.

On Saturday evening I moved up the valley
four miles to Jones Chapel, and began a series of
meetings that continued for more than a week. I
left the meeting on Monday for my home, with the
promise that I would return soon. In waiting for a
train at Knoxville Junction that night, I suffered a
great deal from the cold, having to wait out of doors
for several hours. The Lord sustained me and kept
me up. On Tuesday morning I ran up home, but
started back next day by driving twenty-one miles
to Peter Matthews', where I remained over night.
The next day being Thanksgiving-day, I drove
fourteen miles, reached Jones Chapel, when I found
my meeting all ablaze. I remained until Monday,
when we had had five conversions. I left Brother
Bailey, a Freewill Baptist preacher, in charge.
After I left there were seven more conversions,
making twelve in all.

After staying at home a few days, I set off

horseback to meet my appointment at Oakdale Iron Works, where I preached the second Sunday in December, morning and night. Two persons united with our Church, and I baptized two young ladies at the altar. I was suffering intensely with a severe cold. December 14th I set off for my first quarterly-meeting at Frost Bottom. I drove thirty miles, and staid one mile above Oliver Springs, at Brother Cannon's. The next morning I drove up into Frost Bottom, where I met Brother Peters and congregation. We continued the services until Thursday night. There were four conversions and two accessions to our Church. I baptized ten infant children. I then ran down the valley, preached at Jones Chapel, attended meeting at Oakdale, and preached on Sunday at Oakhill, on the Emory Gap Circuit. I drove home the day before Christmas.

I am now closing up the year. God be praised! That I shall live through another, God only knows. I am not anxious about that. If the good Lord permits me to live, I want to live to his glory; and when I die, to throw back the mantle of a happy Christian triumph. I want that to be the grandest victory of my life. I am now sixty-two years old. My years are sitting heavily upon me. I can best express my feelings in the language of a certain poet:

"If, in this feeble flesh, I may
  Awhile show forth Thy praise,
Jesus support the tottering clay,
  And lengthen out my days.

If such a worm as I can spread
  A common Savior's name,
Let Him who raised thee from the dead
  Quicken my mortal frame.

> Still let me live, Thy blood to show,
>> Which purges every stain,
> And gladly linger out below
>> A few more years of pain."

During the year I have preached two hundred times, have witnessed sixty-one conversions, have received twenty-nine into the Church, have baptized thirteen adults and twenty infants, have preached the funerals of thirteen persons, and have married three couples. I enter upon a new year, praying the Lord to make me humble, meek, and holy in all conversation. If I am not stricken down again with sciatica, I trust to witness during the year one hundred conversions. May the Spirit of the Master rest upon me! And now, 1888, farewell; while to 1889 I say, Good morning, and a Happy New Year.

Early in the year God's approving smiles rested on the work. I left home in the rain, January 4th, drove thirteen miles to Wartburg, preached there at night, and baptized at the altar a young lady. The next day I drove about seven miles in the rain, and took up for the night at James Goddard's. The next morning I drove nine miles, and as I could not reach my appointment at Frost Bottom, I called in at Middle Creek, where a Freewill Baptist preacher was holding, and at his request I preached. In the afternoon I drove into the town of Oliver Springs, where I preached at night in the Presbyterian church, at the request of the pastor. During the week I preached several nights at Middle Creek for the coal-miners, where four young ladies were converted. Here is located the Big Mountain coalmines. I also preached one night at Frost Bottom during the week. I drove down the valley, and preached on Saturday night at Jones Chapel. I preached twice on Sunday at Oakdale, in the morning a funeral sermon. Two persons joined our Church, and a number came forward as penitents.

On Monday I drove thirty miles to my home. Early in February, I began to feel an attack of sciatica in my right hip and leg, instead of my left, as it was the winter before. However, we had some good meetings. In coming home from this round, I rode twenty-two miles in six hours, through a heavy storm of wind and snow, coming from the north, and blowing in my face. I was suffering so much, and was so lame, that I did not reach my appointments at Oakdale and Jones Chapel on this round; but early in March, I set off almost half dead, my right side and right limb being almost paralyzed. I reached Frost Bottom, and preached on the first Sunday.

I remained in that neighborhood during the week; but how much I suffered, the good Lord only knows. I preached again, however, on Thursday in the afternoon. The following Saturday and Sunday was the occasion of my second quarterly-meeting at Oliver Springs. Brother Peters was present, and did the preaching. On Sunday afternoon I drove out four miles, and remained over night with Samuel Russell. The following day I drove home, fully resolved to remain there until I should get better or die, and so I did not reach my appointments at Oakdale and Jones Chapel in March.

Feeling better, on the 5th of April I left home to reach my appointment at Frost Bottom on the first Sunday of April. I preached, and in the afternoon rode eight miles and preached at Field's school-house. I remained in that country during the week. On the second Sunday of April I preached at Oliver Springs and Middle Creek. The following Wednesday and Thursday I preached at Jones Chapel, and on Friday and Saturday at Oakdale. The following Sunday being Easter, I held an Easter service in the morning at Jones Chapel, and in the afternoon an Easter service at Oakdale, with happy results at both services. At the former place a young lady joined our Church. I drove home the next day.

On the first Sunday in May I preached a missionary sermon at Frost Bottom, and took a collection of $17.15 for the cause of missions. In the afternoon I rode eight miles, and preached at Field's school-house, and took a collection of $10.75 for missions. On the following Wednesday I attended the Commencement exercises of Roane College. On Thursday I preached in the morning at Oliver Springs, and in the afternoon at Middle Creek, taking missionary collections at both places, amounting to $4.65 at the former place, and to $12.35 at the latter place. On the third Sunday in May I held a missionary meeting at Oakdale, and took a collection of $9.80. In the afternoon of that day, I held a like meeting at Jones Chapel, and took a collection of $10.30. The fourth Sunday, I preached again at Jones Chapel and Oakdale. At the former place a young man joined our Church. My third quarterly-meeting embraced the second Sunday in June at Jones Chapel. Brother Peters was present, and preached with acceptability. On Sunday night I held a Children's-day service at Oliver Springs.

The third Sunday in June I preached the funeral of Mikey Duncan at Frost Bottom. I went down to Travisville, in Middle Tennessee, and preached the funeral of Mrs. Crabtree on the fifth Sunday in June. The second Sunday in July I preached twice at Frost Bottom. In the afternoon of the following Saturday I preached in a little log school-house in what they call the Cove, to a small congregation. I stopped with a Mr. Simpson, who told me that there were people living near him, in four miles of Oliver Springs and in sixteen miles of Clinton, the county-seat of Anderson County, who had raised up girls to be grown and married, and who are now raising children of their own, that up to two years ago had never been inside of a school-house or church. I would not have thought that such a place could have been found in East Tennessee.

My first basket-meeting was held at Middle Creek, embracing the third Sunday in July. I held until Friday, when five souls had been converted and one person had joined our Church. I left the meeting in the hands of Brother Tedford, a Free-will Baptist minister, who continued for several days and nights, when six more were converted.

My second basket-meeting was held at Jones Chapel, embracing the fourth Sunday in July. I continued the meeting seven days. Four souls were happily converted and three persons joined our Church.

I held the first Saturday and Sunday in August at Oakdale. Some of the people had been talking about each other so greatly that, although there were a number of penitents at the altar, the prospect for a revival was not good, and so I closed on Sunday afternoon, and drove home on Monday.

My fourth quarterly-meeting was held at Oliver Springs, embracing the second Sunday in August. Brother Peters was present, and continued the meeting for several days and nights without any material results. I began my basket-meeting at Frost Bottom on Saturday before the third Sunday in August, and continued it until the following Friday in the afternoon. There were nineteen conversions and ten accessions to our Church. I preached twelve times, and baptized nine adults and thirteen infants. My basket-meeting at Field's school-house embraced the fourth Sunday in August, continuing one week. Six souls were happily converted. I did not receive any persons into the Church, because no denomination is allowed to organize at that place. It is my honest conviction that in many portions of the counties of Anderson and Rome the people are educated against the Methodist Church, many of them having been taught from childhood to regard it as a bad thing.

Methodism has been greatly misrepresented in this country. I love the Methodist Church, and I know that the Lord does not cast out devils through Beelzebub. I had an appointment to hold a basket-meeting at May's school-house in Roane County, embracing the first Sunday in September; but as Brother Joe Wilson, a Baptist minister, was holding a meeting with some success near by, I canceled my engagement and occupied the time in Frost Bottom.

On Monday, September 2d, I started for home, drove down through Oliver Springs, and out to Dan Kelley's, six miles from Wartburg, where I remained over night. The Baptists were holding a protracted meeting at Union Church near Brother Kelley's. I preached for them at night, and drove home the next day. I am now at home on this second Sunday, September 8th, having a rest Sunday, writing up my journal. I discover that I omitted to mention some things at the proper time, and will now relate them. I preached the funeral of a babe of Mr. Russell, in Scott County, on one Sunday in June.

On August 15th, the day before I left home for my basket-meeting in Frost Bottom, I received a note from Mrs. Dr. Hungerford, stating that the doctor was very feeble and wished me to call on him. He had been stricken down with palsy for some time. He was my near-door neighbor in Sunbright. I visited him that afternoon, and found him quite penitent, almost believing unto salvation. I talked and prayed with him, until he was happily converted to God; and on my return home, after some time, September 12th, at his own request, I baptized him while he sat up in his bed, and received him into the Methodist Church. Brother Ogle, pastor of the Methodist Church at Sunbright, being present, administered the sacrament of the Lord's Supper to the people present, Methodists and Baptists communing together. Dr. Hungerford had been an able physician, and an avowed infidel prior to his afflictions. He had been brought up under Baptist influence, but when converted he desired to be a Methodist.

On Wednesday after the third Sunday in September, the Kingston District Conference convened in the new Methodist Church in Sunbright, and held over Sunday. On Sunday morning, at nine o'clock, I held the funeral service of a babe of Brother and Sister Ward, recently from Ohio. That day at eleven o'clock, Rev. T. C. Carter, D. D., of Chattanooga, preached an able sermon and dedicated our new church in Sunbright, raising by cash and subscription more than one hundred dollars to liquidate the entire indebtedness. This is the same church that I had toiled so hard to build two years ago. Dr. Carter is one of the able men of American Methodism. On the fifth Saturday in September I preached at Oliver Springs, and received six persons into our Church. On the following Sunday I preached at Jones Chapel, and baptized three persons by immersion, three persons by pouring, and an infant.

This closes up an eventful year's work on Oliver Springs Circuit, with the follow happy results: Sixty-nine conversions, forty-one accessions, twenty-eight infant baptisms, and three adult baptisms.

On October 8th I took the train at Sunbright and ran down the line to Dayton, Tenn., where our Conference was to convene the next day. I staid that night with my highly-esteemed old brother, W. H. Rogers, at Captain Gibson's. The Conference convened at the appointed hour in the new

Methodist church, Bishop Joyce presiding. I was assigned to stay at Dr. Williams', by whom I was treated with great kindness. Mrs. Williams is a daughter of my old friend Dr. Story, who also lives in Dayton. The Conference session was harmonious and attended with great spiritual power. On Friday night I preached at the Southern Methodist Church with happy results.

On account of my declining health, I did not take pastoral work, but was appointed financial agent for Sunbright Seminary. I did not do this from a lack of religious zeal, for I never felt more overwhelmingly endowed with the Holy Ghost upon leaving an Annual Conference, than I did on leaving this. I fully determined to go and to preach all that I could, and to offer Christ more earnestly than ever before.

The Conference closed on Monday afternoon. I took the train on Tuesday morning for Sunbright, and having been delayed nine hours on the road, by a wreck near Nemo, I reached home in the afternoon.

CHAPTER XVII.

MT. VERNON.

ON the third Sunday in October I preached in Crooktown, Scott County, then walked two miles and baptized an old man by pouring while he was kneeling in the water. That night I preached at Black Wolf Church, when quite a number of penitents came to the altar. One lady was converted and two persons joined our Church. This was a good Sabbath-day's work.

On Monday I took orders for books, and at night I went back to Crooktown, and made a prohibition speech, several persons signifying their purpose to stand by the cause. On Saturday night before the fourth Sunday in October I attended a temperance supper at Young's Chapel in Morgan County. The following day I preached at the same place, and afterward, while holding class-meeting, a young lady was converted. I baptized a babe and preached again in the afternoon, when four more persons were converted, and one joined our Church. I went back and preached again the next day. The Church got in good working order, and sinners were converted, but we closed.

The first Sunday in November I attended Brother Peters' meeting in Sunbright, and I held an educational meeting at night. This was my natural birthday, I being then sixty-three years old. God be praised for his mercies through an eventful life! The second Sunday in November I preached at Byrd's school-house, three miles from Sunbright, with good results. Embracing the third Sunday in November, I preached three days and nights at the old camp-ground in Scott County. The weather was very cold, and rain and snow fell all the time. A number of penitents were seeking salvation, and two young ladies were happily converted. One of them joined our Church. Before conversion they had been great enemies, and would not speak with each other, but after conversion they were great friends.

Embracing the fourth Sunday in November, I preached two days at Young's Chapel. The people of God shouted for joy, while penitents wept. I baptized a young lady at the altar. The first Sunday in December I attended preaching by the Southern Methodist pastor at Mt. Vernon. The second Sunday in December I preached at Byrd's school-house, but I was suffering greatly with cold and shortness of breath. The following Saturday I drove into Scott County, and delivered a number of books, and the following day preached at the old camp-ground to a good audience. On Monday I distributed books, and held a family meeting at Matthew Young's, and also baptized a young lady by pouring. The fourth Sunday in December I preached at Mt. Vernon with prospects of good, and on the fifth Sunday I preached at Rome to a good audience.

I now reach the close of the year 1889. Time speeds away, and how short the years do seem! My system is becoming more and more feeble. I find upon every attack of affliction of any kind, even a bad cold, that my system falls down a notch lower, not to rise until my body is raised immortal from the grave. I have now outlived the age of my fathers. Why my days are lengthened out, the good Lord knows. When I look back through the past year I see a great many suffering hours and days; but, thank God, I see a great many happy ones. During the time I have preached one hundred and forty-nine times, witnessed forty-four happy conversions, received twenty-four persons into the Church, baptized twenty-three adults and nineteen infants, have preached the funerals of nine persons, and married one couple. I am wearing the world about me as a loose garment. I have nothing to live for but to glorify God.

The first quarterly-meeting for Sunbright Station embraced the first Sunday of January. Rev. J. A. Ruble, the presiding elder, was in attendance, and preached for a week with great power. He insisted on my traveling the Mt. Vernon Circuit the present year, and I agreed to do so. I do not feel contented without preaching all that I am able to do; and so I enter at once upon the work, praying God to bless my labors with one hundred conversions during the year. I began the work at my first quarterly-meeting, held at Mt. Vernon, embracing the third Sunday of January, and continuing six days. Brother Ruble was present three days, and preached four times. The result of the meeting was twenty-one happy conversions to God, and seventeen accessions to our Church, while a number of penitents were left at the altar.

On Saturday night before the fourth Sunday in January, I preached at Young's Chapel with happy prospects of great good. On Sunday morning I preached in Rugby, where a number stood up for prayers. On Sunday night I preached again at Young's Chapel, with a number of penitents at the altar. The first day of February I set off for my furthest appointments, Banner Springs and Bruner's Chapel. After riding ten miles, a cold rain set in, and I took up at Brother Cherrie's. It continued to rain, and I went no further that day. The next morning I rode eight miles to Banner

Springs, aud preached to a good congregation in a neat and comfortable church. Five men came to the altar for prayers. In the afternoon I rode eight miles more, and preached at Bruner's Chapel. Here was a good congregation, penitents were at the altar, and the saints of God rejoiced. The next day I preached again at the same place, and licensed a young man to exhort. Several penitents were at the altar, and a lady united with our Church. That night I preached at Banner Springs to a crowded house. Five men and two ladies came to the altar for prayer, and one man was converted. The next day I rode home, passing through Deer Lodge, a prosperous, growing young town. I stopped awhile in the printing-office of the *Southern Enterprise*, and enjoyed a pleasant time with the editor.

The second Sunday in February I preached at Deer Lodge in the morning, and at Rome in the afternoon. On the third Sunday in the morning I preached at Mt. Vernon, when two young men joined the Church. In the afternoon I preached at Bethlehem, and received two persons into full connection. Several penitents were at the altar, and the Christians were greatly rejoiced. The fourth Sunday in February I was rained out from both my appointments at Young's Chapel and Rugby; but I was happy to learn that a man and his wife, who had been penitents at my meeting at Rugby four weeks before, were happily converted at their home.

On the last day of February I left home for my western appointments. I rode eight miles, and stopped for dinner with Brother Martin Watts. In the afternoon a cyclone of cold, sleety fog arose from the north, and I rode through it eight miles, when I was chilled almost through and through. I arrived at the home of Brother Cherrie, suffering greatly with the cold. I was to preach at Oak Grove, two miles from there, that night; but I had suffered so much during the day, and the night was so bitter cold that Brother Cherrie insisted that I should not go out, and sent his son John, a young man, to tell the people who came that I would preach there the next day. The weather continued very cold, but I preached the next day to a small congregation, and in the afternoon rode eight miles, suffering greatly from cold, and staid at Luke Hall's. The next day I preached at Banner Springs; but the weather was so cold that the congregation was not large. Five men came to the altar for prayer. I rode eight miles in the afternoon, and preached at night to a good congregation at Bruner's Chapel. I preached again the next day at the same place. Several penitents were at the altar, and I baptized three persons, and received them into full connection. In the afternoon I rode seven miles, and spent the night with Brother Francis Atkinson. The next day I rode home, passing through Deer Lodge.

On Saturday night before the second Sunday in March I held services at the family residence of Brother G. W. Kemper in Deer Lodge. He is a widower, and has no family but himself and two little girls, one twelve years old, and the other ten. That night he and his little girls joined our Church, also three other persons by letter and one on probation. I baptized the youngest daughter of

Brother Kemper and another lady, and organized our class in Deer Lodge that night. The next day I preached in a church in the town, and in the afternoon at Rome. On Saturday night before the third Sunday in March I preached at Mt. Vernon; but the weather was so cold that only a few were out. That was regarded as the coldest night of the winter. I stopped with Brother Henry F. Peters. I preached again the next day at Mt. Vernon in the morning, and in the afternoon at Bethlehem. My afternoon congregation was lessened on account of a funeral service near by, and because of the intense cold. The fourth Sunday I preached to two good congregations at Young's Chapel in the morning, and at Rugby in the afternoon. I spent the fifth Sunday at home, writing up my life journal.

My second quarterly-meeting was held at Bruner's Chapel, embracing the first Sunday in April, I left home on Thursday before, rode horseback to Deer Lodge, and stopped for dinner with William R. Ross. Mr. Ross is an intelligent, well-to-do Northern man, whose wife is a member of our Church. In the afternoon I took deeds for two church lots, one in Deer Lodge, and the other in Rosslyn. That night in Deer Lodge I held a meeting for the Christian Endeavor Society. The following day, Brother Watts, an exhorter of our Church, and myself set off for the quarterly-meeting, and, after riding twelve miles, I preached at night at Banner Springs. The night was very dark and rainy, and there were not many out. The following day we rode ten miles to Bruner's Chapel, where I preached to an attentive audience.

Brother Ruble was not present, and so all the duties of the occasion fell upon me. I preached in the afternoon of Saturday, and held the Quarterly Conference. We had a happy Conference session.

On Sunday morning, after a short Sunday-school, we had a good, old-fashioned Methodist love-feast, taking around the bread and water. Afterward quite a number of both men and women bore testimony for Jesus, giving soul-stirring Christian experiences. I preached again, and administered the sacrament of the Lord's Supper to a large number of communicants. I also took a public collection for the benefit of the presiding elder, and preached again at night. Some were seeking salvation at the altar, while a number of Christians shouted aloud for joy. This was Easter Sunday, and as was my custom on such a day, I preached on the resurrection of Christ. During the two days I preached four times, besides rendering other duties, and preaching on the way, and on Monday rode home twenty-five miles. For several days I felt quite indisposed from overwork.

The second Sunday in April I preached in the forenoon in Deer Lodge, and in the afternoon at Rome. On the third Sunday in April I preached in the forenoon at Mt. Vernon, and in the afternoon at Bethlehem. At the latter service a number of people were seeking salvation at the altar. The fourth Sunday in April was my time to preach at Young's Chapel and Rugby; but having been requested to attend the funeral of Dr. Hungerford in Sunbright on that day, I did not fill either appointment.

The first Sunday in May I preached at Banner Springs. The day was very rainy; but we had a good meeting, and a number of penitents were at the altar. In the afternoon I rode eight miles, and preached at Bruner's Chapel; also preached there again the next day. On the second Sunday, I preached in the forenoon at Deer Lodge, and in the afternoon at Rome. At Rome a brother united with our Church by letter. The third Sunday, I preached at Mount Vernon in the forenoon, and at Bethlehem in the afternoon. At both places there were seekers of salvation.

The reader of this journal will notice that I am not preaching on missions and taking collections during the month of May, as heretofore. The reason is, that the Mount Vernon charge, which is a mission field, is without an appropriation the present year, and the people are unwilling to contribute to missions. The presiding elders of the Conference form the Missionary Committee, and it is thought that they are not always wise and just in the appropriation. My own zeal for the cause has not abated, and I shall preach missionary sermons, and do my best for the collections before the year closes.

On Saturday before the fourth Sunday in May I preached at Young's Chapel. The next day I rode four miles to Rugby, and preached in the morning, and rode back in the afternoon to Young's Chapel and preached again; then rode home six miles, making a ride of fourteen miles, and preaching twice during the day. I was very tired at night, but slept well and rested.

On Saturday, the last day of May, I left home

for my appointments at Banner Springs and Bruner's Chapel. I reached Banner Springs in the afternoon of that day, and preached to a good congregation. The next morning I drove ten miles to where Rev. R. Pierce, a presiding elder in the Central Tennessee Conference, was holding a quarterly-meeting, my appointment at Bruner's Chapel having been consolidated with this. After Rev. Pierce had preached, I administered the sacrament of the Lord's Supper. I went back two miles to Harve Peters' for dinner, and drove eight miles more in the afternoon to Banner Springs, and preached to a good congregation. I called for penitents, when twelve persons came to the altar for prayer. After laboring with them for a time, I closed; drove two miles more, and staid for the night with F. M. Atkinson. The next day I drove home. Mrs. Craft, a widowed lady from Tustin City, California, accompanied me to these appointments, and did good work in talking to and praying for penitents, and looking after the education of some girls who expect to attend college next year. My prayers and best wishes will follow this Christian lady back to her distant home in California.

On Friday evening before the second Sunday in June I preached at Deer Lodge, and the next morning rode nine miles to Potter's Chapel, to hold a quarterly-meeting for Rev. J. A. Ruble, for Oakdale Circuit, J. M. York being the preacher in charge. I preached twice on Saturday, and held the Quarterly Conference. On Sunday morning I preached, administered the sacrament of the Lord's Supper, and took a public collection for the benefit

of the presiding elder. In the afternoon I rode to
Rome to fill my own appointment; but becoming
lost on the way, I was delayed, and the congregation was dispersed before I reached the church. I
took supper with Brother Kincaid, late from Ohio,
who lives near the Church, and rode home eight miles
afterwards. This day's work was a heavy task on
my system.

The third Sunday in June I held Children's-day
services at Bethlehem in the morning, and at Mount
Vernon in the afternoon, and took an educational
collection at each place. The fourth Sunday in
June I preached missionary sermons—in the morning at Young's Chapel, and in the afternoon at
Rugby—and took a missionary collection at each
place. On Saturday before the fifth Sunday in
June I drove nineteen miles to Banner Springs, and
preached in the afternoon. The following day I
preached in the morning at Bruner's Chapel, and in
the afternoon at Banner Springs, and took a missionary collection at each place, making a drive of
sixteen miles, and preaching twice on this day.

My third quarterly-meeting was held at Rome,
embracing the first Sunday in July. Brother Ruble
was present, and preached. On account of some
misunderstanding in my appointment at Little Crab,
I staid at home on the second Sunday. My son,
Rev. J. C. Wright, preached in Sunbright on that
day. On Friday before the third Sunday, I left
home for a funeral appointment on the Three Forks
of Wolf River. I went the first day eighteen miles
to Brother Stockton's, near Jamestown. The next
morning I rode into town, and found the Southern

Methodists engaged in a Sunday-school Conference.
I went in, was introduced, and called out in several
speeches. In the afternoon I rode down to the head
of Wolf River to William Pyle's, an old friend and
neighbor, and spent the night. The next morning
I rode to my appointment at a new Methodist
church, in less than one hundred yards of where I
joined the Church, met a congregation of about five
hundred people, and preached the funeral of John
Coile. I preached again that afternoon at the same
place, and baptized six young ladies at the altar for
Brother Creel, the pastor. The next day, Brother
Creel and I rode to his home at Allardt, and staid
over night. The following day I went back to
Brother Stockton's, and preached to a small congregation at his house. The power of the Lord was
present. Four young ladies were earnest seekers of
salvation at the altar. I rode home the next day.

My first basket-meeting was held at Young's
Chapel, embracing the fourth Sunday in July, and
continuing five days. There were four conversions
and one accession to the Church. I also baptized a
young lady, and received four persons into full
connection.

My second basket-meeting was held at Banner
Springs, embracing the first Sunday in August. It
continued nine days, and resulted in twenty-four
conversions and fifteen accessions to our Church.
I baptized two young men and six young ladies at
the altar, and preached four funeral sermons during
the meeting.

On Saturday before the third Sunday in August,
in company with John Davis, my brother-in-law, I

boarded the early morning train at Sunbright, and went down the line to Harriman Junction. We walked out over the new city of Harriman, saw the great progress being made in building up a new town, formed some acquaintances, and met a number of my old friends, whom I had served as pastor in other years. We rode in a wagon three miles up the valley to Brother Ed. Roberts'. We found this excellent family greatly afflicted with malarial fever, Brother Roberts himself and five of his children having been stricken down with this dreaded disease. However, they are all convalescent. We took dinner, and having prayed with the family, we walked out to Webster, where we found Mrs. Wood, a merchant's wife, and Fillmore McCartt, his clerk, both prostrated with fever, though somewhat improving. We staid over night at Mr. Buckheart's, whose wife is in the last stages of consumption. The next morning we boarded the train, and ran up the line three miles to Oakdale Iron Works. We took supper at the home of Buck Taylor, a section boss, who is very low with fever. We preached in the church that night, after which we staid with I. W. Legg.

The next morning being Sunday, I preached the funeral of Levi Morgan, from Isaiah lx, 19, 20. A number of penitents were at the altar, and a young lady was happily converted. I preached again at the same place in the afternoon. We boarded the night train, and ran down the line to Harriman, where we staid over night at Howard Carter's. The next morning we ran up the line to Sunbright. God be praised for a busy life! My third basket-meeting was held at Mt. Vernon, embracing the fourth Sunday in August. It continued for ten days. The power of the Lord was present to save. Forty-six souls were powerfully converted, twenty persons joined the Church, and the membership was gloriously revived. Rev. Martin Watts held charge during the last three days, as I had to fill other engagements. I left the meeting on Friday afternoon, and drove fourteen miles to Banner Springs, and preached at night. A young man was a penitent at the altar, and there was one accession to our Church. I staid that night with Brothers Ramsey and Wright. I felt greatly wornout from excessive labor. The next morning I drove two miles to Clear Fork, and baptized five persons, two men by pouring, and three ladies by immersion. Having passed through heavy labor, and having lost a great deal of sleep by being up late at night, and having been in the water a great deal of late baptizing people, I was greatly indisposed. In the afternoon I drove nine miles to Bruner's Chapel, and preached to a good congregation.

Brother Carter, of the Central Tennessee Conference, and I had arranged to hold this meeting together. He arrived on Saturday afternoon. We preached alternately until Wednesday afternoon, when I left. Up to that time there had been two conversions and two accessions to our Church. Brother Carter continued the meeting until Thursday afternoon, when there were four more conversions, making six in all. My fifth basket-meeting was held at Bethlehem Church, embracing the first Sunday in September. I left the meeting on Wednes-

day afternoon in charge of Brother Watts, who
continued it two days longer. There were six conversions and seven accessions to the Church. My
sixth basket-meeting was held at Rome, embracing
the second Sunday in September. The people were
busy with their fodder, and sinners were very ob-
stinate, and so I held meeting only two days.

On the third Sunday in September I had an
appointment to preach a funeral at Cedar Grove,
Fentress County, about twelve miles below Jamestown, in a very broken country; but I was so
prostrated from labor that I felt unable to make
this trip, and so canceled the engagement. I occupied this time in a protracted service at Deer
Lodge. I preached on Saturday night and on
Sunday morning. Brother Mosier preached in the
afternoon, and I preached again at night. The congregations were large and attentive, but the Christian people were dead to all work, and sinners were
unmoved. I took up Monday in visiting, and
preached again at night, without any visible results.
At this place the different denominations are not in
good fraternal spirit with each other, and are, therefore, in poor condition for a revival.

My fourth quarterly-meeting was appointed for
Young's Chapel; but on account of the measles
prevailing in that settlement, it was moved to Mt.
Vernon. It embraced the fourth Sunday in September. Brother Ruble was present and preached.
We had a very interesting quarterly-meeting occasion. This closes another Conference year. During the year I have witnessed one hundred and
fourteen conversions, received eighty persons into

the Church, and baptized thirty-five adults and nine infants. To God's name be all the glory.

I am now feeling the infirmities of age, though during the past year I have been free from sciatica, and have enjoyed as good health as I could expect for one of my age. The good Lord has been very kind to me, and has given me many sheaves to my ministry. I am close on to sixty-four years of age. I have been a professed Christian and a member of the Methodist Church for more than forty-seven years. I have been a Methodist preacher for more than forty-two years; but if I had life to go over again, I would travel the same road. God be praised that life's toiling pathway is to be traveled but once. O may mine end in glory!

During the Conference year I have read 6,138 pages in a course of study. I spent the first Sunday in October at home in praying and in writing up my journal. On Saturday before the second Sunday in October I left home, and rode horseback thirteen miles to Henry Branstetter's, where I staid over night. The next day, at his residence, I preached the funeral of his father, Levi Branstetter, from Rev. xx, 12. A number of anxious penitents were at the altar.

Our Annual Conference met in Greeneville, Tennessee, October 8th, with Bishop Walden to preside. I did not feel inclined to attend, as there was a most unpleasant feeling existing between some of the leading ministers of the Conference. The characters of some of these were to be arrested and tried, under what I have always believed to be false charges. The unholy ambition for leader-

ship was the great sin of these brethren—the same
trouble that disturbed the disciples when they con-
tended who should be the greatest in the kingdom of
heaven, and also the same sin that caused Satan to
fall from heaven. May these brethren learn les-
sons of wisdom and grace from God's Word! I
am unwilling to hear the discordant notes of these
troubles. I want my life to be full of sunshine
instead of clouds.

Brother Ruble had asked me to take charge of
Mt. Vernon Circuit another year, and I had written
him a letter stating that I would do so. I had only
had charge about eight months of the past year, and
we had such glorious success that a number of people desired my return. I felt that I would like to
go back another year. However, at Conference they
cut up the Mt. Vernon Circuit, and divided it out
among three other charges, and put young men in
charge. So I was left without any pastoral work
at all. I was appointed financial agent of Sunbright
Seminary, which is only a nominal appointment.
As I have been in the pastoral work so long, I feel
quite blank to be left without work. I much pre-
fer to be in pastoral work while the good Lord
sheds his smiling approbation upon my labors as he
did the past year. I know I am getting old; but
there are men much older than I in the effective
work. I have prayed and wept over it, and must
make the most of my position that I can.

After Conference, Brother Ruble wished me to
take charge of the Jamestown Circuit, a very large
and broken work, that required much more labor
than one of my age could do, and so I declined it.

I am praying the Lord that I may see one hundred conversions this year, to be added to some Church or other, though I shall have to go under my own direction. I want to sell a great many good books during the year.

I think a great many of our old men, while God is crowning their labors with the greatest results, are pushed out of work to make place for untried and inefficient foreigners, who remain only a few years, and then pass away. It is some consolation to know that, while men may err, God can not err in dispensing rewards to the worthy. I expect to take winter quarters at home during the coldest part of the winter; but I must not lose any zeal for the Lord's cause.

CHAPTER XVIII.

NEW RIVER.

ON the third Sunday in October I attended Church at Mt. Vernon, and heard Rev. Creels, their new pastor, preach. In the afternoon I rode six miles to Bethlehem Church, and preached at night. Several came forward and gave their hands as seekers of salvation, and two persons united with our Church. On the fourth Sunday I attended Brother Creels' first appointment in Sunbright.

The first Sunday in November, being the day before my birthday, my youngest son came up from Rockwood to visit me; also my daughter from Mt. Vernon came, and we had a kind of family reunion, and so I remained at home. The second Sunday I rode six miles to Mill Creek, and preached to an attentive audience. I preached again at night at the same place. On Monday I took orders for books, rode over into Scott County, and preached at the camp-ground at night. Several came forward for prayers. The third Sunday I attended Sunday-school and class-meeting in Sunbright. On the fourth Sunday I held the funeral services of a little boy of G. W. Kempton, at Huffman's Switch. On Saturday before the fifth Sunday, I left home on horseback for Taylor's Chapel, two miles from Allardt. In the afternoon I arrived at the home of Hon. J. C. Taylor, and preached at the chapel at night. Rev. W. L. Patton was pastor of the Methodist Episcopal Church, South, at this place. I preached on Sunday and Sunday night. A number of penitents came to the altar, and two persons were converted, while the saints of God shouted for joy. I remained over Monday, preaching, laboring with penitents, and taking a number of book orders, the interest increasing all the while.

On Tuesday morning I left the meeting in the hands of Brother Patton, and returned home. The services went on until Thursday, resulting in nine conversions and four accessions to the Methodist Episcopal Church, South. Others will yet join. The reader will note that, as I am not in pastoral work, I am doing independent labor to build up any good Church. I pray God that I may see one hundred conversions this Conference year. I love my Church as well as any man should love his Church; but as I am left without pastoral work this year, I do not know that I shall take any members

into the Church, but shall work earnestly for conversions, and let them join where they wish. I
must say that my true friends at Taylor's Chapel—
members of the Methodist Episcopal Church,
South—paid me liberally for my services at that
place.

The first Sunday in December was a very cold,
rainy day, and so I remained at home, read, prayed,
and wrote up my journal. On the second Sunday
I attended pastoral preaching in Sunbright with my
wife. On the third Sunday I had intended to go to
the camp-ground in Scott County; but having been
disappointed in obtaining a lot of books for distribution in that neighborhood, I did not go, but remained at home.

I am somewhat disturbed in mind with the conviction that I am not preaching as much as I ought
to do in bringing lost souls to Christ. I presume
it is a feeling common to all old men, when laid
on the shelf from itinerant work. It seems to me
that, since a number of much older men than I are
in pastoral work, I might have been in charge a
little longer. The position to which I was appointed is nominal, and amounts to nothing. It is
not a question of salary; for my two younger sons
are single men, and are making money fast, and
supply all my needs; but it is strictly a question
of religious duty that disturbs me. After taking
winter quarters at home, if the good Lord will
bear with me, I want to break out afresh in the
spring, like the spring bird in his early song. I
must be content to know that I am becoming old,
and can not do so much for the Lord's cause as once

I did. Perhaps my zeal is running ahead of my strength. I now begin to realize that what further work I do for the Lord in this world I must do quickly, or not at all. In the end of life I want the approbation of "Well done, thou good and faithful servant; enter thou into the joy of thy Lord."

I had an appointment to preach at Mt. Vernon on Christmas, but the day was so rainy and cold that I did not go. I am so troubled with asthma that I have to avoid exposure in bad weather. The fourth Sunday I remained at home. After a long life of abundant labors, I feel very restless without employment.

I am now at the close of another year. Farewell to the year 1890! I am now sixty-four years old, and have outlived nearly all the companions of my younger life. The Lord has been very good to me. Blessed be his holy name! O how fast time speeds away! The years do not seem half so long as once they did. I know that I shall soon leave this world. Shall I live to see the close of 1891? God only knows. I am not anxious about that; but I want to die in the ranks, and fall on the field of battle.

During the year 1890 I have preached a great many sermons, witnessed a large number of happy conversions, and have baptized and received a great many into the Church. I was in charge of a circuit a little more than eight months. To God be all the glory!

I now enter the year 1891, the first year of the last decade of the century, with a system running down-grade in strength.

"Shrinking from the cold hand of death,
  I soon shall gather up my feet—
Shall soon resign this fleeting breath,
  And I my fathers' God to meet.

Numbered among thy people, I
  Expect with joy thy face to see;
Because thou didst for sinners die,
  Jesus in death remember me.

O that without a lingering groan,
  I may the welcome word receive,
My body with my charge lay down,
  And cease at once to work and live!

Walk with me through the dreadful shade,
  And, certified that thou art mine,
My spirit, calm and undismayed,
  I shall into thy hands resign."

The Lord help me to be faithful to him this
year, if I should live through it, that I may walk
worthy of my high vocation in Christ Jesus! I
have trials of which no one outside of my family
knows—great trials; but I ask God for great grace
to endure as seeing Him who is invisible. O for
grace to resist the evil and cleave to the good!

Embracing the first Sunday in January, the first
quarterly-meeting for Sunbright Circuit was held in
Sunbright. On Sunday I assisted Brother Ruble
in the communion service. The second Saturday
and Sunday in January I preached each day at Mill
Creek Church, six miles from Sunbright. We had
a very interesting worship each time. I staid on
Saturday night with my dear old friend and brother,
Jesse B. Ketcherside, who is nearly one year older
than myself; but he wears a great deal of the cheer
and courage of youth. We make it just as heav-

enly as we can when we get together. It is a great
feast to my soul to meet and spend some time with
my old Christian comrades. I had an appointment
to preach on Saturday night before the third Sunday in January at Taylor's Chapel, in Fentress
County. I left home on Saturday morning in my
buggy in a slow rain. The rain increased as I traveled, and afterwards turned to a heavy snow; and
so, when I got near Mt. Vernon Church, I took
up at Dennis Hull's for awhile, and took dinner.
In the afternoon I drove thirteen miles through
some snow, it turning very cold in the latter part
of the day; and just before night I reached J. C.
Taylor's. I preached at night in the chapel near
by, and also on the next day, with happy results.
I baptized two young people, and afterward Brother
Patton, the pastor, received them into the Church.
In the afternoon I rode out seven miles to Brother
Stockton's, and remained over night. The follow-
ing day I came back to Brother Field's for dinner.
On Sunday afternoon and Monday morning I suf-
fered greatly from the severe cold weather. On
Monday afternoon I drove home.

For some time I have been very busy taking
orders and delivering books. I have sold a great
many valuable books. I never sell any book of
doubtful moral teaching. The Lord help me to be
useful in some way! On the fourth Sunday I attended pastoral preaching in Sunbright. The day
before, I preached for the Baptists at Pilot Mountain, at the request of their pastor.

On the first Sunday in February, by request of
some excellent people of Crooktown, in Scott

County, I preached the funeral of Rebecca Davidson Birch, a lady who had emigrated from England
to America a few years ago. She was a good Christian woman. I attended the prayer-meeting in the
afternoon, and preached again at night, with happy
prospects of a revival of religion.

The second Sunday in February I attended pastoral preaching in Sunbright. The third Sunday
in February was very rainy, so I staid at home
that day. In the afternoon of the following Monday I preached the funeral sermon of a little boy
of William R. Staples, in Sunbright. The next
day I went to Crooktown, in Scott County, and
preached at night. The people insisted that I
should protract the meeting, but as their pastor was
absent I thought it the better not to do so. The
fourth Sunday I attended meeting in Sunbright.
O I do feel so much out of place when not in pastoral work!

The first Sunday in March being a very cold,
wintry day, I remained at home until in the afternoon, when I went down the railroad to Lansing to see a sick son. The second Sunday
there was a wonderful tide on the waters, so I remained at home. The third Sunday I left home in
my buggy, drove nine miles to the camp-ground
in Scott County, where I preached for the pastor,
W. D. Gorman. We took dinner at Brother Baker's together, and drove two miles to Crooktown
in the afternoon, where I preached for him again at
night. The fourth Sunday I preached in Sunbright
for the pastor, who was conducting a successful protracted meeting at Young's Chapel.

On Friday before the fifth Sunday I left home on horseback to hold for Brother Ruble the second quarterly-meeting on the Jamestown Circuit, at Banner Springs. I rode ten miles and remained over night with Brother Cherrie. The next day he and his family accompanied me eight miles to the quarterly-meeting. We reached the place in due time, and I preached to a good audience. Rev. J. M. York is their pastor. He is a young man, a good preacher, and well received by the people. This is his first year as an itinerant. We held all the services common on a quarterly-meeting occasion, except the sacrament of the Lord's Supper, which was omitted because the elements were not prepared. During the two days I preached three times and labored with penitents at the altar. Two persons joined our Church by letter from the Baptist Church.

The first Sunday in April I attended Sunday-school in Sunbright. The second Sunday I rode out ten miles, and preached morning and afternoon at Bethlehem Church. At each service penitents came forward for prayers. The third Sunday I boarded the train and ran up the line six miles to Glen Mary. I attended Sunday-school there, and heard the pastor of the Congregational Church, Rev. Marsh, preach. Rev. Stanley Pope, a Congregational minister from Harriman, then organized a Congregational Church at that place. The basis upon which it was built was so different from that of the Methodist Church that it looked very meager to me. I walked out to Crooktown and met the Methodist pastor, Brother Gorman. Rev. Mosier, of Sunbright, preached there that afternoon, and I preached again at night at the same place.

The fourth Sunday I was to go down the line and preach, but on Saturday morning I was taken down with a congestive chill, which lasted five hours, and was followed with high fever and great suffering I was so prostrated that I was confined to my home the next day. Rev. W. D. Gorman, pastor of New River Circuit, was wanting me to take charge of his work, insisting that the people on the charge desired it, and, without seeing the presiding elder, I agreed to fill a round on the work.

On the first Sunday in May I boarded the train, ran up the line twenty-eight miles to Winfield, and met and preached to a fair congregation, though they were not looking for me until I arrived. We had a good meeting. After dinner I visited several families, and prayed with them. I ran down the line six miles to Oneida, and preached at night. The next day I visited among the people, but O what a lifeless state of religion I find at this place! It has declined so much in interest since I left it four years ago.

The second Sunday in May I boarded the train and ran up the line eighteen miles to Helenwood, where I met and preached to a good audience. I visited several families in the afternoon, and again took the train and ran down the line five miles to New River, where I met and preached to a fair audience; however, they were late in gathering. At the two last-named places they were looking for me, but O how lifeless the state of religion seems at all these places! The Lord pity and replenish Zion!

During the coming week I was severely attacked with a heavy cold, or, as others call it, la grippe, which produced severe coughing, with great hoarseness, so that I could scarcely talk or go. However, I set off on horseback on the third Sunday, rode nine miles to the camp-ground, and preached. Several came forward for prayers. I went one mile for dinner, but had to lie on the bed part of the time. In the afternoon I visited and prayed in some families, rode two miles further, and preached at night in Crooktown.

The fourth Sunday I drove in my buggy nine miles, and preached at Black Wolf Church, both morning and afternoon, with some indications for good. I have scarcely ever found a work so dead religiously as New River Circuit seems to be; but, God helping us, we will weep between the porch and the altar, until the good Lord rains salvation down.

On the fifth Sunday I ran up the line to Glen Mary, walked out to Crooktown, attended prayer-meeting in the afternoon, and preached at night.

On Saturday before the first Sunday in June I took the train, and ran up the line to Winfield, where I spent the day in visiting from house to house. I preached there the next morning, and came down to Oneida in the afternoon; but it stormed and rained so hard that I did not preach there at night. The second Sunday in June I ran up the line, and preached at Helenwood in the morning and at New River at night, taking collections at both places for the Freedmen's Aid and Southern Education Society of our Church.

On Saturday before the third Sunday I left

home on horseback, rode nine miles, and preached in the afternoon at Young's school-house. The next day being Sunday, I preached at the same place in the morning, and at night I preached in Crooktown. The fourth Sunday I rode horseback nine miles, and preached at Black Wolf Church in the morning. Several penitents were forward for prayers, and two persons united with our Church from the Baptist Church. I rode three miles and preached that afternoon at Rugby Road. The third quarterly-meeting for the charge was held at Helenwood, embracing the first Sunday in July. This was the first quarterly-meeting held since my taking charge of the work. Saturday, the first day of the meeting, was the fourth day of July, and there was a great stir of the people in celebrating the day. Brother Ruble was present, and preached at all the services with the power of the Holy Ghost sent down from heaven. A number came forward as seekers of salvation. In the afternoon of Sunday I ran down to New River, and preached at night. After I had preached, a number came forward for prayers. Brother Ruble remained at Helenwood, and preached at the same time. I occupied Monday in visiting and praying with a number of families at New River. That day, in stepping into a dry-goods store where an excellent young lady was clerking, and in talking to her in the interest of her soul's salvation, I found that she was deeply penitent. I knelt down on one side of the counter and she on the other side, and I prayed for her while she wept and prayed.

The second Sunday in July, I preached at Byrd's

school-house, three miles from Sunbright. Several penitents were at the altar, and one young lady was happily converted to God. Two young ladies united with the Church, and I baptized one of them at the altar. On the following Wednesday, at the request of Rev. W. L. Patton, pastor of the Methodist Episcopal Church, South, I baptized for him two infants and seven adults—five by pouring, and two by immersion. This brings me to the beginning of my basket and protracted meetings, the reports of which will come next on my journal.

On Saturday before the third Sunday I began my first basket-meeting at Young's school-house in Scott County. The meeting continued nine days, reaching over the fourth Sunday, and resulted in ten conversions and five accessions to the Church, with the membership greatly revived.

Embracing the first Sunday in August, I held a meeting of three days and nights in Crooktown. Our white congregation there seems very hard to move. On Sunday afternoon I preached for the colored congregation. They had a happy, shouting time, and several were forward for prayers. Embracing the second Sunday, I held, at New River, preaching of nights, beginning on Saturday night and closing on Wednesday night. One lady was happily converted, and united with our Church. The Church in that place is in a lifeless state. The Lord pity them!

Embracing the third Sunday, I held at Black Wolf Church. I held there nine days and nights, over the next Sabbath. Up to that time there had been six happy conversions and two accessions to our Church. I took sick, and had to leave the meeting on Sunday afternoon; but left it in the hands of Rev. W. D. Gorman, a former pastor, and Rev. A. L. Williams. After I had gone, during the next six days and nights, there were twenty-five more conversions, making, during the meeting, thirty-one conversions and seventeen accessions to the Church. The good seed for a glorious harvest had been sown before I left, and the altar was being filled with anxious penitents. I suffered greatly during those six days with catarrh of my head and lungs. I could scarcely eat, sleep, or rest. The next Sunday, in a feeble state of body, I drove back in my buggy to the meeting, and preached for them. This service closed a meeting of sixteen days.

On the last Sunday of the meeting the stewards of the Church raised a good public collection of money, and gave it all over to Brother Gorman. I was the pastor of the Church, and had labored faithfully for the people with scarcely any remuneration. I mention this to show that the right things are not always done even by the Churches. I had no objection to giving Brother Gorman money, but a Church should meet its obligations before it makes gifts. The good Lord will make it all right in that day when we stand before the great white throne. I was compelled, on account of poor health, to take a rest of two weeks before engaging in another protracted meeting. The first Sunday in September I remained at home, quite unwell. Embracing the second Sunday, I held a meeting of several days at Helenwood. Rev. W. L. Patton assisted me. We had a good meeting.

My fourth quarterly-meeting was held at Crooktown, embracing the third Sunday. My son being very sick, I could not remain, but left the meeting in the hands of Brother Gorman, who continued the services after the presiding elder had gone. The meeting resulted in a glorious revival of thirteen conversions and the same number of accessions to the Church.

The fourth Saturday and Sunday in September I held a meeting in Oneida, with good results. The first Saturday and Sunday in October I held a meeting at Young's school-house, preaching on Sunday night in Crooktown. This closed my work on the circuit.

On the second Sunday in October I preached in Sunbright, and on the third Sunday I preached at Potter's Chapel, fifteen miles from Sunbright, the funeral of Catharine Davis, from John xi, 25, 26. I preached at the same place again at night. Some men came forward for prayers, while the people of God shouted for joy. On Tuesday evening after the third Sunday, in company with Rev. J. M. York, I boarded the train at Sunbright, and set off for our Annual Conference at Chattanooga. That evening we ran down the line twenty-three miles to Oakdale, and staid over night at Robert Harmon's. Soon after our arrival I was informed that the people expected me to preach that night at their small Sunday-school room, which I did with flattering prospects of much good.

The next morning we took the early accommodation train, and ran down the line eighty-four miles, arriving at Chattanooga soon after Conference

had convened.   I was assigned my boarding place
at the Merchants' Hotel, run by A. L. Ross.   The
Annual Conference was one of great spiritual power.
Dr. S. A. Keen, an evangelist from Cincinnati, held
a few pentecostal meetings in the First Presbyterian Church.   A number of the ministers of the
Conference professed the higher life of entire sanctification.   By the grace of God I was one of the
happy number.   I pray God that I may ever be a
faithful witness of this blessed experience the remainder of my life on earth.   The Conference was
presided over by Bishop Ninde, and was one that
settled some very grave troubles that had existed
for some time between belligerent brethren.   Glory
be to God!   We elected Drs. Carter and Spence
delegates to the General Conference, to meet at
Omaha.

At this Conference I was granted a superannuated relation, which makes me feel sad of heart
to think that I am not able to do effectual service
for the blessed Christ.   I am fully resolved, however, God sparing my life, to hold as many protracted meetings as I can, and see souls happily
saved to him.

While in Chattanooga I visited the cyclorama
of the great battle of Atlanta, Ga., fought in the
year 1864.   I also went up on Lookout Mountain
by the incline railroad, and took a view of its wonderful scenery.   The hotel on top of the mountain
is several hundred feet above the Tennessee River,
just below it.   I visited a number of places of interest on the mountain.   On Sunday morning of
the Conference, Bishop Ninde preached an able

sermon to a large audience from Isa. lii, 1. On Tuesday morning I ran up the railroad line one hundred and eight miles to Sunbright.

CHAPTER XIX.

A SUPERANNUATE.

ON the last day of October I left home for a ride on horseback of twenty-five miles to J. C. Taylor's, near Allardt. I reached Brother Taylor's just before night, and the next morning, in company with him and others, I rode nine miles down into the Buffalo Cove, in Fentress County, the county of my birth and raising, it being the first Sunday in November. We met a congregation of about five hundred people, and in a beautiful grove I preached the funeral of O. P. Cooper, the old county trustee, from Hebrews ix, 27, 28. A number of ministers, both Methodists and Baptists, were present. At the close of the sermon several persons came forward and gave their hand as seekers of salvation, and quite a number of God's people shouted aloud for joy. I preached again at night at the home of the widow of Mr. Cooper, and several persons came to the altar for prayer, and God's people rejoiced together in his praise.

I returned home, and on the second Sunday rode horseback twelve miles down the railroad line and preached the funerals of two sainted children of Isaac and Sarah Jane Jones, from Jeremiah ix, 21. On Friday afternoon before the third Sunday myself and wife boarded the train at Sunbright and ran down the line to Rockwood, where our youngest son lives. We remained over night at J. H. Tate's, the principal clerk in the company store of the Roane Iron Company. Our son boards at Mr. Tate's. The next day I went to the Baptist Church in Rockwood and heard Dr. Anderson, an able minister of Nashville, Tenn., preach.

After taking dinner at Dr. Gaines', I took the local freight-train and ran up to Emory Gap, where I met and preached to a good congregation. The next day being Sunday, I preached again at the same place, to a large congregation, the funeral of Mary Ann Bane, from Rev. xx, 12. I preached again at night, when two young ladies were powerfully converted, and the people of God shouted his praise. I preached again on Monday at the same place. There were seekers of salvation. In the afternoon I ran down to Rockwood, and the next morning my wife and I ran up the line home to Sunbright. The fourth Sunday I attended pastoral preaching in Sunbright at the Methodist Church.

On Friday afternoon before the fifth Sunday I set off horseback, rode eight miles, and remained over night with Henry Peters. The next morning I rode twelve miles to a new church just erected in five miles of Jamestown, that we named Pleasant Vale, where I met a congregation and preached to them twice on that day with prospect of much good. I preached again twice on Sunday, when a number of penitents came to the altar for prayers.

On Monday I preached twice again when ten souls, five men and five ladies, were happily con-

verted to God. Five persons united with our
Church. The people brought provisions to the
meetings each day, and we remained on the ground
all day. I staid each night at Brother B. R. Stockton's, who lives two miles from the church. They are
most excellent people, and well-to-do in this world.
It was my good fortune to see both the parents
converted and to receive them into the Church years
ago. I celebrated the rites of matrimony between
them, and have baptized all their children in infancy, seven or eight in number. God be praised
for his goodness to this family!

I organized a Sunday-school and prayer-meeting for them, and rode home on Tuesday. I feel
very clearly the seeds of death sown in my system by
this distressing and increasing asthma, that makes
me suffer so often almost sleepless nights, but the
Lord sustains me. The first Sunday in December
being feeble in health, after a restless night with
asthma, I remained at home and wrote up my journal.
The second Sunday I attended the Baptist Church
in Sunbright. The pastor, Rev. B. L. Summers, invited me to preach, but I declined. He preached,
and I followed with an exhortation. There was a
good fraternal spirit manifest in the congregation.

The third Sunday I preached a sermon on holiness at Mt. Vernon, and there was a shout in the
camps of Israel. This brings me to my sixty-fifth
Christmas, it being on Friday after the third Sunday. I am nearing the close of another eventful
year. The fourth Sunday I preached at Sunbright,
in the Methodist Church, in the place of the pastor. In the afternoon of the following Tuesday I

ran down the railroad line to Emory Gap, and after a walk through the mud to the academy, I met and preached to a good congregation. The following day I preached in the morning, and at night at the same place. The power of the Lord was present upon the people.

On Thursday morning, being the last day of the old year, I ran up home to Sunbright. And now I bid farewell to the year 1891. In retrospecting the year, I find that it has been one of a great deal more sunshine than shadow, although I have suffered some with afflictions. The good Lord has been with me in great blessing. Twice in my life I had felt the sweet breezes of perfect love; but failing to bear testimony to it as I should, I did not retain the evidence; but, God be praised, at Dr. Keen's pentecostal meetings held in Chattanooga on October 23, 1891, I received such a wonderful baptism of the Holy Ghost that I realized fully what it is to be made perfect in love, and before the meeting closed I made a public profession of the blessing of entire sanctification. Since that time the Lord has sweetly kept me. I had said at the altar when received into full connection in the Conference, that I expected to be made perfect in this life, and I now realize what I was then seeking after. I would now exhort everybody to seek the sweet blessing of entire sanctification.

I am now sixty-five years old. I have lived much longer than I had calculated when I was a young man; however, I would not recall a single day of my life if I could. I feel that the evening of life is the sweetest part of my life. God be praised!

"Hail, blest old age, when life well spent is crowned,
With years and honors, loved, revered, renowned,
Earth's noblest state, where all ripe virtues blend,
And life's best hopes in rich fruition end."

During the year 1891 I preached one hundred
and nine times, witnessed sixty conversions, baptized thirteen adults and ten infants, preached the
funerals of nine persons, and received a number
into the Church. I now enter upon the year 1892,
with a system somewhat more enfeebled than in former years, earnestly praying the good Lord that, if
I should live through the year, I may witness
many precious souls happily converted to him. The
first Sunday in January I had an appointment to
preach at Pleasant Vale, about twenty miles from
Sunbright; but on account of the very bitter cold
winter weather I did not go. In view of my age I
can not now endure so much severe weather as once
I did, and being sorely afflicted with asthma, I am
compelled to take winter quarters. If the good Lord
spares me until spring and warm weather, I want
to go as an evangelist, and witness more good, the
Lord sending salvation down, than at any time before of my life. The first Sunday being so cold, I
remained shut in at home, writing up my journal, reading, and praying. I praise God that I
have the sweetest peace in my soul of the Divine
presence.

Beginning with the second Sunday, for about
ten days we have had the most severe winter
weather, so that, as I am afflicted with asthma, I
have had to stay indoors at home. I do not cal-
culate that I shall preach much through January

and February; but, the Lord helping me, I expect
to make the time all up when the spring opens. As
I am now a superannuated preacher, and standing
upon the last hilltop of life, I will take a review
of my life's work, which I can now look at with a
great deal of pleasure.

I was born just thirty years after Tennessee became a State, and before there were any railroads
or telegraph lines. The section in which my parents lived was comparatively a new country. The
mode of living was primitive. The people of the
rural parts lived in log houses. A cook-stove was
an unknown luxury. The people cut their small
grain with a reap-hook, and thrashed it by tramp-
ing it out with horses. Wild animals were abundant. Many a night have I heard the wolves howl
about our home. Deer were plentiful, and wild
bears were not unusual. Wild turkeys were to be
found in large flocks. There were no public schools
in Tennessee when I was born. I remember when
the first public schools were taught. The people
used the products of their own hands both for food
and for clothing, there being very few manufac-
tured goods of any kind. The Methodist Church
was then made up of large circuits. There were no
city stations, nor easy places. A Methodist preacher's
life was one of toil and personal sacrifice. It took
the best preachers in the Church to receive a salary
of more than one hundred dollars per year, and
yet consecrated men were not lacking to do the
work.

A great change has come to this country since
then. While I linger with happy memory of those

good old days, yet I rejoice at the great progress that the country has made. My life has been spent among the mountain people of Southern Kentucky and Middle and East Tennessee. Clinton and Wayne Counties in Kentucky, and Overton, Pickett, Fentress, Cumberland, Morgan, Scott, Anderson, and Roane Counties, in Tennessee, have been my parish. A truer-hearted people than these people of the mountains can nowhere be found. Among them I was born, and with them I have lived, and in the sweet soil of these dear old mountains I want to rest when I die. I have preached in their homes and in their school-houses and in their rudely-equipped church-houses.

Often have I seen the glory of the Lord among the people as we worshiped in the groves, nature's first temples. I have married the parents, baptized the children, preached the funerals of old and young, and shared the hospitality of this people. O the happy years that I have lived among them! Long years my parents, and nearly all of my brothers and sisters, have been sleeping in the dust. I have outlived nearly all of the companions of my youth. The Lord has been very good to me in letting me see a great many happy conversions to him.

During the first two years of my itinerant life, I witnessed four hundred and ninety conversions, and received about the same number into the Church. I pray God that I may realize what the psalmist means when he says: "They shall bring forth fruit in old age, they shall be fat and flourishing." The Lord give me a clear sky for the setting sun of my life! The month of January for this year was noted for hard winter weather. On the third Sunday I attended Sunday-school in Sunbright. The day was very cold. That Sunday night, Brother J. M. Brown, the Sunday-school superintendent at Pleasant Ridge, and a steward of our Church, died as the Christian only dies.

On the following Tuesday I was called to preach his funeral. A heavy snow fell all that day; but I rode more than three miles out to Pleasant Ridge Church, and as the friends were not ready for the burial, I rode back home late in the afternoon. The following day I went back and preached the funeral, to a large audience, from 2 Tim. iv, 7, 8. The day was very cold, and I suffered greatly from the weather. That night I had an attack of la grippe, and for several days I suffered intensely, which shut me indoors for some time.

I spent the fourth and fifth Sundays at home. Having been so active all my life, it is like fire shut up in my bones to be compelled to take winter quarters from age, or to be prostrated by affliction. The Lord help me! I remained at home the first, second, and third Sundays in February. However, on the fourth day, while yet struggling with la grippe, I rode out to Pleasant Ridge, where Brother Gorman was holding successful revival services; and at his request, I preached. Several persons came to the altar for prayers.

I left home February 17th, and drove in my buggy about twenty-five miles, running over into Fentress County, and distributing books for which I had taken orders. I staid the first night at Brother Stockton's. The next morning, he and I rode out and visited a number of families. In the afternoon I drove four miles to Brother McClellan's, near Allardt. This is a good Christian Methodist family. The following day it rained all day long, and so I remained with this family until Saturday morning, when I drove home. The fourth Sunday in February I rode seven miles, and preached at the house of Rev. J. M. York. He was absent on his circuit, but his wife requested that I should preach for her benefit at their home. In the afternoon I rode back, a part of the distance through rain. The following day I rode six miles to Young's Chapel, and preached the funeral of Aunt Susan Carpenter, while she lay a corpse in the church altar. She had requested of me more than twenty years ago to preach her funeral if I should outlive her, giving me her funeral-text, it being Rev. vii, 13, 14. I used this text in preaching her funeral.

The first Sunday in March I had an appointment to preach at Byrd's school-house. It rained so hard all day, and having been so recently sick, I did not go. The second Sunday I rode out to Pleasant Ridge, and preached to an attentive audience. The third Sunday I remained at home. It had snowed nearly all the week before, and had made the deepest snow that we had had for many years. To spend so many Sundays at home unemployed, while so many souls are perishing for the bread of life, makes me feel sad. May the good Lord save dying sinners! The fourth Sunday I had an appointment to preach at Rev. J. M. York's; but it rained so much that I was afraid to turn out after my recent severe affliction, and so I remained at home. It will be seen that I have been kept from my appointments several times during the past winter, on account of the severe weather.

On Saturday before the first Sunday in April, at the request of Hon. R. Walton, I attended the memorial services of Dr. Kemp, at Rugby, in Morgan County, and preached the funeral sermon to an attentive audience. Hon. S. E. Young, Judge Rogers, Judge Parkerson, Hon. W. A. Henderson, and Hon. Underwood followed with speeches. I had never mingled with so many judges and lawyers before on a funeral occasion; but it was a very pleasant meeting, and I had quite an enjoyable time with the legal profession. The same day, at night, I preached at Young's Chapel for the pastor, and also for him again on Sunday afternoon at Pleasant Ridge.

On Saturday before the second Sunday, I boarded the train at Sunbright, and ran up the line to Whitley Station, in Pulaski County, Kentucky. The weather had turned so very cold that I suffered a great deal that day. The station was new, and the people rather poor, and had no church or school-house sufficiently comfortable in which to hold a meeting at so cold a time. A Baptist preacher, Tapley by name, had an appointment to preach that night at the house of Uncle Middleton B. Holloway. By request, I preached to the people that night, and also the next day at the same place. The rooms of the house were crowded with an attentive audience. On Sunday morning, before preaching, myself and Uncle Holloway walked out one-half mile to the grave of Lucy Carpenter Holloway, his first wife, and also an aunt of my wife. We knelt down by the grave and prayed, and then sang a verse of the hymn, "We shall sleep, but not forever." In the afternoon I boarded the train and ran down home to Sunbright.

The following day I received a telegram to come down the line to Emory Gap, and to go over near Kingston the next day, to preach the funeral of old Brother Gilford Delozier, who had died on Sunday night. I boarded the train that afternoon, ran down the line to Emory Gap, walked one mile, and staid for the night at George H. Delozier's. The next morning I rode horseback four miles to Pine Grove Church, and preached the funeral to an attentive audience, from Psalms xxxvii, 37. In the afternoon I rode back to Rev. F. K. Suddeth's, near the station, and staid over night. I boarded the train next morning, and ran up home to Sunbright. The third Sunday I rode horseback seven miles to Young's Chapel, met a large audience, and preached the funerals of three infant children of Wesley and Mary Ann Peters. I also baptized a babe. It will now be seen that I am constantly employed again in the work. I am also selling a great many good books.

The fourth Sunday I attended the Baptist Church in Sunbright, and heard Elder Madaris preach. In the afternoon I rode out two miles, and preached at Samuel Jones'. The first Sunday in May I preached twice at Scutcheon Church, eight miles from Sunbright. There were several penitents seeking salvation, and two persons joined the Church. On Friday before the second Sunday I left home in my buggy to fill an appointment in

Frost Bottom. Samuel Paul, a young minister, went with me. We drove twelve miles to Wartburg, and took dinner at the Cumberland Hotel. In the afternoon we drove thirteen miles, and staid over night at Samuel Russell's. The next morning we drove through Oliver Springs and up Poplar Creek twelve miles to Frost Bottom, where I preached four days.

On Sunday I preached the funeral of Margaret Duncan to a large audience. I was feeling very much indisposed from severe cold, and so I left the meeting in the hands of Brothers Koon and Paul, and went home. Up to the time of my leaving, there had been a number of conversions. On the third Sunday I attended the Sunday-school anniversary at Pleasant Ridge. The fourth Sunday I attended pastoral preaching at the Methodist Church in Sunbright, and in the afternoon rode out three miles and preached at Bird's school-house. Several gave their hands to be prayed for. The fifth Sunday I rode to Montgomery Mills to preach. The day was very rainy and only a few persons were out. I lectured the Sunday-school only, and preached at the same place at night to an attentive audience. Several persons stood up for prayers.

The first Sunday in June I preached at Scutcheon in the morning, and in Sunbright at night. On the following Tuesday, in the Methodist Episcopal Church in Sunbright, I preached the funeral of an infant babe of Mr. and Mrs. P. J. Neal. On the second Saturday and Sunday I again preached in Frost Bottom. The third Sunday I attended the quarterly-meeting services for the Sunbright charge at Mill Creek. The fourth Sunday I rode eight miles on horseback to Rome Church and preached to an attentive audience. The Children's-day services, a very delightful entertainment, was held just before I preached. They carried out the program as furnished by the Board of Education, the children rendering their parts nicely. We had an interesting meeting. Near the church I found my old friend and brother, Thomas Wheeler, who emigrated from Cincinnati to this country a few years ago, very sick. He is now in his eighty-second year, and I do n't think will live a very great while. I had a good time of handshaking with my old friends, mostly emigrants from the North and Northwest.

The first Sunday in July I had three appointments for the day—the first in the morning at Scutcheon, the second in the afternoon at Montgomery Mills, the third at night in Wartburg. It stormed and rained so much during the day, and, my wife being very sick, I did not reach any of them. When I was a younger man, I rode through all kinds of weather to reach my appointments; but now that I am growing old and feeble in health, I can not do so. It makes me sad to think this. The good Lord knows that I want to be doing some good while I live.

The second Sunday I had an appointment to preach at Oakdale; but my children coming to visit me, I deferred the appointment until a future occasion. The third Sunday I preached twice at Byrd's school-house; also on Monday, with some prospects of good. On Saturday afternoon before

the fourth Sunday I boarded the train and ran down
the line twenty-three miles to Oakdale, where I
preached Saturday night, Sunday, and Sunday night,
and Monday night in their new school-house. They
have but little preaching at that place, and I think
it will take a great deal of it to move the people
much. We had some indications for good, and I
took several orders for books. The fifth Sunday I
rode eight miles on horseback and preached at
Scutcheon. Several penitents came to the altar for
prayer.

On Saturday morning before the first Sunday
in August I left home in my buggy and drove
eighteen miles over a very rough road into Fentress
County. After taking dinner at B. R. Stockton's, I
went two miles to Pleasant Vale Church, and
preached. I preached at the same place twice a
day until Wednesday evening, with happy results.
On Sunday there were two conversions, on Monday two, on Tuesday seven, and on Wednesday
two, making a total of thirteen happy conversions.
A goodly number united with the Church. I baptized two adults and an infant of the Methodist
pastor. On Wednesday night I preached in Allardt, also on Thursday and Thursday night. On
Thursday night a young lady was converted, making
fourteen conversions in a few days. I returned
home on Friday, but had been there only a short
time when I was called to go out eight miles and
hold the funeral service, on the following day, of a
sainted child of William Bullard. Although feeling
great prostration on account of excessive labors, I
went and held the service. On the second Sunday

I remained at home, rested, and wrote up my journal. The third Sunday I rode out four miles to Pilot Mountain, and preached the funeral of Elizabeth Bunch, from John xi, 25.

On Friday before the fourth Sunday I left home on horseback, rode twenty miles to Hon J. C. Taylor's and preached that night at the chapel near by; also next morning at the same place. In the afternoon I rode thirteen miles down into the head of Poplar Cove to see my oldest sister, Mrs. Price, a widowed lady. In the last few months she had had two children to commit suicide—a son by shooting himself through the head, and just one month from that date her daughter, Mrs. Crouch, a widowed lady, hung herself. She was a member of the Methodist Episcopal Church, and was a most devoted Christian lady, but became demented. She left a son eighteen years of age.

On Sunday morning I walked out a few hundred yards to view the place where she hung herself. She had gone above the cleared land, up a deep ravine in the forest, to where a slim, tall black-walnut grew about ten feet above the center of the ravine. Beside the walnut was a large limestone rock, about three and one-half feet high. At the lower side a redbud grew up about two feet below the walnut, forking about two feet above the ground, one fork turning back over the ravine, and the other running up and pressing against the walnut about four and a half feet above the top of the rock. I was told that she got on the rock, wrapped a leather rope twice around her neck, then once around the walnut and the redbud, then once again around the redbud only. Taking the ends of the rope in her hands, she stepped off. The straightness of the walnut, and the rope being around the redbud right at the walnut, pressed her face and hands tightly against the walnut; so that it was impossible for her hands to loosen on the ropes, and in that condition she was found dead. She hung herself about ten o'clock in the morning, and was found about four o'clock in the afternoon. My old sister, in her eightieth year, rode down the Cove three miles with me, where I preached to a large audience in a grove. Several penitents were at the altar. Brother York, of Kentucky, preached in the afternoon. I exhorted, and called penitents. Two young men were converted that afternoon. I held there until Friday afternoon. The result was thirty-eight happy conversions. Rev. W. W. Newberry, of the Methodist Episcopal Church, South, was with me several days, and received eleven accessions to his Church. At his request, as he was not ordained, I baptized five persons for him. Going as an evangelist, I leave all the taking into the Church to the pastors.

On Saturday morning I went down the Cove four miles to Cedar Grove, a Baptist Church, and preached the funerals of Aunt Susie Beatty and her son Aley S. Beatty, to a large congregation. I preached at the same place in the afternoon, when a young man was happily converted. The next day, being the first Sunday in September, I preached the funerals of three ladies and one child at Linder's schoolhouse to about five hundred people. I preached at the same place in the afternoon. During the day there were eight happy conversions. Rev. J. B. Cobble, pastor of the Methodist Episcopal Church, received six persons into the Church; and as he was not ordained, at his request, I baptized them for him.

During the week there were forty-seven conversions, seventeen accessions, and eleven baptisms. I rode home on Monday through rain nearly all day. I felt greatly fatigued. The second Sunday in September I rode eight miles horseback into Scott County, and preached the funeral of a babe of William J. and Malinda Lewallen. I rode back home in the afternoon, but was very sick the following day.

On Friday before the third Sunday I drove in my buggy to Wartburg, thirteen miles, and delivered a number of books. I put up in old Montgomery for the night. Brother Hartley, a Baptist minister, was holding a protracted meeting in Wartburg. At his request, I walked back, and preached for him that night; but was very tired. The next day I drove seven miles up Emory River, to Pleasant Hill Church, where I preached twice on Saturday and twice on Sunday. The saints of God shouted aloud for joy, and two souls, a man and his wife, were happily converted.

On Saturday before the fourth Sunday I left home on horseback for Banner Springs, a distance of twenty miles. I reached there in the afternoon, and on the following day, to a large congregation, I preached the funerals of two children of Luke Hall. Two persons were happily converted at this service. The first Sunday in October I preached the funeral of a babe of Joseph Epsey Lewallen, at Young's Chapel, from Rev. xxi, 3, 4.

I had an appointment on the second Sunday to preach some funerals in Middle Tennessee; but as it was thought best by the friends, I deferred it two weeks. I rode horseback to Mt. Vernon on that day, and heard Rev. A. C. Peters preach in the morning. I preached at the same place at night. The Holston Conference met in Morristown, Tenn., Bishop Foss presiding. I did not attend. On the third Sunday I preached at Byrd's school-house, when a number of persons came forward for prayers.

On Friday before the fourth Sunday I left home in my buggy, drove twenty-six miles into Poplar Cove, and remained over night at Joseph Campbell's. After leaving Jamestown, I had to drive down a long, steep, rough, rocky mountain to get there. The next morning I drove down through the Cove, and across Obed's River, by the roughest road, and up and down very steep hills for ten miles, to reach what I thought to be the funeral appointment of Louisa Beatty, but before reaching the place I learned that the appointment had been deferred. I stopped at Hiram Beatty's, and took dinner. Brother Beatty's mother, who lives with him, is very old, and quite afflicted. I sang several hymns, and talked and prayed with her, then drove two miles, and stopped with an aged couple, Jacob Cooper and wife, who were greatly afflicted. I sang for them that good old hymn,

"And let this feeble body fail,
And let it faint or die,"

and prayed with them. I felt that I was doing a good work in these families, visiting and worshiping. I drove four miles more that afternoon, and stopped for the night with my old friend and brother, Elias Bowden. I had driven over a very rough country that afternoon, making a drive of sixteen miles for the day. The next morning being Sunday, was cloudy and rather cool. I drove five miles up the river to Buffalo Cove school-house. The last two miles were along a deep ravine, where the mountains rose almost perpendicularly, like walls on either side. Sometimes there were great cliffs or rocks, between fifty and a hundred feet high. Some places, trees nearly a foot in diameter grow out of the rocks on the side of the cliff, lifting their stately heads up the side of the mountain, and making the grandest scenery. I thought, surely this is the handywork of the Lord. I met at the school-house about five hundred people. A great many of the ladies of the Eastern Star degree of Adoptive Masonry were in attendance; also the Master of Jamestown Lodge of A. F. and A. M. These marched in order, with books and flowers, to the grave of Sister Viann Stephens, and went through all the ceremonies for a funeral occasion of the Eastern Star degree, after which we went to a large new school-house near by, and I preached her funeral sermon to an immense audience, from Isa. lx, 19, 20. Her young husband, father and mother, brothers and sisters, and a large train of relatives, were present. The people had brought bountiful provisions on the ground to supply this large congregation.

In the afternoon I drove up a long steep mountain, and out six miles, and remained over night at

Brother McGee's, a most excellent family, who live two miles from the town of Allardt. The following day I drove twenty miles to my home. The fifth Sunday I preached at Mill Creek, six miles out from Sunbright. The first Sunday in November I preached in the Methodist Church in Sunbright. November 3d, I passed the sixty-sixth mile-post of my life. The second Sunday I rode horseback nine miles, and preached at Young's school-house, in Scott County, in the morning. After preaching, I rode out three miles to Brother John Young's for dinner, and back again, to preach at night at the same place. There were prospects of much good at these services. I staid for the night at Brother G. M. Baker's.

The next day I rode home, nine miles, making a ride of twenty-six miles and preaching twice in two days. The third Sunday I remained at home, and attended Sunday-school in Sunbright. O how time speeds away! But I shall soon exchange time for eternity! My prospects are bright. On November 24th, this being Thanksgiving-day, I preached a Thanksgiving sermon in Sunbright, from Psalms xcii, 1. The fourth Sunday was a very wet day. I had an appointment to preach at night in Lansing, nine miles below Sunbright on the railroad, but it rained so severely that I did not go. My youngest son, Asbury, from Rockwood, spent the day with me at home.

On the first Sunday in December, having received a card from Rev. M. M. Sumner, Congregational pastor at Glen Mary, requesting me to fill his pulpit for him that day, I boarded the morning train, ran up the line six miles to Glen Mary, and preached for him to a small but attentive audience. On Saturday afternoon before the second Sunday, though it was quite a cold day, I rode out eight miles on horseback, and preached at Young's school-house at night. I walked a mile, and staid over night at G. M. Baker's. The next day I went back, and preached to a full house of people, and rode home in the afternoon.

The third Sunday I remained at home, and wrote up my journal. I begin to feel that I must keep my journal well written up all the time, as I am becoming old, and know not when the Master will call for me. My time on earth now is very uncertain; but, praise the Lord, I am ready. The fourth Sunday was Christmas-day, I rode out horse-back three miles, over ice, sleet, and snow, in a very cold day, and preached at Byrd's school-house, returning in the afternoon. It was a very distress-ingly cold and freezing time. A great many were visiting us during Christmas, which made a hard time on me. I did not care for this when I was young; but since I have become old it annoys me greatly. I am always glad to see my two younger sons; but when they come, others come that should not. The first day of the new year was the first Sunday in January. It came in very rainy and stormy. I wish now to say, in my declining old age, to 1892 a solemn last farewell:

"Farewell to its labors, farewell to its cares,
    Its thousand temptations, misfortunes, and snares."

The old year has been fraught with a great many events that write themselves eternally upon my

memory. In the early part of the year I was
brought down very low with la grippe, almost face
to face with death; but I feel sure that the good
Lord had other work for me to do, and I did not
die. I am perfectly resigned to the Lord's will in
all afflictions. In retrospecting the past I am con-
strained to adopt the sentiment of the poet:

> " When o'er our vanished days we glance,
>   Far backward to our young romance,
>   And muse upon unnumbered things
>   That crowding come on memory's wings."

But sweetly looking forward by faith I sing:

> "There everlasting spring abides,
>   And never-withering flowers;
>   Death, like a narrow sea, divides
>   That heavenly land from ours."

In the coming in of this new year I have walked
nearly two months toward my sixty-seventh mile-
post of life. O how fast time steals away! On the
first Sunday in January I had an appointment to
preach at Mill Creek; but the day was so stormy that
I did not go. I am greatly distressed with asthma,
and can not expose myself to any severe weather.
I was once a very strong man, and had no regard
for weather; but time has made changes for me.

During the year 1892, although a superannuated
preacher, I preached eighty-eight times, witnessed
seventy happy conversions to God, baptized fourteen adults and two infants, preached the funerals
of twenty-three persons, and married one couple.
I did not receive any persons into the Church; for I
went as an evangelist, and left that work to the
different pastors with whom I labored.

Beginning now the duties of a new year, I wish to consecrate my whole soul, life, and all my ransomed powers to the service of the blessed Christ! If God should lengthen out the feeble thread of life to me through another year, I trust to see a great number of souls happily converted to him. The good Lord be my strength and support in this great work. I will now give the number of baptisms, adults and infants, the number of funerals preached, and the number of persons I have married since my ordination as a minister, up to the beginning of the year 1893. I have baptized 494 adults by immersion, 466 adults by pouring, and have baptized 352 infants; making a total of 960 adult baptisms, and a grand total of all ages of 1,312. I have preached the funerals of 355 adults and 214, infants; making a total of 569 funerals preached. I have celebrated the rites of matrimony between 84 couples. I wish I could here give the number of conversions I have witnessed, the number of persons received into the Church, and the number of sermons that I have preached; but they are all written down in my life journal. If I should ever have a Biography written out, 1 hope that my Biographer will have all these things in round numbers. I do praise God that my ministry has reached over so long a train of years. Hallelujah, God be praised!

The second Sunday in January I had an appointment to preach at Young's school-house, in Scott County; but the day was so bitter cold, and there was such a deep snow on the ground that I did not go. The reader will notice that I do not expose myself now as once I did. My age and afflictions forbid it. We are having a most intensely severe winter of deep snows and cold weather. I do not expect to preach much until the return of spring and warm weather. I have covenanted with God to preach and do all that I can for the building up of his kingdom, and I am praying him that I may see a great many souls converted during this Conference year.

The third Sunday there was a very deep snow on the ground, and although the day was clear, it was very cold. There has been up to this time the most severe winter that we have seen for years, and so I am at home writing up my journal. O how restless I feel while confined at home on account of severe winter weather and age! The Lord help me to discharge every known duty. The fourth Sunday I attended Sunday-school in Sunbright, and at the request of Rev. W. D. Gorman, the pastor, I preached in the Methodist church to an attentive audience. God be praised! On the fifth Sunday I held the funeral service of a small babe of Dr. Rains, in Sunbright, in the afternoon of the day. Death nips the tender bud.

On Friday evening before the first Sunday in February, at the Baptist Church in Sunbright, I preached the funeral of an infant of Melvin and Ellen Johnson. The first Sunday in February my wife was sick, and I was not feeling well, and so I remained at home. On Saturday evening before the second Sunday I rode eight miles, and visited old Brother Matthew Young, who was very low with dropsy. In all probability he will soon be with bright angels in heaven. He says his prospect is unclouded for a heavenly inheritance. I staid for the night with his son-in-law, George M. Baker. The next day being Sunday, I preached in the morning at Young's school-house, and rode home in the afternoon. The third Sunday I remained at home, rested, and read.

The fourth Sunday I attended pastoral preaching in the Methodist Church in Sunbright. I think that spring is now near at hand, so that I can soon get out and preach some every week. It seems almost like fire shut up in my bones to be compelled by age and affliction to remain at home, while souls are perishing for the bread of life. The first Sunday in March I remained at home. There was quite a cold spell of weather for March, with snow on the ground. I am now sending out my appointments to begin with the opening spring. During the year I am taking and reading some of the best religious papers that I have ever read. Some friend is sending me the *Michigan Christian Advocate*, edited by Dr. J. H. Potts, published in Detroit, Mich., a large sixteen-page paper, one of our very best Church papers. Also the *Christian Witness*, an advocate of Bible holiness published in Boston, a glorious, large eight-page paper. Also the *Christian Herald*, a Presbyterian paper edited by Dr. Talmage, in New York, a large sixteen-page paper. I also take two monthlies, the *King's Messenger*, an eight-page paper from New York, and the *Revivalist*, a four-page paper from Cincinnati. I also take a secular weekly paper published at Allardt, Tenn., the Allardt *Gazette*, a large four-page paper. I also take *Christianity in Earnest*, a thirty-two page magazine published by the Church Extension Society in Philadelphia every two months, edited by Dr. Kynett, secretary of the Society. So it will be seen that I am reading a great deal of current literature. I am also reading a great many books. I think that I am doing more reading than at any time before in my life.

The second Sunday I attended the Baptist Church in Sunbright, and affiliated with their pastor, Rev. B. T. Summers. The third Sunday I rode horseback seven miles to Mt. Vernon and preached in the morning to an attentive audience, returning home in the afternoon of the same day. On Saturday before the fourth Sunday I rode horseback eight miles into Scott County to see my old friend Matthew Young, who is still lingering on earth in the last stages of dropsy. After delivering a number of books, I staid over night with Brother Baker. The following day I preached at Young's schoolhouse to an attentive audience. The first Sunday in April being Easter Sunday, I drove in my buggy eight miles and preached at Rome Church to a good congregation.

The second Sunday I attended Church at Mt. Vernon and heard Rev. A. C. Peters preach a sermon on the mode of Christian baptism. I gave a short talk also myself. The third Sunday I rode horseback to the camp-ground, preached to a good audience and returned in the afternoon. The fourth Sunday I attended Church in Sunbright, and heard Rev. W. D. Gorman preach. The fifth Sunday I preached at Byrd's school-house, and organized a

Sunday-school for that place. On Saturday before the first Sunday in May I rode horseback eight miles and preached at Scutcheon Church, both in the morning and in the afternoon. I preached again at the same place the following day in the morning, when quite a number came forward for prayers, and two persons united with our Church. I preached that afternoon for an aged man and his wife, who were near death's door in a low state of affliction. They live two miles from Scutcheon Church. I rode home that night.

On Saturday before the second Sunday I rode eight miles on horseback and preached in the afternoon at Young's school-house. On Sunday morning we held an old people's experience-meeting, and after I had preached we held an old-fashioned class-meeting of fifty years ago with closed doors. Several shouted aloud the praises of God. To God be all the glory! On Saturday before the third Sunday I rode horseback seven miles to Deer Lodge, and took dinner with Brother Kemper and his two little daughters. In the afternoon I rode six miles and preached at Pine Grove school-house, staying over night with Wash Neal. The following day I preached in a pine grove near by as the school-house would not hold the people. Several manifested a desire for salvation. I preached that evening again in the school-house. A number of young men knelt at the altar for prayers. I staid on Sunday night at Rev. John Stowers', a Freewill Christian Baptist minister and well-to-do merchant. Some of the neighbors gathered in, and sang until a late hour. I rode home the next day.

On Friday evening before the fourth Sunday, myself and wife took the train at Sunbright, and ran down the line to Rockwood, where my youngest son lives. On Saturday morning he took me to the company's store and presented me with a fine suit of clothes. On Sunday morning Rev. S. B. Hillock, pastor of the Methodist Episcopal Church, preached a memorial sermon for the Grand Army Post in the opera-house. In the afternoon the Knights of Pythias decorated the graves of their dead. At night I preached in the new Methodist Episcopal church, although it was a very rainy night. On Monday night was the closing exercise of the high school at that place. Eight graduates, seven girls and one young man, received diplomas.

On Tuesday morning myself and wife boarded the train at Rockwood, with our son, W. D. Wright, and ran up to Sunbright, It was Decoration-day in Sunbright, and my son Willie made a splendid speech for the Post at that place. The first Sunday in June I rode horseback seven miles, and preached at Young's Chapel, in Morgan County, to an attentive audience, returning the same day. The second Sunday I rode four miles horseback, and preached at Pleasant Ridge, taking dinner with a young widowed lady, Mrs. Mary J. Brown, an excellent Christian lady. I rode home in the afternoon. The third Sunday I rode horseback nine miles and preached at Scutcheon Church. I preached at the same place again in the afternoon, when several persons came forward and gave their hands as seekers of salvation. O what sweet enjoyments I realize in working for the blessed Lord! I rode

one mile and staid over night with Mrs. Holloway, a widowed lady, and rode home the next day.

On Friday evening before the fourth Sunday,
myself and wife boarded the train at Sunbright and
ran down the line nine miles to Lansing. We drove
in a buggy four miles to Wartburg, where our son,
Will D. Wright, lives. We staid where our son
boards, at the Mountain Hotel, Hon. J. H. Lewallen being the proprietor. On Saturday afternoon I
conferred the Eastern Star Degree of Adoptive Masonry on about twenty-five gentlemen and ladies.
A large dinner was set in the hall, and quite a number partook of it. I attended the Masonic Lodge
meeting awhile that night. The next day being
Sunday, I preached both morning and evening in
the Presbyterian Church. I trust the seed fell in
good ground. The next morning we were kindly
brought by my son and Mr. Lewallen to the depot,
where we boarded the train and ran up home to
Sunbright.

On the first Sunday in July I rode horseback
seven miles to Mt. Vernon, and preached in the
morning. After preaching, I rode two miles to Rev.
A. C. Peters', and celebrated the rites of matrimony
between his daughter, Miss Bertie Peters, and Mr.
Gilbert Young. I rode home that afternoon. The
second Sunday I preached at Byrd's school-house, and
lectured the Sunday-school. The third Sunday I rode
horseback eight miles to Young's school-house, in
Scott County, and preached to a large congregation.
Brother Cobble, the pastor, preached in the afternoon. We continued the services over Monday,
with prospects of good; but on account of a great

deal of sickness in the neighborhood, we closed. I attended an educational meeting of Dr. J. F. Spence in Sunbright, on the fourth Sunday.

On Saturday afternoon before the fifth Sunday I rode horseback eight miles, and preached at Scutcheon Church. After preaching, I rode two miles further, and remained over night with Brother Buxton. The next morning I rode three miles into Wartburg, and preached the funeral of old Sister Cochran. After taking dinner at the Cumberland Hotel, I rode four miles more, and preached in the afternoon at Scutcheon Church, with some indications of good. After staying over night one mile from the church, I returned, and preached the next day. The people took their dinners to the ground and remained all day. A number of penitents were at the altar for prayers, and one young lady was happily converted. I rode home in the evening; but returned the next day, and preached again. Three young ladies were at the altar for prayer; but there was such a falling off in the attendance of the people that I closed the meeting. I really think that there was a glorious prospect for a sweeping revival at that place if the Church people had given the work their proper support.

The first Sunday in August I remained at home, read, rested, and wrote up my journal. I now have arrangements to spend a few weeks in Wayne and Clinton Counties, Kentucky, in evangelistic work. I also expect to preach a number of funerals. I drove in my buggy the first day to Jamestown, my grandson, James Peters, accompanying me, where we staid over night with O. C. Kanatsur. I had

written to a friend in Jamestown some time before
that I would preach there that night. Court was
in session at that time, and a little ten-cent show
was held in town that night. These called off the
people so much that I did not preach. I think
Jamestown is joined to her idols. The next morning we drove ten miles down on to Wolf River,
where we came upon a large congregation of people
at a new church on the road. We entered the
church just as the preacher had taken his text to
preach. After the sermon, one person came to the
altar seeking salvation, and was happily converted.
A great many people bore testimony to entire sanctification. We had a heart-cheering time of handshaking with happy Christians.

We took dinner near the church, at Brother
Pyle's, and drove that afternoon over Poplar Mountain, into Wayne County, Kentucky, and remained
over night at Brother Dalton's. He and his family
are members of the Methodist Church. He is also
a merchant, a large farmer, and a well-to-do man in
worldly affairs. The next morning we started early
for our appointment ten miles away. On the way
we encountered a heavy rain, and drove under a
large oak-tree for protection. After stopping at
Brother Edwards' a short time, we drove on, reaching Bethel Church a little late; but found the people singing, praying, and waiting for us, so that they
received us gladly. I preached an introductory
sermon, and preached there again in the afternoon,
with prospect of much good. This neighborhood
abounds with a great many of the Guffeys. They
are nearly all warm-hearted, shouting Methodists.

We staid that night with my wife's nephew, her sister's son, Louis Shelley. His mother, Elizabeth Shelley, who is now in her seventy-first year, with her daughter and youngest son, had come eighteen miles to meet us there. I had not seen her for about twenty years. O how time and age change our beings! I preached to a very large congregation on Sunday in a grove, as the church could not hold the people, preaching the funeral of Matilda J. Guffey Choate, to a large train of connections, a widowed husband, and five motherless children. I continued the services there at Bethel until the next Saturday evening, with a glorious, happy meeting. The people brought their dinners and ate on the grounds; and so we had an all-day service each day. Twelve souls were happily converted and thirteen persons united with the Church.

On Saturday afternoon we moved four miles over into Clinton County, and at Walnut Grove Church I preached an introductory sermon on Saturday night, to a very large audience. On Sunday, at the same place, in a grove near by, I preached the funeral of Celia Jane Franklin Clarke, to an immense audience. Religious impressions were deep, and penitents flocked to the altar. I rode three miles in the afternoon to Davis Chapel, a large church; but as it would not hold the congregation, I preached again in the grove, preaching the funeral of William Guffey. I had secured Rev. Frank Mills to preach at the grove in the afternoon, so as to make no break in my meeting there. A deep religious interest grew rapidly. The congregations were large, and the people brought provisions to the ground each day. I continued the services until Friday evening. The result was twenty-eight happy conversions to God and twenty accessions to the Church. I baptized eight persons—six by pouring and two by immersion. The first person to join was a Baptist minister, joining by letter. I had an appointment on the following day to meet the people at Jones' Mills, on Otter Creek, to baptize some persons.

On Saturday morning we drove five miles to that place. Soon a heavy rain began falling, and I preached to the people at the private residence of Mrs. Jones. I have been acquainted with this family for many years. They are most excellent people. I baptized three ladies by pouring, and one gentleman and five ladies by immersion in Otter Creek. I staid that night at Mrs. Jones'. This is an excellent place for rest and comfort.

On Sunday morning, being the fourth Sunday in August, I had an appointment to preach the funeral of James Hicks at Edwards Chapel. After a drive of eight miles over a very rough road, I met a large congregation. Although the church was large, it would not hold the people, and I preached again in the grove. The children of Brother Hicks were unwilling to have his funeral preached at Edwards Chapel, and insisted that I should drive up Otter Creek three miles to the Dishman graveyard, near the oil-works, where their father is buried, and preach his funeral that afternoon, which I did, to a large congregation. After preaching, I drove four miles over a very high, rough, rocky mountain, and down on to Carpenter's Fork, where I again staid over night with Brother Dalton, traveling that day fifteen miles over a very rough and broken country, and preaching twice in the open air. I was very tired at night. The next morning we set off for home, driving over Poplar Mountain, a very rough mountain indeed, and back into Tennessee.

After driving nine miles, we stopped for dinner again with Brother Erasmus Pyle. We walked out near by to the same church we had stopped at as we went on to Kentucky. Brother Burks, a holiness man, was now holding a very successful meeting at this place. At his request, I preached for them. Several persons came to the altar seeking pardon, and several seeking entire sanctification. Many of the saints of God shouted aloud for joy. We drove that afternoon up on the mountain near Jamestown, and staid for the night with Ambrose Parmley. The next day we drove by noon to Brother Henry Peters', and took dinner. In the afternoon we drove home. I found my family well. God be praised! In about two weeks' time I had preached twenty-seven times, baptized seventeen persons, received thirty-three into the Church, preached the funerals of ten persons, witnessed forty-one happy conversions, and traveled one hundred and seventy-five miles in a buggy over a rough country. To God be all the praise!

The first Sunday in September I attended Church in Sunbright, and heard Rev. Bingman, a Disciple, preach. On Saturday before the second Sunday in September, I left home on horseback, rode thirteen miles to Wash Neal's, took dinner, and delivered

him a book which he had ordered. After praying
with the family I rode thirteen miles more, and
preached at night, at Potter's Chapel, to an attentive, large audience. After preaching, I rode two
miles in company with Rev. J. M. York, the Methodist pastor, and staid over night with Brother
Potter. A great many people staying there that
night, and their getting off to bed very late, and
making considerable noise, I did not sleep much
that night; but rose early the next morning, and
began preparing for a heavy day's work of funeral
preaching. I rode two miles to Potter's Chapel,
and at the morning service preached two funerals,
and at the afternoon service I preached five funerals. The people brought provisions on the ground
for dinner, and remained for both services. I held
an altar service for penitents in the afternoon. I
rode three miles, and staid that night at Mrs. Williams', a widowed lady. I was very tired, but had
a comfortable rest in this pleasant home. The next
day I rode twelve miles to my home. God be
praised!

The third Sunday I attended services at the
Baptist Church in Sunbright, and heard Rev. B. T.
Summers, the pastor, preach. On Friday evening
before the fourth Sunday, myself and wife drove in
the buggy to Tobias Peters'. The next morning
I rode horseback seventeen miles to Jamestown,
falling in company with Rev. J. C. Taylor three
miles from town. We went on together, took dinner, and rested for a while at the Crowley House.
In the afternoon we rode twelve miles down on to
Obed's River, and staid for the night at old Uncle

William Reagan's. The next morning we rode one mile to the river, where I baptized two men by pouring, and Rev. P. E. Johnson baptized six persons by immersion. We rode one mile further to where I preached the funeral of my cousin, Louisa Beatty, to a large audience, in a beautiful grove. I noticed a wonderful change in that country to what it was several years ago, by almost everybody being converted, and living a happy Christian life. We took dinner at my cousin's, Abe Beatty's. We rode that afternoon seven miles to Poplar Cove school-house, where I baptized two men by immersion for Brother Taylor, after which we rode one mile, and staid for the night at J. F. Wright's. His wife is my niece, a daughter of my oldest sister, who was there that night. She is very old, but stout for one of her age. The next day I rode eighteen miles, a part of the way through rain, and stopped for dinner at Rev. A. C. Peters'. In the afternoon I rode three miles to my son-in-law's, put my horse in the buggy, and my wife and I drove home. I was very tired.

On Wednesday morning before the first Sunday in October, I boarded the train at Sunbright, and ran up the line sixty-four miles to Burnside Station, in the forks of the Cumberland River. After stepping off the train, I walked down to Mr. Duncan's eating-house. To my surprise, I found that he and his wife both knew me. They gave me a hearty welcome to their table free of charge. After praying with the family, Mrs. Duncan and I walked out a short distance to see Mrs. Frost, a lady who also knew me well. That afternoon I drove down in a

carriage that was sent for me twenty miles to Monticello, on a pike road, being a little late reaching that
place. I staid that night with my old friend and
brother, B. W. S. Huffaker.

The next morning I left early on the mail-hack
for Gap Creek, a distance of twelve miles. I reached
there about ten o'clock. I had been invited by the
Baptist Church at that place, of which my dear
cousin, Elder B. Wright, was the pastor, who is an
older man than myself. It was a very happy occasion for myself and cousin, to mingle together in a
revival service. The meeting was a most glorious
service, resulting in thirty conversions and about
that number of accessions to the Baptist Church.
The people treated me with great kindness, paying
me liberally for my time and traveling expenses.
We closed the meeting on Thursday, October 5th.
Brother John Shearer sent me in a buggy twelve
miles to Monticello that afternoon, where I preached
at night, stopping with T. J. Markham.

I took the early stage the next morning for Burnside Station. After running five miles, we stopped
at the first post-office. At this place a man named
Kelsey was lying very low with consumption. His
stay on earth was very brief. At his request, I got
out of the stage, went into his house, and held a
short service with him, the stage waiting on me. I
found him very ready for the change. It was a
Bethel to my soul to hear him talk of his home in
heaven. We parted with the express understanding
of meeting in heaven, our glorious home. We arrived at Burnside station about twelve o'clock. I
stopped again with Mr. Duncan. After dinner,

Mrs. Duncan and I walked out a short distance to visit a man right at death's door, in the last stage of dropsy. He had been converted the day before, and said that he was ready to die and be with the Lord. I talked and prayed with him, and left his wife and three little children in tears. Sister Duncan wished me to stay and preach his funeral, as they were looking for him to die every minute. I told her I would go down home, and they could telegraph me when he died, and I would return, and attend to the funeral. I boarded the train, and ran down home that afternoon; but rode out next morning eight miles to Young's school-house, to hold a protracted meeting, arranging with the mail-carrier to bring me any telegram that might come to me that day. None came that day, but one came the following day. I did not receive it in time to go, but have written to them.

Embracing the second Sunday in October, I held a meeting of three days and nights at Young's school-house. There were several penitents, but no conversions.

CHAPTER XX.

A GOLDEN SUNSET.

I HAVE followed the life-story of my sainted father, as given by himself, through childhood, manhood, and age. The story has been that of a life of ceaseless labor and great personal sacrifice for the cause of the Master. He might have taken high position in some earthly calling; but called of

God, as was Aaron, to the toiling life of the ministry, like the great apostle he conferred not with flesh and blood, but laid his all upon the altar. Perhaps no man ever lived up to the rule more than he : "Never be idle; never be triflingly employed." He fell on the field of battle, with his face to the foe. He died, as he had lived, in the midst of revival work, almost amid the shouts of victory of souls new-born into the kingdom. It had ever been his desire thus to die. He died in the midst of his loved employ. "He ceased at once both to work and to live." The thousands that he led to salvation will rise in the great day of eternity to be stars in his crown of rejoicing. Many were the great victories won from the enemy in his great basket and revival meetings.

Who that ever saw him amid these exciting scenes does not recall the fire of battle in his eye, and the flush of victory on his cheek, as sinners came flocking to the altar, and mourners arose happily converted, and the Church was led on to greater heights? His one aim of life was to lead souls to Christ. He never desired nor sought what the world calls pulpit ability; but he sought and obtained the higher art of leading sinners to the fountain of blood. He knew the way of salvation, and taught it to others. He believed that an aggressive, mighty gospel consists more in work than in word. His life journal closed with a protracted meeting at Young's school-house, in Scott County.

The following Sunday, being the third Sunday in October, he preached the funeral of old Mother Goddard, at Pleasant Hill, on Emory

River, in Morgan County. Here he preached his last sermon from the text: "Thou shalt guide me with thy counsel, and afterward receive me to glory. Whom have I in heaven but thee? and there is none upon earth that I desire beside thee. My flesh and my heart faileth: but God is the strength of my heart and my portion forever." (Psalm lxxiii, 24–26.) This was the last text he ever used. He had a number of unfilled appointments out when his translation came. Among these was the arrangement to hold a protracted meeting in the Methodist Episcopal Church in Sunbright, in connection with his beloved cousin, Elder Ballinger Wright, of the Baptist Church in Kentucky. On Friday after the third Sunday, he wrote a letter to the writer, in which he complains at some Conference action, held in Maryville a few days before; but consoles himself with the expression: "I shall soon receive my reward in heaven." Doubtless he had a premonition of the coming event.

October of the year 1893 was a very dry month. All the smaller running streams of the Cumberland Plateau dried up as usual. The stream where he was accustomed to water his horse had gone dry. On the opposite side of the railroad from our old home there is a small spring that remains during the dryest seasons. When other places failed, he was accustomed to water his horse at this spring. On the fateful afternoon of Saturday, October 21st, he was riding his horse to water at that spring, when crossing the railroad track where there is not a usual crossing-place, his horse caught the hind part of his shoe under the railroad-track iron, and stumbling forward and partly falling, threw him forward over his head. Being a man of considerable weight, he struck the ground heavily on his right shoulder, fracturing his right clavicle bone. He was also considerably shocked by the fall; but arose, and without any assistance, returned home several hundred yards distant. He was cheerful and patient, though suffering greatly. The family telegraphed our youngest brother, Asbury, living in Rockwood, of his injuries, who at once boarded the train, accompanied by Dr. George, and ran up to Sunbright. Dr. George set and dressed the fractured bone, ascertained that he had received no other serious injuries, and left him doing well. The doctor returned during the week, and found his condition satisfactory, no complications having occurred. Our youngest brother also returned to see him, and found him still improving. For two weeks he remained in this condition, doing as well as the family expected under the circumstances. During the time he read a great deal, remained in the house and about the premises, and talked much of his children and of their future. He seemed to be forgetful of himself in his interest for them. He also talked a great deal of the Methodist Church and of its future in this country. He greatly regretted the strife that had come about in his own Conference. His position was for peace between the warring factions.

On November 4th, our brother, Will D. Wright, with the purpose of remaining a week or two with him, came to the old home, and found some serious complex indications in his condition.   He had a severe recurrence of his usual asthma, as also a symptom of heart-failure.   There was a general giving way of his system, with alarming symptoms. Our brother William, thinking that these conditions would pass away, did not think it necessary to notify the family friends of his immediate danger until on the following Tuesday afternoon.   At that time his symptoms became so alarming that he telegraphed Asbury at Rockwood, and myself at Maryville, to come at once.   Our sister, Mrs. Peters, was also notified, and was at his bedside.   I arrived at the old home late in the afternoon of Wednesday, and found him suffering with a severe attack of asthma, and also with some indications of heart-trouble.   He seemed to be recovering from his recent injury, and was cheerful.   Dr. George, his physician, was present, and believed that he was in no imminent danger.

I was the last of the old family to arrive.   I remained with him alone on Wednesday night, gave him his medicine, and waited on him. He suffered a great deal throughout the entire night with shortness of breath, was thirsty, and drank a great deal of water.   He slept very little, and talked a great deal.   It was an easy matter to gather from his conversation that he believed that his end was near.   He frequently called for William, who was sleeping in an adjoining room.   He spoke of his journal, saying that he had written it up to the time of his injury, and then said: "You can finish it."   Death had no terrors for him at all. Heaven to him was a great fact.   There was not a waver in his faith to the very last. It was to him like taking a journey from his family rather than death. Not a murmur fell from his lips, nor a wish that his condition were otherwise. He had been accustomed to family prayers from the beginning of his home, and when the usual hours for the morning and evening services came around, he called the family together for prayers. To our precious mother he said: "Your boys will care for you when I am gone." Many were the beautiful things that he said.

On Thursday afternoon he seemed so much improved, having slept a great deal during the day, that we were all confident that he was better, and so I left him for my own home, my son being very sick at the time, with the promise to return after the following Sabbath, and spend a week with him. Our youngest brother Asbury had returned to his home the day before. On parting with him, the last thing that he said to me, as he pressed my hand, was: "God bless you in your noble work."

I was required to remain over night in Harriman so as to make connection with the Knoxville train the next morning. Mr. F. H. Dunning, of Sunbright, came in to spend the night and wait on him. All the family had retired except Mrs. Peters, our sister, who, with Mr. Dunning, was in the room with him, when about ten o'clock at night he was seized with a great difficulty of breathing. He called for brother William, who came at once to his bed. He asked William to raise him up a little, which he did, holding him in his arms. He had scarcely been raised when his head fell over on brother's shoulder and he said faintly, "O Willie, this is the end;" and he was gone at once without a struggle or an apparent pain.

"So fades a summer cloud away,
   So sinks the gale when storms are o'er;
So gently shuts the eye of day,
   So dies a wave along the shore.

Life's duty done, as sinks the clay,
   Light from its load the spirit flies,
While heaven and earth combine to say,
   How blest the righteous when he dies!"

The fitful dream of life was over, and his happy spirit had entered the city of God. Doubtless, loved ones gone before, and many spiritual children, were at the portal to welcome the storm-scourged old pilgrim as he moved into the quiet haven of the glory-land. Happy spirit safe in glory! Dear father, we would not recall you to earthly sorrow and toil again. We would not bring you back to this world of broken hearts and suffering. We would not take the well-earned crown from your head; but some sweet day, when our earthly toil and battle are over, we expect to come over and live with you forever. We hope to meet you on the plains of glory, and walk with you 'mid scenes of eternal day, where

"No chilling winds nor poisonous breath
   Can reach that healthful shore;
Sickness and sorrow, pain and death,
   Are felt and feared no more."

Having been notified by telegram at Harriman, I returned the following morning with my brother Asbury to Sunbright. Our dear old home was

shadowed in sorrow. Our venerable and loving
father, who had so often met us at the door with a
warm, loving welcome, had gone out, and the old
home, robbed of its glory, was not what it used to be.
A beautiful casket was procured, and the loved form
was laid to its long repose. Beautiful and lovely
was he in death, the large and manly form looking the very picture of health. His large, open
face clad in a beautiful smile, and his broad marble
brow crowned with flowing locks of snowy white-
ness, he looked like a king. His glorious depar-
ture occurred at ten o'clock on Thursday evening of
November 9, 1893. On the following Saturday
morning we bore his body to the Methodist Episcopal Church in Sunbright, attended by relatives,
neighbors, and a long train of Masons, where the
funeral service was held by Rev. A. C. Peters,
preaching from the text, Joshua i, 11. A large audience was present, and when the opportunity was
given them to look for the last time upon the kindly
face of their old friend, many were the sobs and
tears. Afterward, in long funeral train, we bore
him seven miles to Mt. Vernon churchyard to lay
his body away to its long sweet rest, where he sleeps
in hope of a resurrection-day.

He was buried in the honors of Masonry according to their beautiful service, an unusually large
number of the Craft being present, representing several Lodges. He had been a Mason from early manhood, and was a great lover of the Order. The day
was a lovely autumn day. It seemed that all nature had put on her loveliest and best to make the
day indicative of the beautiful life that had just

closed. A large audience of his old friends and neighbors and spiritual children were present to do him honor. As the golden sun was sinking to rest behind the Western hills, we took the farewell look upon his dear old face, and laid him gently down to sleep, while the master of the Lodge said: "Earth to earth, dust to dust, ashes to ashes."

Sleep on, dear father, heedless of summer's heat and winter's cold. The soft zephyrs of spring may whisper above your narrow bed, and the storm-cloud may gather, and the thunders may roll through the heavens and shake the earth, but they do not disturb your sweet repose. We will plant flowers ever blooming above your bed, and while the rolling years come and go we will come to stand above you, drop a tear, think of you, and say: "Dear father, we will never forget you."

No more lovely place can be found than where he sleeps. 'Mid forest-trees of primeval glory, and blooming flowers, and the sweet notes of singing birds, he sleeps where the worshipers come on each Sabbath to sing the sweet songs of Zion. Fit resting-place is this for this grand old preacher of the gospel. We turned away from the place, orphans in this world. O how we miss him! No more his dear, loving letters come to cheer us on to battle and to victory. All that we have left to remind us of our sweet childhood is our precious mother. How our hearts gather about her, now that he is gone! Sadder still, it means the breaking up of our dear old hearthstone. Our old home is no more. The place where we gathered from life's storms to find father's sympathy and mother's love is gone from us forever. O how dark the world is now! But heaven is brighter.

At a regular meeting of Sunbright Lodge A. F. and A. M., held soon after his death, the following preamble and resolutions were adopted:

In Memoriam.

ABSALOM B. WRIGHT—A MASTER MASON.

BORN NOVEMBER 3, 1826.
DIED NOVEMBER 9, 1893.

"BRETHREN,—The duty assigned us is both pleasing and sad; pleasing, in that we have an opportunity of presenting a few of the many virtues and good qualities of our departed brother; and sad, in that he is no more with us, and that we shall nevermore hear from him words of admonition, warning, and encouragement. After a short illness, caused by a fall from his horse, Brother Wright died at his home on November 9, 1893. He was born in the adjoining county of Fentress, where he made his home during the greater part of his life. While a young man, he married Miss Cynthia A. S. Frogge, of the same neighborhood, with whom he lived in loving companionship for nearly half a century. She, together with a daughter and three sons, still survives him, honored and respected in their several homes. With the widow and the fatherless we sincerely, deeply, and most affectionately sympathize, and pray that the God of consolation may comfort and sustain them in this trying hour.

"The Grand Master has called our brother from labor. His work completed, his Sabbath of eternity has begun. Truly, the bereaved ones may look back upon his life with an affectionate and honest pride. In his early life, his twenty-second year, he gave himself to the work of the Great Master above; and as a minister of the Methodist Episcopal Church, he labored throughout all this mountain country, and wherever he labored success attended his efforts. Both as a Churchman and as a lover of our Fraternity, he was a faithful Craftsman; and the beautiful designs which he drew upon the Trestleboard may be found throughout his extended itinerancy. He was gentle, kind, and amiable to a remarkable degree, winning the friendship and affection of all with whom he became associated. He always sought to win the convictions of his congregations by soft and mild pleadings, and conversions so obtained were the more permanent because of the manner by which they were obtained. One of Christ's ministers, he was truly devoted to his ministerial work, and also to our beloved institution, which is the handmaid of Christianity. He never laid aside his armor, nor permitted the fire upon the altar of his heart to go out.

"Grandeur of character is wholly the force of thought, moral principle, and genuine love. It is the force of thought which measures intellect, and so it is the force of principle that measures moral greatness, that highest of human endowments, that brightest manifestation of the Deity. The greatest man is he who chooses the right with invincible resolution; who resists the temptations from within and from without; whose reliance on truth, on virtue, and on God is most unfaltering. Measured by these Masonic rules, we do not hesitate to call our brother great. His precept and example were always found tending to promote every good work. Masons ever rejoice at the elevated character of their members, and it is extremely gratifying to them to be able to point to such a man, while living, and say, ' He is one of us;' and when dead, to refer to his life as an example, and to embalm his memory in their hearts.

"As Masons, we point with pride to Brother Wright's life and character. Early in life he sought and obtained admission into our Order, and for more than a quarter of a century he gave his influence and energies to our beloved institution, of which he always spoke in terms of love and veneration. He became a member of Sunbright Lodge by affiliation, March 8, 1890, and was our chaplain during 1891. He has left to the Craft the fragrance of a pure and holy life, the best treasure he could have placed in our archives.

" He fought the good fight, he finished his course, he kept the faith, and there awaited him the crown of righteousness. He was one of those of whom it is written, ' Blessed are the dead who die in the Lord from henceforth, yea, sayeth the Spirit, that they may rest from their labors, and their works do follow them.' Truly, Brother Wright's works are many, and they continue with us. Many souls once shrouded in darkness, to-day thank God for the light that came to them through the ministrations of our brother.

"After the solemn services of his Church, escorted by the Fraternity of Sunbright Lodge and many of the brethren of sister Lodges, the mortal remains of our brother were conveyed to the beautiful city of the dead at Mt. Vernon, where, after the impressive ceremonials of our Craft had been performed, his body was consigned to mother earth to sleep that calm, sweet sleep which comes only to those whose walk has been upright. There we leave him until his hope ends in fruition, and on the glorious morning of the resurrection his body rises as immortal as his soul.

"In Brother Wright's death our Lodge has lost one of its brightest jewels. It is therefore,

"1. *Resolved*, That in testimony of our love and veneration for our brother, and to aid in some little degree in perpetuating the memory of his virtues, this preamble and these resolutions be placed upon our records.

"2. That we commend the life and example of our brother to the Fraternity as an illustration of that eminence that may be reached by the well-directed and constantly-pursued purpose of doing good in whatever place in life we may be called to act.

"3. That our sympathies be tendered the family in their bereavement.

"4. That this memorial be published in the Sunbright *Dispatch*, a copy be sent to the family, and that we wear the badge of mourning for thirty days.

"(Signed,)   S. E. FRANKLIN, ⎫
               W. B. CARLOCK,   ⎬ Committee."
               THOS. MITCHELL, ⎭

At the following session of the Holston Conference, Methodist Episcopal Church, the following memoir was read and adopted:

Memoir.

"Rev. A. B. Wright was born in Fentress County, Tennessee, November 3, 1826. His early opportunities for an education were very limited. It is very possible that he never attended school, all told, more than three months. He was converted, August 28, 1843, at a camp-meeting held by the Cumberland Presbyterians, in Poplar Cove, Fentress County, and joined the Methodist Episcopal Church, October 1, 1843. Was licensed to exhort, August 10, 1844, and was licensed to preach, July 31, 1848, by Rev. Thomas Lasley, at Five Springs Camp-ground, Clinton County, Kentucky. He was ordained deacon by Bishop George F. Pierce, at Cleveland, Tennessee, October 15, 1854, and ordained elder by Bishop Calvin Kingsley, in Knoxville, Tennessee, October 6, 1867. He was married to Cynthia A. S. Frogge, May 27, 1849. To these parents were born six children, four sons and two daughters.

"During the Civil War he was a pronounced Union man, and never faltered in his loyalty and faith in the General Government during the darkest days of that strife. Embracing the first opportunity, he left the Methodist Episcopal Church, South, and re-entered the Methodist Episcopal Church in 1866. He joined the Holston Conference in October, 1867, and received appointments as follows: 1867 and 1868, Jamestown; 1869 and

1870, Montgomery; 1871, Jamestown; 1872, Madisonville (this charge he did not travel, however, but traveled the Cumberland City charge, in the Kentucky Conference); 1873, Jamestown; 1874, Wartburg; 1875, Crossville; 1876, Wartburg; 1877, Jamestown. In August, 1878, he was elected County Court clerk of Fentress County, which position he filled with efficiency and fidelity for four years, during which time he held a supernumerary relation. In 1882 he again entered the active work and served the Wartburg charge; 1883, Sunbright; 1884 and 1885, Kingston; 1886, New River; 1887, Sunbright; 1888, Oliver Springs; 1889, financial agent of Sunbright Seminary, and traveled Mount Vernon Circuit; 1890, agent for same institution, and served as pastor for part of the year on New River charge; 1891, at his own request he was granted the relation of a superannuate, which relation continued up to death.

"He was thrown from his horse, October 21, 1893, receiving injuries which, together with other complications, resulted in his death, November 9, 1893. During the nine months immediately previous to the fatal illness, he had preached more than a hundred times, witnessing under his ministry more than seventy-five conversions. 'He died at his post.' His end was peaceful. To him heaven was a great reality. He talked much of death and of the glorious future with a faith truly sublime. Rev. A. C. Peters preached the funeral sermon in the Methodist Episcopal Church at Sunbright, after which he was buried with Masonic honors in the Mount Vernon Cemetery.

"Brother Wright was well endowed by nature, and was in the best sense a popular preacher. Quick and clear in perception, possessed of a pleasing and flexible voice, and ever giving evidence of the presence and power of the Holy Spirit, the people heard him gladly. He believed in the doctrine and polity of the Methodist Episcopal Church, ever preaching the one, and defending the other. As a preacher he was evangelical, so that conversions at his regular preaching services were not unusual. 'Never be unemployed, and never be triflingly employed,' was his rule. He was a student to the last. The Bible was his chief book; but biography and Church periodical literature constantly found a place in his reading, so that he kept well informed touching important movements in Church and State, at home and abroad. He diligently circulated good books.

"Following his track extensively, the writer makes the statement that he has found more books in more homes, put there by this sainted brother, than by any one else of whom he has knowledge; and it is due the memory of this grand hero to say, of all the many books circulated, not one could be found of doubtful moral teachings. His ministerial labor, for the most part, was in sections and under circumstances involving sacrifices, hardships, and privations; but who ever heard him complain, and who will say that amid all he was not cheerful?

"He was pre-eminently a peacemaker. If any criticised him unkindly, which rarely occurred, his only reply was the charity of silence. If his brethren became estranged from each other, he sought by impartial tears of brotherly love to unite them in friendly Christian fellowship. Ever the ardent friend of education in general, he was diligent and laborious in helping the schools of his own Church. Such was his estimate of the importance of good Christian education that he, with limited financial ability, gave his three sons good educational advantages; and now the eldest, Rev. J. C. Wright, stands deservedly in the front rank in his Conference, while the others, W. D. and Asbury, are attorneys at law, with a brief but successful career.

"Brother Wright has left us; but faithful in life, victorious in death, we are richer for the blessed moral legacy he has left us. 'Mark the perfect man and behold the upright; for the end of that man is peace.' JAMES A. RUBLE."

Recently a marble monument of beautiful design has been placed by his grave. On one side is the inscription: "Our Father and Our Mother." On another side: "Rev. A. B. Wright was born in Fentress County, Tennessee, November 3, 1826, and died in Sunbright, Morgan County, Tennessee, November 9, 1893." On a third side is the inscription: "I have fought a good fight, I have finished my course, I have kept the faith: henceforth there is laid up for me a crown of righteousness, which the Lord, the righteous judge, shall give me at that day." (2 Tim. iv, 7, 8.) Just above this inscription is the cross and crown. The fourth side is left vacant for our mother.

CHAPTER XXI.
ENTIRE SANCTIFICATION.

FOR those who may survive me in this life I wish to make a few statements of how I was enabled to rise above a low type of Christian living, and to soar into the clear, unclouded element of full consecration, of perfect love, basking in the sunshine of entire sanctification. I have all the time believed that sanctification is the grandest doctrine of Methodism, clearly taught by our illustrious founder, as well as by the Word of God.

When, as a traveling preacher, I stood before the altar to be received into full connection into the Holston Conference by Bishop Levi Scott, I was asked the following questions: "Do you expect to be made perfect in this life?" I answered: "I do." "Are you going on to perfection?" I answered: "I am." "Are you groaning after it?" I answered: "I am." I felt and meant all that these questions and answers meant.

In August, 1871, it being the fourth year of my itinerancy, at Mt. Zion Church, in Morgan County, while souls were being converted at the altar, the Lord came powerfully into my heart, and filled me with a joy unspeakable. I shouted aloud his praise at the top of my voice. A good brother came to me at the close of the service, and asked me what made me shout so loud? I told him that, if I had not shouted, every log in that house would have cried out. I felt that every evil propensity of my heart was rooted out, and my whole soul was filled with love. I was so exceedingly happy for days that I could scarcely refrain from shouting aloud at any time. At the next session of our Annual Conference, in the love-feast meeting, I arose, and testified to an emancipation from all inbred sin and to full salvation. I gradually declined to bear testimony to this great salvation, and, of course, I lost the evidence, and got into Doubting Castle to such an extent that I began to think that I had never reached that high standard.

I staggered on in this way until August, 1885, when I was traveling the Kingston Circuit. I had not witnessed a great many conversions during the year, and was becoming somewhat discouraged; but before beginning my basket-meetings, I went as a deep penitent before the Lord, laying all upon the altar. I asked the Lord, as a token that I was wholly his, that, in the next two months on my work, I might witness one hundred conversions to him. Glory be to his precious name, in that time I saw one hundred and five happy conversions to him in my meetings!

In Hine's Valley, just below Rockwood, where between thirty and forty souls were converted, the Lord again filled me unutterably full of the Holy Ghost, and I shouted aloud his praise. For many days I felt that I was walking in Beulah-land, and yet I did not bear constant testimony to the all-cleansing power of the Holy Ghost in my heart. Had I borne the testimony properly, there would have been no necessity for my going again to the altar to seek this great second blessing in Christian experience. Any child of God can greatly darken, if not entirely destroy, his assurance of Divine acceptance by failing to bear testimony for Christ as he should.

I was never backward to testify to God's converting power in my soul, and yet I can hardly account for my hesitancy in believing for full salvation, or for my timidity in bearing testimony to full salvation—saved from head to foot. In the early part of the year 1890 I was requested by Rev. J. A. Ruble, presiding elder of the Clinton District, to take charge of Mt. Vernon Circuit, with eight appointments, for about two-thirds of the year. I took charge of the work, and again asked the Lord, as a token of my full acceptance, that I might see one hundred souls converted to him; and, God be praised, I saw one hundred and fourteen conversions at my meetings during the remainder of the Conference year!

Glory be to God for such marvelous evidence of his love to me! So many glorious answers to my prayers by the blessed Christ more and more confirmed my faith in my being fully consecrated to God, and in my attainment unto this second great blessing. Had I then borne testimony to the full cleansing blood, I needed not to have been splashing along in Doubting Castle.

The Holston Annual Conference met at Chattanooga, Tenn., October 21, 1891. I attended it; and without any knowledge of Dr. S. A. Keen's being there to hold pentecostal meetings, on the first afternoon of the Conference, seeing people gathering at the Second Presbyterian Church, just across the street from our stone church, where the Conference was being held, I asked some one what it meant?

He said they were holding pentecostal services there. I said at once, then I will attend these meetings. When I entered, Dr. Keen was in the pulpit, talking. I took a seat about halfway down the aisle from the door. I had never seen Dr. Keen before, and did not know whether he was a Presbyterian or a Methodist preacher; however, it did not take long to understand that he was a Methodist preacher, full of the Holy Ghost, and running over with perfect love.

His explanations given of the doctrine of entire sanctification, as taught in the Word of God, were plain and easy to understand. I took in all that he said without any criticism. It seemed that the way into the Holiest of Holies was plainer to me than ever before. When he made the proposition to all who hungered and thirsted for full salvation to come to the altar, I went at once. It seemed that almost the whole house was moved forward to the altar. There was truly a moving, melting time. I felt as though I could lay everything on the altar, and I realized that God accepted the offering; and though I felt in my heart the joy divine of the Holy Ghost, yet there seemed to be in my soul a hungering and thirsting for higher joys and undoubted assurance. These meetings were continued each evening during the Conference.

On the afternoon of October 23, 1891, I cried from the depth of my soul, O Lord, if thou wilt only fill me with the Holy Ghost this evening, I will never be delinquent again in bearing testimony to the fact of full salvation wherever I go; and, God be praised, when I approached the altar that afternoon, I felt that I was sinking into the arms of perfect love. Such power of the Holy Ghost came upon me that I rejoiced with joy unspeakable and full of glory. O what sweet peace of soul and mind I have since enjoyed! On the last evening of these meetings I rose and testified to full salvation. I have ever since confessed it publicly and in letter-writing. I pray God that I may never fail to bear testimony of the great power which God has bestowed upon me.

I have witnessed great and glorious results to my feeble efforts in preaching Christ through my past life; but I now feel that I can offer Christ as a Savior more fully than ever before. At a number of my meetings, after my return from Conference, the Lord powerfully converted a number of souls. O how I wished that I had realized this full salvation in early life! My sheaves, though many, would doubtless have been many more. I find that, with all the sanctifying grace of God, this life is to be a constant battle.

Temptations will come, and though carnality be removed, I often find my own depravity such that I abhor myself. I once flattered myself that I could grow into a state of Christian perfection, but by a more thorough understanding of God's Word I am convinced that all divine good comes by faith in Christ. If faith could be gradual, then the attainment of Christian perfection could be gradual; but as faith is an instantaneous assent of the mind, perfection must be instantaneous. I know that there are degrees in faith; but the crowning act of faith realizes a last moment when we have not attained, and a first moment when we have attained. The desired goal must be instantaneous. If the conversion of the soul be instantaneous then the higher blessing is an instantaneous work. If conversion be gradual, then sanctification is gradual. In conversion there must be a last moment when sin reigns and and a first moment when righteousness reigns. I do love that Christ that we can go to in an instant. And now I do bless God with all my heart for the happy state of entire sanctification. I expect, erelong, to go to my happy home in heaven. I feel now that I am ripening for glory. It is no hard matter to walk with God when the Holy Ghost reigns in the soul. I now daily sing:

> "This is my story, this is my song,
> Praising my Savior all the day long."

To allow that we can not live without sin, and that Christ can not save us from the desire to sin, robs him, and is in conflict with the following Scripture: "Wherefore he is able to save them to the uttermost that come unto God by him." (Heb. vii, 25.) "But if we walk in the light as he is in the light, we have fellowship one with another, and the blood of Jesus Christ, his Son, cleanseth us from all sin." (1 John i, 7.) We are admonished by the Master: "Be ye also perfect, even as your Father in heaven is perfect." (Matt. v, 48.) "The disciple is not above his Lord, but every one that is perfect shall be as his Master." (Luke vi, 40.) Paul predicts a time when perfection shall come: "But when that which is perfect is come, then that which is in part shall be done away." (1 Cor. xiii, 10.) He also represents the child-life and man-life of Christian experience in the same chapter. The different stages of the Christian life are beautifully set forth in 1 John iii, 12, 13, 14.

God has been pleased to set forth the full type of our Christian life in the word sanctification. Christ prays for his disciples of all the ages: "Sanctify them through thy truth." (John xvii, 17.) Paul says: "And now, brethren, I commend you to God and to the word of his grace, which is able to build you up and to give you an inheritance among all them that are sanctified." (Acts xx, 32.) He also declares: "This is the will of God, even your sanctification." He prays God to sanctify the Thessalonian Church wholly. He also testifies to his own sanctification: "By the which will we are sanctified." (Heb. x, 10.) These are only a few of the many Scriptural texts supporting this great doctrine. Whenever one says that he can not live without sin, he detracts from the mercy and power of the Lord Jesus to save, and claims that sin and the devil are mightier than God. What nonsense! The word sin and the word righteousness are opposites. Never can the two principles be blended so as to be one. If a Christian sins, he is not a Christian in that act, but a sinner; for sin is of the devil, and not of God. Therefore, "Christ came into the world to put away sin by his own death;" and if the blood of Christ by his own death is not sufficient to put away sin out of the heart of the truly consecrated child of God, then the mission of Christ is a failure, which is presumption.

It is claimed that St. John says that "if we say

that we have no sin we deceive ourselves," and therefore we must go along through life sinning. This text teaches that no man can claim natural purity, but that by nature he is a sinner. The purity that we urge is wrought out by the blood of the Lord Jesus. The Savior taught his disciples to pray that his will be done on earth as in heaven, and unless we can and do live without sin, there can not be any similitude between the two, for there is no sin in heaven. If we can not live without sin, then the blessed Savior has taught his disciples to pray for an impossibility. I would not be understood as teaching Adamic nor angelic purity or perfection, yet there must be a similitude between the perfect of both worlds; for the Savior says: "Blessed are the pure in heart for they shall see God" (Matt. v, 8); and the apostle says: "Follow peace with all men and holiness, without which no man shall see the Lord." (Heb. xii, 14.)

CHAPTER XXII.

THOUGHTS ON REVIVAL WORK.

1. LET the minister who conducts the meeting be very serious and earnest in all of his conversation with the people. Let him strictly avoid an air of lightness or of jest. His every deportment, both in the church and out, should indicate a burning zeal for the salvation of souls. Remarks for the purpose of exciting fun or laughter from the pulpit should be carefully avoided. An ounce of diver-

sion to a congregation seriously inclined will destroy a pound of religious interest.

While I would not have the minister put on an air of sadness, I am satisfied, from years of experience in revival work, that worldly lightness will not only impede, but possibly destroy, the success of the revival. The minister can not manifest too much seriousness in the beginning of a revival. He should be as solemn as though some one were lying dead in the congregation.

2. At an early stage of the meeting, the minister should duly impress his audience of the great need of a revival, endeavoring to fasten the conviction upon their minds that the meeting must prove either a savor of life unto life, or of death unto death; that the Holy Ghost will leave no soul where he finds it at the beginning of the meeting; that the people will either be nearer heaven or nearer hell at the close than at the beginning of the meeting. Let him put his own seriousness and earnestness upon them, and then he will be in a fair way for a revival.

3. Let the minister, by earnest effort, impress the Christian element to enter into earnest work and labor for the salvation of their unconverted friends. Induce them into praying for their friends in public, at the family altar, and in secret; and, if possible, induce them to go to them in the congregation and ask them to seek salvation. But teach them how to approach them successfully. Whenever he can get the Christian element to work in this way, and can get them properly enthused, he need have no fears about a revival. He will soon witness the

waves of salvation rolling high, and shouts of victory rending the air. Sinners can not resist such power. They may endeavor to overcome the influence, but they can not succeed; for one shall chase a thousand, and two shall put ten thousand to flight. No influence can equal that of earnest Christian influence.

4. The minister, if a Methodist, at an early stage of the meeting should hold a class-meeting, and, so far as possible, have a talk with each one in the house himself. This will give him the opportunity of knowing who are Christians and who are not, and who really want to become religious. He will then know whom to approach, and how to successfully approach them. No other means of grace can furnish him such information as this one. When the meeting has progressed a few days, he should hold an old-fashioned love-feast meeting, having as many as will to bear testimony for Christ, either voluntarily or by calling them out by name. Have them always to stand up when they talk.

If there be young converts, call on them to testify. Intersperse the testimonies with appropriate verses of song. Encourage all to talk. Let the testimonies be short and plain. Allow no long, tiresome talks. I have seen this kind of meetings ruined by such talks. Allow no one to speak of unpleasant feelings in his heart toward any, nor to speak of injuries from others. The class-meeting is the place to talk of these things, and not the love-feast. A feast of love should never be embittered with sour herbs. Let no love-feast meeting extend over one hour and a half, unless the interest be such that it should be continued. I have frequently found it necessary to continue the Disciplinary time. The best time of the day for these meetings is in the early morning, the people being then more restful and freer to speak.

5. The minister should insist on all the people to sing. Let one-half hour before each service be used in spirited song. If the meeting be a camp or basket meeting, let a number of good singers be selected to occupy the recess-hours in song. Induce the people during the recess-hours to talk only on religious subjects. Don't allow them to discuss worldly matters, and especially politics. Let them know that this is no place for discussing such topics. Keep their minds on religious subjects. The minister should visit and hold religious services in as many families as possible. When in the families, become acquainted with the young people and the children in the homes; learn their names, and find out their state of heart. Always urge their attendance upon the meeting.

Convince them that you are greatly interested in their salvation. Many young, unconverted people in the congregation feel that the minister is not concerned about them, because he does not know them by name and is not acquainted with them. He overcomes this difficulty by visiting and becoming acquainted. When he becomes acquainted with them, he can approach them easily. If the minister is not well acquainted with the people, let him obtain a good religious pilot to go with him in this work.

This work should be done at an early stage of

the meeting. A good way is to divide the Christian element, and send them out in different directions to hold religious services in the families. I have frequently followed this plan, and never knew it to fail of powerful awakenings, followed with numbers of mighty conversions.

6. It is presumed now that the Christians and the minister are at work for the salvation of souls, and that the minister has effectually secured the love and confidence of the people. In making appeals to the unconverted, he should not use abusive language. He can show the ugliness of sin without doing this. By using harsh terms, he only excites resistance in the sinner. I have never known such methods to win souls for Christ; but on the other hand, to drive them away. I have seen good revivals broken up in this way. Dr. Adam Clarke, one of the greatest divines, calls such ministers "croakers," who are continually crying out, "Ye are fallen, ye are fallen!"

The minister should faithfully uncover sin, but do it in such a way that he may convince the sinner that he loves him. He should constantly verify the apostolic statement, "Knowing, therefore, the terror of the Lord, we persuade men." He should labor to impress them that life is precarious, and that the present responsibility is great. He may relate instances of the sad death-bed scenes of unconverted people, and earnestly exhort them to avoid such an end. More than all, let him powerfully urge the claims of Christ upon the human life.

7. In inducing sinners to take up the Cross and seek salvation, it may be better, in some instances,

in the beginning of the work to ask them to stand
up, as an evidence that they desire the prayers of
the Church, or they may be induced to come forward and give their hand in token of penitence;
but the best way, without doubt, is to induce them
to come to an altar of prayer, where Christian people may encourage them, and pray for them, and
where they can better think and pray for themselves.

I do not believe that any one will be thoroughly
converted until he is entirely willing to come to the
altar and kneel down and ask God to save him from
his sins. I believe in the old-time repentance and
the old mourners' bench.

In the altar suitable hymns should be sung, and
the relatives and friends of the penitents should be
induced to come around and instruct them. In
some instances I have found it work well to lead
the sinners by degrees, by first inducing them to
stand up for prayers, then to come forward and
give their names, and finally to come to an altar as
seekers. It is fortunate for the minister to be able
to know which of these methods to use, and when
to use it.

It is always best to work by the best policy.
Should he fail on any proposition to the unconverted, he will find it harder to succeed on that
proposition afterwards.

Here he must use much wisdom if he succeeds.
When the minister can induce an influential person
to the altar, this may be the means of leading a
number of others to follow; and yet the minister
must not be partial toward the souls of men. He

must labor for the greatest good to all. Penitents should not be kept kneeling too long at the altar at one time. Let them stand to their feet while some suitable hymn is being sung, and shake hands with their friends, and with the Christian people, and with each other. If necessary, let them kneel again.

The minister should know how to direct the exercises for the best advantage. A minister should learn how to conduct an altar service.

8. It is very material to the meeting that the minister know when to begin and when to close a service. Penitents should never be kept too long at the altar. While showers of blessings from clouds of mercy are falling upon the people, and revival influence is all ablaze, the sermon should be short and to the point. Avoid all preliminaries in sermonizing. Let the time of preaching not exceed thirty, or at most, forty minutes, and never let the entire term of service run over two hours. What can not be accomplished in that time would hardly be accomplished in longer time. Never wear out the people and run the interest down with long services. This can be easily done. Sometimes it is better not to preach at all. When penitents come into the church praying and earnestly seeking salvation, turn the service at once into a prayer and altar service. I have seen preaching on such an occasion do much harm.

I was once holding a revival service in connection with my fourth quarterly-meeting. A man living in the neighborhood had bitterly opposed his children seeking religion. On one morning he came into the church greatly convicted, weeping, and praying. I thought the meeting should have been turned into an altar service at once for the benefit of this man; but the presiding elder, who was in charge, went into the pulpit, sang, prayed, and preached a long, dry sermon. I sat beside the man, and tried to keep him interested in the meanwhile; but with all that we could do he lapsed, and never again was he in condition as he was on that morning when he came into the church; for in a few weeks he was thrown out of his wagon in a runaway of his horses and instantly killed, in an unsaved state. I believe that man would have been saved on that morning but for that sermon.

In closing a service, sing as a doxology something appropriate for penitents; such as, "But drops of grief can near repay," etc.

Charge the people to allow no conversation during the intervals to divert the minds of penitents from their salvation-seeking. It will be well to have some of the more pious Christians take the penitents home with them, and hold an altar service with them in the homes. I have seen many converted in the homes in this way. A good way is to have all the penitents stay at one place if possible, and have some good Christian workers and singers stay with them, and hold a service at night with them. Let the services be held as often as at all convenient. I have known a good revival injured, if not ruined, by resting a day. This is not a good policy. When you get the devil on the run, follow up your blows fast. Don't give him time to rally. When meetings are held in towns or cities, there are a great many business men and operatives in factories and shops who can only attend services at night. In that event you will have need to hold a night service. In rural parts the best plan that I have found is, to have the people to bring provisions for dinner on the grounds, and remain for an all-day service.

In this way they can meet at ten o'clock in the morning, and hold services until twelve o'clock. Then, after an adjournment of one hour and a half for dinner, services can be held from half-past one o'clock to half-past three. The people can then go home, and make all arrangements for the following day. They lie down and sleep all night, and are refreshed for the work of next day. In this way you will not wear the people out, and will keep the work going well.

9. It is not good policy to preach on controverted doctrine during a revival. The minister may support the peculiar doctrines of his Church in a positive and mild way, so as not to offend any one. It may be proper for the minister to give the opportunity to young converts, a few times during the meeting, to join the Church which he represents; but always to do so with proper courtesy towards other denominations. The minister should urge young converts and all others to join the Church of their choice; also urge them to do so at once.

By putting off this matter, they usually come to feel very little restraint, and almost invariably backslide. All young converts should join some good Church at once. Before the close of the meeting, if there be a number of young converts, the minister, by first giving a notice of the same a day or two beforehand, should hold a young converts' meeting. Let them assemble in the altar; then let the minister point out to them the difficulties and temptations with which they are soon to meet. Let him also urge upon the Church the duty of training them properly. Many young Christians fail because the Church does not do its duty. It might be well for the minister to follow this meeting with a penitent's meeting, if there be several of them.

I have known this kind of meeting to result in the happiest way. Old chronic seekers, when brought into this kind of meeting, have laid hold upon the Lord Jesus for salvation. It is my experience that one minister only should conduct the meeting. He may employ all the ministerial help that he can obtain; but he himself should always preside.

There is no place in the Church where leadership is more needed than in revival work. It is better for one man to do the most of the preaching. He should be very cautious about whom he puts in the pulpit. I have seen the interest of meetings killed in this way. It is not well to have a strange minister preach. Curiosity may take the place of worship in this case.

If an able minister should come around, much abler than the man in charge perhaps, no matter how desirable to have him preach, let him wait for some other time. Urge the young converts to receive the ordinance of baptism at once, if they have not already been baptized. It is well to have them bound by the baptismal covenant at once. They need all possible restrictions thrown around them.

10. Now as the revival meeting is coming to a close, let the minister duly impress the older Christians with the grave responsibility of properly caring for the young converts. Have them to fully understand that, by the omission of duty upon their part, the blood of souls will be upon them in the great day of judgment. It is possible that two-thirds of the apostasy of this world might have been prevented if the Church had been true to duty. When a young convert makes a misstep let the older Christians go to him, and, in tones of love and tenderness, beg him to return, instead of denouncing and abusing him in his absence. Assure him that others have erred and have been reclaimed, and are now bright and shining lights in the Church. Cause him to believe that the Cuurch is interested in him, and is praying for him, and that he can live a true life.

If very small children have been converted, they will need very tender nursing. If persons of dissipated habits are among the converts, let the Christian friends rally to their support in preventing their relapse into former habits. If they should make several blunders, do not give them up; persist in holding them for God. Never let a soul be lost from a lack of Christian care and nursing. If they should finally go back, as Peter calls it—"The dog to his vomit, and the sow that was washed to her wallowing in the mire again"—let their Christian friends follow them to the very outposts of the enemy's camp. Sould there be penitents at the altar remaining, as is usually the case, let the minister urge their constant seeking until they are converted. Give them to understand that they may effectively seek salvation in the home, on the highway, in the closet, and anywhere. It will be well to bind the Christian element and the penitents into a covenant of handshaking to pray for each other.

If a number of young men have been converted, it will be well to organize them into "A Young Men's Prayer and Council Meeting," to meet once a week. Have as many young converts lead in public prayer as possible. The minister should organize a prayer and class meeting for the whole Church once a week.

Where a revival can be left all aglow with such class and prayer meetings as these, there need be no fears of the revival interest declining. A congregation that strictly adheres to these duties will not retrograde. The congregation that neglects these important means of grace can not prosper. The Lord help every minister and his congregation to properly attend to this kind of work! O for a baptism of the Holy Ghost upon every pastor, local preacher, and exhorter, that signs and wonders may follow their labors until glorious victory, in shouts of triumph from one wing of the army to the other, shall flash all along our lines; until "a little one shall become a thousand, and a small one a strong nation! I, the Lord, will hasten it in his time." (Isa. lx, 22.)

Then peace and righteousness shall kiss each other, and our land shall yield her increase (Psalms);

then shall the tree of life bloom in all its beauty on earth, and the millennial glory shall dawn upon this sin-cursed world. O that God may make all of his ministers a flame of fire, clothing his priests with salvation; then shall the saints of God shout aloud for joy! Then shall there be one universal revival, reaching from the equator to the poles, and one universal shout shall exclaim: "Hallelujah! hallelujah! the Lord God omnipotent reigneth! Amen and amen!"

And now, inasmuch as I have, in a short way, laid down some rules or methods for conducting revival-meetings, let me add, by way of supplement, a few thoughts on the importance of pure evangelistic revivals, and of God's favored instruments in affecting them. I would say, in the first place, that revivals of religion are essential, not only to the growth, but to the prosperity of the Church. Without them, the Church would soon die out. I know that an objector says that there is too much excitement in revivals, and that people are startled by a dread of hell-fire; that the fear of punishment, more than the desire to do the right thing, actuates them; that we frighten children and weak-minded women almost to death to start a revival. The above objections, in the aggregate, are not true. Such things, in some cases, may be the exception, but never the rule. We endeavor to plant serious thoughts in the minds of the unsaved by pouring out the terror of the law, and by every way to have the unsaved see themselves just as they are by nature, and what they must become by Divine grace, or be miserable to all eternity.

This awakening is necessary for the good of men, as taught in God's Holy Word. (See Isa. lviii, 1; also Ezek. xxxiii, 7–11; and 2 Cor. v, 20.) If this world by nature is unsaved, and man is represented as being dead, asleep, should he not be awakened? If this awakening is a necessary antecedent to his salvation, let him be awakened by any available process. I should like very much to have his judgment as well as his passion awakened.

There are very few persons who have been slumbering in sin, and who have suddenly been brought to see themselves in their true condition, who are not more or less excited because of their eminent danger. All persons are not constituted alike in regard to their impulsiveness. Experience has taught me that it would be impossible to awaken some persons to a proper sense of their awful condition in sin without some excitement. I think it to be wrong to try to avoid it. Have their judgment keep pace with the excitement! God has so constituted them, and they can not be saved in any other way. There are others that, under the same amount of Divine influence, will make no display. The psalmist says: " Be glad in the Lord, and rejoice, ye righteous, and shout for joy, all ye that are upright in heart." (Psa. xxxii, 11.) We are also admonished by St. Paul to "quench not the spirit, despise not prophesyings."

When our Lord was riding into Jerusalem, and the disciples were shouting and praising God, the long-faced Pharisees were offended, and desired the Master to quiet his disciples; but he said: " If these should hold their peace, the very stones would cry out." I think that the Christian should have as much liberty as the sinner.

If the sinner may rejoice and shout over worldly interest, why may the Christian not rejoice over eternal interest? St. Paul says that, when the Lord shall come the second time without sin unto salvation to gather his people home, "the Lord himself shall descend from heaven with a shout, with the voice of the archangel," etc.

Will not his second coming frighten those greatly who can not endure shouting in this world? Shouting God's praise is a license which we get from Heaven. Almost invariably new recruits come into the Church from revival-meetings, or afterward as fruits growing out of some revival. Should we cease to have revivals, we should cease to have a Church. It is estimated by some statistician that the heart of some member of the Methodist Episcopal Church ceases to beat every half-hour. Unless these vacancies are filled up by new recruits, the Church will soon pass away.

O how alert the Methodist ministry should be in recruiting our great army from the world! It should not only be a purpose to recruit the decimated ranks, but to increase our numbers until our beloved Zion shall take the world for Christ. Our distinguished founder said, "The world is my parish." I rejoice that the income of our Church is about three times that of our loss by death. Loss by death does not mean entire loss, but a loss only to the Church militant and a gain to the Church triumphant. The birth-rate of the world is about one-fourth greater than the death-rate, while the income rate of our Church is about three times our death-rate.

Our blessed Lord has not sent a workman into his vineyard but that signs and wonders have followed his ministry. The best way to discern a call to the ministry is to track the minister by his conversions. This rule applies to all ministers who labor in Christian lands. Some of our truest and best ministers have labored in heathen lands for years without any apparently great success. A minister who preaches for years without this Divine token has a right to question his call, and the world may look upon his work with suspicion. All may not be equally successful in this way, but each minister should feel that success of this kind, in some measure, is due him. He should not be contented without it.

I am aware that a great many of our most eloquent ministers have not been successful in revival work, but while these men may be useful to the Church they are by no means so useful as that humbler class of men who live so near the Cross that they have power with God and with men to such a degree that their appeals move and stir the Church to greater faithfulness, and cause sinners to tremble under a sense of guilt. That minister who can not animate and stir the human heart preaches only to the head; and, while he may amuse the fancy and get to himself a great name for his eloquence, yet he is not so powerful for good as that minister who, under God, is successful in revival work.

While I believe that the Church needs a variety of ministerial power, yet I must believe that God

pre-eminently owns the labors of his successful revival preachers. Some believe that all ministers are
not specially fitted to be revivalists. I believe
that the essential qualification for a revivalist is entire consecration and unreserved dedication to God.
Wherever one is wholly given to God's work, and is
willing to spend and be spent for the Lord, without any regard to his own interest, the Lord owns
such a sacrifice, and will use that one for his own
glory in soul-saving. The grandest work in the
universe is to be instrumental under God in soul-
saving. No other work can compare with it. It
has its great reward in eternity. "They that turn
many to righteousness shall shine as the stars for
ever and ever."

When the good Lord shall take us from our
labor and toil to our eternal reward, then it will be
that we shall rest from our labors, and our works
will follow us. While many of God's most efficient ministers do not trumpet their success to the
world, and are but little known, it is a glorious consolation to them to know that the Lord understands
every ounce of influence that they have used to
turn sinners from the error of their ways to the
Lord Jesus. The religious press may often attribute
the success to the wrong one, yet God knows and
will make the proper awards for service done him.

Some of God's most useful servants may be
shut up to a narrow world of appreciation by men,
yet in the kingdom of heaven they may come into
the richest rewards. The distribution that God
may make of spiritual children may not harmon-
ize with that which men make. While some are

claimed as legitimate children, God may show that they are only under a stepfather in this world. While all men labor in their various professions for a reward, none labor with more certainty of reward than those who engage in soul-saving.

Banks may fail and the hard earnings of years may be lost in these failures, but the reward from soul-saving is never lost. Souls eternally saved as stars in our crowns of rejoicing is the currency with which God rewards his laborers, and is much better than the currency of this world that perishes with its using. One has said that in this world we live on the interest of our capital in heaven.

How great that reward must be! John says: "It doth not yet appear what we shall be; but we know that when he shall appear, we shall be like him; for we shall see him as he is." O what a glory it will afford us when we reach our blessed home in heaven, to be daily and hourly receiving our reward for laboring for God in this world, in souls brought to Christ through our influence as they reach their home in heaven! O, may the hope of such a reward stimulate our jaded spirits while toiling for God in so grand a work! Amen.

CHAPTER XXIII.

THE DIFFERENT STAGES OF LIFE.

THESE thoughts on the different stages of human life I dedicate and leave to my children, hoping, when I am cold in the ground and my blood-bought spirit is in heaven, that, simple as they are, they may be valuable to those of them who may survive me. If such shall be, I shall be highly compensated for the work. May God bless my dear children!

Thoughts on the different stages of human life, from the earliest moments to old age, can not form a subject of little importance. Some stages of life, and especially old age, are deprecated and dreaded. All young people desire to live the longest period of life; and yet they come to look upon old age as very undesirable—a gloomy part of life. Because Solomon says, "Remember now thy Creator in the days of thy youth, while the evil days come not, nor the years draw nigh when thou shalt say, I have no pleasure in them," they come to regard old age with horror; but Solomon does not describe the old life which has been true to God in this place. What I want to do in this treatise is to give each stage of life its full value, and also to note its mistakes. I should then begin with the tender babe at birth. Of all animals, it is the most helpless and dependent, and its life most hazarded at birth. The first month of its life is almost without thought. The first exercise of mind seems to be to take notice of its mother or nurse. Its first movements are its instinctive seekings after food from the breast of its mother, impelled by hunger. Thoughts and mind come so gradually as to be almost imperceptible to the parents. With time the improvement increases. As the mind begins to expand, there is in the expression of the child's eye an affection for mother and father and friends. In the earliest beginning the mind of the child is susceptible of culture and improvement.

There is not so great difference in the natural endowments as in the wise and early training of the child. While the passions of love and joy and dislike and hatred are natural dispositions, yet they can be changed either by proper training or improper training. The evil passions accumulate, to the injury and ruin of the child. Solomon has said: "Train up a child in the way he should go, and when he is old he will not depart from it." The first lesson that the child learns is to imitate others older than itself.

The mind of a child that is not under a constitutional defect is susceptible of vast and fast improvement. There is in the sparkle of the eye the expression of love, of joy, and of intelligence. Its attention is called to everything that it sees, and it claims for its own everything about it, and this without regard for the rights of others. Its mouth is the pocket or receptacle for everything it can grasp. As they grow older they are vain of fine clothing, and begin to cultivate pride. No one is vainer than the little boy with his first trousers. They also become very fond of palatable food. When they reach the age of six or seven years, the tastes of the little boy and the little girl begin to

diverge. He has a desire for a penknife, a ham-
mer, some nails, a hatchet, a horse, or for stock;
while she has the desire for scraps of calico, a pair
of scissors, a doll, some small dishes, or flowers.
This is the leading of nature for their future life.
They have a longing desire to be large, and suppose
that, if they were only so large as their older brother
or sister, they would be happy. This is, however,
a grave mistake.

All children are, more or less, bad by nature.
Some have a more stubborn and uncontrollable will
than others. Some are very rebellious to parental
authority, and greatly desire their own way. They
even think that they could make life much better
if they could only have their own way about things.
This is another grave mistake.

There are a great many advantages for enjoyment in childhood that scarcely belong to any other
age. They have not the harassing care of what
shall we eat, or wherewithal shall we be clothed,
that comes to other years. Self-reliance is not
forced upon them. They have no care about life's
support. Their greatest trouble is that they are
required to labor, and that Sunday seems so long in
coming. Should they die in childhood, they are free
from a condemning conscience, and also from the
care of earthly goods to be left behind. In childhood the imagination is very strong, and its whole
life is full of calculations of what it is to do or be
when it reaches maturer years. In early school-
days they enjoy many a happy hour spent in play,
much more sometimes than in acquiring an education; and often they complain of being kept so long

at their books. They even complain at their parents and teachers, supposing that they are afflicting them, while they are working for their good. This is another mistake of childhood.

Affection for each other is in most cases very strong, as also rage and anger, when kindled. They often go to extremes either way. Small children can become so furious as to use deadly weapons on each other should they be at hand, and yet no stage of life is one of so much merriment and joy. They regard their parents, or those who train them, as knowing more than any one else. They almost invariably believe everything told them by their parents or teachers. Childhood faith typifies manhood religion, which brings upon parents or guardians great responsibility.

It should be a blush to Protestant Christianity that they are not so industrious in training their children in the true worship of God as the Roman Catholic in planting spurious doctrines into their minds. But we must follow the child until he merges into the young man or the young lady. There is a transient period between childhood and manhood, known as boyhood and girlhood, when they begin to think themselves about as large as any one.

2. *Young Men and Young Women.*—This is a period of great responsibility. Childhood anticipations, in a large measure, have not been realized. 'Hope deferred maketh the heart sick," and much courage will be necessary for bracing the character. This period of life is open to many mistakes. Let us study the young man first. The young man

meets with the danger of either overrating or of underrating himself. But more danger from the former. He is sure to have an inclination to follow the evil appetites of his nature. Yielding to one temptation weakens him in the effort to overcome others. His safety from evil depends largely upon his companionships and the places which he may frequent. The strength of temptation depends largely upon the surroundings.

A Scriptural conversion to God, a full consecration to his service, and holy living are essential to any young man's success in life. Right here he should take a wise view of life by looking through its future telescope. He must have will power sufficient to say to the evil habits that blast life's fair noon: "I will not indulge you." The forbidding habits to success are profanity, dram-drinking in any degree or kind, gambling in any form, lying, stealing either directly or indirectly, bad company, visiting evil places, or whiling away time in idleness.

The young man should set his face like a mountain against the great sin of fornication or in any way the indulgence of fleshly lusts. Here he will find his greatest temptation. He should not use tobacco in any form. By indulging in any of the above evils he will blast his physical manhood, and sow the seeds of death in his own body, which will ripen into a premature grave. He should have a strong thirst for a complete mental education, should learn to be economical in his expenditures, and very early learn the useful lesson of self-reliance in his temporal affairs, and in his soul's interest rest entirely upon Christ. He should observe sound health rules by avoiding late hours, either with company or in study. So far as possible he should have regular hours for meals, for sleeping, and for proper physical exercise. His mind and happiness will be greatly regulated by a sound body. He should advise with the best experienced on life's work. So soon as possible he should master and enter upon his life occupation. Every energy of his being should be bent to his profession.

Idleness and indifference to success in a young man is fatal. Industry is essential. It is of immense worth that he be courageous, and not easy to falter and despair. He should be kind to his parents and his sisters. It is a great mistake in a young man to be impolite with his own sisters. He should not permit himself to be more so to others than to them. It is one of the great mistakes of a young man to think himself wiser than his father, and refuse counsel from him. His own literary training may far excel that of his father; but his father's greater experience in the real duties of life far excels his, and is of invaluable worth to him.

It is not at all safe to turn the young man loose into an idle life with plenty of money. Nothing will start him down life's grade faster than this. Let him work himself up life's hill upon self-reliance, and then he can hold his ground. Above all, let him sow the crop in youth that will bring a happy reaping in old age.

> "While beauty and youth are in their full prime,
>   And folly and fashion affect our whole time,
>   O let not the phantoms our wishes engage!
>   Let us live so in youth that we'll blush not in age!"

Now we will give the young lady some attention. It has been unfortunate for women that a prejudice growing out of the darker ages has been unfavorable to her equal development with man, as God designed for her. She is properly a helpmate for man. It is unjust and unwise to think of giving the girl a less education than the boy. The character of the young lady is as easily soiled as a piece of white linen, and when once soiled it is difficult to restore.

A misstep in a young girl may destroy the happiness of all her future life. Society makes it much harder for an erring young lady to restore herself than for a young man to do so. Nothing short of early piety and a full consecration to the service of God can save the young lady from the snares and pits that lie in her way. While it is true that many young ladies go through life in a respectable way without professing Christ, it is also true that they owe all their success to the teachings of Christianity.

It is of the greatest importance to a young lady that she be greatly on her guard against the seductive influences of young men. Her ears should be closed to all flatteries. Virtue is her citadel of power. She should be amiable, mild, and gentle in all her deportment. Nothing is more detestable in a young lady than to be selfish or haughty in her disposition, or to be irreverent toward her parents or old people. She should be kind towards her brothers. One of her greatest mistakes is to be disobedient to her mother, especially if her mother be a Christian. Kindness in every word which she utters is very becoming in her. She should never call her mother the "old woman," nor her father the "old man." They should ever be to her " my father" and " my mother." The lady who wishes to maintain dignity of character should never be found in the dancing-room, the theater, the circus, nor the saloon. They tend to degrade character to its lowest depths. No young lady who goes to such places for even mere amusement can ever rise to much in this life. She will always grade with her associates and her places of resort. In her precious youthful time she should store her mind with useful knowledge that will be helpful to her in coming years.

A young lady should cultivate a love for home and its inmates. She should endeavor to make home as charming as possible with the sweet strains of the piano or organ, rendering heavenly music, or with the songs of vocal praise to God. She should make home a delightful place in this way. She should be kind to her little brothers and sisters, and give them all needed instruction. She should not read novels of any kind, but daily read the Holy Bible. She should delight in the Sunday-school and in the divine service of God's house. She should be an angel of mercy to the poor and afflicted all about her. By a strict observance of such rules she will march up life's hill safely, will marry some worthy good man, live happily, and ripen into a contented old age.

3. *Old Age.*—Some people seem to reach this stage earlier in life than others. When the strong man bows himself, and the infirmities of years begin to weigh him down, the iron nerves begin to weaken, and the strength of the body begins to run

low, then it is that he realizes that he is turning over the western slope of life. It has been said that one-fifth of the human race die in infancy. No good man or woman should be sad when they feel the infirmities of age stealing upon them.

If the other two stages of life have been prop-erly lived, a ripe Christian old age, having a clear moral sky, with an unclouded evening sun, yields the richest harvest of enjoyment. While it is true that the infirmities of age cause more or less bodily sufferings, yet while the soul is in sweet communion with God, the thought of soon reaching his heavenly home fills the soul with rapture, and lifts him above the cares and sufferings of life. Human life begins and ends in great weakness; nevertheless the mind retains so many happy memories of life's journey as to afford one much enjoyment.

The experiences of life are worth a great deal to old age. Nothing in this world can be compared with it. While memory is almost invariably treach-erous, and does not serve for recent events, yet the incidents of childhood and middle life come up vividly; and if of worthy deeds, they bring the sweetest recollections and comfort; but if of deeds unworthy, they bring shame and remorse. A travel in foreign countries stores the mind with the richest treasure of enchanting scenes: so life's happy mem-ories of years gone by is a book which old age can read with delight. Life's happy experiences more than compensate for the infirmities of old age. I regard this period as the crowning glory of life's long day. It will afford a richer harvest to the mind to keep a journal of life by writing down the incidents that occur in one's life from childhood to old age, especially those worthy of note. If we should record every mistake which we have made, and bequeath it to our children, it would likely prevent them from making the same mistake.

Our life experience, as well as our religious experience, together with a thorough education, are the richest heritage that we can leave to our children. If every person would write down a complete journal of life, it would blaze out the proper way of life for those coming after. Life, in this way, would become better known, and fewer fatal mistakes would be made.

Some old people have a great spirit of restlessness, while others have one of great contentment. These conditions depend largely upon the proper estimate one takes of this life and of the life to come. When an old person, compelled by necessity, has lived a life of great labor and hard toil, the inclination to continue this kind of life is very common. They do this even when they would have good comfort without it. Force of habit is doubtless the proper explanation of this. Covetousness long cultivated may have something to do with it. To make old age full of sunshine will require a great deal of care, watching, and praying.

Great allowance is sometimes made to old people for having refractory and bad tempers; but I do not see the reason for this. It is true that the mind and dispositions will greatly sympathize with the infirmities of the body; but by culture, prayer, and consecration to God, the most gentle and pacific tempers may adorn old age. Those who have been accustomed to use ardent spirits, tobacco, coffee, or any other stimulants, will find great difficulty in keeping a good temper. Persons of such habits are very likely to be disagreeable in old age.

A good, quiet, Christian grandfather or grandmother may be esteemed as a great blessing to the younger household. They will be held in love and esteem by all the grandchildren and their parents. The stories of early life are a matter of much interest to the children, as they listen in breathless silence to grandpa or to grandma talk. They give perfect credence to whatever the grandparents say. It is very comfortable to have the confidence and love of grandchildren in this way. Unkindness or indifference from children or grandchildren toward their aged sires is a great trial to old people. This should never occur in a Christian land.

The thought to the aged that they must soon leave this world should never bring sadness; for if they are ready for that change, it ought to bring the greatest happiness; for they are soon to be released from a world of toil and suffering, and to enter their home of eternal rest. Sometimes, even to the Christian, the thought of death may have some forebodings. This should not be, because, if there be a proper understanding of the transit from mortal to immortal, it will remove every sense of gloom from death.

Living closely to God, the aged one may say, like Paul, " For me to live is Christ, and to die is gain;" also, " For I am in a strait betwixt two, having a desire to depart and to be with Christ." A good, aged Christian would not call back one day of his time if he could do so. Now, by God's help, I have in some measure portrayed the different stages of life—morning, noon, and evening; childhood, youth, and old age.

Life in this world is coveted by most people, yet I am sure that a happy old age is more divorced from the world than any other stage of life. In the view of Paul, one is more crucified to the world, and the world crucified to him. It may be thought, because I am an old man while writing these thoughts, that I give an undue importance to old age. I do not think so; for, taking it all in all, I regard a ripe Christian old age as the happiest period of life. With the journey nearly ended, the race nearly run, with no unpleasant conviction of misspent time, the aged pilgrim, pointing upward, can say:

> "Yonder's my house and portion fair,
> My treasures and my heart are there—
> There's my abiding home."

The sooner out of this life, the sooner into heaven. Amen and amen!

CHAPTER XXIV.

THE FUTURE STATE.

IN March, 1888, I was stricken down with nervous prostration and sciatica, so that I could scarcely walk, even with the aid of a walking-stick. I suffered greatly at times, and could have no relief from pain in any position. I was shut indoors for a time. Sixty-one years of life have placed me on the western slope of my journey; and adopting the language of St. Peter, "Knowing that shortly I must put off this my tabernacle, even as our Lord Jesus Christ hath showed me," it seemed that my mind was drawn out with the following inquiries about heaven:

1. Having, in the autumn of 1858, consigned to the silent grave my dear babe, little John Wesley, not one year old, and wishing to gather all the light and understanding about the heavenly world that I could from God's Word and the inspiration of the Holy Ghost, the following thoughts were suggested. If they shall prove helpful to my dear children after my body is laid in the grave to rest, I shall feel that I have not labored in vain in writing these thoughts under much bodily pain. O may we all reach that heaven of which we are all thinking so much!

There are some thoughts about the future state that we have a great desire to understand, which are not explicitly taught in the Divine Word, and yet are too far out of reach of human understanding to be otherwise well known. For instance, I can scarcely suppress the uprising inquiry in my mind, in reference to our sweet babe who died in infancy, whether in heaven they will still be infants, or will they be matured in body? Will their mental powers be as inferior to the matured mental powers as here upon earth? Will their immortal minds be an undergrade from those dying in matured age who died gloriously? Shall they, with the adults, know as they are known? Christ said of the child, "Of such is the kingdom of heaven." Does that refer to their moral qualifications only, or does it refer to their mental and physical also?

A poet of our day says: "A babe in glory is a babe forever." Shakespeare speaks of "babes in heaven dandled on the laps of angels." We need not have any anxiety as to whether they shall be large or small, or that their minds are inferior or equal to those of maturity. Our blessed Lord makes them the very type of heavenly excellence. In this I think that the Lord intends us to understand that they are not inferior in knowledge; and as to their bodily size, we should have no anxiety; for among the different races of men in this world there is quite a difference in size, in some instances as much as exists between parents and their infant children. Some adults as well as infants, by some misfortune, have bodily deformities, and die in that condition. St. Paul quiets our anxieties for these ill-shapes in the words : "It is sown in dishonor, it is raised in glory. It is sown in weakness, it is raised in power. It is sown a natural body, it is raised a spiritual body." Although Paul says that one star differeth from another star in glory, yet, since the child is made the example like which we are to become in our happy conversion, the pattern will be

as lofty as the one typifying it. The Savior him
self makes this order without any reference to the
child's working in his vineyard. O may we meet
our precious babes in bright glory! Amen.

2. Will kindred relationships be retained in
heaven? Will the family relations be the same in
heaven as upon earth—parents and children, brothers and sisters, husbands and wives? Or will the
transcendent joys of heaven obliterate all the relationships of earth? Jesus says: "Whosoever doeth
the will of my Father which is in heaven, the same
is my brother and sister and mother." When the
Sadducees came to Christ, tempting him with the
story of the woman who had married seven brothers,
the Savior said: "In the resurrection they neither
marry nor are given in marriage, but are as the angels of God in heaven." Are we to learn from this
that all relationships may be retained in heaven
except that of husband and wife? Such a conclu-
sion would certainly mar the attractions of heaven
to the affectionate husband and wife.

If all of heaven are of equal kinship, then all
who go from earth to heaven from the different
races of earth will be of equal kinship. If this be
true, then the will of God should be done on earth
as in heaven, obliterating all caste and aristocracy
lines. Let us search God's Word for light on this
subject. When good old patriarchs died, it was said
of them that they were gathered unto their fathers.
This certainly referred to their deathless, immortal
spirits, and not to their unconscious, slumbering
dust; for sometimes they were not buried at the same
place. The relation of Abraham to Dives, lost in

hell, was the same as to the living Jew, "Father
Abraham." By this paternal relationship he is still
known to the Jewish world. The relationship of
brotherhood had not been broken by death to Dives
and his five brethren. He says: "For *I have five
brethren*," etc., though he was then in the spirit
world of death.

The Savior's answer to the Sadducees, of the
woman and the seven brothers, does not discard
kindred relationship, but properly answers their
question; for they did not ask Christ of kindred
relationship in the resurrection, but of legal relationship, giving them to understand that marrying
and giving in marriage is an earthly, and not a
heavenly institution. How first, or second, or any
other number of marriages are to be understood
in heaven I do not know. There are many mys-
teries of heaven that will so remain while we live
upon earth. A poet has said:

> "Till death thou searchest out in vain
> What only dying can explain."

Every law of our nature, as well as God's inspired
Word, assures us that kindred relationship is retained in heaven. The mother of Zebedee's children
came to the Savior to ask that her two sons might
have the distinguished honor of sitting, the one on
his right and the other on his left in his kingdom.
She certainly, if she understood the nature of
Christ's kingdom, anticipated her sons' brotherhood
in that kingdom. As she had been just before
worshiping the blessed Christ, she certainly had
a clear understanding of his kingdom, although

the Savior told her that she did not understand what she asked, that is, such a distinguished favor.

In the seventh chapter of Revelation we are told of the twelve brother patriarchs constituting the twelve tribes of the children of Israel, of twelve thousand of each tribe, and with them the great multitude which no man could number, of all nations, and kindreds, and people, and tongues, stood before the throne, and before the Lamb, clothed with white robes, and palms in their hands. Take notice that it says "kindred" or kinship.

The Lord says, by the mouth of the prophet: "Leave thy fatherless children, I will preserve them alive; and let thy widows trust in me." (Jeremiah xlix, 11.) There are many instances in which God has favored dying saints with views of their departed friends meeting them in the hour of death, in which there is the clear recognition of kinship. There is a beautiful story told of the wife of "Little Wolf," a chief of the Iowa Indians. While she and her husband were on a mission to Europe, their babe died, three others having died before. Her sorrow was so intense that it brought an affection of the lungs. Before she died her husband tried to console her; but to all of his consolations she said: "No, no; let me go. My four children recall me. I see them by the side of the Great Spirit. They stretch out their arms to me, and wonder that I do not join them." She soon died gloriously. "Even so come, Lord Jesus!"

3. Will there be degrees of reward in heaven? If so, is it possible that there will be dissatisfaction on the account of the different rewards? or

shall each one receive his penny, and not complain?
Will those who labor through the heat and burden
of the day receive more than those who labor but
one hour? Will the pennies of reward be of the
same value?

If we are to be rewarded according to the deeds
done in the body, will not those who have made
the greater sacrifices, and toiled the more for Jesus
and his cause, receive the greater reward? Doctor
T. O. Summers says: "Some will scarcely be saved.
They will pass, as it were, unobserved into some
comparatively obscure nook in Paradise, wondering
themselves at their admission. Others, who have
done some good service for the sacramental host of
God's elect, shall have an ovation decreed them."
Will the rewards in heaven be in proportion as
they have been faithful in the different spheres in
which God has required them to work, as pastors,
local preachers, exhorters, class-leaders, etc.? Will
the approbation be as great to those under a limited
as to those under a greater responsibility? Shall
the having rule over ten cities imply greater power
and enjoyment than the having rule over four cities?
Shall there be higher and lower seats in heaven?
or shall some be permitted to be nearer the King in
his beauty than others? Will not heaven be equally
full of light throughout all of its glorious domain?
Will not the Lord God be the glorious, luminous
light of the whole city? There is to be no night
there; but one unclouded day forever.

As we are not there yet, and can not in this
mortal sphere comprehend all the laws, government, and beauties of the eternal city of God, we

must be content with the information about that desirable country that the blessed revealed Word of God in the Holy Scriptures has given us. We should not worry, nor become impatient, nor envy our brother his crown, who may be living the life of self-sacrifice and toil. Let us live so as to receive the King's approbation : "Come, ye blessed of my Father, inherit the kingdom prepared for you from the foundation of the world." As to the question of rewards, we need not be over-anxious. The human mind is so finite that awards of merit in this life are often imperfectly given. The Judge of all men is of infinite understanding, and will do right in this matter.

The communication made to Saint John on Patmos was: "Behold, I come quickly, and my reward is with me to give every man according as his work shall be." This Scripture certainly and plainly teaches that we are to be rewarded according to our works. There can be no mistaking its meaning. The pennies given to the workmen certainly have reference to the reward of pardon enjoyed in this life, as the different hours of the day represent the different ages of coming to Christ. Paul says in the sixth chapter of Hebrews: "For God is not unrighteous to forget your work and labor of love, which ye have showed toward his name, in that ye have ministered to the saints, and do minister."

The mercy and justice of God both indicate that God will reward every man according to the deeds done in the body. To the servant who had doubled his five talents, rule was given over ten cities; but to the one who had doubled his two talents, rule was given over four cities.

Ten is more than four, but each man received the proper number of his capacity. Each one in heaven will be filled. The pint measure can be filled just as full as a gallon measure, and a peck measure just as full as a bushel measure. All may be equally full, but hold different amounts. The amount of happiness to each Christian in glory will be the measure of his capacity.

In the pure element of heaven no one will envy another his reward. Wesley, Whitefield, Coke, and Asbury, whose unbounded labors for God will give them a high place in glory, will have no envy from my heart, if I am so happy as to meet the King's approval. There will be no room for envy; but with great emphasis I can sing:

> " I rode on the sky, freely justified I,
>   Nor did envy Elijah his seat;
>   My soul mounted higher in a chariot of fire,
>   And the moon it was under my feet."

4. Will those who reach heaven know all about what is transpiring in this world? Can it be that the misfortune and wretchedness of friends on earth can be a sorrow and grief to loved sainted ones in glory? Warm affection for friends here on earth is certainly not lessened in the hearts of the saved in glory. Can sainted ones communicate to us in any way so as to save us from impending dangers unseen by us? Paul says of them: "Are they not all ministering spirits, sent forth to minister to them who shall be heirs of salvation?" This communication of angel help must come in the way of

spirit acting upon spirit, and not by spirit acting through inanimate matter as the modern spiritualists teach us. Can we find in the Word of God where ministering angels have interposed to save their friends from danger? This would bring heaven and earth into very close communion, and yet it is the plain teaching of God's Holy Word.

Can we feel assured that our sainted loved ones are near us when we are passing through sore trials, or when we are groaning under the weight of condemnation at an altar of prayer? May we believe that they are near us to sympathize with us in our sorrows? Would it not be a great happiness to us to know that this is true? Do they see us at all times, and restrain and prevent many a sinful act in our lives, and thus become a greater hindrance to our doings of evil than the thought, "Thou, God, seest me?" Heaven must be full of unlimited knowledge of God and rapturous praises to him, as well as a knowledge of all earthly things. God grant that we may all attain to such exalted knowledge in heaven!

The Bible abounds with instances of angelic ministries. Angels revealed to Lot the destruction of Sodom, and urged his immediate escape. An angel stayed the hand of Abraham, about to slay his son as a sacrifice. Angels ministered to Christ after the temptation. An angel strengthened him in the garden of sorrow. On the Mount of Transfiguration two saints of God came to earth and talked with him—Moses and Elias. Our earthly woes and sorrows can not be a grief to our sainted friends; for although they doubtless love us with a love sincere, yet are they too infinitely happy to sorrow at all. Upon their entrance into heaven, "God shall wipe away all tears from their eyes, and there shall be no more death, neither sorrow nor crying; neither shall there be any more pain : for the former things are passed away." While they can not sorrow over our misfortunes, they rejoice over our successes, especially when we have great moral victories. For "there is joy in the presence of the angels of God over one sinner that repenteth."

If we are to know even as also we are known, we shall certainly know of earthly transactions just as God knows of them. For our knowledge is made equal to his in the expression, "Knowing even as also we are known." No doubt our sainted loved ones are near us in time of danger. Joshua saw the angel standing with a drawn sword in his hand for the help of Israel. This angel might have been Abraham or Jacob, or some other saint who was intensely interested for these people. What a blessed thought to believe that loved ones are hovering near us! O how sweet to think that fathers and mothers, brothers and sisters, husbands, wives, and children in glory are near us to cheer us on to victory! How they rejoice when we do the right things! We are struggling to reach their happy home in the skies; to greet and sing with them their everlasting song of praise: "Unto him who hath loved us and washed us from our sins in his own blood, unto him be glory and honor and power and dominion forever!" Amen.

5. Will we know each other in heaven? Will the sense of recognition be lessened or increased in heaven?

Will it be possible that our glorified knowledge will be so great that we will have no desire to know each other in heaven? Shall we not know each other better in heaven than we could possibly know each other in this world? Shall we only know those whom we knew in this life, or shall we know every one? Does it mean the reviving and strengthening of memory only, or does it mean a larger knowledge? Shall we not know all the heavenly host by this extended knowledge, and not need a friend to introduce us to Abraham and Isaac and Jacob, the prophets and apostles, and all the ancient worthies of God?

If recognition in heaven be a fact, it makes that glorious land more attractive and desirable. Without it, the anticipations of heaven would be greatly marred. What a glorious change from mortal conflict and suffering to such a heavenly bliss of recognition in glory! How the belief in this precious doctrine mitigates the sorrow as we take the farewell look upon faces that we love at an open grave, and know that we shall see them in beauty again! That they shall appear as they did on earth is not the question; for "they may be sown in dishonor, but raised in glory." The glory that beams in one angelic face will flash in another angelic face.

The sweet image of loved ones long parted from us is indelibly written upon our memory, and we long to see them again. In visions and dreams they often come back to us. In heaven it will not be a vision only, but a sweet reality.

"Then friends shall meet again
Who have loved.
Our embraces will be sweet
At the dear Redeemer's feet,
When we meet to part no more,
Who have loved."

The long time that friends have been separated from each other in this world will only enlarge their bliss when they meet and know each other in heaven, sweet heaven. O how desirable it is that whole families meet and know each other in glory, where

"Sickness and sorrow, pain and death,
Are felt and feared no more!"

God grant that all of my precious family may meet in heaven! Heavenly recognition is plainly taught in God's Word. If the rich man, in lifting up his eyes in torment, knew Lazarus and Abraham in heaven—Lazarus, whom he had known in this world, and Abraham, whom possibly he had never seen before—may we, who reach heaven, not only know our earthly friends, with whom we have toiled and labored, but even all the ancient and more modern worthies whom we have not seen in this life? Most assuredly the mind that contains the source and power of recognition in this life will be stronger and more capable of knowing in glory than here upon earth.

God's Word assures us that the mind is immortal, and will not die with the body. Solomon says: "In the way of righteousness is life, and in the pathway thereof there is no death." The Savior said to Martha: "Whosoever liveth and believeth in me shall never die." It is certain that these Scriptures do not refer to the body, but they must refer to the real man, which consists in the moral, mental, and intellectual man, which does not die with the body. The human mind, the active principle of the soul, does not die. It lives to have all its faculties enlarged in heaven; such as reason, will, memory, recognition.

It is sometimes said that such a one has lost his mind. This is not a correct expression, but means that the medium through which mind manifests itself has been broken. The telegraph wire of his mind has been broken down somewhere, while the electric battery at the other end is intact. This immortal mind can not be confined to this earth, but when interest is involved it leaps out into the expanse of the eternal. Why should the dying pilgrim, when in the last moments of mortal conflict, while bidding adieu to earthly ties, request them to meet him in heaven, if there is not an inspiration in his soul that assures him that they shall know each other in that happy meeting?

If our faith in this precious doctrine, so truly taught in God's Holy Word, be unwavering, our joys and anticipations of heaven are greatly augmented. I feel assured that we shall know, not only our earthly friends, but that we shall knowingly sit down with Abraham, Isaac, and Jacob in the kingdom of heaven. Let this doctrine be a sweet solace to our souls in time of sorrow, when we consign to the silent grave our loved ones, and take a last look at their faces, so that we can say, with the utmost assurance: "We shall see you again." That we shall know them in heaven as our fathers and mothers, brothers and sisters, and as our precious children, kindles heavenly rapture in the soul. Though we have been deprived of their presence for long and many years, yet the meeting and knowing will compensate for all.

Heaven is the only place where our broken families can be reunited. Here we are separated by worldly conditions, one here and another there, so that sometimes thousands of miles intervene between us; but in heaven there will be no separations. Saint Stephen, in the dying hour, was permitted to see Jesus, and knew him. Saint John, on the Island of Patmos, saw him in his glorified state, and knew him. Surely we shall know our glorified friends in heaven.

> "O how sweet it will be
> In that beautiful land,
>   So free from all sorrow and pain,
> With songs on our lips,
> And with harps in our hands,
>   To meet one another again!"

We shall meet, to go out no more forever. Amen.

APPENDIX.

THE following is a list of the baptisms, funerals, and marriages in which my father officiated:

I. BAPTISMS.

1. BY IMMERSION.

Pleasant D. Gatewood.
Sarah C. Crouch.
Nancy Davidson.
Levi Shepard.
Henry Moles.
Elizabeth Jennings.
Rhoda Jane Jennings.
Rhoanna Simpson.
Mary Huddleston.
Reuben Harmon.
Evaline Harmon.
Jennetta Evans.
Angerine Rich.
William Pevyhouse.
Margaret Pevyhouse.
Rebecca R. Pevyhouse.
Mary Buck.
Serenia C. Dishman.
Roena C. Dishman.
Mary Jane Wilson.
Margaret E. Wilson.
Ailcy C. Dixon.
Sarah Ann Neal.
Mary Ann Neal.
William Jeff.
James M. Hester.
Amanda Vickery.
Nicholas Pickard.
Sarah Pickard.

Mary Ann Ferguson.
Margaret Ferguson.
Martha V. Cowan.
Margaret E. Campbell.
Esther B. Smith.
Winnie E. Solomon.
Mary H. Cowan.
Luvica L. Dawson.
Elizabeth W. Cargyle.
Joseph C. Taylor.
James Taylor.
Catherine McGee.
D. C. Lawhern.
Franklin Lawhern.
Virginia Lawhern.
James B. Ward.
Sarah Ward.
Patient Ward.
Elizabeth Ward.
William R. Shelton.
George W. Shelton.
Elizabeth Shelton.
Birdine Young.
Malissa Young.
Andrew Young.
Mary F. Young.
Brooks H. Walker.
John M. Dishman.
Matilda Jane Young.

Malissa Young.
Annie Shelton.
Mary Daniel.
Emily Bolen.
George B. Davidson.
William Davidson.
James Owen.
William L. Smith.
John Smith.
Isaac Smith.
Jonathan Shockey
Virginia Owen.
Anna Smith.
Rebecca Ann Cowan.
Mary Fite.
Nancy Jane Fite.
Jemimah Fite.
Jefferson Pyle.
James C. J. Moon.
Elizabeth Bookout.
Marth Ann Buck.
Rebecca Wilson.
Margaret Duncan.
Matilda Moles.
Sarah Moles.
Millie Emiline Flowers.
Amos M. Koger.
Newton Walden.
Humphrey Walden.
William C. Savage.
Stephen Coil.
Thomas Hays.
Elizabeth Hays.
Juliza Ann Cowan.
Hiram Ferguson.
Minerva Ann Ferguson.
Margaret Elzuria Davidson.
Abigail Beatty.
Mahala Beatty.
Catherine Beatty.
Mary E. Gauney.

Martha Ann Gauney.
Delilah Kannatsier.
Susan M. Robins.
Amanda Pritchard.
James H. Carter.
Ellen Carter.
Thomas Brown.
Malissa Jane Brown,
Mary Lillie Davidson.
Keziah Jane Huddleston.
Landon C. H. Rich.
William B. Simpson.
Winnie Jane Simpson.
Thomas J. Clarke.
Margaret Ann Clarke.
Cynthia Beatty.
Timothy Gauney.
Elizabeth Gauney.
Cynthia Adeline Fite.
Sarah Dorcas Rich.
Mary Evaline Richardson.
Sarah Parmelia Davidson.
Susan Welch.
Elizabeth Wright.
Laura Sublett.
Lorania Flowers.
Nancy Huldah Brown.
Ruth M. Stonecipher.
Mary E. Brown.
Evaline Singleton.
John W. Mulinax
John T. Wright.
James Choate.
Samuel W. Mullinax.
Cumanzy Mullinax.
John A. Beatty.
Hiram Beatty.
Margaret Owen.
Mary Jane Beatty.
John W. Bowden.
Emma Bowden.

Rosetta Bowden.
Landon B. Bowden.
Rufus J. Stephens.
George W. Franklin.
P. J. Smith.
Clementine Paul.
Permelia Branham.
Margaret Smith.
Balaam Beatty.
Matthew Owen.
Susan Smith.
Winney Atkins.
Margaret Mullinax.
Pheriba Kannatsier.
Nancy Gauney.
Mary Ann Kane.
Permelia C. Zachery.
Caroline Zackery.
Nancy Hale.
Elizabeth Penicuff
Marion Brown.
Martha Wayne Pearcy.
Abigail Pearcy.
Millie Morgan.
Anthony C. F. Allred.
Pleasant Hogue.
Jane Turner.
Francis Turner.
Lucinda C. Upchurch.
Delilah Upchurch.
William C. Tipton.
William H. S. Stephens
Jacob Beatty.
Jane Beatty.
Tennessee Smith.
Headly Franklin.
Mary Franklin.
Nellie Whitehead.
Sarah P. Felkins.
Joel Reagan.
Catharine Reagan.

Rachel York.
Mary Kannatsier.
Sarah E. Mullinax.
Jacob Choate.
John Choate.
James B. Mullinax.
John C Albertson.
Alexander Cooper.
James Wright.
Nancy Cooper.
Peninah Jane Wright.
Isaac Hurt.
Louisa Hurt.
Alfred Thompson.
James R. Beatty.
James Price.
Sarah Ann Price.
Mary Kannatsier.
Mary Massingill.
George B. Davis.
Elizabeth Davis.
Minerva Davis.
Sarah Ann Wright.
Peninah Wright.
Freely Anne Wright.
Prissa Morris.
Barbara A. Adkins.
Senia Pearcy.
P. Jane Stephens.
D. P. Livingston.
Elizabeth Livingston.
Sarah Hood.
Hettie J. Stephens.
George W. Stephens.
William J. Taylor.
Lydia Turner.
Malinda J. Whitehead.
George W. York.
J. Patrick Gillentine.
George W. Matthews
Matilda Jane Gauney.

Clara Flowers.
Clementine Flowers.
Lucinda Hatfield.
John Huff.
Sarah Jane Huff.
Thursa Jane Moody.
Kamanza Dishman.
Millie Crouch.
Margaret L. Crouch.
Elvira Crouch.
Mary Ann West.
Rachel Story.
Lucinda Lawhern.
Louisa Jane Lawhern.
Sarah M. Hicks.
Sarah Elizabeth Smith.
Jeannette C. Smith
Sarah Jane Amos.
Julius Potter.
Rhoda Potter.
Sarah Jane Potter.
Macom A. G. Jones.
Rachel Kannatsier
William C. Hayes.
Mary M. Polson.
Luvernia Ann Helms.
Rachel Coil.
Elzira H. McFarland.
Wesley Catron.
Jaduthan Asbury.
Mahala Smyntha Smith.
Greenbury Polson.
Elizabeth Polson.
Uphama Dishman.
Mary Malissa Dishman.
Leann Polson.
Mary Louisa Dawson.
Ruth Roanna Davidson.
Martha Braswell.
George W. Massengill.
Rosie Ann Massengill.

Calvin Davis.
Nancy Bond.
Francis M. Ellis.
Francis M. Aytes.
Henry T. Branstetter.
Solomon Potter.
Isaac B. Haun.
Rufus W. Bishop.
Sarah Bishop.
Alexander Bishop.
Mary Jane Melton.
John W. Potter.
Martha M. Potter.
Lewis C. Potter.
Elizabeth Ann Potter.
Mary E. Hickman
Elizabeth C. Jett.
James E. Jett.
Harriet M. Jett.
William Riley Shannon.
Francis Flowers.
Mary Holder.
James W. Melton.
Sarah E. Huddleston.
Isabella Huddleston.
Sarah Ellen Burriss.
Mary C Wade.
Eliza Strunk.
Hannah E. Rice.
Ellen Louisa Dennie.
Phœbia Davis.
Elizabeth Westmoreland.
Martha Ann Kempton.
Lucinda Jane Upchurch.
Sarah Elizabeth Upchurch.
Adaline Craig.
Martha Emeline King.
Mary Jane Beatty.
Peninah Jane King.
Malvina Davis.
Millie Ann Davis.

Ann Albertson.
Mary Ann Whittenburg.
Marcia P. Whittenburg.
James A. Whittenburg.
Adam Reed.
Joseph S. Crouch.
Martha E. Crouch.
Sampson Fowler.
Elina Alice Fowler.
Adalaide Malissa Crouch.
Margaret C. Beatty
Mahala Garrett.
Sarah C. Jennings.
Rebecca Goldman.
Sarah N. C. Goldman.
Elizabeth Crouch.
Eli Coulter.
Lucinda Coulter.
Catherine C. Dowdy.
Susan Victoria Dowdy.
John A. Culver.
Frances E. Bishop.
Sarah Jane Hickman.
Matilda Ann Taylor.
Thomas Taylor.
Sarah Amanda Bishop.
Arbarilla Pemberton.
Naomi Jane Jett.
Elvira Jane Cox.
Nancy Ann Cooper.
Delilah Tennessee Gooding.
Mary Jane Whittenburg.
Rebecca E Harmon.
James S. Stonecipher.
Precinia McGuffey.
Malinda Hall.
Walter J. Andrews
James Houstin.
Amanda Ray.
Alfred Wyatt.
William R. Hyder.

Mary Emma Hyder.
David Walker.
Samuel Walker.
Ruth E. Walker.
Amilla C. Wyatt.
Malinda Jane Thomas.
Berry Wilson.
Naomi Wilson.
Thomas A. Miller.
Margaret Harmon.
Margaret Jane Harmon.
Warren Ray.
John Hall.
Joel Hall.
John W. Angel.
Mary Jane Angel.
William Jewitt.
Sarah C. Blakely.
Arbarilla Barnett.
Julius J. Nitzschke.
Benjamin F. Nitzschke.
Elizabeth A. Davidson.
Sarah Adaline Brown.
John C. Harmon.
George W. Harmon.
James Edward Rich.
Rachel Kannatsier.
Julius Johnson.
Luvernia Johnson.
George A. Markum.
Emeline Reed.
Tennessee Moore.
Mary Ellen Upchurch.
Alexander Wright.
Crayton T. Wright.
John Davidson.
Archibald Dishman.
John W. Crouch.
John F. Upchurch.
Sarah Ann Davidson.
Louisa Bell D vidson.

Alexander Wright.
Nancy Ann Beatty.
Zylphia Jane Beatty.
Elizabeth Ann Wright.
Emerson Brown.
Jabez A. Brown.
Florence Brown.
Jeptha A. Brown.
Tillie Dennie.
Milton Morgan.
Nathan Morgan.
Martha Morgan.
Cenia Morgan.
James Brake.
Elizabeth Brake.
Reuben Dishman.
John Privett.
Caroline Pearcy.
Lurinda Davis.
Victoria Privett.
Martha Buttram.
General W. Wright.
James Slagle.
Emerine Upchurch.
Mary E. Jones.
Alice Evans.
Delitha Powell.
Ida Evans.
Mary Denton.
Margaret Dabney.
Mary Owens.
Anna Orick.
Amanda Odle.
Arminda Polston.
Annette Smith.
Rebecca Smith.
Mary Rebecca Bandy.
Martha Stockton.
Hannah Hayes.
Malissa Savage.
Lucretia Craig.

Sarah York.
Martha Savage.
Dona Savage.
Mary Stockton.
Artemia D. Huddleston.
Daniel W. Wilson.
Alfred K. Pritchard.
Theo. Earnest Pritchard.
Mary E. Bond.
Malinda Jane Huddleston.
Mary Ludora Flowers.
Lucinda Lawson.
Margaret Ann Holding.
Mary Ann Holding.
Nancy E. Hysaw.
Alice Belle Beatty.
Francis M. Smith.
Flavil M. Huddleston.
Mary Benson.
Guinn B. Bowden.
Avey Frances Bowden.
Zylphia Beatty.
Theo. Earnest York.
Margaret Ann King.
Layton L. Tipton.
Tennessee Wilson.
Susan Perdieu.
Malvina Emeline Gauney.
Louisa Catherine Burns.
Addie Viola Bagby.
Sarah Ann Murry.
Sarah Monday.
Alice S. Kelley.
Anthony W. Simpson.
Francis Paralee Simpson.
Margaret Ann Simpson.
Laura Laveda Cardwell.
Emma Haygard.
Keziah Range.
Rufus Aiken.
Mary Ann Aiken.

Margaret McCulley.
Amanda Jane Simpson.
Frances Belle Simpson.
Edward C. Roberts.
Harriet Roberts.
Oliver E. Burns.
Sarah Fine Pickle.
Catherine Eblen.
Emira Suddeth.
Roscoe McCarroll.
Keziah Jane Hatfield.
Clayborn Lloyd.
Josephine Morgan.
Vestina Morgan.
Charles Edward Scandlyn.
Malinda C. Scandlyn.
Robert Marion Day.
Rivulet T. Murray.

Scott W. Galbraith.
Anna Storie Hogue.
Martin B. Babcock.
Mary May Wright.
Maude Anna Wright.
Nancy Jane Owens.
Pernetta Ann Albertson.
James L. Rector.
Alice Jane Simms.
Allen F. Simms.
Lucy M. J. Frost.
Mary E. Guffey.
L. E. Guffey.
Emma E. Jones.
Polly A Davis.
John Delk.
John Norris.
Total, 503.

2. By Pouring.

Margaret Logston.
James Steward.
Elizabeth Davidson.
Mary E. Davidson.
Jacob Wilson.
Ann Jeannette Young.
Elizabeth J. Campbell.
Susan Walker.
Amanda Lewallen.
Amanda Richardson.
Thursa Fowler.
Harriet Rich.
Martha Claiborne.
Josephine Claiborne.
Edith Jeff.
Rachel Craig.
Dicie Smith.
Ellen Savage.
Susan Pyle.
Nancy McGinnis.

Diadamia Taylor.
Rebecca Pruitt.
Susan Evans.
Mariba Shelton.
Amanda Smith.
Sarah Dawson.
Artemia Ray.
Mary Ann Scarboro.
Elizabeth Walden.
William L. Gillentine.
John R. Wright.
Hiram R. Whittenberg.
James I. Richard.
Delphia Pyle.
Elizabeth Pyle.
Naira Pyle.
Lavina Pyle.
Martha Taylor.
Amanda Taylor.
Fannie L. Gaudin.

Annie Lewallen.
Nancy M. Lewallen.
Mary Ann Lewallen.
Rachel Davidson.
James W. Taylor.
Thomas Reagan.
Lucy Choate.
Lodemia Choate.
Drusilla Bowden.
Susan Erwin.
Orlena Young.
Caroline Hull.
Mary Jane Hull.
Mary Ann Goodin.
Martelia Owen.
Lydia Beatty.
Mitchell York.
Sarah Ann York.
James J. Pearcy.
Luvernia Pearcy.
Julia Ann Clarke.
Balaam L. Stephens.
Susan Tipton.
Elizabeth Franklin.
Sarah Franklin.
Margaret Tipton.
Nancy Jane Tipton.
Lodemia Culver.
Luvernia York.
Jane Whitehead.
John C. Greear.
Zylphia J. Kirklin.
Zylphia Beatty.
Sarah Ann Choate.
Louisa Tipton.
Susan Bowden.
Mary Jane Beatty.
Mary Hoover.
Jane Smith (a mute).
R. Dowell Peters.
Tabitha C. Peters.

Mary Franklin.
Susan Franklin.
Celia Jane Franklin.
Mary Jane Williams.
William York.
Agnes Allred.
Ellen York.
John Albertson.
Jane Albertson.
Amanda Beaver.
Henry Atkinson.
Rachel Atkinson,
Lucinda Atkinson.
Joel Atkinson.
Lucinda Eliott.
Tempie Upchurch.
W. D. Lowe.
Barthenia Pearcy.
John Mariday.
Catherine Jane Young.
Matthew M. Langley.
Elizabeth Eastridge.
Margaret D. Erwin.
James F. Taylor.
George H Taylor.
Andrew J. Taylor.
David A. Taylor.
James M. Galloway.
Ann Eliza Galloway.
Clara Flowers.
Maria Langley.
Minerva Langley.
Mary Langley.
Celia Ann Young.
Abigail E. Young.
J. C. Logston (before his execution).
Edith Morgan.
Nancy Morgan.
Tabitha Morgan.
Mary Jane Ward.

Winnie Ward.
Viann Beatty.
Mary Ann Beatty.
Engletine Atkinson.
Mary Ann Choate.
Jiles Anderson.
Elizabeth J. Morgan.
Jasper Morgan.
Millie Ann Davis.
Luvina Jane Pearcy.
Hiram Guffey.
L. T. Guffey.
Martha Ann Guffey.
Matilda Jane Guffey.
Sarah Jane Guffey.
John H. P. Guffey.
George M. Guffey.
Ephraim G. Guffey.
Ephraim M. Guffey.
Martha E. Guffey.
John M. Walden.
Delilah Savage.
Margaret Jane Rains.
Andrew Martin.
Harrison Massingill.
Martha Belle Davidson.
Mary C. Patton.
Catherine E. Fulton.
Edley P. Galloway.
Lucy Ann Galloway.
Marion B. Culver.
Lucinda Ellen Ketcherside.
John C. Ketcherside.
Rebecca Holloway.
Amanda Holloway.
Nancy Williams.
Emily J. Vann.
Talitha C. Vann.
Louisa E. Vann.
Calvin R. Vann.
Emily C. Brown.

Rhoda Ann Johnston.
Charlotte A. Phillips.
Julia Ann Guffey.
Laura M. Crumble.
Lewis J. Hall.
Sarah Ann Hall.
Sarah Jane Erwin.
Nancy Potter.
Barbara Jane Taylor.
Emily Jane Dawn.
Mary Ann Howard.
Elizabeth Jane Holloway.
Martin Neal.
Rufus Jones.
Patience Jones.
Emeline Bolin.
Mary S. York.
Clarissa M. Shook.
Sarah Cobb.
William Lee.
Elizabeth Lee.
Rachel Elvira Lee.
James Asbury Hale.
Sarah Elizabeth Hale.
Mary Jane Hale.
Sarah Jane Hale.
Rebecca E. Wyatt.
Margaret Jane Tabor.
Mary Loretta Tabor.
Drusilla Hays.
George W. Miller.
William L. Miller.
James C. Miller.
John A. Burnett.
Nancy Jane Webb.
Sarah Wellington.
Emma Wellington.
Martha C. Lee.
Margaret Davenport.
Martha Brown.
Flora Ann Miller.

William F. Ashburn.
Nancy Bond.
Birdie Walker.
Rhoda Ann Davidson.
Joseph C. Vann.
Teresa F. Nitzschke.
Joseph E. Long.
Dillia Catherine Scott.
Sarah E. England.
Nancy Hamby.
Minerva Jones.
Ruth C. Jones.
Barbara Ellen Paul.
Mary S. York.
Tennie Ann Todd.
Mary Rosa Nitzschke.
Sarah Jane Crumble.
Elvina Alexander.
Mary Jane Paul.
Catherine E. Galloway.
Anna M. Galloway.
Andrew J. Craig.
Rufus L. Dawson.
Clarinda Kidd.
Elvira Malinda Kidd.
Mary Lucinda Fletcher.
James H. Berry.
Sarah Berry.
John W. Guffey.
Lucinda C. Guffey.
Miles Beach,
Elizabeth Ann Rigney.
Rebecca P. Crabtree.
William L. Rigney.
Stokely R. Crabtree.
Kansas America Rains.
John Marion Rains.
General Sherman Rains.
Carter D. Dalton.
Moses Upchurch.
John Dishman.

Mary Dishman.
Margaret Wright.
Balaam Pearcy.
Bayless Pearcy.
Clarinda Pearcy.
Tranquilla Pearcy.
Mary Pearcy.
Sherrod Pearcy.
Ambrose Pearcy.
America Pearcy.
William Champ Pearcy.
Thomas Millsaps.
Matilda Viann Millsaps.
James B. Dishman.
Elizabeth Wright.
Sarah C. Carter.
Jane Stockton.
Nancy Elizabeth Todd.
John Henry Tinch.
Martha Jane Wood.
David Sherman Bowden.
Spencer A. Bowden.
Shadrick Beatty.
Pharisina E. Beatty.
Moses Upchurch.
Benjamin H. Albertson.
Emeline Chaney.
Martha C. Ketcherside.
Pharisina M. Enos.
P. Clementine Enos.
Charlotte Isabelle Enos.
Mary Jane Moore.
Pernetta Guffey.
Anna C. Lewallen.
Julia Ann McCoy.
Lydia Frances Holder.
J. Wiley Peters.
Zachariah T. Scott.
Mary Scott.
David K. Eastridge.
Rebecca Ann Jones.

I. F. Human.
Missouri Patience Chaney.
William Catlett Hurt.
Sarah Young.
Margaret E. Ketcherside.
Robert Miller.
Caldonia Landrum.
James W. Johnson.
James W. Langley.
Margaret E. Langley.
Lucretia P. Jones.
Mary C. Spurlin.
Nancy Jane Spurlin.
Isabel Paul.
Nancy Jane Paul.
Margaret Paul.
Martha Lee Floyd.
Susan Tennie Lingo.
Mary Jane Phillips.
George W. Day.
Josephine Isham.
Rowena Poland.
Henderson Robb.
Nancy Ann Robb.
Nancy Ann Able.
Mollie Alice Able.
Lillie Belle Henderson.
Minerva Kirkland.
Lillie Thompson.
Thomas Smith.
Thomas Millsaps.
Miranda Millsaps.
Susan Harriet Millsaps.
Martin Millsaps.
Ferrell J. Pickle.
Vernia Pickle.
Mary Ann Pickle.
William E. Pickle.
James Rufus Pickle.
Mattie Pickle.
John L. Pickle.

Callie Hutson.
Mary J. Williams.
Isaac Barnum Babb.
John C. Martin.
Lizzie Ferguson.
Susan Martin.
Sallie Frazier.
Laura Stephens.
Elizabeth R. Clifton.
Martha E. Thomas.
Winifred Young.
Sarah Lorinda Sherwood.
Lizzie Goddard.
Sarah Caroline Lyle.
William Green McCarroll.
Susan McCarroll.
Charles Isham.
Lillie Brown.
Robert Israel Eblen.
Eliza E. Delozier.
Minerva Suddeth.
Franklin K. Suddeth.
Mary Bain.
Gilford Delozier.
George H. Delozier.
Ellen Staples.
Nancy Jane Capp.
Sarah Ellen Claiborne.
Nancy Ann Hinds.
Sarepta Taylor.
Keziah Chitwood.
Martha Stanfield.
Thomas F. Russell.
William A. Todd.
James M. Sheppard.
Rebecca Young.
Louisa Lewallen.
Lucinda Young.
Elizabeth Young.
Lurania Lewallen.
Icia Hawn.

Lucinda Young.
Eddie Landrum.
John H. Lewallen.
Mary Jane Lewallen.
Salina Young.
Ella Lawrence Chitwood.
Martha Florence Chitwood.
Alsie Rhoanna Dyden.
Anna Sarepta Dyden.
Lodusky Griffey.
Joseph F. Davis.
Tempie Guffey.
Rachel Elizabeth Davis.
Nora Carter.
Sarah Belle Lane.
Maggie McCoy.
Lizzie Jones.
Esther Hughes.
Catherine Green.
Nancy Lizzie Morgan.
Dora Calfernia Saffles.
Levi Morgan.
Sallie Grant.
Nancy E. Hoskins.
Ella Legg.
Fatina Legg.
Margaret Isabel Duncan.
Margaret Jane Duncan.
Jolly F. Duncan.
Cordelia Mattie Duncan.
Jacob L. Duncan.
George W. Duncan.
Lewis Patterson.
George Hungerford.
Mary E. Hambree.
Wiley M. Barger.
Mollie Peake.
William Louden.
Martha E. Lewallen.
Lydia Landrum.
Clara Ann Hammond.

Hattie Jones.
Ollie Ann Galloway.
N. C. Galloway.
Callie Patching.
Harry Hammond.
Luvernia Young.
Laura Bertha Kemper.
James Solomon Young.
Pearl Coventry.
Vandora Todd.
Mary Ellen Wright.
Littleton Williams.
Edia Belle Rains.
Florida Rains.
Laura Mullinax.
Mary A. Mullinax.
Charles M. Hall.
Beththerie Huddleston.
George Franklin Brown.
Sarah Jane Alexander.
Minnie Alexander.
Mary M. Alexander.
Matilda Young.
Nancy Wayne Atkinson.
John L. Rosenbaum.
James Alvin Ramsey.
William J. Young.
Gractina Todd.
Warren E. Taylor.
Lydia M. Ward.
Laura A. Owens.
Eliza E. Owens.
John W. Owens.
Clara Belle Owens.
Mary Jane Morris.
Sarah J. Lewallen.
Thomas A. Brown.
Amanda L. Overstreet.
Henry Hall.
Thomas Stepp.
Isaac Crabtree.

William S. Norris.
Louisa Norris.
Thomas M. Newberry.
William Pearcy.
Rachel Pearcy.
Bailey O. Bowden.
Ann S. Hogue.
Delvina Greear.
Caroline Greear.
Matilda Jane Cooper.
James Clarke.
Archibald J. McCoy.
James H. Lane.

Nancy Jane Lane.
T. C. Clarke.
Letetia E. Clarke.
Nancy E. Clarke.
Matilda Clarke.
Desonia Clarke.
Sarah M. Guffey.
Esther L. Kennedy.
Sallie Ann Choate.
Hattie Smith.
Eli Hinds.
Alvin King.
Total, 468.

3. INFANT BAPTISMS.

John G. Jennings,
Miriam M. M. Jennings.
James Alvin Crouch.
John Wesley Crouch.
Milly Ann Kidd.
Robert Story.
Rebecca V. Richardson.
Margaret J. Walker.
Sarah E. Walker.
Celia Ann Clark.
Elizabeth Brown.
William W. Sheppard.
James M. Sheppard.
Nimrod E. Sheppard.
Jemimah J. Sheppard.
James B. Frogge.
Pharisina Lewallen.
Mary S. York.
Rebecca A. Richardson.
Mary E. Richardson.
John F. Richardson.
William H. Richardson.
Thomas Owen.
Arminda Jane Smith.
Martha Ann Savage.

Deborah V. McGinnis.
James C. McGinnis.
Rebecca Lean Crouch.
George L. D. Carpenter.
Luvica Ward Frogge.
Mary Etta Koger.
Martha Ellen Koger.
Nancy Ann Koger.
Sarah Wilburn Savage.
Sidonia Savage.
James Robert Smith.
George Amos Smith:
Mary Elizabeth Owen.
Wesley C. Peters.
Mary Catharine Allred.
William A. Allred.
Martha R. A. Allred.
Pleasant Byron Allred.
John William York.
Hamilton Tipton.
James C. Stephens.
Cynthia J. W. Lewallen.
John G. Lewallen.
Malinda Young.
Latin W. Young.

28

William H. Young.

John G. Young.

Arnold W. Young.

Mary F. Jones.

William Jones.

Sarah Jane Jones.

Julia Ann Jones.

Rhoda Ann Smith.

Wesley Iredel Peters.

William R. Peters.

Emma P. Peters.

Lydia E. Scott.

Nebraska McCart.

Nancy Jane Peters.

Worcester O. Peters.

Nancy Jane Davis.

Nancy M. York.

Mary E. York.

Andrew M. York.

James Absalom York.

Absalom B. W. Eastridge.

James M. W. Goddard.

Victory McCart.

William Wright McCoy.

Alice McCart.

Minerva Alice McCart.

James Preston McCart.

Elizabeth Langley.

Emily Langley.

George W. Langley.

Celestia Victory Peters.

Mary Malone Davidson.

Absalom B. W. Young.

Meno Rhufina Young.

Lucinda Malvina Lewallen.

William A. Williams.

John William Lewallen.

Matilda Helen Dail.

Henry Grant Dail.

Mary Ellen Dail.

Martha Florence Dail.

Rufus M. Dail.

Greer Johnson Skaggs.

Christopher Beatty.

Putman Beatty.

Hiser Beatty.

James Melvin Paul.

Elizabeth Butram.

Nancy Jane Catron.

Delitha L. A. J. York.

Matilda E. Guffey.

Mary Jane Martin.

Serenia E. Martin.

Martha E. Massingill.

Samuel Walker Paul.

Mitchell Whittenburg.

Pearson Whittenburg.

Edmondson Whittenburg.

Elizabeth Whittenburg.

Joseannes Davidson.

Mary Ida Davidson.

Martha I. Davidson.

William Massingill.

Mack Massingill.

Martin Van Buren Guffey.

Fannie Jane Savage.

John Wesley Galloway.

Absalom B. Peters.

Rachel Annis Peters.

Josephine C. Young.

Anna C. Lewallen.

Absalom F. Lewallen.

Elisca Orlenia Dail.

Mary J. E Farmer.

Nancy Hannah Perdieu.

Joseph E. Ketcherside.

Jessie L. Ketcherside.

Sarah Ellen Cochram.

Franklin Perry Galloway.

John Boyd Peters.

James Arlo Peters.

Elustus A. Washington.

William D. Eastridge.
William F. Atkinson.
Dailey Wesley Atkinson.
James R. McCart.
Sarah Jane Todd.
Engle Todd.
Josephine Todd.
Lawrence E. Roberts.
Julius G. Miller.
Lewis H. Mosier.
Joseph W. Wardell.
Charlotte E. Davis.
Miles Taylor Paul.
James Franklin Young.
Minnie Belle Peters.
Robert K. Peters.
William Ryley Hull.
Henry Latin Galloway.
Artemecia Galloway.
Lewis Willie Nitzschke.
Sarah Agnes Bales.
Charles Husky.
Allie Davis Perdieu.
William E. Perdieu.
Charles G. Shaver.
William B. Atkinson.
Keziah V. V. Atkinson.
Haywood B. Carter.
Wilburn C. Carter.
Maritta Belle Hughes.
Celia E. Upchurch.
Florence M. Goff.
Anna E. Stonecipher.
Samuel G. Young.
Hollis O. Lewallen.
Thomas W. York.
Granville L. Young.
Henry F. Davidson.
Susan F. Davidson.
Elizabeth Belle Dawn,
James P. Atkinson.

Polly M. Butram.
Susan L. West.
C. D. West.
Leo Upchurch.
George W. Upchurch.
Luvernia N. Williams.
William A. Butram.
John M. Butram.
Isaac A. Franklin.
George G. Franklin.
Lemuel D. Franklin.
John M. Franklin.
Wheeler W. Johnson.
John W. Atkinson.
Mary A. Beach.
John H. Paul.
William D. Lee.
Cora E. Lee.
Joseph S. Rains.
Charles C. Rains.
Cyril W. Rains.
Mary I. Greear.
Susan Jane Butram.
Cyril Scott.
Joseph Kelly Stockton.
Rutherford Hays Peters.
Julia Florence Scott.
Orlena Ollie Albertson.
Rosetta Jane Albertson.
Nancy E. Albertson.
Hillary S. Young.
Lucy Jane Stonecipher.
Orlando H. Lewallen.
Calvin Kingsley Lewallen.
John Landen Johnston.
Ruha Isabel Peters.
Gilbert Kingsley Beach.
William Haskell Shaver.
Rebecca F. Shaver.
Theodore Barden Young.
Alice Victoria Young.

Dwight L. Tipton.
Lelor Dell Tipton.
Willie C. Sloan.
George W. Paul.
James A. Paul.
Permelia A. Paul.
Andrew F. Paul.
Timothy D. Paul.
Frances M. Paul.
Lauressa Etta Peters.
Lusetta L. Goff.
Lewis S. Atkinson.
Henry S. Stockton.
George L. C. Stockton.
Ida Willard Beach.
Alonzo H. Lewallen.
Jessie Howard.
Abraham Lee Buxton.
Sarah Loretta Howard.
Minnie Belle Davidson.
Florence Belle Albertson.
Stanley Matthews.
Augusta Matthews.
Timothy C. Young.
Jennie E. Justice.
Bessie A. McCart,
Mary V. Shannon.
Rebecca Belle Shannon.
Hezekiah Shannon.
Charles Oliver McCart.
George Houk Buxton.
Maggie Ann Perdieu.
William Charles Barnett.
Eddie L. Paul.
William Asbury Peters.
Ida Maloney Peters.
Margaret Ann McCart.
Maggie C. McCoy.
Nathaniel G. M. McCoy.
Leroy Houk Shannon.
Eugene M. Ketcherside.

William H. Young.
Henry Latin Young.
Bernetta Ann Young.
Zachariah McCart.
Minnie Belle McCart.
Hattie V. Kington.
James M. Stockwell.
Victoria Alice Paul.
Jennie June Bullard.
Callie Isham.
Frank Allen Young.
Victoria Isham.
Mary Amanda Stockton.
Emma Cordelia Beach.
Cynthia E. Jones.
James Goddard.
Harvey Goddard.
Joan M. Crow.
Maud E. A. Crow.
Laura Jackson Crow.
Willie Larkin Crow.
Lewis H. Suddeth.
Mary Suddeth.
Willie F. Suddeth.
Hilton Burk Millsaps.
Nannie J. Millsaps.
Ida May Millsaps.
Robert L. Millsaps.
Marcus D. Millsaps.
John Carpenter.
Martha C. Burns.
Timothy V. H. Peters.
Elizabeth Young.
Nancy E. Kington.
Nancy E. Dyden.
Martha R. Dyden.
John A. Dyden.
Jacob Noah Dyden.
Jessie S. Hamby.
Jacob A. Rogers.
James N. Rogers.

George D. Rogers.
Minerva L. Rogers.
Clarke E. W. Peters.
Robert Duncan.
Cynthia Duncan.
Widdie Duncan.
Louisa Duncan.
Jasper Newton Duncan.
Michael Duncan.
Henry Duncan.
Dock Duncan.
Mary Duncan.
Isaac Duncan.
Arthur Logan Duncan.
Nancy Jane Duncan.
Cassie Duncan.
Sarah E. Duncan.
Andrew Duncan.
Carrie Ann Duncan.
Jolly Monroe Duncan.
Alfred Duncan.
Eddie Duncan.
John Smith.
Tollis N. Jones.
Hallie May Jones.
Sallie Myrtle Jones.
Debbie Ray Galloway.
Nancy E. Galloway.

Lousianna I. Galloway.
Cordelia J. Galloway.
George T. Galloway.
Minnie G. Young.
Louie Crozier.
Sarah S. Waddell.
Benton A. G. Stockton.
Doshea A. Stockton.
Richard T. Stretmatter.
Winnifred Stretmatter.
Andrew Stretmatter.
Winchester C. Stretmatter.
Deborah May Peters.
Ralph F. Galloway.
Ermine P. Galloway.
George L. Birch.
John W. Watts.
Winnie A. Watts.
Grace A. Heaps.
James P. White.
Archibald White.
Virgil White.
Adam P. White.
Jennie S. Hamby.
William E. Cobble.
James Roy Young.
Arbanna Young.
Lenora Young.

Total, 352.   Grand total, 1,323.

II. FUNERALS.

1. ADULTS.

Mary Jennings.
Thomas Huckaby.
Mary Sandusky.
Franklin Pruitt.
Thomas Brown.
Larkin Brown.
Mary Sanders.
Elizabeth Gentry.
Abraham Brown.
Joseph Grimes.
Joseph Millsaps.
Cynthia Rains.
William Huckaby.
Barbara Paul.
Elizabeth Dishman.
Jeremiah Nicholas.
William Crouch.
John Rich.
Sarah Ann M. Harris.
Elizabeth Moles.
John Vann Hoosier.
Nancy Hoosier.
Margaret L. Jackson.
Allen Beatty.
Martha Savage.
Rachel Helm.
Frances M. Butram.
John Buck.
Permelia Craig.
Alexander Hays.
Elizabeth Hays.
Isham Simpson.
Ransom Smith.
Hannah Hays.
Elizabeth Whittenburg.
Uriah Range.
Sylvester Hicks.

Charles Hick.
Catharine Hurt.
Nancy Solomon.
Thomas Pyle.
Leo. Upchurch.
Moses Upchurch.
Catherine Upchurch.
Tabitha Horton.
Alfred Helm.
Robert McGee.
Mariah Miller.
Elizabeth Smith.
Elijah Brummet.
James M. Coyle.
Isaiah Wright.
Mary S. Ellis.
John Pruitt.
Lavina Mace.
George Y. Carpenter.
Clarinda Dalton.
Brient Smith.
Granville Smith.
Nancy Crabtree.
Jane Savage.
Moses Dishman.
Millie Dishman.
Celia Ann Bridewell.
Robert Whitehead.
Robert S. Evans.
Isaac Scarboro.
Alexander Hays.
Isabel Frances Dawson.
Lydia Ward.
Richard Ward.
Mahala Hatfield.
John Halbert.
Stephen Halbert.

Mary Young.
Robert Wilson.
Henry G. Wilson.
Miles Privitt.
Anna Atkinson.
Lucinda G. Atkinson.
Thomas Riley.
Millie Ann Riley.
John M. Smith.
Joseph M. Perdieu.
Henry Perdieu.
George W. Robbins.
Henrietta P. Simmerman.
Leanders J. Peters.
Nancy Cowan.
Granville G. Beatty.
Pleasant W. Beatty.
Jeremiah Polson.
Jeremiah Coile.
George Huckaby.
Jessie Robertson.
Solomon Albertson.
James Coulter.
Joseph Coulter.
G. W. Upchurch.
James Craig.
Jane Craig.
Missouri Clarke.
Walter Davis.
Rhoda Davis.
Mark Pearcy.
Esquire Buck.
Vincent Coleman.
Fannie Coleman.
Andrew B. Hull.
Morgan H. Hull.
John A. Beatty.
Thomas Beatty.
Green Beatty.
William Beatty.
Elizabeth Jennings.

Rebecca Davis.
Minerva Slavy.
Elizabeth Jennings.
James Patterson Walker.
Margaret Walker.
William H. Brooks.
Consider Carpenter.
Elizabeth Owen.
Constant Guffey.
Rev. John M. Guffey.
David M. Cowan.
Rebecca Jane Bond.
Louisa Jane Zachery.
Samuel R. Littrell.
Lucy Galloway.
Catherine Galloway.
William Flowers.
Sarah Beatty.
Philip H. Beatty.
Catherine Rich.
Evaline Singleton.
Nancy York.
Lucy Ann York.
Avey York.
Rebecca Holloway.
Luvica G. Hamby.
Albert G. Morgan.
Martha Todd.
Jennette Evans.
Sarah Catron.
George Miller.
Elam Huddleston.
Calvin Logston (just
    before execution).
Michael Brown.
R. J. Jones.
Amanda Jane Eastridge.
Nancy E. Peters.
John E. Kannatsier.
William H. McGee.
Nancy Wright.

Mary Ann Polson.

Elizabeth J. Morgan.

Sarah Pearcy.

Frances Pearcy.

Thomas Souder.

Sarah Ann McGhee.

Elizabeth Beard.

Uphama Hays.

James Hays.

James Bookout.

Christina Ridenour.

Jefferson Ridenour.

Robert Ridenour.

Malitha C. Frogge.

Malissa Jane Asbury.

Julia Ellen Threat.

Alice Eliza Wheaton.

Timothy C. Vann.

Rev. Andrew Lewallen.

Sarah W. Gould.

Johnson Jones.

Mary Davis.

Rebecca Wilson.

John W. Simms.

Sarah Simms.

Lucy Grogan.

Hannah E. McCoy.

Mary B. Dail.

Thomas Crabtree.

Jessie L. McKeathan.

Martha Ann Davidson.

Elijah Cross.

Barbara Erwin.

Samuel Taylor.

Catlett G. Fairchilds.

Frances Hull.

William Cooke.

Jane Cooke.

Zebah Wright.

Sarah Duncan.

Mary Miller.

A. M. Allen.

Lucinda Hatfield.

Caleb Harmon.

Uphama Harmon.

Elizabeth Jane Koger.

Austin Wilson.

William Wilson.

Mary Ann West.

Sarah Ann Hale.

Sarah Crabtree.

Barnett Dawn.

Anna Young.

Mary S. Goff.

Rebecca Evans.

Delphia Williams.

Mary Jane Howard.

Vashtina Upchurch.

Sarah Adaline Allen.

Elizabeth Jane Guffey.

Creacy M. Allen.

George W. Upchurch.

Nancy Guffey.

Joseph McCoy.

Rhoda York.

Millie Lewallen.

Susan McCormick.

Nancy C. McCormick.

Nancy Holloway.

Sarah Cobb.

Martha Hurt.

Jonathan S. Bowden.

Landon C. H. Bowden.

John T. W. Upchurch.

Mary Savage.

Ellen Savage.

James Edward Rich.

James King.

Anna Jennings.

James Choate.

Ephraim M. Guffey.

Lucy Choate.

Michael Hale.
Henry L. Beatty.
Emsley Butram.
Elizabeth Butram.
Rebecca Guinn.
Timothy A. West.
Jane Polston.
Robert W. Holding.
Rev. Calvin R. Vann.
Martha Belle Pyle.
Clarissa Tennessee Hicks.
Elizabeth Lane.
Charles Lane.
William Lane.
Michael D. Upchurch.
Elizabeth Hancock.
Charles Dabney.
Amanda L. Stewart.
Mary M. Polson.
Bodicia Johnson.
Rebecca Johnson.
John Alvin Johnson.
Mary Ann Jones.
Dorcas Hatfield.
Thomas R. Turner.
Jessie Kennedy.
Sarah C. Buck.
Lavinia Ridenour.
Absalom C. Guffey.
Jefferson York.
Artemia Wilson.
William Perdieu.
William Brown.
Mary Jones.
Emma Bowden.
Elijah York.
Elizabeth Lavender.
Noah Buck.
Sarah Jane Crouch.
Mary Ann Choate.
Samuel Cobb.

Rhoda A. Griffey.
Rachel Rutledge.
Anna Young.
Julia G. Sargent.
Elizabeth Guffey.
Benjamin H. Albertson.
Elizabeth Peters.
Francis M. Goddard.
Robert Davis.
Sarah Davis.
Sarah Price.
Ruth Duncan.
Craven Duncan.
Aaron Grindle.
Salina D. Todd.
Luvica F. Peak.
Sarah E. Russell.
John Eblen Bailey.
Ann Jane Summers.
Michael Millsap.
Mary Ann Brown.
James Young.
John Range.
Sallie Jennings.
Braxton Lane.
Christina Love.
Tennessee McCart.
Vardamin Bird.
Elizabeth Bird.
Dolly Hungerford.
Elizabeth Morgan.
Belle Peake.
Abigail Young.
Letitia Strange.
William J. Kellin.
Cordelia Hungerford.
Jeremiah Wright.
Nancy A. Davidson.
Margaret Langley.
Sarah Bishop.
Martha Potter.

Charlotte J. Russell.

Nancy Jane Duncan.

Mary Ann Jones.

Michael M. Duncan.

Elizabeth F. Crabtree.

Louisiana Galloway.

Elisha Cheney.

Epsie Bird.

George Hungerford.

Mary B. Wright.

John Coile.

Catherine J. Alexander.

Sarah Ann Alexander.

Rev. Charles E. Atkinson.

William T. Atkinson.

Levi Morgan.

Levi Branstetter.

Rebecca D. Birch.

Thomas Wright.

Catherine Davis.

Oliver P. Cooper.

Mary Ann Wright.

Mary Ann Bain.

John Brown.

Susan Carpenter.

Gilford Delozier.

Doctor Kemp.

Margaret Duncan.

Elizabeth Bunch.

Susan Beatty.

Ailey S. Beatty.

Francis Smith.

Sarah Beatty.

Emeline Smith.

David F. Hall.

Amanda E. Hall.

Viann Stephens.

Nancy P. Hall.

Mary R. Lyle.

Catherine C. Cochran.

Matilda J. Choate.

Celia Jane Clark.

William Guffey.

James Hicks.

Mary Malinda Taylor.

Rev. Michaiel M. Shaver.

Mary E. Smith.

Texas S. Lavender.

Samantha E. Justice.

Tennessee Louisa Beatty.

Aggie Goddard.

Total, 389.

2. FUNERALS OF INFANTS.

Jasper Huckaby.

Barsha Huckaby.

John Pruitt.

Hannah Pruitt.

Mary Westmoreland.

James M. Edwards.

—— Crabtree.

—— Crabtree.

Dorothy Crabtree.

Mary Lewallen.

Emma Lewallen.

Nancy Jane Fowler.

—— Fowler.

Nancy Price.

Mary Jane Jackson.

John Grimsley Jackson.

Lucinda E. Helm.

Matilda Jane Helm.

Benjamin Neal.

Shelby Neal.

James F. Crabtree.

—— Crabtree.

—— Crabtree.

—— Craig.

—— Craig.
—— Craig.
Marcillo Whittenburg.
James Rains.
Martha Ellen Hurt.
Andrew F. Smith.
—— Smith.
Sarah Jane Jennings.
Bolin E. R. Jennings.
John S. Smith.
Abel Miller.
Edith Miller.
George W. Riggs.
—— Riggs.
—— Coil.
Lincoln L. Braswell.
Belzuria E. Brown.
Cordelia Whittenburg.
Epsy Ellen Dishman.
—— Dishman.
—— Dishman.
—— Dishman.
—— Dishman.
Malinda Smith.
Nancy Jane Boiter.
Dorcas Ann Dawson.
Rebecca R. Young.
Eli Marion Young.
John G. Smith.
Pleasant A. Polson.
Mary C. Pruitt.
James E. Pruitt.
Elvira Pruitt.
John H. Pruitt.
Moses W. Matthews.
Mary Alice Johnson.
Elisha M. Mosier.
Lucinda Jane Mosier.
Nancy Ann Mosier.
John G. Lewallen.
Rhoda E. Lewallen.

Sherrod Brewster.
Pheriba E. Brewster.
—— Clarke.
—— Clarke.
James B. Franklin.
Pleasant B. Allred.
Latin R. York.
George W. York.
Rachel Freely York.
Mary Belle Coulter.
Mary E. Guffey.
Pheriba E. Dowdy.
William R. Dowdy.
Mary Jane Galloway.
William B. Galloway.
Mary M. Branstetter.
John Allen.
Adeline Allen.
Sarah E. Morgan.
William G. Morgan.
Margaret A. Morgan.
Epsie M. Morgan.
Mary Jane Morgan.
Albert G. Morgan.
Benjamin T. Young.
Julia Ann Hicks.
James A. Hicks.
Elizabeth Ann Mosier.
Sarah E. A. Alexander.
Malvina Evans.
Mary Frances Evans.
Ervinia Catron.
John Matthews.
Lou Ann Pyle.
Mary Jane Pyle.
John B. Pyle.
—— Peters.
Susan M. Hurt.
Russel Hurt.
Sarah Jane Stinson.
John M. Buttram.

James W. Catron.
William F. Atkinson.
—— Threat.
Elizabeth H. Jones.
—— Simms.
Nancy L. Galloway.
Martha Jane Matthews.
Susan C. Crabtree.
Manson Crabtree.
Eliza Jane R. Crabtree.
Thomas P. Crabtree.
George W. Crabtree.
Jessie W. McKeathan.
John Mann Young.
Martha Jane Jones.
Frances Jones.
William F. Atkinson.
Sarah Ann Taylor.
George W. Hays.
Nancy Jane Wilson.
Willie Cross.
Catherine E. Todd.
William M. Todd.
Engle Todd.
Margaret Ann South.
General H. West.
Mary E. C. Bond.
Ulysses Grant Felkins.
Lewis B. Mosier.
Josie Annis Davidson.
John Henry Howard.
Henderson Upchurch.
Delilah E. J. Upchurch.
Benjamin York.
Henry W. Lewallen.
Henry O. Jones.
Jacob Bowden.
David Graham Lewis.
Robert Ward.
—— Beatty.
—— Choate.

John Wright Hale.
Louisa Jane Alexander.
Virginia Holding.
Tennessee Holding.
Alonzo V. Hull.
Smith Hoover.
Thomas Hancock.
Mary A. Hancock.
John P. Polson.
—— Steward.
Rosie Lee Franklin.
Anna E. Stonecipher.
Flora M. Young.
Eugene C. Whitney.
Martha Jane Jones.
Florence Jones.
Indiana Jones.
Flora Jones.
Tennessee E. Jack.
Bertha May Guffey.
William Ferrill.
Thomas M. Clarke.
John Mann Paul.
Nancy A. Brown.
Fannie L. Lavender.
John Wright McCart.
Freddie C. Paul.
Viola McCart.
Robert Tupman.
Emmett McCart.
Esau Peake.
Samuel M. Bailey.
Media I. Millsaps.
Callie E. Lane.
Minnie E. Kinsen.
Josie M. A. Kinsen.
Samuel D. Scott.
Franklin Underwood.
Joe Franklin Tupman.
Myrtie E. Jones.
Young H. Staples.

John Hurt.

Mary Jane Hambright.

Freddie Suddeth.

Lula Underwood.

Margaret J. Dishman.

Rosie Jane Russell.

Evia Dudley.

Leroy A. Ward.

James Spurlin.

Delilah Jane Staples.

Susan A. Tupman.

Maude Mitchell.

Solomon Jones.

Lucinda C. Jones.

Lloyd H. Staples.

—— Lacy.

Mattie L. Peters.

Arthur C. Peters.

Armond C. Peters.

Leo Allen Neal.

William A Bullard.

Parisinna Lewallen.

Jane Beatty.

Monnt. H. Lewallen.

—— Rains.

Mary J. Johnson.

John S. Tracy.

Mary E. Wright.

Martha Ann Wright.

Benjamin Wright.

—— Wright.

Nancy A. Clarke.

Samuel G. W. Clarke.

Arie C. Smith.

Total, 222.   Grand total, 611.

Those whose first names are not given were unnamed infants.

III. MARRIAGES.

James West	to Sarah Slagle.
Thomas Kempton	to Malissa Crabtree.
Sampson Pruitt	to Malinda Smith.
James H. Story	to Rebecca Pevyhouse.
John R. Morgan	to Elvira M. Crouch.
William Stinson	to Rhoda Ann Sloan.
Benjamin S. Barton	to Margaret Evans.
Jasper J. Campbell	to Lucinda J. Carpenter.
Rev. Willet G. Sherman	to Fannie Latham.
Julius Johnson	to Luvernia Crouch.
John Carpenter	to Peninah J. Wright.
Jesse L. Robinson	to Nancy Young.
Rev. T. C. Peters	to Rebecca B. Frogge
George Catron	to Lean Kannatsier.
Archibald Penicuff	to Mahala Westmoreland.
John C. Bookout	to Maria E. Witt.
Moore Medlock	to Harriet Riley.
Thomas Riley	to Millie Ann Smith.

Rev. B. L. Stephens	to Sarah Moredock.
Joshua F. Wright	to Z. Angeline Price.
James Campbell	to Martha Richardson.
William Hurt	to Serinia C. Dishman.
Robert P. Garred	to Sarah Ann Allen
Thomas Hays	to Margaret Pevyhouse.
Isaac D. Campbell	to Martha E. Cullom.
John R. Wright	to Emeline Westmoreland.
William Looper	to Mary E. Kidd.
David Greear	to Malissa M. Jennings.
George W. Ward	to Eliza Bookout.
Alexander Williams	to Loretta Kidd.
Elias T. Bond	to Rebecca Cowan.
David Butram	to Amanda Gray.
Wilson Dewett	to Alsie Gilreath.
Franklin D. Hull	to Catherine Galloway.
Alfred Lawson	to Eliza Ann Smith.
E. J. Price	to Celestia C. Springer.
John E. Savage	to Nancy C. Reese.
George S. Kington	to Elizabeth C. Gould.
McKager York	to Sarah J. Smith.
A. B. Williams	to Mary Jane Littrell.
John C. Barger	to Mahala Stonecipher.
Ellis H. Crouch	to Ruth Luster.
Rev. J. H. Carter	to Sarah E. Dawson.
Rev. William S. Hill	to Selenia Brown.
Dan C. Young	to Hannah N. Galloway.
James W. Peters	to Elizabeth Eastridge.
G. W. Crouch	to Millie Ann Dishman.
James C. Butram	to Sarah Franklin.
Wright Meroney	to Elizabeth Duncan.
J. S. Stonecipher	to Nancy M. Lewallen.
Reuben B. Lee	to Nancy Ann Crofts.
William Key	to Eliza Jane Baldwin.
James F. Paul	to Anna Woolsey.
Miles Beach	to Sarah Jane Paul.
John Taylor	to Martha Delk.
Alfred Markum	to Malissa Jennings.
B. R. Stockton	to Palina Shillings.
Mark Jennings	to Catherine Wright.
James L. Williams	to Matilda J. Kannatsier.

Lewis Lovelace	to Matilda Cupaheffer.
John C. Abbott	to Amanda Brown.
General Manson Guffey	to Nancy C. Carpenter.
Bartholomew Lee	to Sarah Mullinax.
W. A. Houfland	to Mary Jane Ray.
Rev. J. V. Brown	to Abigail Williams.
John E. Fulton	to Frances D. Brown.
James F. Paul	to Malissa Kannatsier.
S. V. Bowden	to Clara I. Lacy.
J. J. Clinch	to Mary C. Neal.
Rev. A. C. Peters	to Peninah C. Allred.
James T. Goff	to Luvernia Kannatsier.
John E. Hooper	to Roenia Swift.
Elisha Wright	to Mary Ann Jones.
Calvin R. Baird	to Etta C. McCart.
William J. Roberts	to Florence Fordham.
Phelbert Jennings	to Mary Walker.
George J. Smith	to Nannie Abel.
Henry Tracy	to Hettie Jones.
Samuel F. Hanson	to Lillian Ellis.
G. S. Dudley	to Laura Mosier.
James T. Guthrie	to Rebecca Ann Jones.
William A. Overstreet	to Nancy Belle Jones.
Joseph Lewallen	to Epsie J. Galloway.
William C. Overstreet	to Mahala Franklin.
Thomas A. Brown	to M. C. Paul.
Samuel G. Young.	to Bertie Peters.

Total, 87 couples.

www.ingramcontent.com/pod-product-compliance
Lightning Source LLC
Chambersburg PA
CBHW022020110726
47901CB00006B/1596